**Suzanne Wright** lives in England with her husband and two children. When she's not spending time with her family, she's writing, reading or doing her version of housework – sweeping the house with a look.

She's worked in a pharmaceutical company, at a Disney Store, at a primary school as a voluntary teaching assistant, at the RSPCA and has a First Class Honours degree in Psychology and Identity Studies.

As to her interests, she enjoys reading, writing, reading, writing (sort of eat, sleep, write, repeat), spending time with her family, movie nights with her sisters and playing with her two Bengal kittens.

**To connect with Suzanne online:**

Website: www.suzannewright.co.uk
Facebook: suzannewrightfanpage
Twitter: @suz_wright
Blog: www.suzannewrightsblog.blogspot.co.uk

# SHADOWS

## SUZANNE WRIGHT

piatkus

PIATKUS

First published in Great Britain in 2019 by Piatkus

3 5 7 9 10 8 6 4 2

A CIP catalogue record for this book
is available from the British Library.

ISBN 978-0-349-41631-1

Typeset in Goudy by M Rules
Printed and bound in Great Britain by
Clays Ltd, Elcograf S.p.A.

Papers used by Piatkus are from well-managed forests
and other responsible sources.

Piatkus
An imprint of
Little, Brown Book Group
Carmelite House
50 Victoria Embankment
London EC4Y 0DZ

An Hachette UK Company
www.hachette.co.uk

www.littlebrown.co.uk

*To everyone who has taken a chance on the Dark in You series—I'd kiss you all if I could, but I think there might be a law somewhere against kissing strangers (the world can be so uptight sometimes, right?)*

# CHAPTER ONE

It was the sharp ache in the back of her neck that woke her. Or it could have been the churning in her stomach, or even the awful throbbing in her head.

Too tired to open her eyes, Devon Clarke let out a quiet moan. God, she felt so unbelievably heavy. Her mouth was bone dry and her throat felt raw, but she wasn't sure she could summon the energy to even reach over to her nightstand and grab her bottle of water.

Sleep threatened to tug her under once more, thick and compressing. Her inner demon nudged her hard, a sense of urgency in its manner that pricked at her hindbrain. The fog started to slowly clear from Devon's mind, and she became aware of a dull ache in her wrists, shoulders, and ankles.

Brow creasing, she tried opening her eyes. Failed. She was just so incredibly tired and drowsy. *Unnaturally* tired and drowsy. She might have fallen back asleep, but the pain kept her from drifting and forced the last bit of sleep-fog to dissipate.

Her eyes fluttered open, but her world was a blur. She double-blinked, struggling to bring things into focus, and she realized she was looking at her jean-clad thighs. She also became aware that she was sitting on a chair, her head drooped forward, her long, ultraviolet ringlets hanging around her face like a curtain.

She slowly lifted her head, wincing at the stiffness in her neck. She went to give it a soothing rub, but she couldn't move her arm. In fact, it was weirdly stretched behind her and—

Reality slammed into Devon, making her mind snap to full alertness. She glanced over her shoulder and, *shit*, her wrists were bound together behind the chair. Not by simple rope. No, it was a pure white energy rope that buzzed against her skin. She felt that same buzz against her ankles and realized that, yep, both were tied to the legs of the chair.

Her heart stuttered, and then it was racing like crazy. *Shit, shit, shit.* Devon tugged at the rope binding her wrists, and pain lanced through her stiff shoulders. There was no give in the energy knot whatsoever; it was so damn tight that her fingers were numb from poor circulation.

Fear gripped her tight and squeezed her insides. The dark power inside her stirred and uncoiled, wanting to be free, but it was trapped. And she realized that the energy ropes weren't only keeping her bound, they were blocking her from using her abilities. *Motherfucker.* She hadn't felt this helpless since—

Devon slammed the door on the memories.

Her gaze darted around the small room, and she sucked in a breath. She was in what looked to be a cabin. Slices of sunlight streamed through small holes in the wooden roof planks, casting light on the dust motes that floated in the air. The place stank of mold, pain, fear, and the old blood that stained the floorboards—some were reddish brown dots; others were larger and darker. The only furniture other than her chair were a stool and a work table on which lay safety goggles, gloves, and an array of torturous implements.

What. The. Fuck? Had she been taken by some psychopathic Dexter-wannabe or something?

The last thing she remembered was driving home from the grocery store. As she'd stopped at a red light, the front passenger door had swung open, a stranger had slid onto the seat, and then . . . nothing. Absofuckinglutely nothing.

She couldn't smell drugs on her, so she was guessing she'd either been dealt a psychic blow to the head or she'd been spelled to sleep just as she'd been spelled to the chair. That meant her captor was either an incantor—no other demonic breed possessed and wielded magick—or a practitioner.

Her inner demon wasn't afraid. The emotion was something it rarely felt, and it didn't find fear unpleasant anyway. But the feline was baring its fangs, filled with an ice-cold anger that wouldn't be sated by vengeance. Yeah, well, hellcats were a terribly vindictive bunch.

Her demon, like every one of its kind, was a cunning, conscienceless predator that possessed an addictive personality and felt no remorse, empathy, or love. It especially liked power and control, so to have another person subdue it and Devon this way? Yeah, the feline was beyond infuriated.

What was this all about? How did she get here? Who took her? Where was the bastard?

Where was the exit?

She couldn't see shit out of the windows, thanks to the dirt smudging the view, so she had no clue where she was or if Psycho Stanley was close. The room only had one door, and that door was currently closed. She doubted she'd be alone for long. Someone would come—the same someone who'd brought her here.

As the feeling of being confined once more seized her insides, awful memories of that day long ago insidiously snuck back up on Devon. Again, she shoved them away. This wasn't the time to reminisce. It was time to get her shit together and *think*. Plan. She needed to get out of this shithole.

She rocked and squirmed, but the chair didn't even so much as creak. Sturdy fucker. Standing as much as the chair would allow, she slammed it back down. She did it again. And again. And again. And again. And—

The sound of hinges squeaking came from somewhere in the cabin.

Devon stiffened, her heart pounding as heavy footsteps came her way, scraping at the creaky floorboards. Moments later, the door was pushed open. A tall, lean male with shoulder-length black hair filled the doorway. *This* had to be Psycho Stanley.

He was still. Watchful. And as she found herself the focus of those soulless gray eyes, Devon swallowed hard. She didn't let her dread show, though. No. Good at hiding her emotions, she kept her face blank as she resumed slamming the chair to the floor over and over, holding his gaze the entire time. If he expected her to shake with fear and plead for mercy, he was out of his mind.

The wooden planks groaned beneath his feet as he walked further into the room. "The chair isn't going to break," he said in a voice so devoid of emotion that it gave her the chills. An incantor, she sensed—and a very powerful one. "Far stronger people than you have tried it," he added.

So, what, he made a habit of kidnapping people and bringing them here to be tortured with those implements on the table? *Twisted.*

"Bet you're wondering why you're a guest of my fine accommodations."

She stilled, wanting an explanation.

"It's nothing personal on my end—I'm just a bounty hunter. Someone will be here to collect you very soon. Someone who'll deliver you to a person who must want you very badly, because they paid me a huge chunk of money to acquire you." He grabbed the old stool from the corner and slid onto it. "But then, this isn't a job anyone would do without the promise of a hefty reward, is it, considering you're a good friend and employee of Harper Thorne?"

Yeah, no one in their right mind would want to upset Harper. The co-Prime of a large demon lair that spanned most of Vegas and even some of California was powerful in her own right. Her mate, Knox, was rumored to be the most powerful demon in all existence, and he *really* hated it whenever anyone upset Harper.

Devon's own lair was small and mostly made up of imps. And since imps lived for pissing people off, her Prime—who was also Harper's grandmother—had a whole host of enemies. It wouldn't surprise Devon if someone was planning to hold her hostage in order to manipulate Jolene. That would be a dumb move. There was no way to manipulate Jolene Wallis.

"There'd be no sense in screaming for help," the incantor went on. "This plot of land goes on for miles and miles. There's no one around who'd hear you. For now, little hellcat, your ass is mine."

It was almost cute that he truly believed that. But why warn him that he was wrong? It would be better to allow him to think that he was on top of the situation.

He cast a quick glance at his collection of knives. "It's a real shame that I can't use them on you. My client paid me extra to ensure you were delivered in one piece. They wouldn't grant me so much as a pinkie finger, which is disappointing. Powdered hellcat bone sells for good money on the black market. I can personally attest to the fact that it does indeed power spells."

Well, she'd already known that. Her deceased godmother was an incantor, and she'd told Devon plenty about magick.

Stretching his legs out in front of him, he cocked his head. "You're a cool one, sitting there calmly, looking me right in the eye ... as if you're not tied to a chair and completely at my mercy."

At his mercy? Oh, good Lord, he was just adorable.

"Before you try telling me you'll escape and kill me—they all vow that—let me just say that I've done my research on you. Even if my spell wasn't preventing you from accessing your abilities, you wouldn't have been able to call out to your lair members or friends for help—your telepathic range is short."

True, sadly. Devon didn't doubt that her godmother could have untangled the spell effortlessly, since she'd possessed more magick than any incantor Devon had ever met. Millicent was so strong, in fact, she'd imprinted protective wards on Devon's very bones. The wards didn't make her immune to magick, but they did ensure that any spells placed on Devon would wear off fast. Which was undoubtedly why the energy ropes had begun to weaken—the buzz of power was no longer so strong against her skin.

Luckily, Psycho Stanley didn't seem to be aware of that. And she'd need to keep him distracted so that he was less likely to notice. "Well, are you going to tell me what delightful person hired you?" she asked, her voice croaky with thirst.

"I've no idea who it was." And he didn't sound as though he cared. "The deal was done through a broker."

"Surely you at least know what they want with me."

"Something about offering your father an exchange—if he freed their friend, Asa, they'd free you." He shrugged, uninterested. "I suppose this is where you get to find out just how much Daddy loves you."

Well, considering she'd never heard of an Asa and that the guy she *thought of* as her dad wouldn't have the authority to free anybody, this mess had to be related to her biological father, Finn. He was the Prime of a lair in Salt Lake City, and she didn't have regular contact with him. As such, the person who'd arranged all this would have had better luck if they'd kidnapped one of Finn's other offspring. It honestly wouldn't surprise her if Finn refused to make the trade. Which meant she was fucked if she didn't get out of this cabin *fast*.

The incantor's eyes narrowed. "Harper Thorne used to belong to your lair. You've been close friends with her since you were kids, from what I uncovered. Girls share just about everything with their BFFs, don't they? I'll just bet she told you what breed of demon her mate is."

Well, he'd lose that bet. Devon had once asked Harper what Knox was, and the female sphinx had responded, *"You're better off not knowing, Dev, and it's not something I can share anyway."*

By her own admission, Devon was annoyingly curious—it was a hellcat thing—and would badger people for answers. But she also knew when it was best not to push, so she'd let it go.

"What is he?"

Devon arched an imperious brow. "And what incentive do I have to tell you that? You've got nothing to offer me except for my freedom, which we both know you won't give me. You can't even tell me who hired you."

His eyes bored into her, empty and cold. "Why would I offer you an incentive when I could torture the information out of you?"

"You've been instructed to keep me alive and unharmed, remember."

"I can put you through a world of hurt without leaving a single mark on you."

Hmm, was that so? Well, she could return the favor if these damn binds would just fuck right off. He might have done his research on Devon but, like many demons, she deliberately kept some of her abilities quiet. He had no way of knowing that he had, to put it simply, completely fucked up. All she needed was—

She shot forward in her chair as white-hot agony crashed into her gut, twisting it so painfully that stars burst behind her eyes. *Holy fuck* it felt like someone was taking a blowtorch to her stomach. The scorching heat sizzled its way up her chest, settled in her breastbone and, honest to God, she thought it would melt from the heat or at least crack from the pressure.

She looked down, half-expecting to see her skin blistering and peeling away from her body. There was absolutely no outward sign of the fire that blazed in her—

It stopped.

She sagged in her chair, panting and shaking.

"I think I've made my point," he said. "Now, tell me what I want to know."

She blinked, licking her dry lips. "What was the question again?"

Devon hissed as the pain returned. Not like a blowtorch this time. No, now it felt more like a jagged, red-hot knife was carving its way up the column of her throat, and she was genuinely surprised she didn't smell blood. It *felt* as if the blade sliced through her skin as it traveled over her chin, along her face, and toward her eye.

Nostrils flaring, she jerked her head back, but there was no way of avoiding the—

It stopped again.

Devon shuddered out a breath. God, it was going to be so satisfying to watch this bastard die. So very, very satisfying.

The fuck of it was that although the buzzing against her wrists and ankles had faded a little more, it wasn't enough for her to break free. It was, however, enough for her to release a little of her own power.

Slowly and cautiously, she sent out a vine-like tendril of dark power. He couldn't see it, of course. But, as its wielder, *she* could. The hazy vapor slinked its way across the ground like a snake, heading right for him.

At her command, the vapor came to a stop near his foot. It coiled, tensed, ready and raring to pounce. She might have released her hold on it right then if he wasn't a strong incantor. He could easily combat a *tendril* of such power—sadly. She just had to hope that whoever was coming to collect her didn't arrive before the energy rope faded and she could release the rest of the dark force that writhed in her belly.

For the first time, she wished her anchor bond *was* emotionally invasive. To have her mind so strongly linked to someone else's yet be unable to reach out to them ... Fuck if that wasn't shitter than shit at the moment.

All demons had a predestined psychic mate who anchored them, preventing them from turning rogue—something they were all at risk of doing, considering how much of a struggle it could be to maintain dominance over the cruel entity that lived within them. There was nothing sexual or emotional about the bond. It was only a psychic construct, but demons still struggled to be apart from their anchors for long periods of time.

Devon was incredibly close to her anchor—so close, in fact, that Adam and his partner, Hunter, had switched to her lair six years ago. Both guys were uber protective of her, and they'd lose their shit if they could see her right now.

"Had enough pain?" Psycho Stanley asked.

Sensing he thought he'd scared her, Devon couldn't help

it—she laughed. It was a slow, raspy sound that built until her shoulders shook.

His gaze flared. "Something funny?"

"I was just thinking how much of a mistake you made taking this job. It won't matter how strong you are or how carefully you covered your tracks. My disappearance will be traced back to you, and then you'll pay for this."

"No one can trace me."

"Not even a hellhound?" she challenged. "One of Knox's sentinels is a hellhound. He'll find you."

"I assume you're referring to Tanner Cole. Are you forgetting he's also Harper's bodyguard? Knox is hardly going to send him on a mission to find a she-demon who isn't even from his lair. His mate's safety is far too important to him."

"Yeah, but Tanner considers me under his protection." Which annoyed her, in all honesty, but that wasn't something she needed to share with this asshole.

"If that were true, you'd carry his mark. I bound your hands earlier. If you bore his mark, I'd have seen it."

Because hellhounds left their brand in the center of a person's palm. They could only mark someone if both halves of their soul wanted to protect that person. Tanner might be protective of her, but his inner demon wasn't—hellcats and hellhounds had a natural aversion to one another.

That was okay, though; she didn't need or want Tanner's protection. Didn't want his attention either. But the devastatingly hot hellhound seemed intent on driving her insane. Each time his mind touched hers, he whispered teasing comments to her . . .

*How's my little kitty cat?*

*Missing me?*

*Need any cat litter while I'm at the store?*

*I picked you up some balls of yarn—you owe me, kitten.*

She'd been dealing with that shit for *years*. In the beginning, her inner demon had hissed and spat, *outraged* by his psychic touch merely because he was a hellhound, its natural enemy. Nowadays, the feline merely curled its upper lip in a lazy snarl. The demon no longer felt compelled to rip out his lungs, since it was relatively certain that he meant Devon no harm.

"You still haven't answered my question, hellcat. What. Is. Knox?"

"Well ..." The ropes winked out, freeing her. The blood rushed back to her fingers and toes, and it hurt like a mother-fucker. Ignoring the pain, Devon acted fast. She released her hold on the dark power that waited to attack. As smooth, fluid, and fierce as a wildcat, it lunged at him, encased his entire body, and seized him in a crushing vice-like grip.

Eyes wide, jaw tense, he drew in a shocked breath. Before he could even *think* of retaliating, the power squeezed and contracted around him like a snake, exerting more and more pressure on his body and insides. He yelled in agony as bones cracked, veins popped, and skin split.

Her demon's grin was somewhat feral as it observed the nause-ating sight he made. The whites of his eyes had reddened, blood was leaking from his ears and mouth, and broken bones were protruding through his skin. Merciless, the power kept on squeez-ing and crushing him until, finally, his brain exploded inside his skull and he toppled off the stool. Like that, the vapor dissipated.

Devon pushed off the chair and strode toward him, rolling her stiff shoulders and examining the chafed skin of her wrists. *Bastard.* She looked down at where he lay, his bloodshot eyes open and vacant, his body an unholy mess. He'd suffered excru-ciating pain—there was no doubt about it. And she couldn't find it in herself to give a rat's ass.

"Told you that you made a mistake when you took this job. People never listen to me. Why is that?" She tossed a high-voltage ball of hellfire at the little bastard and didn't move from the spot until he was nothing more than mere ashes. Satisfied, she nodded. Now where the fuck was the phone?

*

Standing in the watch room of the old lighthouse, Tanner scraped his hand over his jaw. He wasn't by any means squeamish, and he'd seen worse sights than this. But there was nonetheless something very disturbing about seeing a dead body propped up against a wall, his legs crossed, drenched in blood, holding his eyes, tongue, and ears in his hands.

Outside, sea birds squawked, the wind bounced off the walls, and the rotating light at the top of the lighthouse flashed continuously. Inside, there was only silence as he and the two other demons in the room circled and studied the body.

"Fuck," Tanner finally said.

"Yeah, fuck," said Knox.

"How long has he been dead?" Tanner asked Levi since, as a reaper, the sentinel had a certain affinity for the deceased.

Crouched beside the corpse, Levi replied, "Just over an hour. It wasn't the wounds or blood loss that killed him. He died of a heart attack—one that was brought on by preternatural causes." The reaper looked from Knox to Tanner. "Know anyone who has that ability?"

"No," said Knox.

Tanner shook his head, staring once more at the body. Harry Tomlinson had been a member of their lair whose specialty lay in espionage, which was why he'd acted as a spy for Knox. He'd telepathically contacted the Prime a few hours ago, asking Knox to meet him at the lighthouse—it was the same location they always met at when Harry had important information to share.

After his business meeting was over, Knox had pyroported himself, Tanner, and Levi to the lighthouse . . . only to discover Harry dead. Knox's ability to travel by fire was a secret that only a select few people knew of. Although Tanner acknowledged that it was smart to keep people guessing just how powerful you were, he knew it would drive him crazy to mostly use normal means of transport if he could just pyroport wherever he wanted.

His inner demon, by nature, was no more patient than Tanner. Right then, it didn't want to hang around the lighthouse. It itched to track down whoever had ravaged Harry this way—hunting was what the hound did best.

"This was done to Harry before his death," said Tanner. "The scent of his blood is strongly tainted by pain, fear, fury, and helplessness."

"How many other people were here?" asked Knox.

"Just one. A demon. Their scent . . . it's earthy but *wrong*."

"What does that mean?"

"Some people have scents that are floral. Others are fruity. Or sweet. Or spicy. Or earthy. The list goes on. This demon smells of autumn leaves and sandalwood, but there's a single, small note to their scent that's *off*. Like . . . have you ever tasted something you usually enjoy but, for some reason, it just doesn't taste *right*? Like someone put a spice in it that didn't need to be there, or one of the ingredients was stale? This scent isn't right. Almost seems . . . unauthentic."

"Like someone concealed their scent—either through an ability or with magick—by covering it with a fake one, only they didn't cover it well enough?"

"Yes, exactly."

Knox's brow furrowed. "You don't scent Sloan here?"

"No."

Sloan Monroe was the newly appointed Prime of a Washington lair. He was also a slick motherfucker who'd repeatedly tried to buy the Underground from Knox. The subterranean version of the Las Vegas strip was every demon's idea of paradise, and it brought in a shitload of money every year.

Sloan hadn't been the first to try to buy it from Knox, and he wouldn't be the last. But he was the only demon who'd tried to recreate it. Sloan had built it in Washington, not far from the lighthouse, and he'd named it the Haunt—how original.

Knox didn't care about the competition, but he *did* care that Sloan attempted to coax demons to relocate their businesses from the Underground to the Haunt. That was something they'd learned from Harry, who Knox had planted in Sloan's lair to keep an eye on things.

It was reasonably common practice for Primes to plant spies in other lairs. Knowledge was power, after all—demons were all about power. In fact, Sloan had planted two spies in Knox's lair. The dumb assholes believed they were flying under Knox's radar, and they were blissfully unaware that they were only ever fed false info.

Whenever a Prime discovered a plant, they tended to toss them out of the lair and warn their Prime not to try that shit again. Sometimes they also beat the plant for good measure. They didn't mutilate and kill them.

Tanner slipped his hands in his pockets. "I wonder how Sloan discovered that Harry was a plant."

"Can we be sure that that's *why* Harry was killed?" asked Levi. "I mean, cutting out his tongue, slicing off his ears, and gouging out his eyes seems something of an overreaction."

"Yeah, but it fits," said Tanner. "Seems like a punishment to me. He cut out his tongue for blabbing, removed his ears for eavesdropping, and scooped out his eyes for spying."

"I don't think this was just a punishment; I think he was being silenced." Jaw hard, Knox glanced out of the window that overlooked the deserted beach and choppy water. "Fuck, he didn't deserve this."

No, he hadn't. Harry had been a good guy, and they'd all known him a long time. He hadn't just been a member of their lair, he'd spent years of his childhood in the same home for orphaned demonic children that Knox, Tanner, Levi, and the other two sentinels had. Knox had long ago bought the place, knocked it down, and then built a luxury hotel over its remains.

Whereas the five of them had stuck together on leaving Ramsbrook House, Harry had gone his own way like many of the others. It hadn't been until eight years ago that Harry reappeared in their lives and joined their lair.

Tanner inhaled deeply again, filtering through the smells of rust, stale air, and must to focus better on that fake scent, trying to find a way past it to get just a brief hint of the real scent beneath it. But he hit a wall each time.

His hound was having the exact same struggle. It no doubt would have cursed a blue streak if it had the ability to speak.

A person's inner demon could surface just enough to talk and take control. But hellbeasts, no matter the breed, couldn't use speech to communicate; they used telepathic images or impressions. Though the entities lacked the ability to talk and had all the instincts of a predatory animal, they were more human in their way of thinking. His hound fully understood exactly what had happened to Harry, and it was mightily pissed off that it couldn't yet do anything about it.

Tanner gave the sparse room another once-over. "There's no sign of a struggle." No blood spatter on the walls, no objects flung around or knocked over. "Harry's killer must have somehow subdued him while they did this sick shit to him, but he doesn't have any marks to suggest he was tied down."

"What are your reaper senses picking up?" Knox asked Levi.

"Harry's pain and fear are so prominent they're almost tangible," said Levi, who could read any left-over emotional vibes from death scenes. "But I can still feel faint echoes of other emotions—ones that didn't belong to him, which means they belonged to the killer. Given the severity of the mutilation, I would have expected killing rage, battle adrenaline, or even a mild sense of satisfaction. There's none of that. Just cold determination and an odd sense of righteousness."

"Harry didn't fear much," said Knox.

"He was afraid of whoever killed him." Levi's nostrils flared. "What pisses me off is that we can't confront Sloan over this without admitting that Harry was a plant."

"We can, however, make our displeasure clear by treating his own plants to some pain." Knox's eyes glittered with what could only be described as bloodthirst. "And I don't mind admitting that I'll enjoy that."

Tanner believed him. Knox had a well-earned reputation for being utterly merciless. But then, his breed of demon was a part of the fabric of hell, so he'd hardly be a fluffy bunny. Not many knew what breed of demon the Prime was, and Knox intended to keep it that way.

Tanner's phone began to ring. He fished it out of his pocket and saw a familiar number flashing on the screen. He felt his jaw harden. He could admit he was somewhat tenacious and often got tunnel vision when he wanted something, but this female hellhound had him beat by a mile.

"I'm guessing that's Eleanor," said Levi. "You grind your teeth whenever she calls."

"She's not hearing my 'no.'" Tanner canceled the call and pocketed his phone. "I honestly don't know how I can make myself clearer."

"Female hellhounds are persistent creatures," said Knox. "You know that."

Tanner did know that, so it didn't surprise him that she wasn't initially put-off by his refusal. But it had been three months, and she was *still* bugging the shit out of him.

"You're not even in the least bit tempted by her offer?" asked Knox. "You've walked this Earth for a long time, Tanner. Most hellhounds your age have fathered at least four children by now. You don't even have one."

"It's not like Eleanor's asking you for a relationship—she knows that won't happen," said Levi. "She's more interested in your genes. Female hellbeasts want the biggest, toughest, most badass males to father their offspring. You're an alpha, so it can't shock you that she's not backing down easy."

Tanner sighed. "Like I've already told both of you, I'm not interested in her offer."

"What about your hound?" asked Knox. "Because if it's pushing for you to start your own line—"

"It's not." Tanner didn't doubt that the demon would eventually do it, though.

Male hellhounds rarely committed to one female; they tended to have children with several different partners and were content to be a perpetual bachelor—it was just the primitive way they operated. They weren't family orientated or built for relationships; their inborn purpose was to protect and defend the gates of hell, not families or mates.

Female hellhounds, however, were different. More nurturing and parental. They did the bulk of the childrearing, and they sought a male who met the qualities they were looking for:

strength, power, loyalty, etc. Females often had at least two children before they took a permanent mate, since their inner demon could take a long time to settle down.

"Now, back to the matter at hand," said Tanner before either Knox or Levi could push him any further on the annoying subject. "I guess we'll need to take care of Harry's burial."

Sobering, Knox nodded. "It will need to be a quiet one. Most of our lair had no clue he was one of us. I think it—" He cut off, muscles tensing. He had that faraway look in his eyes that told Tanner the guy was telepathically communicating with someone.

As the air thickened with rage, Levi exchanged a look with Tanner and said, "This is going to be bad."

Knox bit out a curse and turned back to them. "That was Harper. It seems we have another issue."

"What kind of issue?" asked Tanner.

Knox studied him for a long moment. "It's Devon."

Every cell of Tanner's body seemed to brace itself for impact. Uneasy, his hound pushed close to the surface. By sheer force of will, Tanner kept his tone even as he asked, "What about Devon?"

# CHAPTER TWO

Perched on one of the stools around Jolene's kitchen island, Devon felt her lips twitch as Khloë ranted about "dumbass, monkey-loving, goat-fucking, shit-for-brains incantors." Sitting beside the imp, Raini nodded along, her amber eyes hard. Harper, who was on her way to Jolene's house, had been just as pissed when Devon relayed the evening's events over the phone. The four of them had been close friends since childhood, and they all worked together at the tattoo studio that Harper and Raini co-owned.

"Here." Jolene set a steaming mug in front of Devon and then slid onto a stool, patting her perfectly styled updo. No matter whether she was relaxing at home or attending a meeting, Jolene always dressed in a smart blouse, chic skirt, and high heels, emitting an inborn grace and elegance. In her chest beat the heart of a fiercely protective lioness. A rather shrewd, vengeful lioness who proudly let her crazy flag fly and could start a riot at a monastery.

Devon cupped the hot mug with her hands. Steam wafted from the herbal tea and whispered over her face. "Have you heard from your sentinels yet?"

"Only to say that no one has showed at the cabin looking for you. But they will sooner or later."

After dealing with the incantor, Devon had found her purse in the cabin's den and used her cell phone to call a teleporter-friend from her lair, Ciaran. He'd not only teleported her to Jolene's house, he'd then teleported Jolene's sentinels and five members of her Force to the cabin. They were now all lying in wait for the broker's men. They'd also searched the cabin and learned that the incantor had gone by the name of Elliot Maverick.

"My sentinels will make the bastards talk; we'll find out who brokered the deal, and then we'll discover who was behind the kidnapping." Jolene's eyes briefly bled to black, indicating that her inner demon was straining to surface and take control. The Prime might sound calm and composed, but she was no doubt far from it. Devon would bet that the woman was plotting all kinds of delightful ways to punish the fucker responsible.

The Prime didn't possess a lot of scruples. But then, most imps didn't, which was why their lair didn't have the best reputation, and their "laws" were pretty simple. They went along the lines of "Thou shalt not kill without covering up the evidence" and "Thou shalt not steal, lie, or cheat unless thyself is confident thou will not get caught."

Sipping her tea, Devon let her gaze drift around the room. Jolene kept it immaculately clean. There no sauce splatters on the wall tiles or backsplash. No dishes piled in the sink. No crumbs on the tiled floor or cup rings on the cherry wood counter.

Despite being so orderly, the room didn't lack personality. Not with the keepsakes and framed photos that lined the shelves and the hand-drawn pictures that had been attached to the fridge by magnets. A great treasurer of memories, Jolene had mementos and framed photos in almost every room.

Taking the stool beside Devon, Jolene's daughter, Martina, gave her hand a gentle squeeze. The astonishingly beautiful imp was just as batshit as her mother and seemed to find joy in setting things on fire. To each their own.

"Thank God Millicent put those protective wards on you," Martina whispered. "Mom wasn't so happy about it back then— the process is a painful one for all involved in the spell, and you were just a child. But I could understand why Millicent never wanted you to ever again be in a position where magick could trap you."

Devon almost flinched as memories slapped her.

*Her little fists pounding against the rear passenger window.*

*Sweat dripping down her temples.*

*Her mouth dry and sticky.*

*Her voice hoarse from shouting for help.*

*An infant's cries and struggles.*

Martina winced. "Sorry. I shouldn't have brought that up. Sticking my foot in my mouth is sort of my thing, as you know. I just mean that—"

"Do you have any vodka, Martina?" asked Beck, Jolene's anchor. "I think Devon needs something stronger than tea."

The blonde tilted her head slightly. "I'm pretty sure we have some in the outside bar. Let me go check." And then she was gone.

Devon gave Beck a too-quick smile. "Thanks."

"My aunt means well," said Khloë, idly tracing the scars on the wooden surface of the island. "She just doesn't always think before she speaks."

Raini raised a brow at the petite, olive-skinned imp. "Kind of like you?"

Khloë pursed her lips. "Kind of like me," she agreed, unashamed. Yeah, well, Khloë didn't really do shame. Or awkward. Or discreet. Or impulse-control. Or have any hesitation to say exactly what she was thinking.

A fist pounded on the front door.

"That's probably Harper." Raini pushed to her feet. "I'll get it." Her flip-flops slapped the hardwood floor as she strode out of the room, hips swaying. In her faded Harley-Davidson tank, scuffed blue jeans, and plain white flip-flops, the blonde wasn't whatsoever dressed to impress. As a succubus, she didn't need to put in any such effort; she naturally oozed sex.

Devon overheard Raini greeting, "Oh. Hey." She sounded surprised, but not unwelcoming. "Devon's in the kitchen."

Moments later, Adam and Hunter rushed into the room, looking harried. *Well, hell.* She'd held off on calling Adam about what happened, wanting to wait until she had some answers. Clearly *someone* had called him.

The two males were very different but complemented each other well. Adam, a super talented hair stylist, was incredibly fashion-conscious and had an enviable dress sense. Hunter, a fabulous chef who was planning to start his own catering business, probably wouldn't dress so stylishly if Adam didn't go shopping for him so often.

Adam crossed straight to Devon and hugged her. "My girl." He rocked her from side to side. "My poor baby girl." His body vibrated with rage. "Why didn't you call me? I shouldn't have heard this from *Beck*."

Devon shot the blabber a quelling look.

Beck shrugged. "If it was Jolene, I'd want to know what happened."

Sighing, Devon looked at Adam. "I was waiting until I had some info to share. We have a lot of unanswered questions." And she hadn't wanted to send him into a blind panic.

Adam was like a close friend, big brother, and treasured confidant all rolled into one. He was always there for her, loyal and supportive and protective. Of course, he also pried into her private life and could be quite the meddler.

All anchors were possessive of one another, but it probably should have seemed odd that a gay male could be possessive of her, and vice versa. Their relationship ... it was kind of like when you were close and purely platonic friends with an ex—you had no sexual interest in each other, but there was an emotional intimacy there that you didn't get with an average friend. Which was kind of why demons were often jealous of the closeness their mate had to their anchor. Fortunately, Devon didn't have that problem with Hunter.

Whenever she saw the couple together, she was struck by how well they suited. Her demon envied them that, just as it envied Harper and Knox. And Devon had to wonder if that was what had triggered the feline's desire to find a mate of its own—something that spooked the shit out of her. It wanted that same devotion and connection. Wanted a family of its own, which could be a major freaking issue, since Devon had never gone into heat.

Most of her kind first went into heat in their late teens, and then did so three times a year from that point onwards. But here she was in her late *twenties*, and she'd still never experienced it. Which she could only take to mean that she was infertile— something that pained her every single day. But then, if it was meant to be some sort of punishment for what happened so long ago, it was kind of fitting.

She'd never told anyone about her suspicion that she was infertile, and she'd love to never have to. But if she met someone

who she even *considered* taking as a mate, she'd have to tell them.
Would she blame them if they then walked away? No. But it
could certainly lead to her demon lunging for their throat.

For Devon to take someone as her mate, *both* she and her
feline needed to accept him. Like every dark entity that lived
within demons, her feline was incapable of love. It did, however, sometimes form attachments to people—and it never
let them go.

"You look exhausted," said Hunter, reaching around Adam to
stroke her hair. Then he flicked her forehead hard.

"Ow." Devon rubbed the spot to soothe the sting.

"You gave us a scare, Dev," Hunter complained.

"Not on purpose."

Adam released her. "Have you told your parents yet?"

"They're out of town," she reminded him. "I'll wait until they
get back."

Devon had always felt that she had two moms—Pamela, who
loved her but was unable to take care of her, and Gertie, who was
Pamela's older sibling. Both sisters were hellcats and had been
very close as children, which might have been why Gertie hadn't
hesitated to take Devon in and raise her as her own.

Although Gertie and her mate, Russell—one of the most
hilarious imps Devon had ever met—were biologically her aunt
and uncle, they were her parents in every way that counted.
They were currently celebrating their anniversary in New York,
and Devon had no intention of spoiling their short trip.

A foot kicked open the back door and then Martina walked
inside, holding a tray of small glasses. She placed it on the island.
"Shots, anyone?"

The entire table seemed to descend on the tray.

Adam set his empty glass down. "What do we know about
the incantor?"

"Maverick was a bounty hunter who often sold rare objects on the black market—particularly the bones, blood, eyes, or organs of certain demonic breeds," said Jolene.

Recalling the many knives and blood stains at the cabin, Devon suspected he'd often taken a little something from each of the people he'd kidnapped. "Our best bet of finding out who's after me is to get our hands on the broker. Jolene's sentinels searched the cabin and looked through Maverick's cell phone, but they didn't find anything that could help identify the bastard. So far, no one has turned up at the cabin to retrieve me, which is a surprise. I had thought they'd have arrived by now."

"I sent someone to find your car, Devon," said Jolene. "I doubt it will be too far from where Maverick snatched you."

Adam's brow wrinkled. "Wouldn't he have wanted to dispose of it to cover his tracks?"

"His priority will have been getting her to the cabin," Jolene pointed out. "He probably left the car in the woods near the highway where she was taken, intending to go back and deal with it later." She frowned as the doorbell rang three times in quick succession, as if someone was jabbing it hard with their finger.

"That has to be our Harper." Martina's heels click-clacked along the floor as she sashayed down the hallway. Moments later, she said, "Hi, Harper, it's good to see you."

"Where's Devon?" the sphinx demanded.

"In the kitchen."

Footsteps stamped along the hallway. Harper marched into the room, her face like thunder. "What in the fuckety fuck is wrong with the world? Tell me you know who's responsible for this, Grams."

"I wish I could," Jolene told her.

Knox breezed into the kitchen and exchanged nods with

everyone before giving Devon a speculative glance. "You look well for someone who had a run-in with an incantor."

Devon shrugged. "He was instructed not to harm me."

"But he did," Harper ground out, staring at the angry marks on Devon's wrists.

"Really, Harper, I'm fine," Devon assured her.

The sphinx's eyes flashed. "Do not use my own therapist tone on me, Clarke. How can you be fine? *You were kidnapped and held captive.*"

"Yeah, I remember."

"Don't be a smartass, this is serious."

Devon opened her mouth to assure Harper that she was taking it very seriously, but then she stilled as a familiar scent drifted into the room. Her pulse spiked and her stomach twisted into knots. And then *he* was slowly prowling into the kitchen with a fluid, arrogant grace.

He *always* prowled. Broody. Watchful. Intense. Uber-hot.

All eyes immediately landed on him. Well, of course they did. Darkly sensual and deliciously ripped, Tanner Cole was built for sin, sex, and seduction. An apex predator that was dominant through and through—the trait seemed built into every cell, muscle, and bone.

He was all confidence and smolder and masculine power. Exuded a bold, audacious air that said, "I do what I like, I go after whatever I want, and I don't give a hot shit if you approve or not."

*Behold, ladies and gentlemen, the elusive alpha male.*

All six-feet-plus inches of him throbbed with a lethal, animalistic sexuality that could reduce any girl to mush. Devon had been battling it for so long that she'd developed a tolerance to it. Ha! Such wishful thinking. She had *no* such tolerance for it. She was, however, good at hiding how deeply it affected her. That was something.

But, God, it would be a lot easier if he wasn't so dangerously seductive. He possessed a mouth so carnal, she figured it would be an absolute sin not to fantasize about it. His smooth, short hair was just a few shades darker than the light stubble that shadowed his strong jaw. Sleek, tanned skin covered all those lickable, roped, perfectly defined muscles. So many, many muscles . . .

Damn, his testosterone levels had to be through the *roof*.

Oh, had she mentioned that she hated him? Okay, that wasn't entirely true. She *wanted* to hate him. Technically, it should have been easy, considering he latched onto any opportunity to stomp on her hot buttons. He could also be a pushy bastard. A little self-centered and arrogant in a way that skated the edge of assholeness. Which should have been a major turn-off. It wasn't. She couldn't help but respect that he was so supremely comfortable in his own skin that he didn't change his behavior to please others.

He was also currently involved with a female hellhound who'd paid Devon an unexpected visit to—in the nicest possible way—warn her to keep her distance from him. Devon had—in the bitchiest possible way—told Eleanor Owens to fuck right off.

The memory had her grinding her teeth. As a rule, Devon didn't really do jealousy. She felt the occasional twinge of envy here and there, but she was never bitter if someone had something that she wanted . . . until now.

If her attraction to him was just about his looks, she could have ignored it easily enough. But it was more than that. She admired his depth of loyalty, his dedication to his role of sentinel, and how protective he was of those who mattered to him. And yeah, okay, she was as turned-on by his alpha ways as she was annoyed by them.

Although he could irritate her like no one else, he was one

of the few people she trusted. Tanner Cole was not a person who let people down or who took their trust for granted. He was solid. Reliable. Brimmed with integrity. All that drew her like a magnet.

Right then, his attention settled over Devon like there was no one else in the room. He didn't give her his usual teasing smile. It wasn't hard to tell that he was a very unhappy bunny. A barely leashed anger seemed to ripple the air around him.

His gaze heated as it boldly raked over her with a hint of possession that made her bristle. Those eyes were like deep pools of liquid gold. They dug their way under your skin and made you feel exposed.

He prowled toward her, moving with the ease and calmness of a man who knew he could dispatch any threat without breaking a sweat. A man who made things happen. A man who was in control of his own destiny.

Flexing its claws, her feline gave him its usual snarl ... just because.

Devon swallowed hard as he stepped into her personal space. Every inch of his skin seemed to hum with the sheer power that lived within him, as if it were barely contained. When she was close, it whispered over her own skin and called to the power that lived inside her.

Sexual tension charged the air, making the hairs on her nape stand up. It was always like that between them. The dazing sexual chemistry was as visceral as it was electric. There was no fighting it. All she'd ever been able to do was channel it; give it an outlet through their constant conflict.

She suspected that part of the appeal for them both was that, due to their demons' aversion to each other, she and Tanner were each other's forbidden fruit. Demons were all about instant gratification, and they didn't like being denied what they wanted.

He lifted her arm and examined the chafing on her wrists. A dark growl rattled his chest. "Where else are you hurt, kitten?"

God, his voice . . . He could say a perfectly inane sentence with that deep, low-pitched, masculine rumble and she'd still be instantly hot for him. It wasn't just his voice that enticed her, it was the *way* he spoke with calm, assertion, and authority. There was often a punch of command there that made it even hotter.

"She has a little chafing on her ankles too, but not quite as bad," said Jolene.

Tanner's eyes slammed on the Prime. "Do you have any idea who might have sent someone after her?"

"We will when we speak to the men who work for the broker that arranged the deal. My sentinels are waiting at the cabin for them to show," Jolene told him.

Harper plonked herself on a stool. "Give me the whole story. I want *every* little detail."

*

Listening intently as the Prime relayed what happened, Tanner found himself clenching his teeth so hard his jaw ached. Fury rushed through him, making his blood boil, tightening every muscle until they hurt; it was difficult to keep his grip on Devon's wrist gentle.

Some fucker had taken her, bound her, used magick on her, *marked her flesh*. The urge to hunt and kill the son of a bitch was a drumbeat in his veins and battered at his composure.

Knox's mind slid against his. *You're growling.*

Of course he was fucking growling. Devon Clarke was under his protection. She was also the thing he wanted most but could never have. He could, however, keep her safe and erase any threat to her—which he fully intended to do.

*I'm gonna find who wants her and fuck their shit up*, he told

Knox. *You know I take my position of Harper's bodyguard very seriously—*

*As it happens, Harper already told me she wants you to join the hunt for him,* said Knox. *Larkin can guard her any time you're unavailable—she's done it before. But Jolene might not like you partaking in the hunt; she'll want to kill him herself. I doubt Devon will like it either.*

No, the hellcat wouldn't. She often told Tanner to butt out of her business. She'd also rebuffed his offer of protection more times than he could count. *She'll just have to deal with it.*

It wouldn't be the first time she'd chewed a chunk out of Tanner's ass. They'd been "at war" since they first met, exchanging annoying little gifts. She'd bought him things such as milk bones, a dog lead, and even a can of puppy chow. He'd bought her gifts such as balls of yarn, a pretty collar, and a catnip plant. The playful war was an outlet for all their sexual tension, really.

Tanner frowned at something Jolene said. "What do you mean by 'she got free?'" he asked. "She was spelled to a chair."

"He obviously wasn't as powerful as he thought," replied Jolene. "It's not easy to magickly bind any breed of hellbeast—you know that."

Sensing it was more than that, he looked down at Devon, who was staring into her mug. Apparently, she didn't want him knowing how she'd freed herself. It wasn't unusual for demons to keep some of their abilities quiet, but he didn't like that she didn't trust him with the information. "You're sure the bastard's dead?"

Devon's head whipped around to face him, and her angry eyes sparkled like chips of ice. "What, you don't think I have it in me?"

He almost smiled. Perverse as it was, he liked riling her. Liked that he could get under her skin—it was only fair, she seemed to live under his. He didn't know what it said about him that his cock hardened in the face of her anger. "It was just a question, kitty cat. Not everyone has the stomach to kill."

In truth, he had no trouble believing that she'd coldly disposed of the incantor. Every instinct he had told him that she was as dangerous as she was beautiful, like a shower of glass shards.

He'd never wanted anything even half as much as he wanted Devon Clarke. He knew a lot of guys liked slender women, but Tanner preferred curves. Liked to thrust his cock into something soft. Devon had gorgeous curves and a body made to be worshipped. She was all tits and ass. And fuck if he didn't love that ass. And those tits.

Heads never failed to turn when she entered a room. Devon Clarke was a woman who made you sit up and take notice. Gave off an energy that was all sex and mystery and self-assurance.

Her expressive cat-green eyes were framed by long, thick eyelashes that made him think of black lace. An ultraviolet river of shimmering spiral curls spilled down her back, tempting him to fist them tight while he ravished that bow-shaped mouth that was just as succulent as her scent . . . *strawberry candy canes with a hint of vanilla*. That scent was like a warm, slick fist wrapped tight around his cock.

Beautiful women weren't rare—he'd known plenty of them. But Devon held a deeper appeal for him. Fascinated him, even. Maybe it was because she defied stereotypes. There was no way to label her. She was a whole host of contradictions. Responsible yet impulsive. Antagonistic yet restful. Open yet guarded. Mischievous yet serious-minded. She also had a wit he could fully enjoy, and he'd bet she'd be a firecracker in bed.

Why had he never made a move on her? Simple. His hound saw her kind as prey to be hunted and killed. Just their scent alone made his demon strain to be free and give chase.

Tanner had figured that his attraction to her would fade

in time. It hadn't. Hell, the want had evolved into a hissing, spitting ache.

After years of knowing her, his hound had grown to be somewhat tolerant of Devon, and it no longer itched to hurt her. Still, Tanner had never dared act on what he so badly wanted. Although the demon no longer felt the *need* to lash out at her, Tanner couldn't trust that his hound *wouldn't*.

It had come as a complete shock when his demon leapt to the surface with a snarl on hearing what had happened to Devon, raring to avenge her. Tanner hadn't realized his hound was protective of her.

"Finn might be able to tell us who was behind this," said Devon. "If nothing else, he'll be able to tell us who Asa is, so that will be a start."

"Has anyone called Finn yet?" asked Tanner, his eyes briefly darting to the pretty diamond piercings that dotted Devon's outer ear. He'd never been a fan of piercings on a woman, but she worked them—especially the diamonds on her hips and navel; he'd caught glimpses of them whenever her tees rode up.

It was Jolene who answered. "No. I want to look in his eyes when I talk to him. He's Devon's biological father, yes, but that doesn't mean he'll easily talk to her Prime about the goings-on within his own lair. I don't trust that he wouldn't hold back information and then try to take care of the situation himself."

As Tanner didn't know much about Devon's relationship with Finn, he couldn't speculate. It had been a while before he realized that the people she referred to as her parents were in fact her aunt and uncle. She'd always been very vague with him about her past. All she'd told him about her biological mother was that she was "gone."

"I'll arrange to meet with him in the morning," said Jolene. "But I won't tell him you're coming along, Devon, or he'll know something's wrong. I'll let him think it's Prime business. Ciaran can teleport us to the meeting."

Tanner was just about to firmly state that he fully intended to accompany them when Jolene spoke again.

"I'm inclined to think that it was probably Maddox Quentin. The demon is well-known for brokering deals that no one else would dare touch." Jolene sighed. "It won't be easy to get an audience with him. Unless it's business, he has little time for demons outside of his own lair."

Very true. Maddox had little contact with other Primes. He also refused to allow demons to join his lair if they weren't the same breed of demon as him, which was highly unusual.

Maddox was a descendant of The Fallen—angels who'd been clipped of their wings and fell to the Earth eons ago. Many of The Fallen had copulated with humans, producing hybrids known as nephilim. Others, however, had copulated with demons, producing something else altogether; beings that were highly dangerous and unstable. After centuries upon centuries of mating with demons, they were more demonic than angelic and, as such, were considered a breed of demon in their own right. But they were only ever referred to as "descendants."

Harper folded her arms across her chest. "I'm looking forward to having a *long* chat with both Finn and Maddox."

Jolene gave her granddaughter a steady look. "Harper, you know that can't happen. I understand you're upset, and I know this has been something of a shock for you—it stunned us all. But I have to be seen to deal with this myself."

Eyes flashing, Harper leaned forward slightly. "Someone targeted one of my girls—I'm not down with that, Grams."

Jolene sighed. "And how many times have you told me that I'm not allowed to avenge any slights on you because, as a Prime, you need to be seen to deal with your own problems? The same applies here. I know you love Devon, but she's one of mine."

Knox put a supportive hand on his mate's back as he spoke to Jolene, "I agree with you that, as Devon's Prime, you need to deal with this yourself. But it would also be good for our lairs to be seen working together on this. Primes rarely work together, yes, since it doesn't always go well and often leads to power struggles. But it concerns me that someone was as ballsy as to go after someone so close to Harper, risking her wrath and, by extension, mine."

Jolene eyed Knox. "Define 'working together.'"

"Take Tanner with you when you question Finn and Maddox; let people see my sentinel at your side while you deal with this matter."

*Son of a bitch.* Devon kept her expression carefully blank, refusing to betray any emotion. Being around someone you wanted but couldn't have was hard enough. When said guy knew all your buttons and could play your body with his voice alone, it was just best to spend as little time as possible with him.

Devon kept her tone even as she said, "His presence on the hunt—which is essentially backup—would make Jolene look weak, just as Harper's interference would."

Tanner snorted. "It would take a lot more than that to make Jolene Wallis look weak. Even if Finn can point us to whoever hired Maverick, the broker still needs to be dealt with. You know what Maddox is, kitten, and you know his kind are very insular. He will probably talk to Jolene, but he won't do it in a hurry. He likes to make people wait. He won't make me wait."

"Why not?" Devon asked.

"He and I have an understanding." Tanner's face was a pure taunt as he added, "Look, I know that close contact with me makes it hard for you to deal with your feelings for me."

"Feelings?" Her nostrils flared. "You mean the colossal, infinite, bottomless hatred?"

Smiling, Tanner teased, "There's a fine line between love and hate. Don't be embarrassed that you don't trust you can resist me."

"I don't trust that I won't annihilate you."

"Annihilate? Is that what they're calling it these days?"

Devon hissed. It was the purest temptation to snatch one of the pans that dangled from the rack and bash him over the head with it. And then his mind brushed hers, strong and determined.

*You may not like it, kitten, but you're under my protection. An attack on you is an insult to me. You won't push me out of this, so there's no point in trying. If you really don't want me working with you and Jolene to find whoever wants you, fine, I'll try tracking him alone. Whoever gets to him first will be the one who kills him.*

Devon narrowed her eyes. *Not fucking likely.* Because there was every chance that he'd find the culprit first.

*Then we work together. Which will also mean finding him faster.*

She hated that he made sense. "You're an asshole."

"The majority of the time, yeah, I am."

Well at least he wasn't lacking in self-insight.

Tanner turned to Jolene. "Do you have an issue with me joining the hunt for the bastard behind the kidnapping?"

Jolene delicately shrugged one shoulder. "So long as I get my hands on whoever wants Devon, I don't give a rat's ass who tags along. Provided, of course, you understand *I'm* the one running the show."

Devon silently cursed at her Prime's agreement. Another familiar mind slid against hers, humming with warmth and amusement.

*I must admit, watching you and Tanner interact is quite entertaining,* said Adam.

Devon shot her anchor a glare. *Fuck off.*

Adam's laughter floated around her head. *He's hot. All that alpha energy is totally flipping my switch—and yours. Admit it.*

Admit it? She'd rather swallow glass. *He's a hellhound, I'm a hellcat.*

*Ah, forbidden love.*

Biting back a curse, Devon glanced at her watch. "It's been a while since I was taken. It's possible that the broker's men aren't coming for me. Maybe someone tried telepathically contacting Maverick, got no response, figured something was wrong, and decided not to take any chances."

"I had the same thought," grumbled Jolene. "I'm just hoping I'm wrong. Why don't you go home and get some sleep—I'll call if anyone appears at the cabin."

Nodding, Devon pushed to her feet. "Has my car been found yet?"

Jolene's gaze turned inward, signaling she was communicating telepathically. Then her eyes came back into focus. "No, unfortunately. But it will be found."

"I'll drive you home, kitten," said Tanner. He held up a hand when she went to object. "Haven't we done enough arguing for one night?"

Devon snorted. "No."

He smiled. "I had a feeling you'd say that."

# CHAPTER THREE

She let him take her home. Mostly because fighting him on it only made him smirk and accuse her of being nervous around him. *Asshole.*

Riding shotgun, Devon couldn't help but be excruciatingly hyper-conscious of every gloriously masculine inch of him. Tanner might get on her last goddamn nerve, but that didn't stop her body from reacting to him—stomach knotting, pulse quickening, skin charging with a familiar sexual buzz that made her nerve endings tingle in awareness.

It was senseless to give herself a hard time about it. Her defenses didn't stand even the tiniest sliver of a chance against all that alpha energy.

Maybe it was like calling to like or something, but her libido always did the mambo for fellow hellbeasts. They liked rough sex—there was often a lot of biting and clawing. That wouldn't be so bad if they weren't venomous.

Devon often had to be careful not to bite her sexual partners, since she didn't want them writhing in pain or being struck by temporary paralysis. But as hellbeasts were immune to each other's venom, there was no need to hold back with them. There was something very freeing about—

"It's not like you to be quiet," he said.

"I'm thinking."

"About me, right?"

Devon forced a snort. "You're not that interesting."

"Hey, it's okay, kitty cat. I have plenty of impure thoughts about you. I can just imagine us in bed together ... Reading. Watching TV. Playing UNO. Doing totally nonsexual things."

"Do you ever wonder what life would be like for you if you weren't such a fucking weirdo?"

"You're not gonna convince me that you don't like me, kitten. I've seen how you look at me. It's not nice being ogled and objectified, you know. I need a little warmth, sensitivity, and connection."

She rolled her eyes. "Come back when you've grown some pubes, pooch. We both know that could take a while." He let out a throaty chuckle and, honest to God, her nipples pebbled. She wondered if the guy gargled grit or something—how else could he make his voice *that* gravel-rough?

Devon turned back to the window, relaxing slightly as she noted how close they were to her apartment building. She was mega tired and needed to crash *badly*. She also needed to breathe in air that wasn't filled with the pooch's scent.

"You always do that when you're not the one driving."

Blinking, she looked at him. "Do what?"

"Rest your hand on the door handle, as if you'll leap out at any moment."

*Her little fists banging the car window, her breaths sawing at her dry throat—*

Pushing back the memories, Devon licked her lips. Honestly,

she didn't like being in cars at all. Had found them confining since that day all those years ago. That was *why* she'd forced herself to learn to drive—it was about facing her fears. As the driver, she was in control, so it wasn't so bad. But being a passenger always made her nervous.

For months after that terrible day, she hadn't spoken a word to anyone. Had been terrified to go to sleep as she'd known the nightmares would take her. Had suffered flashbacks that seemed triggered by the smallest things. Had been unable to even look at a photo of her mother without wanting to scream.

Without Gertie, Russell, and her girls, Devon might never have recovered enough to live a life that wasn't haunted by that day. The nightmares still came now and then, and she had the occasional flashback during periods of stress, but she was as close to okay as she had the potential to be. She'd even been able to have a relationship with her very fragile mother who, unlike Devon, had never moved past what happened.

"No response to that?"

"Was there a question?" She mentally crossed her fingers, hoping he'd let it go—this really wasn't something she could stomach talking about right then. Seconds of tense silence ticked by, grating on her raw nerves.

Finally, after what felt like minutes, he sighed. "All right, we'll drop it. For now. Tell me about you and Finn."

Devon grimaced. That wasn't exactly a cheery topic either, but it was better than the first. "Finn's Prime of his lair and a very strategic businessman who's built himself an empire over the years. He's nowhere near as rich as Knox, but he certainly has money to burn." He also didn't think much of her line of work. Finn was all about logic, reason, and ballpark figures. To him, tattooing held no value and was a waste of time. He felt she could do better with her life.

"I know that much, kitten. I never asked about him, I asked about *you and him*. I take it you're not close, since you refer to Russell Clarke as your dad."

"No, we're not close. Finn and my mother had a meaningless, one-night stand ... and I was the result. She didn't tell him about me. She didn't tell me about him. Kept his name secret from everyone. I was eight when Jolene found out Finn was my father. She contacted him."

"And then what happened?"

"Not much. I'd been living with Gertie and Russell for years by then. I thought of them as my parents, and I was happy there. Finn didn't want to force me to go and live with him—in fact, I think it suited him just fine that I didn't want to. His partner had left him, so he had a family to win back; it would have made it a fuck of a lot harder if I was living with him."

There was a whole lot of information there, Tanner thought. But there was also a lot of holes. "How did your mom die?" he asked, his tone gentle. Nonetheless, she bristled.

"I thought you wanted to know about my relationship with Finn."

Tanner felt his mouth tighten. His hellcat sure had a lot of no-go subjects. But after the day she'd had, he'd be a fucking asshole if he pushed her to open what was clearly a raw wound. "Finn has other children, right?"

She nodded. "Three." Like Finn and his partner, they were harbingers whereas Devon took after her mother, who was a hellcat. It was one of many things that set Devon apart from her paternal family, but she didn't lament that.

"What's your relationship with them like?"

"Complicated," said Devon just as he pulled up outside her building. And he immediately tensed. Yeah, she'd figured he wouldn't like what he saw. Looking at the tall, rundown, graffiti-stained building, she almost sighed. She wished she could say it looked better on the inside than it did on the outside, but that would be a lie.

"You live here?" Tanner asked, voice strangely flat.

"Yep," she replied, going for nonchalant. He'd given her rides home in the past—mostly when she'd been smashed after a girls' night out—but she'd shared a place with her cousin back then. It was only when her cousin got serious with some guy that Devon moved out to give them space.

This part of North Las Vegas was far from a good area, but there were worse neighborhoods. The complex might need some major TLC, but it was structurally sound. Sort of.

"Thanks for the ride." She hopped out of the Audi before he could say a word. It was just as she skirted the hood of the car that he slid out of the driver's door, his body uncoiling like a snake.

"I want to give the place a once-over," he said.

She blinked. "What's that now?"

"There's a chance that the broker's men came here. I want to check there aren't any surprises waiting for you up there."

Devon's mouth thinned. "No one who is a threat to me could get inside the walls of my apartment. An incantor from my lair pretty much lavished protective wards all over it."

"Wards can be undone—I've seen it happen." He prowled toward the building before she could argue further.

Cursing to herself, she followed him. "This really isn't necessary."

Stopping outside the main door, he said, "Humor me."

She went to object again, but then she snapped her mouth shut, knowing she'd be wasting her breath; there was no way of shooing along someone like Tanner Cole. "Fine—have at it."

Devon unlocked the door, and in they went. As the scents of

pot, alcohol, urine, and mouse shit wafted over them, a lick of shame brushed over her skin. She'd never seen Tanner's home, but she knew from Harper that he lived in one of Knox's swanky apartment buildings. She'd bet his stairwells weren't littered with empty beer bottles, cigarette butts, and other debris. Would bet the paint wasn't peeling from the walls that were riddled with cracks, holes, and splotches of black mildew. Would bet he wouldn't hear rodents skittering, see doors chained shut, or find squatters here and there.

She spared him a brief glance; his jaw was tight, and his eyes were hard as he scanned their surroundings. Her pride took a hit, but she kept her head high as she led him up the stairwell to her floor and then over to her apartment. She unlocked the door, stepped onto the beige carpet, and then moved aside for him to pass.

He came in and closed the door behind him, his nostrils flaring. "There's a lot of powerful magick here. I can feel it. Smell it. The incantor sits high on the power spectrum. Just where do you sit on it, kitten?"

Devon snorted. "Do I look slow to you?" Unless they were stupid, no demon revealed something so personal. To answer "low" or even "in the center" was to admit to being vulnerable on some level. Demons were predators. You didn't admit weakness to a predator. Even to answer "high" wasn't good. It would intrigue the predator, who might then see them as a potential challenge or feel the need to establish themselves as the dominant figure.

As such, Tanner's question was the equivalent of asking her to strip naked.

Not that she'd have been particularly opposed to stripping naked for Tanner if things had been different and his demon didn't ache to gut her open.

"Wait here while I do a walk-through of the place." He stalked off before she could respond, fully *expecting* her to do as he'd told her.

Devon snorted and headed into the kitchen/dining area. It was too late for coffee, so she'd settle for hot chocolate. Preparing the drink would give her something to do and distract her from the annoying fact that Tanner was in her apartment.

It made her antsy to have him there. For *years* she'd made a point of keeping him out of her world as much of possible. Which hadn't been easy, given that he was not only her friend's bodyguard, he was ridiculously nosy and seemed to orbit around her . . . as if testing her defenses or something. And now he was in her private sanctuary, searching every room, probably touching her things. She didn't like it.

Having added toppings to her drink, she propped herself on the counter and picked up her mug. It wasn't long before he entered. She didn't hear him—Tanner rarely made a sound as he moved. But she smelled him, felt his energy charge the air around her. Her inner demon swished its tail at him in a put-out gesture. It didn't like having people in its territory.

Devon spooned some marshmallows and whipped cream. "I take it you didn't find any intruders hiding in my wardrobe or anything."

"The place is clear." Propping his hip against the counter, Tanner felt his cock twitch as her tongue lapped the cream from her spoon. He could think of far better things she could do with that tongue, but he kept that thought to himself. He just settled in and enjoyed the show as she ate the marshmallows and cream, not even caring that she was pointedly ignoring him. Tanner was just content to have finally made his way into her home.

The apartment had a completely different tone to that of the rest of the building, which didn't surprise him—Devon would never live in filth. Although the rooms were small, they were also cozy and warm. No grime on the windows or dubious stains on the walls. Her furnishings weren't top-notch, but they were quirky and clean.

She'd made the best of what space she had, and she'd managed to give the place a surprisingly welcoming feel. There were pictures here, there, and everywhere. Most featured her parents, Harper, Raini, Khloë, and adoptive brother who also happened to be her cousin. It was as if the hellcat liked to surround herself with memories of the people important to her.

Devon Clarke had bags of attitude, but she was also sweet as she smelled—though she hid that soft underbelly from the people outside of her little circle—and never too busy for those she loved. Always made time for them and rushed to their side if they needed her. In his opinion, she didn't put herself first often enough, which he didn't like.

He also didn't like that she lived in this shitty building. Every instinct he possessed urged him to get her out of that hellhole; to put her in a place that didn't need mouse traps, heavy metal locks, or magickal wards. A place where she wouldn't be surrounded by what must seem like paper-thin walls to a hellcat's enhanced hearing.

If he thought for a second that trying to order her out of here would achieve anything, he'd go for it. But Devon wasn't a person who'd appreciate or allow that kind of interference in her life—something he respected, even as it sometimes annoyed him.

Tanner made a mental note to ask Knox if there were any empty apartments in any of the buildings the Prime owned. Devon didn't have to be part of their lair to rent one—anyone could. He didn't say that to her, though. Making disparaging remarks about her home would only poke at her pride.

"You can go now," she said.

Lips twitching, he heaved a mock sigh. "Always so eager to get rid of me. I'd be offended if I didn't know you are violently in love with me."

She gave him a pitying smile. "Being delusional doesn't help anyone now, does it?"

"Delusional?"

"Sorry, was that too big a word for you? How about 'pathetic'? Have you heard that one?"

He put a hand to his heart. "That hurt. You should make it up to me. Naked. In bed."

"Are you kidding? I wouldn't even fuck you for practice."

He laughed. "God, kitten, you can be such a bitch."

Devon might have sniped at him for that comment if he hadn't said it with approval. "It comes naturally to me. And you really should go. Surely you have stuff to do, places to be, people to see." *Like Eleanor,* Devon almost added. No, she wouldn't mention that heifer, unable to trust that her jealousy wouldn't seep into her words.

"I like it *here.* It smells of you." He dipped his head close to her neck and inhaled deeply. "Your scent makes my mouth water."

She narrowed her eyes. "You think you're charming, don't you?"

"The charm comes and goes."

Devon gave him an indignant huff. "Shouldn't you be off chasing your tail or something?" Her stomach clenched as his mouth curled into a sensual, panty-dropping smile.

"You're doing it again," he said.

"What?"

"Making me want to bite you," he replied, dropping his voice into bedroom territory. His gaze raked over her in a way that made her pulse spike. "Hmm, I'd like to mark all that pretty skin."

"And your hound would like to rip it to shreds."

"At one time, it happily would have skinned you alive. But it's grown to tolerate you and your demon."

Okay, that shocked her.

"I'd say your feline has probably grown to tolerate me just the same."

"Well, it would no longer like to snack on your heart, but it probably also wouldn't care if said heart abruptly stopped beating. Does that count as 'tolerating' you?"

"Yeah, it's good enough." Tanner eyed her soft curls, thinking they'd look good fanned over his pillow as he pounded into her. His cock, already hard and heavy, twitched at the visual.

As he inched a little closer to her, his gaze dropped to the chafe marks on her wrist. The sight made his teeth grind all over again. He took her hand and brushed his thumb over her palm. "If you'd been wearing my mark, the incantor wouldn't have been so quick to take the job."

Sipping her drink, she gave him a look that questioned his sanity. "You wouldn't be able to mark me unless your demon considered me under its protection, which it doesn't. It might have grown to 'tolerate' me, but it's not going to give a flying fuck what happens to me."

"You're wrong about that."

She snorted. "Our kinds *hate* each other. There's no way your demon would offer its protection to a hellcat."

"It's pissed about what happened to you. It wants to avenge you."

"Yeah," she drawled, all skepticism. "Right."

Tanner didn't blame her for doubting him. "I can prove it." He tightened his grip when she tried snatching her hand back. "If you really don't believe me, where's the harm in letting me try?"

Looking bored, she took another sip of her drink. "Even if it *did* work—which it absolutely would not—no one would buy that the mark was real. They'd think it was a tattoo."

"A closer look would be enough to tell them that they're wrong." The mark would be nothing more than a small, innocuous-looking symbol in the center of her palm, but it would also glisten and smell of him—something no tattoo would do. Better still, it would glow whenever she was in danger *and* psychically alert him that she needed help, no matter how far apart they were. "You don't need to worry that being marked would hurt. It might sting a little, but that's all."

"My demon would view any pain from you as an attack. It'd rise and retaliate."

"No, it wouldn't. It can sense that I won't hurt you." Tanner breezed his thumb over her palm again. "Tell me the truth, kitten, why does the idea of being marked by me bother you so much?"

"Who *wouldn't* it bother? Hellhounds are insanely proprietary over whatever they mark, which is why Knox didn't want you to leave one on Harper—she told me."

He gave a slow nod. "And you don't like possessiveness. But it's more than that, isn't it? You feel that accepting my protection will be like surrendering to me in some sense. It won't, kitten. It won't be a show of weakness." He gave her hand a little squeeze. "Come on, put your money where your mouth is; let me try to mark you."

She heaved a sigh of sheer exasperation. "Why bother? You know it won't work."

"If you're so convinced of that, let me try."

"Will you leave if I do?"

"Sure."

Sighing again, she shrugged and put down her mug. "Knock yourself out, I guess." Devon almost snickered at the triumphant look on his face. God, he truly was delusional if he thought this would work. He linked his fingers with hers and dug his thumb into the center of her palm. Nothing happened, just as she'd known it wouldn't.

Devon smirked. "See? You should have listened to—" Power, hot and raw, zapped her skin and scorched it like a branding iron. *Sting, my ass.* It goddamn *burned*. She tried snatching her hand from his, but he held tight. That was when her inner demon charged to the surface.

Tanner tensed when Devon's eyes bled to black and the room temperature lowered. Her demon didn't attack, didn't struggle, but it held razor-sharp claws to his throat in warning. He didn't flinch, didn't pull back. "She's safe with me," he told it, knowing it would fully understand every word. "I'd never hurt her. You can sense that, or you would have slit my throat instantly."

It narrowed its eyes and pressed its claws closer to his flesh—it wanted him to let Devon go, and this was apparently his final warning.

"People could come for her," he said. "We both want her safe, so let's call a truce and work together to make that happen."

An image flashed in his mind—an image of Devon kicking the ass of a faceless foe, her eyes totally black. Tanner nodded at the wordless telepathic message. "Yes, I know she has you. I know you can protect her. But being powerful isn't always enough. I just want her to have my help in case she *does* need it."

The demon didn't react, didn't pull back its claws. Just stared at him.

Tanner felt his jaw tighten. "You might not like or trust my kind, but you do trust that I'd never harm her." Still no reaction. And he sensed that only the truth would get him what he wanted. "She's important to me. Let me help you keep her safe."

Long moments of silence ticked by, winding him tight. Then

the feline lost some of its tension and slowly retracted its claws. It gave a slow nod, and another image flashed in his mind—one of him and the hellcat standing side by side while Devon stood behind them. Understanding the feline was agreeing that they could work together to protect her, he inclined his head.

The demon then subsided, and piercing green eyes met his. Devon, seeming somewhat stunned, looked down at her palm. There, as if they'd been stamped onto her skin, were three, black, very small tribal-like lines set into a thin circle. The same mark was featured on the gates of hell—the brand of a hellhound.

Satisfaction settled over Tanner. He took an easy breath for what felt like the first time in days. She was marked now. Was officially under his protection. Wore his scent on her skin. He'd *feel* it if she was ever in danger. All that gratified him on a very primal level. He couldn't have her for himself, but he could ensure she was safe.

"There, done," he said. "Does it hurt?"

Shocked to the bone, Devon closed her hand. "It's fine." Proud that her voice came out strong and steady, she gave herself a mental pat on the back. "How the . . . I don't understand."

"I told you, my hound considers you under its protection."

Devon would never have believed that. *Never.* But the proof was right there on her palm.

Totally thrown, she raked her hand through her hair. Surely her feline should be raging that a hellhound had marked Devon. Surely it should be hissing, snarling, and raring to strike out at him. It wasn't. It also wasn't convinced that his help was needed or that he wouldn't withdraw his protection at some point, but it saw him as a valuable ally. It intended to use him for as long as he was available. Cold, sure, but that was how the entity operated.

Devon suspected her demon would work with anyone if it would keep her safe. Why? Because it had never forgotten how utterly helpless it had felt while unable to free six-year-old Devon from the magickly warded car. Had never forgotten how close she'd come to dying right along with the infant in the car seat.

It wasn't that the entity was haunted by regret or guilt—it couldn't feel such emotions. But it resented that it had been unable to protect Devon. Was embittered by the powerlessness and sense of failure it had felt. The demon didn't intend to experience such things ever again. And if working alongside a hellhound would help ensure that, the feline would do it.

Devon, however, wasn't so at ease with the idea. She wrenched her hand free, cursing beneath her breath. If she'd thought for one second that he'd be able to mark her, she'd never have agreed to let him try. She didn't want to wear his goddamn brand. But there'd be no washing it off, no tattooing over it, no ridding his scent from that spot on her skin. It wouldn't fade until either he or his demon withdrew their protection. And now she was *livid*. Livid with herself, with him, with his motherfucking hound.

"I don't need or want your protection," she ground out.

"Too fucking bad—you have it." There was no heat in his voice, just a firm resolve. "I told you before, it's not weak to accept someone's protection, kitten. Hell, I've never met a more powerful demon than Knox in all my existence, and he has a damn bodyguard, because it's just plain smart."

She couldn't deny that, which was seriously fucking annoying. "It makes no sense to me that your demon would offer a hellcat its protection. I mean, I can see it not wanting me to be harmed purely because I'm a close friend of your Prime—if someone hurt me, it would hurt Harper, and your hound wouldn't want that for her. Is that what this is?"

He shook his head. "This isn't about Harper. It's about you."

She snickered. "You truly trust that your hound would protect me if need be? Because I sure don't."

His eyes bled to black, and a disgruntled growl vibrated in the demon's chest. The room temperature instantly plummeted, and goosebumps swept across her skin. *Shit.*

Obsidian eyes stared down at her—cold, hard, and so empty of emotion they were like black voids of nothingness. Really, it was like being caught in the gaze of a cobra, and it sent a tingle of fear skittering down her spine. Apparently, the entity didn't like that she'd questioned its integrity.

Her inner feline surged close to the surface, watching it closely, prepared to defend her if necessary. But Devon didn't give an inch to the feline; she intended to remain in control and show the hound that she didn't need her own demon's protection. Intended to make it understand that she could face it herself just fine. So, even though she felt chilled all the way to her soul by that unwavering, reptilian glare, she didn't once look away.

It tilted its head slightly. Assessing her, she thought. It seemed confused, and she wondered if it had expected her to cower and behave like prey purely because it considered all hellcats to be exactly that.

Just to drive home that she was nobody's prey, Devon raised a sardonic brow. "You done staring at me, Fido?"

Another growl vibrated in its chest. Something flashed in those dark eyes. Something that might have been approval, but it was gone too quick for her to be sure. Then the demon did a slow blink, and she was once more looking into a pair of golden eyes.

"You're a ballsy little thing, aren't you?" Tanner took her hand and stroked her palm with his thumb, his face lazy with satisfaction as he stared at the mark. She didn't like that satisfaction *at all*.

Devon jutted out her chin. "Just to be clear, this mark is only that—a mark. It's for show. A deterrent to the people who might mean me harm. I don't care how territorial it incidentally makes you feel, it gives you *no* rights to me. None. Is that understood, pooch?" She expected a growl, a frown, some sign of annoyance. Instead, his mouth ever so slowly curved.

"Ah, kitten," he said, his voice soft. "You're oblivious to your . . . value to me, aren't you? 'Territorial' is a mild word for what I feel toward you, and it has nothing to do with that mark." He released her hand and took a slow step back. "Get some rest. You've had a rough day. I have the feeling that tomorrow's not going to be any easier."

Tanner would have insisted on staying the night to guard her, but his fiercely independent hellcat would never go for that. Her protective wards were strong, and he'd be psychically alerted if she was in any danger—that would have to be enough. "Stay safe." With that, he left.

Outside, he headed for his Audi. He clocked the two imps watching the building from the shadows; approved that Jolene had sent people to guard Devon. That didn't stop him from making a call to a member of his Force and ordering them to stand watch through the night.

In the car, he switched on the ignition and telepathically reached out to Knox. *You can assure Harper that Devon's home, safe and sound. Or as safe as anyone can be in the shabby building where she lives.*

*Harper tells me she's been trying to convince Devon to move, but the hellcat likes to be close to her parents,* said Knox. *The only other nearby empty apartments are in far worse condition than the one she's living in.*

Well, if Devon wanted to live near her family, she wasn't likely to move to one of Knox's buildings. Tanner would still take a shot at convincing her to relocate, though. *Just so you know, I've stationed Enzo outside her complex. I trust the imps to be vigilant, but I want someone watching her who'll report back to me.*

*Our Force is big enough for us to spare him. I'll clear it with Jolene. I also want him and Lex to guard the tattoo studio tomorrow.*

*I understand your need to be sure she's safe, Tanner, and I'm not opposed to making it clear to the demon population that I'll take an attack on Harper's friends seriously. But be careful—your hound could get annoyed by the attention you're paying to the hellcat.*

*No, it won't, because it wants her protected.* Tanner decided to hold off on informing Knox that he'd marked her. Knox would tell Harper, who'd immediately call Devon and ask her about it; then Devon wouldn't get the rest she needed.

*If you say so.* Knox didn't sound whatsoever convinced. *We'll talk more tomorrow.*

*Sure thing.*

# CHAPTER FOUR

The sound of the alarm blaring pierced Devon's dream. Upper lip curling, she blindly reached out to the nightstand and slapped at her phone until the dreaded noise stopped. She was not what anyone would call a morning person. *Everything* irked her when she first woke—the sunlight seeping over the edges of the blackout blind, the sound of her own breathing, the tacky taste in her mouth, the gnawing sensation in her stomach.

The most irritating thing about every morning? Knowing she needed to get up.

Until she'd had her first caffeine-fix of the day, her friends never spoke to her. Or made eye contact with her. Or tried getting her attention. Or made any sudden movements that she might misinterpret as a challenge.

It was as the sleep-fog began to clear from her brain that snapshot-memories of the previous day sucked her under—the cabin, Maverick's death, Tanner bringing her home, Tanner *marking her.*

Well, fuck.

Honestly, she wasn't sure what pissed her off more—that she'd been snatched by an incantor, or that she now wore the pooch's mark. Probably the latter.

Knowing she'd need to call Jolene and find out what time they were meeting with Finn, Devon lazily grabbed her cell. Her Prime had texted her an hour ago to say that she and Ciaran would arrive at Devon's apartment at 8:45am, since the meeting with Finn was scheduled for 9am. Jolene had also added that Devon's car had been found but was an utter wreck. *Groan.*

Either Maverick had purposely put it out of commission, or some kids had found and had their fun with it. In any case, it would be taken to the local mechanic shop this morning, where some of her lair worked.

With yet another snarl, she returned the phone to the night-stand. It was a good ten minutes before she summoned the energy to get out of bed. Eyes half-closed, feet dragging, Devon made her way into the bathroom and did her business.

A short while later—washed, dressed, and wearing a subtle layer of makeup—she shuffled to the kitchen. Two cups of coffee and a Danish pastry later, she was no longer feeling like a zombie. She'd just finished rinsing her mug when Ciaran and Jolene appeared in the middle of her kitchen.

Devon almost jumped. "You need to give a girl some warning before you go teleporting into her home."

Khloë's twin brother raised a brow. "Where would be the fun in that?"

Jolene glanced around. "No Tanner? I told him to meet us here at exactly eight—" She cut off at the knock on the door. "Ah, good." The Prime disappeared down the hallway. Moments later, she returned with the pooch in tow.

The moment his golden eyes landed on Devon, all her hormones sighed in feminine appreciation. Her stomach twisted as he gave her a slow, intense perusal that was nothing short of an eye-fuck.

He flashed her a crooked smile. "Here, kitty, kitty."

Her inner demon rolled its eyes and huffed in annoyance. Devon bared her teeth at him and sniped, "Clearly the lifeguard wasn't looking when you dived in the gene pool."

He chuckled. "Such a cranky kitten."

"Such a mangy mutt."

Ciaran chuckled. "You two argue like . . . well, cat and dog."

"Funny." Devon put her hands on her hips. "Where are we meeting Finn?"

"At his home," replied Jolene. "You ready to leave?"

Devon nodded. "Whenever you are."

And so, mere minutes later, her father's butler was showing them into Finn's parlor. Like the rest of the oversized house, it was spacious and immaculately clean. Sure, it was beautiful with the crown molding, expensive chandelier, and baby piano, but the parlor made her think of a showroom. It just didn't have any personality.

Devon sank into the sofa, frowning when Tanner took up a position behind her . . . like a sentry or something. Jolene and Ciaran, however, took a turn about the room. Devon was just about to ask them not to steal anything when two people elegantly strode inside.

Tall, lean, and well-groomed, Finn wore his usual imperious frown. The beautiful, curvy woman at his side—his adviser as well as his partner—always wore the ghost of a smile . . . but that smile never failed to slip from Leticia's face when she was in the company of Devon. Really, given that Devon's mom had the one-night stand with Finn while he was in a relationship with Leticia, who could blame the woman for resenting the sight of the child who came from that one-night stand?

She wasn't a bitch to Devon, though. Never took out her hurt on her or tried cutting her from Finn's life, which was more than Devon would have expected.

Finn's pace faltered slightly when he saw her, and his frown briefly smoothed out. "Devon? I didn't realize you were coming." He took in the other people in the parlor, and his questioning gaze danced back to her.

It probably should have been sad that he hadn't given her a hug, a smile, or even a hello. But she and Finn had never had a father-daughter relationship. He was more like a distant uncle who'd do something for her out of some sense of obligation, but not out of love or loyalty.

She'd never felt like she'd "missed out." For one thing, Russell was fucking awesome. For another, Finn wasn't exactly *fatherly* with his other kids. He was the cliché workaholic who had a corner office and never took a day off unless the circumstances were dire—as in someone was dying.

Jolene stepped forward, all smiles and grace. "Ah, Finn, Leticia, always a pleasure. You both remember my grandson, Ciaran, don't you? And I'm sure you've already met Tanner Cole at some point or other."

"Yes, I have." Unfailingly polite no matter the circumstances, Finn greeted both males before looking down at Devon once more. "Is something wrong?"

Devon gave him a weak smile. "Kind of, yeah."

Leticia narrowed her eyes on Jolene. "You said that you and Finn had something important that needed to be discussed."

"We do." Jolene lifted her chin. "It concerns Devon, and she should be here for this discussion."

The door opened once more. Two of Finn's sentinels, Eric and Reena, entered. The stunning redhead bore a very strong resemblance to her mother, Leticia. When she caught sight of Devon, her mouth thinned. "Devon," she greeted.

"Reena." As she'd told Tanner, Devon had a somewhat complicated relationship with her three half-siblings. It was less awkward with Spencer as he was so much older than her and completely focused on the family businesses. He didn't resent her for being the product of their father's betrayal, but Reena did. The youngest of the trio, Kaye—who was only two years older than Devon—wasn't as bitchy, but she wasn't exactly accepting of Devon either.

Reena had made it clear that she thought Devon disloyal for not joining their lair. Honestly, though, Devon had a hard time believing that Reena really wanted her there.

Spencer, Reena, and Kaye all considered her job to be an absolute joke, since they didn't place much stock in tattoos or piercings. And she knew it embarrassed them that their half-sister was part of Jolene Wallis's lair, since that lair had a bad reputation.

Like Finn and Leticia, they were all about "appearances" and placed a lot of importance on social status. They liked to be seen at the right places with the right people. Liked chic clothes, fast cars, fine wine, and posh restaurants. It wasn't that they were shallow, they were just far too concerned with what others thought.

Devon, however, didn't place any value on social status. She didn't go to Michelin star restaurants or wine tasting events. She liked takeout food, vodka, and bar-crawling. Though she liked pretty clothes as much as the next person, she didn't feel the need to keep up with the latest fashion trend—she wore what she liked.

"Why are these people here?" Reena asked her father.

"We're about to find out," said Finn, his expectant gaze locked on Jolene.

Ralph, the butler, offered them drinks, but everybody politely declined. The moment the door closed behind Ralph, Jolene spoke.

"I'll get straight to the point. Devon was kidnapped last night."

Finn did a slow blink, and his entire body went rigid.

"She freed herself, obviously," Jolene went on. "But now we need to find out who arranged the kidnapping, and so we have some questions from you."

Finn turned to Devon, his eyes hard. "You were kidnapped last night . . . and I'm only hearing this *now?*"

"It was my call to keep it from you until we could speak face-to-face," Jolene told him.

Finn rounded on the other Prime. "Why?" he bit out. "You don't trust that I'll answer you truthfully?"

"No, I don't. Because I suspect you may find my questions . . . uncomfortable."

Flushing, he took an aggressive step toward her. "You had no right to keep this from me, Jolene. *None.*" Raking a hand through his hair, he looked down at Devon, seemingly at a loss for what to say to her. "Are you okay?" he finally asked.

"I'm fine," replied Devon. "Just eager for answers."

"Where do *you* come into this?" Reena asked Tanner, belligerent. "Is it connected to your Primes? Did someone take her to get at Harper?"

Tanner's hound bared its teeth, not caring for the female's tone. It didn't much like her indifference toward Devon either. Although Tanner had known in advance that she and Finn weren't close, he'd expected more concern from the other male. Finn seemed more bothered by the fact that he'd been kept in the dark than he did by the threat to his daughter.

"I'm here because Devon is under my protection," Tanner told Reena. He cut his gaze to Finn. "From what her kidnapper told her, the person connected to the kidnapping intended to contact you."

"There was supposed to be an exchange—me for a guy called Asa," said Devon. "You wouldn't happen to know anything about him, would you?"

Finn's expression went utterly blank.

Devon narrowed her eyes. "Don't even think of lying to me, Finn. Not about this."

"It's lair business," said Reena.

"And it touched Devon," Tanner cut in, "which makes it *her* business." And these people were out of their fucking minds if they thought he'd leave without the answers she was due. "Keeping your shit private is really more important to you than finding out who targeted Devon? Really?"

Nostrils flaring, Reena turned to face Finn. "Dad . . ."

"Who. Is. Asa?" asked Devon.

Leticia sighed. "You should tell them, Finn. They can't protect her if they don't know the facts."

Reena's eyes widened. "But—" She broke off at the cautioning look her mother shot her.

Finn's shoulders lowered. "Asa was part of my lair. But when I denied him a position on my Force for a third time, he left. Became a stray. He also banded together with other strays and started . . . an operation, of sorts."

Devon's brow furrowed. "Operation?"

"They would kidnap the child of a demon within our lair, and then they would threaten to kill that child if the demon didn't do something they'd otherwise never do—cheat on their mate, kill their most trusted friend, hand over one of their other children. It was a game to Asa."

"Sick bastard," Jolene muttered.

Devon had to agree. Demons *always* got revenge, but this was fucked-up even for them.

"Apt description." Finn sank into an armchair. "We captured Asa and locked him up. As you can imagine, the people he hurt are enjoying exacting their vengeance on him."

"What about the others in Asa's group?" asked Jolene.

"He gave up their names under torture. They've all been killed."

"He couldn't have given up all of them, because someone wants him freed," Jolene pointed out. "Only one of his group could possibly want that."

"He swore there were no others. I believed him. That was my mistake."

"We all believed him," said Eric.

Ciaran spoke for the first time. "But how many others *can* there be? One? Two?"

"Probably just one, or they wouldn't have needed to hire someone else to do the kidnapping," said Devon.

All eyes jumped to the parlor door as it swung open. Devon watched as yet *another* redhead waltzed inside. Just as stunning as Reena but without the badass vibe, Kaye always looked as if she'd just walked off a commercial shoot for cosmetics.

Kaye smiled at Devon—it was the kind you'd gift a distant relative merely to be gracious. "Ralph said you were here and . . . my, my, this looks official."

Reena sighed. "Kaye, we're kind of busy here; you need to go."

Kaye's smile slipped from her face as her gaze darted from person to person. "Something's happened. What is it?"

Finn took a deep breath, turned to his youngest daughter, and spilled the beans.

Her mouth fell open. "Oh my God." She eyed Devon. "You look okay, but you must be a little shook up. I don't get why they took *you*. I don't mean it in a bitchy way. It's just that, well, you're not a big part of Dad's life. Shouldn't they have gone after me or Reena or Spencer?"

Reena shot her sister a look that called her an idiot. "We're better protected than Devon. She made an easier target."

"I don't think it was that," said Jolene. "I think they thought there was more chance of Finn agreeing to free Asa if he had

pressure coming at him from other people to make the trade."
She looked at Finn. "Knox and I would have demanded you
take whatever action necessary to see that Devon was returned
safely—I think someone was counting on that."

Finn rubbed at the back of his head. "Devon, I . . . " Exhaling
heavily, he dropped his arm. "You're welcome to stay here until
all this is over."

Reena's spine snapped straight.

"I'll be fine, but thanks," Devon said to him.

Finn's lips thinned but he inclined his head. "I can take things
from here, Jolene. I'll find out who—"

"That's not how this is going to work, Finn," said Jolene.
"I've already had this conversation with Harper. I don't feel like
having it again with you."

"Harper's merely her friend. *I'm* her father."

"But not her Prime."

"Only because she refuses to join our lair," Reena chipped in.

Jolene slowly arched a brow. "It's never bothered any of you
before that Devon isn't your responsibility. I don't see why it
should bother you now."

"Ouch," said Kaye, her lips quirking. "She makes a good
point, though."

Reena's upper lip curled. "*Kaye.*"

Leticia silenced her daughters with a dark look.

"If you really want to help, talk more with Asa," Jolene told
Finn. "Do whatever you have to do to find whatever names he's
been hiding from you. We intend to talk with Maddox Quentin
later tonight. It seems most likely to us that he brokered the deal.
I'll call you after I've spoken with him and we can compare notes."

Finn gave a curt nod. "You'd better not hold back any information from me, Jolene."

The imp smiled. "I was just about to say the same to you."

Turning back to Devon, he swallowed. "You're sure you wouldn't rather stay here for a while?"

"I'm positive." Devon pushed to her feet. "But I do appreciate the offer."

He inclined his head again. "Call if you need me."

Devon nodded, but he gave her a look that said he didn't believe her. He was right not to. This man might have played a part in her conception, but he wasn't the man who'd helped her with her homework, taught her to ride a bike, or shot at any teenage boys who upset her. Russell was her dad, and he was the only man she trusted with her fears and vulnerabilities.

Reena stepped close to Finn's side and lifted her chin, staring hard at Devon. Her mind nudged Devon's. *This wouldn't have happened to you if you'd just moved to our lair where you'd have had better protection.* She didn't add, "You have no one to blame but yourself," but Devon heard it in the female's tone.

*You say that as if I'd have been warmly welcomed into it,* said Devon. *But we both know you never wanted me to move here—let's not pretend differently.*

A warm hand splayed on her back. "Time to go, kitten."

Yes, it really was.

\*

A short while later, Devon unclipped her seatbelt as Tanner pulled up outside one of Knox's nightclubs. The place was highly popular with humans, who had no idea that the Underground was located beneath it. The club itself was closed to humans during daytime hours, but the Underground was a hub of activity twenty-four/seven.

"You weren't kidding when you said your relationship with your half-siblings is complicated," said Tanner as they walked toward the club.

Devon shrugged. "Plenty of people can say the same."

"They could have at least expressed a bit of fucking concern about the issue of your safety. We practically had to drag information out of them."

She blinked at the vehemence in his voice. "Blood relative or not, I'm an outsider; they're not going to want to share lair business with outsiders."

Tanner entered the club first and led her down the basement stairs and over to a door that was guarded by two powerfully built demons. With a respectful nod at Tanner, they parted and punched in the keycode for the elevator behind them. The metal doors instantly slid open.

Devon put her hand on the rail as the elevator began to smoothly descend. Already, the tension inside her started to ebb—heading for work always did that for her. She knew she was lucky to be able to claim that she *adored* her job. Although she specialized in piercings, she'd also been Raini's apprentice for a while. Her apprenticeship had ended four months ago, and she was now a fully-fledged tattooist.

Tanner folded his arms. "You don't seem to get along well with Reena."

"We're close in age, so I think she felt threatened when I first came into the picture. Like I'd replace her in Finn's affections or something. She was competitive, which got annoying fast. She lost the petty streak over the years, but she never 'took' to me."

"And Kaye?"

"Kaye's pretty much indifferent to my existence. She's a free, directionless spirit who's wrapped up in her own world. So long as Finn continues supplying her with credit cards and paying for her condo, she'll be blissfully happy."

"What about the oldest, Spencer?"

"He's very self-focused, and all he really cares about is

preparing himself to take over from Finn one day. If I asked Spencer for a favor, he'd probably do it for me. But not out of love, and he'd no doubt try to extract a favor from me in exchange."

Moments later, there was a *ping*, and then the shiny doors slid open once again. *Hello, demonic paradise.* There was a seemingly endless strip of stores, bars, casinos, clubs, eateries, restaurants, hotels, and strip clubs throughout the Underground—most of which didn't have front walls, allowing people to see inside. There were also things you would not expect to find, including a rodeo and a combat circle.

Tanner walked in front of Devon, protecting her from being bumped by pedestrians. It wasn't long before they arrived at the tattoo studio. As it was next door to the cutest coffeehouse and wasn't too far from the shopping mall, Devon considered Urban Ink to be very nicely situated. She usually met up with the girls at the coffeehouse before work of a morning, and she was bummed that she'd missed it.

Two scowling, badass looking males stood near the studio's front door, their expressions *daring* the world to come at them. They nodded at Tanner in greeting.

"Devon, meet Enzo and Lex," said Tanner. "They're members of my Force, and they'll be watching the studio today."

She barely had time to say hello before the pooch splayed his hand on her back and herded her toward the door. The bell above her head jangled as she pushed it open. She stepped inside, releasing a long breath as the familiar, comforting scents of ink, paint, and disinfectant swirled around her, smoothing over the sharp edges of her antsy mood and settling her feline.

Urban Ink was like a second home to Devon. She loved everything about it—the artsy/biker/rock theme, the checkered glass partitions between the tattoo stations, the metal art on the white walls that were also enlarged copies of tattoos. She wasn't sure which of the latter she preferred best—it was a toss between the Chinese dragons and the flock of ravens.

Behind the large, freakishly tidy reception desk that doubled as a jewelry display cabinet, Khloë looked up and saluted them. "Hey, muchachos."

The young male on the sofa snorted a laugh and then went back to scanning one of the tattoo portfolios. A burly guy sat stiffly at Raini's station, warily eyeing the buzzing tattoo gun in her hand. Each of the stations looked similar with the black leather recliners, wall mirrors, framed licenses, and sketches and photographs of tattoos that had been tacked to the wall.

"You're here, good," said Harper, standing at the rear of the studio. She tipped her head toward her office. "Both of you come tell me how the meeting went."

Devon hung her jacket on the coat rack near the vending machine and then headed to the office with Tanner hot on her heels. Inside, they brought the sphinx up to speed.

Harper blew out a breath. "Jesus, Asa is one sick puppy. Hopefully Finn can get him to part with whatever names he held back. Are you still planning to talk with Maddox Quentin?"

"Yes," replied Tanner. "We're going to his nightclub later; he's there every night." His eyes slid to Devon. "I'd ask you to wait outside, but I know I'd be wasting my breath."

Devon frowned. "Why wouldn't you want me there? You think he'd hurt me?"

Tanner's snort was all arrogance. "He knows better than to touch anything under my protection. Maddox doesn't kill for shits and giggles, but he doesn't place much value on the life of other breeds of demon—none of his kind do. He likes to toy with people."

Devon narrowed her eyes. "In what sense?"

"He can get into a person's mind, like Knox. He can delete

memories, insert false ones. Can find their worst fears, dig out secrets that they keep even from themselves, and compel them to do things they'd never normally do—and he can even make sure they'll have no recollection of it."

She'd already known that Knox had that ability—he'd used it on her honorary brother. Though she hated to admit it, Drew had brought that shit on himself.

"But unlike Knox," Tanner went on, "Maddox can also do things like plant desires in a person's head, change or erase their fears, make them feel pain, make them *crave* pain. He also likes to use people's fears and hopes and secrets against them—sometimes to intimidate, sometimes for personal gain, and sometimes purely for his amusement."

Devon tilted her head. "Has he ever done any of that to you?"

"He tried. It didn't work out so well for him. He was also stupid enough to try it with Knox."

"Really?" asked Harper, brows lifting. "What did Knox do?"

"Fried one of Maddox's sentinels alive right there on the spot—it took mere seconds. Maddox was pissed, but he respects power. Respects guts." Tanner pinned Devon's gaze with his own. "I don't think I need to tell you to be on high alert today. Whoever hired the incantor could make another try for you, thinking to take you off-guard."

"I noticed you stationed Enzo and Lex outside," Harper said to him. She gave a nod of approval. "Good thinking."

Devon felt her mouth tighten. "That's not—"

"You're not weak, we know that," Tanner quickly cut in. "But Asa's friend now knows that too, since you managed to escape the cabin. Where's the harm in you having backup just in case you need it?"

Khloë skidded into the room. "Okay, the suspense is *killing* me. What did Finn say?"

"Devon will tell you all about it when I'm gone," said Tanner. "Before I go, how's your palm, kitten?"

Devon stiffened. Oh, he just *had* to bring that up, didn't he? "It's fine."

Harper looked at her, frowning. "Did the incantor hurt your hand? Which one?"

"I'm not hurt, I'm fine."

Nose wrinkling, Khloë walked further into the room. "Then why is he asking about your palm?"

"The same reason he chases his tail and licks his own asshole—he's dumb," said Devon.

Tanner chuckled. "You can't keep it a secret, kitten. People are going to notice it."

"Notice what?" Harper seized Devon's hand and studied her palm. She blinked. "He marked you? Seriously? How in the hell did that happen?"

"It wasn't *supposed* to happen," clipped Devon. "He said it would work, but I didn't believe him."

"*I* wouldn't have believed him either," said Khloë. "It's pretty. Is it sensitive or anything?"

"No," said Devon. "It's like a tattoo. Only it glistens. And smells like wet dog."

Tanner's mouth kicked up into a smile as his mind touched hers. His voice flowed into her head. *You like my scent.*

*Not in the slightest, pooch.* Ha, such a lie! He had a rather scrumptious scent. It was dark, rich, and smoky with notes of cinnamon spice.

Khloë looked at him, her face all scrunched up. "Your demon is actually protective of Devon? Really?"

"She wouldn't be wearing my mark if it wasn't," he said.

"Huh." Harper scratched her chin. "And your feline hasn't tried clawing it off?"

Devon shook her head. "It appears to think he'd make a good ally. For now, anyway."

Harper pursed her lips. "Well, it's right."

Tanner glanced at his watch. "I have to go. Enzo and Lex will be outside; they'll keep watch over you," he told Devon. "Don't give them any shit or try sending them off to take a break. No, don't pretend you wouldn't have messed with them. And don't let Khloë mess with them either."

The imp blinked. "What makes you think I would?"

Tanner just snorted and then tugged on one of Devon's curls. "Be good." He said his goodbyes and then headed out.

Khloë exhaled a mockingly dreamy sigh. "You guys would make such a cute couple."

Devon glowered at her. "Don't make me hurt you."

Khloë shrugged innocently. "Hey, I did some digging on Maddox Quentin. None of the things I heard were good."

"By the sounds of it, *he* isn't good." Devon relayed to her what Tanner told her about the descendant's abilities.

"My hackles are rising just thinking of you in the same room as the guy," said Khloë. "You have tough mental shields, but they're not impenetrable. Do you think he'll try getting in your head?"

"Not while Tanner and Jolene are right there—they'd fuck his shit up. Jolene could bring the whole building tumbling down around him—and she wouldn't hesitate to do it, since she could shield me, her, and Tanner at the same time."

"He doesn't sound like a guy who'd let a little thing like danger stop him from doing anything he wanted to do," said Harper.

Yeah, that was what worried Devon.

# CHAPTER FIVE

Knox's main office within the Underground was quite close to Urban Ink, so it was mere minutes before Tanner arrived. The space was sleek and modern with a large window that overlooked the combat circle. There was ample seating with the desk chair, sofa, and cozy chairs—all of which were upholstered in rich Italian leather.

Tanner tipped his chin at Larkin. Sitting near the window with her cell phone wedged between her ear and shoulder, the harpy raised her brows at him in greeting as she chatted to whoever was on the other end of the line.

Looking up from where he was seated behind the executive desk, Knox gave Tanner a short nod. Papers, memos, and stationery cluttered the surface. There was also a top-of-the-range computer, printer, and copier machine.

Tanner took the chair opposite Knox. "Where's Levi and Keenan?"

"They're on their way. How did things go with Finn?" After

Tanner gave him a rundown of the meeting, Knox added, "He might not be a father to Devon, but he cares for her in his way. If Asa is hiding anything, Finn will find out."

Finally ending her call, Larkin gave Tanner a half-smile. "Morning." She took a sip from her takeout coffee cup. "I heard about what happened to Devon. Knox said you took her home last night. How is she?"

"A pain in my ass, same as always." Tanner leaned back in his seat, making the leather creak slightly. "She's also alert, which is good, because there's a possibility that whoever hired the incantor might make another try for her. I've stationed Enzo and Lex outside the studio."

Larkin's eyes widened a little. "I'm sure Jolene already has people watching it."

"She does, but they're hanging near the hotel opposite the building, out of sight." Tanner had spotted them easily enough, though. "In other words, they're happy to use Devon as bait. I'm not. Moving onto lair matters . . . Any issues last night?"

Knox shook his head. "Not one."

Tanner blinked. "Seriously?"

"Not even a case of vandalism or drunken teens," said Knox.

Well that was new. Despite that Knox ran a very tight ship and showed no mercy to any who crossed him, such peace among lair members was rare—they were demons, after all. It was in their nature to push, rebel, and take risks. Still, they were usually careful not to do anything that would require the sentinels to intervene, since that often meant the punishment would be severe. As such, the Force managed to resolve those small issues just fine.

"I have a feeling our lair is going to be on its best behavior for a while," said Larkin. "News of what happened to Devon will travel very fast, and people will figure Harper is seething about it; they won't want to do anything that would attract her attention while she's in a violent frame of mind. With any luck, it will also discourage whoever hired the incantor to back off from Devon."

"It would be the smart thing for them to do," said Tanner. "Especially since she now wears my mark."

Larkin's brows flew up. "How the hell did you get her to agree to that?"

"It wasn't easy. Nothing with Devon ever is."

Knox's eyes narrowed. "You didn't mention this last night."

"Mention what?" asked Levi as he and Keenan strode into the office.

Knox waited until the two sentinels were seated before he explained, "It would seem that Tanner has marked Devon."

Levi looked at Tanner, his brow creased. "I could tell that you wanted to, but I didn't think your demon would go for that. Or that Devon would, for that matter."

"Your hound likes her?" Keenan asked him.

Tanner made a face. "It finds her tolerable."

Keenan snickered. "Coming from your demon, that's undying love."

"On a completely different topic," began Knox, "we need to discuss the matter of Harry's death."

"I visited the crime scene with Larkin after you headed to Jolene's house last night," said Keenan, eyes dulling. "I've seen a lot of bad shit in my time. I've been *responsible* for a lot of bad shit. But what happened to Harry? That wasn't just cruel, it was sick."

Larkin nodded. "Especially with the way the killer posed him like he was a damn doll or something. The killer was most likely one of Sloan's sentinels."

"Most likely," Tanner agreed, eyes dancing from Larkin to Keenan. "Do you either of you know if any of them has the ability to alter or cloak their scent?"

Keenan shook his head.

Larkin pursed her lips. "I'm not sure. I'll ask around and see if anyone knows, but we have to bear in mind that most demons don't make all their abilities public knowledge."

True, but . . . "If we don't check, we won't know. So, what else is on the agenda for today?"

They spent some time discussing what needed to be done—including making important calls, investigating complaints made by business owners within the Underground, and chewing a certain demon's ass out for starting a bar fight that resulted in a whole lot of damage. Said demon would also be expected to cover the costs of those damages.

Tanner looked at Larkin. "I can give Harper a ride home from work, as usual. But the evening is going to be a busy one for me. If she needs to go anywhere—"

"I'll take her," Larkin assured him.

"Do you need one of us to go with you to see Maddox?" asked Keenan.

"It's best if you don't. A group would look confrontational." Tanner pushed out of his chair. "I'll get going. Call if you need anything."

"Before you head out," Larkin began as he walked away, "there's something you should know."

Pausing, Tanner glanced at her over his shoulder and saw that she was staring out of the window. "What?"

"Well, Eleanor's waiting for you near the entrance of the combat circle."

Tanner swore under his breath. He did not have the time, patience, or inclination to deal with her. But then, he never did.

Leaving Knox's office, he descended the stairwell of the small building and yeah, there she was. She gave him a bright smile that lit up her face and could probably stop traffic. There was no denying that Eleanor Owens was astoundingly beautiful. Violet eyes. High cheekbones. Long, silky auburn hair. Sensual mouth. Hourglass figure. He'd soon realized that she wielded that beauty like a weapon. Used it to charm, manipulate, and disarm people. It often worked.

"Tanner, I've been waiting for you." Her expression molded into one of mock reprimand as she playfully tutted. "You didn't answer my calls."

"I had nothing to say. Still don't."

Her smile didn't falter at his flat tone. "Let's take a walk."

Tanner blocked her arm when she tried to link it through his. "There's nothing for you here, Eleanor. Go."

Her eyes hardened. "Why are you being so stubborn? I come from a long line of strong, powerful hellhounds. My family would make good allies. I wouldn't refuse you access to your child or—"

"Eleanor, you already gave me this speech. It made no difference the first time you said it, and it's not going to change things now either."

"You can't honestly tell me that you don't have any inclination to start your own line. You're an alpha hellhound who's centuries old, for God's sake. I'd wonder if maybe you were gay, but I've heard enough rumors about you from women—all good, by the way—to tell me that isn't the case. Is there another woman in the picture?"

"I'm not gay or in a relationship. I'm just not interested."

"What about your hound? Surely it wants to start its own line."

"It doesn't."

"Given your age, I find that hard to believe."

He shrugged. "Believe whatever you want—it doesn't change the facts."

She sighed. "Look, I'll be going into heat again in exactly three weeks—"

"Then you'd better find yourself a male you think is a worthy father for your child. That male isn't me." With that, Tanner skirted past her and stalked off.

If Eleanor wasn't so focused on the physical qualities he possessed, she'd have noticed that Tanner wasn't what anyone would call father-material. He'd been just a toddler when he was placed in Ramsbrook House. He didn't remember his own father, and he'd never had anything even close to a father figure while growing up. He didn't know the first thing about parenting.

Despite that he was a sentinel, he wouldn't make much of a role model. Ramsbrook hadn't been a stable environment to grow up in. The staff hadn't been cruel or abusive, but they'd been incredibly strict in an almost military fashion. They hadn't been warm or affectionate. Hadn't given out hugs or comforting words. Hadn't tolerated any rule-breaking, no matter how small the rule happened to be.

You didn't bother crying, because you knew nobody would come. You didn't bother reporting your problems to the staff, because they'd trivialize or outright dismiss those problems. You didn't dare show any attachment to an object or person for fear that that would be used against you during punishments.

His experiences there had shaped him into a person who even he could admit was riddled with issues. A person who was uncommunicative, volatile, highly private, and disliked relying on people. Someone who was very protective of his possessions, found it difficult to share, and who found it even harder to trust or take people at their word.

He also didn't easily connect with people, just as his hound didn't easily form attachments to places, things, or people. The only people that he and his hound had ever let close were Knox and the sentinels—their shared experiences had bonded them in a way that nobody outside of Ramsbrook could possibly begin to understand.

So, given how fucking messed up Tanner was, he honestly

didn't trust that he or his hound would be able to truly form an attachment to their own child. And they had no business fathering one until they were sure that wasn't the case.

\*

"I still can't believe you let him mark you," said Raini later that day.

Tightening her grip on the brush handle, Devon turned to her. The succubus was staring out of the window at Tanner, who was talking with Enzo and Lex. He'd obviously come to escort Harper home, just as he normally did near closing time.

Plenty of people had spotted the mark on Devon's palm throughout the day. Some had merely raised their eyebrows. Others had made passing comments like, "A *hellhound marked a hellcat— well that's new.*" News of it would no doubt circulate through the Underground like wildfire, just as news of her kidnapping had.

Devon sighed. "I told you, Raini, it wasn't that I *let* him do it. I didn't think it would work for obvious reasons."

"But it did work," Khloë pointed out, wiping down the reception desk. "And if it will make a difference while there's someone out there who wants to get his hands on you, I'm good with it. Besides, the mark's kind of cute."

"Cute but pointless if his demon isn't completely invested in protecting Devon," said Raini, "and it damn well better be. Tonight, you're going into Maddox Quentin's club, which will be full of *his* people. If they all converged on you, you'd be on Shit Street."

"I still think Grams should take me along, but she's being stubborn," said Harper, tidying her station.

"She's being smart," Raini corrected. "She has no choice but to deal with this her—"

"I know, I know." Harper sighed. "I accept that, but I don't like it. You can't make me."

The bell jingled as the door swung open. Tanner prowled

inside, muscles bunching and rippling in a way that almost made Devon shiver in delight. But then he gave her that taunting grin that pricked at her patience.

"Hey kitty cat," he said in that deep, gritty voice. "Have you missed me?"

Devon gave him a mockingly bright smile. "Of course I have. What's your name again?"

The corner of his erotic mouth hitched up. "You don't have to be embarrassed that you're so obsessed with me—these things happen."

She ground her teeth, tempted to swipe out with the brush and knock him off his feet. "If I could just Photoshop your personality, I'd be a much happier woman."

Chuckling, he slid his gaze to Harper. "You ready?"

"Almost," the sphinx replied. "We can give Devon a ride home, right? Her car is still out of commission."

He nodded, turning back to Devon. "I'm always here for you when you need a ride, kitten."

She almost blushed at the sexual innuendo. "My, my, aren't I the lucky one?"

"I'd say so, yeah."

Once she and Harper were ready, he escorted them out of the Underground. He took Devon home first, promising he'd return at 9pm and pick her up on the way to Jolene's house. All three of them would be riding to Maddox's club together, apparently. Whoopdeefuckingdoo.

After dinner, she took a long, hot shower and dried her hair before slipping on her favorite black dress and high heels—perfect club attire. The dress accentuated her cleavage and dipped low at the back.

It was a little before 9pm that Tanner's mind touched hers. *I'm outside, kitten.*

God, it so wasn't fair that even his telepathic voice was like a carnal stroke to her senses. *I'll be down in a sec*, she told him.

When she stepped out of the building moments later, he unfolded from the car, all graceful menace and dark sensuality. And her libido had a mini orgasm or something. Well, in her defense, how did you brace yourself against that kind of concentrated sex appeal? It simply wasn't doable.

He opened the rear passenger door as he blatantly raked his gaze over her, his eyes broody and hooded. The all-too-familiar sexual chemistry sparked to life and thickened the air, making little bumps rise on her flesh. "Well, now," he said. "You—"

"Don't talk, pooch, you'll just mess everything up."

But, of course, he taunted her throughout the journey to Jolene's house. No sooner had he beeped the horn than Jolene came striding down the path with her eldest son, Richie. They appeared to be squabbling about something.

Shit, Devon hadn't thought her Prime would bring Khloë's father along. Hey, Richie was a great guy. A talented artist who could recreate any painting—hence why he made most of his money selling counterfeits. Jolene often called him a "fixer." If something was broke, he'd mend it for you. If something of yours had gone missing, he'd find it. If you needed an alibi for the police, he'd give it to you.

He could also break the bones in your body with a stray thought. Which might have been cool if he didn't lose control of that ability when he was pissed off. Really, he wasn't the ideal person to take along to what would no doubt be a highly tense situation.

Richie opened the rear passenger door for his mother, saying, "Well, see, this is what happens when you don't listen to me. You've known me since I was, what, born—you really should have known what I'd do."

"I don't need an army," Jolene gritted out.

"Probably not. But just in case you do, we'll be close by." He gestured for her to hop inside the car. "You have somewhere to be, remember."

With a regal huff, Jolene slid into the car. "I should have put you up for adoption."

"Yeah, so you always say." Rolling his eyes, Richie gave Devon a quick wave and then shut the door.

Returning the wave, Devon asked, "Everything okay, Jolene?"

"No. That idiot is paranoid that Maddox is going to pull something. I vetoed him coming along, so now he's insisting on hanging close to the club with a large number from our lair."

Tanner pulled onto the road. "It's fine so long as they *stay* outside. Like I said to you on the phone earlier, the smaller our group, the better. Maddox will talk with a small group. If a large bunch of us go in there, Maddox will see it as confrontational."

"It would also make me seem weak to have lots of backup, I know," said Jolene. "Have you told Maddox that we're coming?"

"No. But I don't think he'll be surprised to see us there. News of Devon's kidnapping circulated fast. Given his rep, he'll know we'll consider him an obvious suspect."

The drive to Maddox's club—which was aptly named, the Damned—was relatively short. Unlike most demonic clubs, it wasn't located within the Underground. Tanner parked at the far end of the lot and then led both Devon and Jolene to the club. There was a long line of people waiting to get inside, so it was clearly popular. The bouncers instantly recognized him and unclipped the red rope, allowing the three of them to pass. Well that surprised her.

"Are you and Maddox friends or something?" she asked as they walked inside. It was dark, loud, and jam-packed with people. Strobe lights flashed and sliced through the fog-filled air. Patrons crowded the dance floor, moving to the beat that was so intense Devon could feel it through the soles of her shoes.

He put his mouth to her ear, and she just about suppressed a shiver at the feel of his cool breath. "No," replied Tanner. "Like I said, he and I have an understanding."

Jolene glanced around, her mouth set into a thin line. "Now what?" she asked, speaking loudly enough to be heard over the thumping music.

"Now we find ourselves a table and sit down," said Tanner. "Maddox will see us from the window of his office overlooking the dance floor; he'll come to us."

Devon frowned. "What makes you so sure of that?"

"Maddox is a control freak. He'll know why we're here, and he'll want to take control of the situation. He'll approach us before we get the chance to ask for an audience with him."

Devon managed not to tense when Tanner put a hand on her bare back, his fingers spread out to take up as much skin as possible. The move was nothing short of possessive, but she didn't comment. Now wasn't the time. They needed to be focused on the matter at hand.

He found them an empty table not far from the bar and they ordered some drinks—none of which were alcoholic. All three of them wanted to have a clear mind.

Devon was halfway through her orange juice when someone caught her attention. She gaped. "You have *got* to be kidding me."

Tracking her gaze, Jolene sighed. "I suppose we should have expected this."

Standing a few feet away, Khloë did a double-take that was *totally* false. She sidled up to their table with Raini, who was acting equally shocked.

"Well, what a coincidence," said Khloë, sliding onto one of the empty seats. "Didn't expect to see you here."

Taking her own seat, Raini beamed at them. "My, don't you look pretty, Devon."

Tanner sighed. "You didn't have to do this. Devon's safe with me."

"She's safe with or without you," Raini told him. "We just wanted to be here in case things went tits up." She set her glass on the table. "I like this place, even if I am baking hot."

Fanning her face with her hand, Khloë said, "There are a whole lot of humans here. Poor oblivious humans who don't realize they're surrounded by predators. I'm so used to having nights out at the Underground that I didn't—"

A shadow fell across their table. "Hope I'm not interrupting anything."

Devon looked up at the male standing in front of them. *This* had to be Maddox Quentin. Wow, no one had told her the guy was hot. Like *blistering* hot. Tall, dark, and humming with power, he emanated sex, strength, and danger—a lethal combination for any demon.

He inclined his head. "Tanner, good to see you again."

"Maddox," the hellhound greeted simply.

"And just who have you brought with you?" Maddox looked at Jolene and said, "Ah, Jolene Wallis. I've heard much about you. Some good. Some bad. All entertaining."

"I'll take that as a compliment," said Jolene.

"You should." Maddox's gaze drifted to Devon and sharpened. "You must be the hellcat I've heard so much about today."

Devon felt him then. Like cold fingertips probing at her mind, testing her defenses. "You really shouldn't do that."

Tanner let out a low growl. "*Don't*, Maddox. You fuck with her, you fuck with me."

Maddox didn't seem concerned by that. He gave a careless shrug and then studied the other two she-demons. "Who are your

other friends, Tanner? The little one has the look of a Wallis."
His eyes narrowed on Raini, and then those eyes were glittering
with heat. "A succubus. A powerful one. What's your name?"

Raini lifted her chin. "I don't see how that matters."

Maddox stared at her long and hard, and then his mouth
very slowly canted up in what could have been amusement. He
turned back to Tanner. "Let me guess, you're here to ask me if I
brokered the deal that got your hellcat kidnapped."

Tanner tilted his head. "Did you?"

"No." Maddox took the seat beside Raini. "I hadn't even heard
through . . . shall we call it the broker grapevine . . . about the
deal. If I had, I'd have contacted Knox with the information,
since the hellcat is a close friend of his mate."

"Why? You have no loyalty to Knox," Devon pointed out.

"Very true," said Maddox. "But I like it when people owe me
favors. Having Knox Thorne owe me one? Yes, that would appeal
to me. But as the guilty party in this case *didn't* try to contact
him about the deal, I'd say you're looking for a broker who—for
one reason or another—wouldn't have any interest in extracting
a favor from Knox." His eyes drifted back to Raini, who met that
stare just as boldly.

Tanner studied the male in front of him, unsure whether he
believed him or not. He'd long ago learned that Maddox was a
terrific liar. "And, off the top of your head, just who wouldn't
have an interest in doing that?"

"There's always Roth Lockwood. Knox did torture him and
then kick his ass out of your lair, after all. I'm not saying it wasn't
deserved. I'd have done much worse to someone who was selling
information about my lair to other Primes. But Lockwood now
loathes Knox with a passion—he wouldn't want anything from
him, would he?"

No, he wouldn't. And Roth would sooner set himself on fire

than give Knox any information, whether he'd receive something in return or not.

Maddox looked at Jolene. "Lockwood has also had run-ins with your son, Richie, so he'd probably get a petty kick out of doing something that would annoy you. I'm not saying it *was* Lockwood. Just that he's someone you might want to take a closer look at."

Tanner narrowed his eyes. "It's not like you to be so blunt." The descendant often talked in circles. "Getting info out of you is usually more like dragging blood out of a stone."

Maddox shrugged. "Maybe I'm not in the mood to play."

"Or maybe you want something."

The guy's mouth kicked up into a smile that unapologetically said, "guilty as charged."

"Here's something you might find interesting. You know that one of the areas I excel in is gathering information. People frequently hire me to find intel on others. Three months ago, a male hellcat came to me requesting a dossier be done on Devon Clarke. He said he was looking for potential female hellcats to breed with, and he considered her a prime candidate. It's not uncommon for people to do such a thing, so I didn't think anything of it at the time."

Devon stiffened. "Who was he?" The question was a whip.

"If you want me to break client confidentiality, you'll need to give me a good reason," said Maddox.

Jolene clenched her fists. "I'll destroy you right where you sit if you don't—that's a good reason."

Maddox's smile widened. "It is. But I don't fear death."

Devon sighed, exasperated. "You already know what you're going to ask for in exchange for information. You probably thought it up before we even got here, figuring we'd come talk to you sooner or later. Why not just say it?"

"Direct." Maddox gave a short nod. "I like that." He slowly leaned forward and rested his clasped hands on the table. "You do have something I want."

Tanner bristled. "You're not getting *anything* from her."

"You think I'm going to demand a sexual favor?" Maddox looked affronted. "No, Tanner, I don't operate that way. And I have no taste for unwilling women." His gaze sliced back to Devon. "What I want is very simple. I want a few ounces of your venom." He dipped his hand into his pocket and then placed a small vial on the table in front of her. "You give me the venom, and I'll give you the name of the person who requested the dossier."

Devon cast the vial an uneasy glance. "What do you want the venom for?"

"That's not important."

"If it wasn't important, you wouldn't want it."

A smile touched one side of his mouth. "I have my reasons, and those reasons are my own."

Tanner growled. "You can have some of mine." He went to grab the vial, but Maddox snapped his hand around it.

"I don't want hellhound venom. I want *hellcat* venom." Maddox raised a brow at her. "Well, what will it be, Miss Clarke? Just how badly do you want that name?"

Very badly, but ... *I'm not comfortable giving him my venom when he could use it to hurt someone,* Devon told Jolene.

*He could hurt someone easily enough without your venom,* Jolene pointed out, *so I'm not sure he intends to use it that way. He might just like to collect such things—he wouldn't be the first demon to do so.*

True. And she didn't really have much choice if she was going to get that damn name, did she? Grinding her teeth, Devon held out her hand for the vial.

Maddox gave it to her. "Right decision."

It was easy enough to secrete the venom—she could do it at will. She placed the open vial beneath one of her fangs and filled it with a few ounces of venom, as requested. She capped it and then held it out to Maddox, but she didn't let go until . . .

"Hugo Sheridan," said Maddox. "He's not very powerful, so he shouldn't give you any trouble when you question him. He's from Michigan, but I don't know his address. I'd imagine you can find it out for yourself." Maddox pocketed the vial. "It was a pleasure doing business with you, Miss Clarke." His gaze darted to Raini. "You still haven't told me your name."

"Haven't I?" the succubus asked airily.

Taking Devon's hand, Tanner pushed to his feet and edged around the table. "We appreciate your cooperation," he said, though his words were somewhat stiff.

Maddox inclined his head. "There's no rush for you to leave." But he wasn't talking to Tanner, he was talking to Raini.

The blonde stood and moved away from the table, but she looked at him steadily. "We have somewhere to be."

Maddox pursed his lips and rose to his feet. "Pity."

Raini turned to leave, but then her knees buckled, and she stumbled backwards. Her hand flew to her head as she let out a loud gasp—there was no pain in it, only shock.

Devon whirled on Maddox, about to demand to know what the hell he'd done, but he was staring at Raini, appearing utterly stunned.

Drawing in a long breath, the succubus lowered her arm and looked at him, her eyes flickering nervously. Devon glanced from one to the other. What the fuck?

"Well, well, well," said Maddox, looking nowhere near as cool as he sounded. "Now *that* was a surprise." But the shock seeped away from his gaze and was quickly replaced by what could only be described as a dark sense of ownership. And then Devon understood. *Ah, hell.*

Raini made a beeline for the exit. She wasn't fleeing, no, she was marching out of there like she had beef with the world at large. Devon followed her closely, sensing that Khloë, Tanner, and Jolene were close behind.

In the parking lot, Devon touched the blonde's arm. "You okay?"

Raini shoved a hand into her hair. "I just needed to get out of there."

"He's your anchor, isn't he?"

Raini swallowed. "Yeah, he's my anchor. And he's a guy who does cruel shit like broker the kinds of deals that get hellcats kidnapped. And he might well have brokered the deal that was made for you. He said he didn't, I know, but he's not a person whose word I'd ever trust." She gave a bitter laugh. "And, as my anchor, he's supposed to be someone I can trust above all others. What a fucking joke."

Devon exchanged a worried look with Khloë. Maddox Quentin . . . hell, Devon wouldn't want someone like him for an anchor. Then again, she wouldn't want Knox for an anchor, but he'd been supportive and loyal to Harper even before they began their little fling that turned into a mating.

Jolene put a hand on Raini's shoulder. "Take a breath, sweetheart. Everything's going to be fine. I can't say for sure whether Maddox will want the anchor bond or whether he'll pointedly avoid you like the plague—some controlling males like him go one way, some go the other. Just know that we're here for you and . . . " She trailed off with a sigh as something in the distance caught her attention. "That boy is a pain in my ass."

Devon tracked her gaze and saw Richie heading their way.

"Hey, Pops," said Khloë.

"Hey, trouble." Richie curled his arm around his daughter's shoulders and lifted a brow at Jolene. "Well, what happened?"

Jolene quickly brought her son up to speed.

Eyes hard with anger, Richie hummed. "Who do you plan to speak with first? Roth Lockwood, or Hugo Sheridan?"

"We should talk with Sheridan first, since he seems a very likely suspect," said Devon.

Jolene gave a curt nod. "I agree. But that will sadly have to wait until tomorrow, since he doesn't live locally. I've never heard of him before."

"Nor have I, which is why I contacted Larkin." Tanner tapped his temple, indicating that he meant telepathically. "She'll do some digging and get the information we need on both Sheridan and Lockwood. With any luck, she'll have it by the time I've dropped you off at your place."

But, sadly, that wasn't the case.

As he parked outside Jolene's house, Khloë and Raini both thanked him for the ride, said their goodbyes to Devon, and then slid out of the Audi. They lived close to Jolene, so it made sense for all three of them to pile out at the same time.

Lingering, Jolene said, "Contact me the minute you hear from Larkin."

"Will do," Tanner told her.

She gave Devon a too-quick smile. "Bye, sweetheart." Then the Prime closed the car door.

Only when Jolene was safely inside her house did Tanner pull back onto the road. "Let's get you home, kitten."

A short while later, Tanner whipped the car into an empty parking space in the lot outside her building. He again insisted on doing a walk-through of the apartment, surprised that she—however grudgingly—allowed it. She seemed too distracted to argue with him, as if deep in thought.

He asked her to wait outside her front door while he searched the place, but she headed straight to her living area and plopped herself on the sofa. She was still there when he finished his search and sought her out. She was also staring into space.

"The place is empty," he told her.

She didn't look up at him, and her gaze remained unfocused. "Hmm."

He crossed to her and crouched in front of her. "What are you thinking?"

She double-blinked, finally seemed to see him. "Why would someone want hellcat venom?"

"I doubt Maddox wanted it for nefarious purposes, if that's worrying you. Unlike hellcat bone, it doesn't power spells. It's also not lethal to demons."

"But it is to humans," she reminded him.

"Sure, but Maddox is powerful enough to kill a human effortlessly. Many demons like to collect the unusual. I once heard that some even add small amounts of venom to their drinks— sometimes as a delicacy, sometimes in the hope of building a tolerance to it."

"But if it was something that simple, he would have just said so."

"No, he wouldn't have. Maddox is by no means a simple creature. He'd keep something so small from someone just because he can. And he doesn't explain himself to people." Tanner paused as Larkin's mind touched his.

*I have the info you need on Roth Lockwood and Hugo Sheridan,* the harpy said. *Lockwood isn't willingly a stray demon. He's tried joining other lairs since getting kicked out of ours, but no Prime will take him in because they don't trust that he'll be loyal to them, given that he betrayed Knox. I have his address here. He lives just outside of North Las Vegas. It's a dodgy neighborhood.*

Roth's brokering business clearly wasn't doing so well, then. *What about Sheridan?*

*As Maddox told you, Sheridan lives in Michigan. He also works at a veterinary clinic run by humans. Smart guy. Has a few fancy degrees. Lives with a woman he's been with for almost four years. She teaches at a human school and has a fancy degree of her own. They're both strays; always have been from what I can tell.*

*Sheridan's address?*

Larkin rattled it off. *I'm guessing you plan on going there tomorrow.*

*Good guess.* His blood buzzed with the urge to hunt. The threat to Devon needed eradicating fast.

"Was that Larkin?" Devon asked, snapping him out of his thoughts. "I could see you were having a telepathic conversation—it's not hard to tell."

He relayed what information Larkin gave him. "I'll pass it all on to Jolene after I leave here. We'll pay him a visit tomorrow and find out if he's really our guy."

She tilted her head. "You're not certain it's him? You think Maddox lied to us?"

"I simply don't believe in making assumptions. It's best to be open-minded."

Devon's pulse spiked as he took her hand and uncurled it, exposing the mark on her palm. Eleanor had to have heard about it by now, and Devon wondered just how well the woman had taken it. Then again, if this was a regular thing for him, Eleanor might not care much. "How many people have you marked?"

His eyes snapped to hers. "None."

Sincerely stunned, Devon almost gaped. "None?"

"Hellhounds mark their family members, but I don't have any

family to mark. All the other people under my protection are part of my lair, so it isn't necessary to make a statement like this to the outside world." He wasn't just making that statement to others, though, he was making it to Devon and her inner demon. He could see that his admission had unbalanced her, and it made him smile. "Speechless? That's not like you."

Flushing, she snatched her hand back and stood, forcing him to stand and back up a step. "You should go."

His mouth quirked. "Kicking me out again?"

"You searched the apartment, you can see I'm quite safe."

"I don't know about 'safe.' This building doesn't exactly have top-notch security. An apartment recently became free in one of Knox's buildings. The place is in a good area, and it's close to the entrance to the Underground. It was designed to house demons, so it has thick walls, unlike here. You wouldn't have far to travel for work, which would be a bonus. You'd have modern appliances and a landlord that gives a shit about his tenants. This complex is a shithole, kitten, and you know it."

Devon felt her cheeks go impossibly hot and her stomach curdle with embarrassment. Yes, she knew the place was bad; she didn't need to have that rubbed in her face. He hadn't *maliciously* trampled over her pride, but he'd done it all the same.

It wouldn't have been so bad if he'd done it yesterday when he first saw the place—she'd been braced for it then, could have shrugged it off. But because he'd made no disparaging remarks yesterday, she'd dropped her guard. *Stupid*. So stupid.

It was easy for him to pass judgement—he'd probably had centuries to accumulate the money he now had. It wasn't easy to tell how old a demon was; they moved with the times, adjusted, adapted—it was how they blended. But she'd come face-to-face with his hound yesterday; she'd sensed that it was far older than she ever would have suspected.

"I can take you to see the place tomorrow," he offered.

"I'm not moving." Not only because she couldn't afford to or because she wanted to be near her family, but because she'd be *damned* if she'd let him interfere in any aspect of her life. He wouldn't be satisfied with doing it just once; he'd do it over and over and over.

His jaw hardened. "You can't honestly want to live *here*."

"Not all of us can afford to live in swanky condos."

"And not all of Knox's buildings are 'swanky,' nor are they out of your price range. More importantly, they're secure."

She lifted her chin. "I'm not moving."

His growl was low and deep. "Kitten—"

"Didn't I say that your marking me doesn't mean you have rights to me? I don't need you interfering in my life, Tanner, and I won't fucking allow it." She pointed toward the door. "Go."

"I'm not trying to hurt your pride, kitten—"

"My name is *Devon*. Now get out."

He swore, low and vicious. "It's so bad that I want you safe?"

"Why are you still here? Go home, go to your Primes, go to your girlfriend—I don't care, just *go*."

His brow hiked up. "My girlfriend? I didn't realize I had one."

"That's not what Eleanor Owens believes." And, just as Devon had expected, she was unable to keep a bitter note out of her voice when she spoke the bitch's name.

His shoulders went stiff. "She talked to you? *When*?"

"A few weeks ago. She came here. She said that you're hers, and that I needed to back off. She seemed to be under the impression that I was a threat to your little fling. I'll bet she's not happy that you marked me, huh?"

"I don't care, it's got nothing to fucking do with her. I never so much as kissed her, let alone slept with her."

"Then why did she warn me off?"

"She must think you're the reason why I refuse to father the baby she plans to have, despite that I've told her several times I'm simply not fucking interested. Did she touch you?"

Pushing back the shock and pain she'd felt at hearing what Eleanor was offering him—something Devon could probably never offer any male—she replied, "No, she didn't. Now, seriously, Tanner, get out."

"Kitten."

And then she'd had enough. "*Just fucking go.*" She sent out a wave of dark, thick energy that knocked him so hard he staggered back a few steps.

The weird bastard smiled. "Well, well, well. My kitty's got sharp claws."

Fury whipped through her, and her upper lip curled. "I'm not *your* anything, pooch. You'd better get that through your head, because this possessiveness isn't going to fly with me. And my demon's not going to take kindly to it either, considering it's on the hunt for a mate."

Devon had seen people stiffen. Seen them freeze on the spot. But she'd never seen someone go *literally* as still as a statue until right then. He didn't even look like he was breathing.

His power swept out in a wave that purred against her skin and, oh God, she could *feel* the depth of his anger. Finally, his muscles unlocked, and he prowled toward her, all menace and intensity. The air felt thick and oppressive with the power that continued to pour off him. It took everything she had to stand tall and not back away, especially while his golden eyes stared down at her, glittering with something dark and dangerous.

A long, low growl rumbled out of him. "What did you just say?"

# CHAPTER SIX

She hadn't just said the word "mate," Tanner told himself. She hadn't. No fucking way. That was not what—

"It's on the hunt for a mate."

Rage exploded in Tanner's gut and rushed through his veins. A thread of something that suspiciously felt like panic tightened around his chest, squeezing until he felt like he couldn't quite get enough air.

His hound let out a furious snarl as a dark jealousy clouded the edges of its vision. The demon didn't want to stake a claim on her, but it didn't want anyone else to have her either.

"Is that so?" Tanner bit out, nostrils flaring. He took a long breath, trying to find some measure of calm. It eluded him. His pulse just kept on elevating faster and faster. His anger just kept on burning hotter and hotter. A pounding filled his ears, and adrenaline coursed through his veins as if preparing him for battle.

Looking somewhat nervous, she licked her bottom lip. "Yes, it is."

Another growl vibrated his chest—one that came from both him and his demon. A sick feeling took hold in his gut, and the pounding in his ears seemed louder.

His muscles quivered with the urge to lunge. Take. Taste. *Bite.* And no matter how hard and deep he dug for calm, he couldn't fucking find it.

Brow wrinkling, she swallowed again. "Are you okay?"

Not in the slightest. Because he'd soon have to watch the first thing that he'd wanted for himself in a very long time bind herself to someone else. It was going to happen right in fucking front of him—all of it, from the first date to the decision to mate. He'd have a front row seat to every goddamn phase of it.

Desperation hammered at him, feeding his anger, driving him to do something—*anything*—that would shut this finding-a-mate shit down. "You're young, you've got a lot of years ahead of you, there's no rush to take such a big step."

"My feline has made up its mind; it won't change it."

"So it's just your demon that wants this, not you?"

"No, it's both of us." She shrugged. "I want to mean something to someone, Tanner."

Was the woman fucking blind? He put his face closer to hers and growled, "You mean something to *me*. And that goes both ways, doesn't it?"

"Look, I—"

"*Doesn't it?*" If she denied it, he was going to lose it.

"Considering nothing could come of it, it doesn't really matter, does it?"

Fisting her hair, he dragged her closer and snarled. "It fucking matters to me." He slammed his mouth down on hers and boldly sank his tongue inside. Taken aback, she froze. No, he wasn't having that. He kissed her hard, deep, demanding a response.

A soft, broken moan of surrender poured down his throat, and then she was kissing him back.

Tanner growled, tightening his grip on her hair as he feasted on the mouth he'd fantasized about for too long. His demon would intervene any second now; would rise with a snarl of distaste. Tanner would have to pull back to be sure it didn't lash out at her—it might not like the idea of her mated, but it would have no interest in taking what it viewed as a lesser demon to its bed. But until his demon made its move, he'd make the most of every second he could get with her.

He licked and nipped and consumed her mouth as he skimmed his hands over her, shaping and clutching and squeezing. Her little moans spurred him on, stroking his throbbing cock like slick fingers.

Gripping his hair, she arched into him and whispered his name. With a low growl, he cinched her hip and yanked her closer, grinding his dick against her. The scent of her need spiced the air, and he ached to slide his fingers into that pussy and feel just how hot and wet she was. Ached to strip her naked and shove his cock so deep inside her she'd feel him in her throat.

He tensed as his hound stirred. It didn't barge to the surface. It moved slowly, edging its way close until, finally, it was pressing against his skin. It let out a chuff of disapproval. Snapped its teeth at Tanner in annoyance . . . and then it retreated, uninterested in interfering. He stilled for a few seconds, stunned. And then he lost all control.

Devon gasped as he clawed off her dress with a hungry snarl and backed her into the wall. He shoved his hard cock against her pulsing clit and, *damn*, that was one long, fat dick he was packing.

Stilling, he growled low in his throat. "Your nipples are

pierced," he choked out. He swooped down and sucked one into his mouth, grinding his cock against her clit just right.

Devon's head fell back and smacked the wall. She'd initially frozen the moment his mouth crushed hers, but the kiss had been so hot, wet, and hungry that it quickly sucked all thoughts of protest out of her head. And every ounce of the control she'd managed to exercise over her need for him had just . . . dissipated.

Years, she'd wanted this. *Years.* And she knew by the aggressive desperation in his touch that he'd been fighting that same battle.

She thought her feline would shoot to the surface and attack him. Instead, it had hissed and given her a haughty sniff of disdain, but then it had turned its back on her. And so she'd decided to make the most of however long she'd have before his demon put an end to it. Only . . . his hound didn't seem to be interfering either.

Never passive, she tore off his shirt and splayed her hands on his chest—it was perfectly defined and packed with hard, male muscle. His skin was hot and buzzed with power.

She tugged on his hair as he alternated between playing with her piercings and toying with her nipples—plucking, pinching, and twisting the throbbing buds, sending sparks of pleasure/pain to her clit. "Tanner."

His cock throbbed painfully at the stark need in her voice. Tanner was just as desperate—no, *frantic*—for more. For her. Needed to slake the hissing, spitting need roaring through him before he went crazy with it.

He snapped off her panties and cupped her pussy hard. *So hot.* "Let's see if you're ready for me." He sank two fingers inside her and groaned at how slick she was. "Fuck, kitten, you're dripping wet. Wet enough to take my cock."

He hoisted her up, frantic to get inside her before his demon could change its mind and interfere. "Wrap yourself around me. Good girl." He inched the thick head of his cock inside her. "If this is the only time I get to have you," he growled, "I'm going to imprint myself in your memory."

He slammed into her with a shocking, possessive force that stole Devon's breath, stuffing her full of the long, thick cock now throbbing inside her. She double-blinked. *Jesus.* The pressure of his cock stretching her to bursting was unlike anything she'd ever felt. She could feel every ridge and vein and beat of his heart.

She pricked his back with her claws. "Fuck me. Now." He didn't make her wait. No, he fucked her like he owned her. Hammered into her as if there was a fever pounding in his blood. Every thrust was as savage and ruthless as the mouth that hungrily ate at hers. That was how she wanted him—rough, demanding, out of control.

"I've wanted this pussy since the first time I saw you." Tanner brutally slammed harder, needing to hear more of those little moans. He was hooked on her taste, the feel of her skin, the scorching hot pussy that held him so tight and sucked him back in again and again.

The succulent scent of her need filled his lungs, making him wish he'd taken the time to taste her. He'd been too desperate to wait even a second longer than necessary to get inside her. And there he was, pounding hard, relishing every moan and whimper that mingled with the dick-hardening sound of flesh smacking wet flesh. God, she was so perfectly slick and tight. And so very close to coming. Hell, so was he.

He bit her lip. "I'm gonna make you come so fucking hard."

Oh, Devon believed him. His pace was feverish as he thrust deep again and again, driving her higher, winding her tighter, making her burn so hot she knew—

Devon frowned as his mind shoved demandingly at hers.

"Let me in," he said.

Before she'd really thought about it, she dropped her shields. And then he poured into her, until she could feel him everywhere; until she felt what *he* was feeling—the hunger, the need, the pleasure, a hot slick pussy squeezing him so tight.

Her inner walls quaked around him, and she felt his cock begin to swell. "Tanner, I'm gonna—"

"I know." He plucked one of her nipple piercings just right and growled, "Come." He bit down on her neck, purposely breaking the skin.

Devon winced as his venom leaked into her wounds. *Fuck*, it stung like a bitch. It also threw her over the edge. Digging her nails into his back, she shook violently as waves of blinding pleasure viciously tore through her, arching her spine and wrenching a scream of his name out of her throat. He snarled a harsh curse into her neck as he slammed deep, and she felt his cock pulse over and over as he exploded inside her.

Every bit of strength seemed to seep from her body in a rush, and she slumped against him, resting her head on his shoulder. Mouth dry, chest burning for air, she floated on a post-orgasmic cloud, utterly dazed and completely sated.

It could have been minutes or hours later that she became vaguely aware of him moving, holding her tight in his arms. And then she was falling. No, she thought as she snapped her eyes open, she was being lowered to her bed. Limbs like noodles, she sank into the mattress flat on her back, and her eyelids fluttered shut once more.

She felt the bed dip beside her. Felt him burrow into her side and gently rub at her inner thigh. No, she realized, he was rubbing his come *into* her skin. Shit, they hadn't used a condom.

She tried forcing her heavy eyes open—it didn't work so well. "Tanner."

He kissed the corner of her mouth. "Sleep, kitten. We'll talk tomorrow."

Yeah, that would work, she thought. And then sleep pulled her under.

*

For once, Devon woke before her alarm. She didn't need to open her eyes to know she was alone. Tanner's scent still permeated the air, but it was faint.

Oh God, she'd slept with the fucking pooch.

It had been mind-blowing. Unparalleled. Would be etched into her memory for all time, just as he'd promised it would.

Ordinarily, she liked it when a guy delivered on his promises. This time? Not so much.

Her enhanced hearing picked up the sounds of someone puttering in the kitchen. She let out a tired groan. Hell, he was still there. She would have thought he'd be long gone before she woke, considering he was supposed to be escorting Harper to work. And, God, Devon wished he had left. She just didn't know what to say to him. Didn't know what to expect from him.

Was he regretting it? Was he worried she'd expect more from him? Was he going to ask her to keep it a secret so that Harper didn't get involved? Was he—

Her alarm went off. Fuck, it was time to face the music.

Devon turned off the horrid sound, went through her morning ritual, and then shuffled through the apartment into the kitchen. Her demon huffed at the sight of Tanner sitting at the small dining table, reading something on his phone while he drank coffee, looking *far* too at home.

He also looked far too gorgeous and edible—which only grated on Devon's prickly mood.

He looked up. "Morning, kitten." He gave her one of his slow, sexually charged perusals that made her all tingly. "How are you feeling?"

Devon held up a hand and mumbled, "Don't talk to me." She needed caffeine before she had any hope of holding a conversation with him. And she certainly wasn't capable of civility until she'd had her fix.

She was just about to head for the half-full coffee pot when something caught her attention. There was a little saucer of milk on the island.

Tanner glanced at it, his eyes dancing. "Thought you might be thirsty, kitten."

And that was enough to jab at her foul morning temper. She sharply flicked her hand with a snarl. Power crackled through the air and zapped his ear hard enough to make his head jolt. "It'll be your balls next," she warned.

Even as a little blister formed near the tip of his reddening ear, the masochistic bastard smiled. "And there are my kitty's sharp claws again."

Devon narrowed her eyes at his possessive tone. Caffeine, she needed caffeine to deal with this shit.

It was as she moodily snatched a mug out of the cupboard that her cell phone rang. The chiming ... God, the sound was so piercing right then, it was like having an ice pick shoved down her ear. She dug the phone out of her pocket and looked at the screen. *Adam.* She tapped the answer icon and snapped, "What?"

There was a brief silence. "You haven't had coffee yet, have you?" Adam asked, a smile in his voice.

She grunted.

"Just wanted to check how you were doing."

"Fine," she bit out, watching through narrowed eyes as Tanner crossed to the coffee pot. If he tipped that precious liquid down the sink, she was *so* going to slit his throat.

"I actually intended to come check on you before I headed for work. You can imagine my surprise when I saw the hellhound's Audi parked outside your building."

Devon snarled at the note of amusement in Adam's tone.

"I guess I don't need to ask if you got much sleep last night."

"Eat shit, asshole." She ended the call on his laugh.

Tanner slowly approached her and poured coffee into her mug. "There."

She grunted again.

"You're welcome."

Why was he still talking? Right then, she'd kill people for less. Ugh.

Devon lazily crossed to the table and sank into the chair. Cradling the hot mug in her hands, she drank her coffee quietly, enjoying the blessed silence, acting for all the world like she was completely alone.

It wasn't until she'd drained the cup that she finally met the gaze of the male opposite her. And then memories of last night crawled all over her. Memories of his hot mouth eating hers, of his skilled fingers playing with her nipples, of his long cock driving so deep inside her it almost hurt. That quickly, the air snapped taut with that good ole sexual chemistry. "Stop staring."

"But you're such a pretty view."

Whatever.

"Jolene called me a few minutes ago. She said Finn told her that Asa was ... uncooperative. The prick swore to Finn that he'd already given him the names of everyone from his group."

Devon ground her teeth. "Finn should hand the fucker over to Jolene—she'll get him to talk."

"Jolene made that same suggestion, but Finn turned her down; said he'd get the information. He also said he'd never heard of Sheridan. He intends to ask Asa about him."

"Finn probably doesn't trust that Jolene won't kill Asa." Which was a good hunch, because Devon was pretty sure her Prime would subject Asa to a truly agonizing death—and probably hum a merry tune the entire time.

Devon rose from the table, grabbed a Danish pastry from the cupboard, and refilled her mug. She didn't need to ask if the pooch had eaten—there was an empty bowl near his cup. Taking a bite out of the Danish, she turned . . . and found herself face-to-face with him. Uncomfortable with the glitter of hunger in those eyes, she chose a neutral topic. "We're going to see Sheridan today, right?"

"Later today, yes. Jolene said Ciaran will teleport us to Sheridan's veterinary clinic just as the place is closing."

Yeah, Jolene wasn't one to question people at their homes where they felt most comfortable. She liked to take them off-guard; mess with their usual safe routines.

Tanner tilted his head. "You planning to pretend last night didn't happen?"

Well, the thought *had* crossed her mind. She just had no idea what to say or do; didn't like postmortems. She found herself blurting out, "We forgot to use a condom."

"I didn't forget."

She tightened her grip on her mug. "You, what?"

"Kitten, I don't forget stuff like that. I didn't want to come inside a condom, I wanted to come inside *you*."

It was a good thing for him that she couldn't reach the knife block, or he'd have one of those blades buried in his chest right now. Now yeah, sure, there was a high chance that she was infertile, but *he* hadn't known that. "It didn't bother you that I might not be on the pill?"

He braced his hands on the counter on either side of her. "You're not in heat—I'd have smelled it if you were, so there was no chance of you getting pregnant."

"Well, did it occur to you that I might not like guys coming in—"

"Stop trying to pick a fight."

"I'm not!"

"You are," Tanner said softly, without judgement. "You're feeling awkward and unsure, so you're going on the attack. You don't need to." He dipped his head and skimmed his nose along her neck, breathing deep, taking her into his lungs. "Your scent makes my dick hard every time."

Surprisingly chilled, his hound lay quiet, watching through hooded eyes. The demon was intense, by nature. Always alert and restless. Wired, even. The only time it was ever so relaxed was after sex, and the effect never lasted long. Right then, though, the demon was as close to content as it had ever been. Or maybe Tanner's own satisfaction at having finally had the thing he most wanted had bled over onto the demon.

She probably had no idea that last night was the first time he'd slept at a woman's house. He'd stayed, because he'd wanted to make the most of what time he had with her—unable to know for sure if his hound's attitude toward her would change overnight. It hadn't.

Tanner wouldn't have thought he'd like sharing a bed. Wouldn't have thought he'd be able to relax enough to sleep deeply. But she wasn't a snuggler, so he'd had his space. She didn't snore or hog the covers. And waking up to the sight of her right there while her scent cocooned him ... yeah, he'd liked that a fuck of a lot.

"We need to talk about last night," he said.

"Our demons didn't interfere. I don't get it."

"It was probably a combination of things. One, they've grown to tolerate each other. Two, your demon has come to view me as an ally and trusts that I won't harm you. Three, my hound

considers you under its protection—I should have figured that
meant it therefore wouldn't hurt you. Your feline had obviously
already worked that out or it would have surfaced to chase me
off. You know what all that means."

Pausing, he brushed his mouth over hers. "It means it
doesn't have to be a one-off." He heard her pulse quicken,
sensed she was going to object. "How long have we both
been struggling with this thing between us, kitten? Too long.
Far too long. It's not going to go away, or it would have done
so by now."

"I don't—"

"A month."

"Excuse me?"

"Years' worth of pent-up sexual frustration isn't going to burn
out fast. One month of you in my bed, night after night . . . yeah,
I think that should do it."

Devon's stomach hardened. She felt as if he'd slapped her
because . . . "Oh, you want to fuck me out of your system."
Hiding how much that stung, she gave him a sardonic smile.
"Well, isn't that nice. You sure know how to make a girl feel
special, pooch."

"You got a better idea, baby?"

"Yeah, go find yourself a fuck-buddy."

He raked his teeth over her lower lip. "Is that really what you
want, kitten? You want another man's hands on you? You want
another woman's hands on me?"

Her claws almost sliced out, pricking the insides of her fingertips so hard she winced.

"Yeah, I figured you wouldn't like it. I sure as shit don't."
Dipping his head again, Tanner dragged his lips down her neck
and over to her rapidly beating pulse. He wanted to feel it beating in his mouth, wanted to bite down on that soft flesh again.

But if he did that, he'd need more. And there was no time—she had to be at work soon. So he satisfied himself with grazing his teeth over her pulse, leaving the slightest mark.

"Look, I don't—"

He lifted his head. "I know it's pure reflex for you to fight me on everything, but what's the sense in fighting me on something you want as much as I do?" He slid his hand up her arm, over her shoulder, and settled it on her neck. "A month. Think about it. You can give me your answer later."

"And if you don't get the answer you want?"

He skimmed his thumb over her lower lip and said softly, "You know me, kitten."

She *did* know him, Devon thought. Knew that he wasn't fazed by rejection, knew he never settled for anything less than what he wanted. He wouldn't tip his hat and walk away if she turned him down. No, he'd be relentless and single-minded in his pursuit. And she couldn't help but feel sad that he wouldn't be in pursuit of *her*, he'd be in pursuit of a brief fling.

Oh, she knew a hellhound and hellcat could have no future together, especially since male hellhounds rarely mated, but it still hurt to know he simply wanted to rid his system of her ... like she was a virus or something. Yeah, there was nothing flattering about that.

\*

It wasn't until much later, when she, Raini, and Khloë were having lunch in the break room, that Devon had a chance to tell them about Tanner's little proposal.

Khloë's brows rose. "A hellcat spending a month in the bed of its natural enemy. What could go wrong?"

Raini picked up her soda. "I doubt his hound would harm her, Khloë. *Unless* it withdrew its protection from her, of course." Her gaze slid to Devon. "Do you think your feline would fight you on hopping into his bed again?"

"It might be okay with another night," Devon replied. "But a month? No way. Not when it's seeking a mate. But that works for me, because I'm not exactly itching to jump into bed with a guy when his objective is to flush me out of his system."

Sure, there was a certain logic in burning out the lust that had held them in a tight grip for far too long. But although she had nothing against a fling, the way he'd put a time-limit on it and said it wasn't about exploring what flared between them but about *ridding* himself of it . . . that just made the whole thing seem so cold. Impersonal sex was not her thing.

"Yeah, I can't say I'd like that either," said Harper. "So, what are you going to do?"

"Tell him no." Simple.

Harper blinked. "You say that like he'll hear and heed you."

Khloë gave a wan smile. "*Hello, alpha hellhound.* Betas of his kind are annoying enough—all bluster and pigheadedness and 'I want my way in all things.' Alphas? They're far harder to deal with, because there's no reasoning with them. Getting them to accept that they won't get what they want . . . yeah, that's always a rough road."

Harper nodded. "Tanner uses whatever method it takes to get his own way—straightforward or underhanded. If it means being sweet, he'll be sweet. If it means playing dumb, he'll play dumb. If it means coming across as harmless, he'll do that too. And right now, what he wants is you. I don't envy you."

Cursing under her breath, Devon rubbed at her temple. She'd never expected to find herself in this position. Never expected him to ever claim that his hound "tolerated" her presence.

"I say you should agree to one more night," said Khloë. "Then you can wow him with all your skills and make it a night he'll never forget so it'll be *impossible* for him to ever get you out of his system."

"Ruthless." Harper chuckled. "I like it. And it'd serve him right."

"Totally," agreed Raini. "I'm all for that idea."

It wasn't such a bad one. Devon hadn't had a chance to use *any* of her skills last night—it had all happened so fast. She hadn't done anything more than hold on tight for the ride. "I'll think about it. For now, let's talk about something else." She tilted her head, regarding Raini carefully. "You haven't been yourself today. Heard anything from Maddox?"

Harper frowned. "Maddox? Why would Raini have heard from him?"

Raini winced. "Oh yeah, I kind of forgot to mention that part earlier when I told you what happened at the club."

It was while Raini was making her little revelation to Harper that Devon's cell phone began to chime. She knew from the ringtone that it was a video call. Seeing Spencer's name on the screen, she headed out of the room and tapped the answer icon.

"Hey," she said to the face staring back at her. Just like Reena and Kaye, he possessed Leticia's almond eyes and prominent cheekbones. But Spencer also had his father's blond hair, lean build, and strong jawline.

"I heard about what happened from Dad," said Spencer. "I wanted to check how you were doing."

Able to tell from the high windows behind him that he was in his office, she suspected the call would be a short one. Spencer was as much of a workaholic as his father. "I'm okay," she replied. "Just frustrated that Asa won't spill whatever names he might be holding back."

Spencer nodded, jaw hardening. "Dad had a *long* talk to him.

Asa refuses to admit there were any others in his group. Don't worry, Dad will get him to cough up the info."

"Jolene could make him talk." And if that failed, Knox would certainly step in.

Spencer snorted. "No one's going to hand Asa over to another lair. You don't know the shit he did, Devon. Dad might have told you the bare facts, but there's so much more. He and his group destroyed lives without even killing anyone. And they did it because they could. Dad's never going to hand over that fucker to someone else."

She sighed. She'd already figured as much, but it was still frustrating.

"He won't let you down on this one, Devon. Trust him to get the answers you need." He paused. "Reena told me that Tanner Cole considers you under his protection. That true?" He didn't seem to believe it.

In answer, Devon held up her palm, showing him the mark there.

Spencer's brows flew up. "Well damn. You realize hellhounds are super territorial of whoever they mark, right?"

"Yep."

He puffed out a breath. "Good luck dealing with him. I'm pretty sure you're going to need it."

Yeah, so was she.

# CHAPTER SEVEN

Resting his clasped hands on the office desk, Knox addressed all four sentinels as he said, "I'm hoping that at least one of you can tell me that your investigations into Sloan's sentinels revealed something interesting about them or their abilities."

"I spoke with my sources, some ex-members of Sloan's lair, and even one of Sloan's old girlfriends," said Tanner, sprawled on the sofa. They hadn't been alarmed by his questions; it wasn't exactly uncommon for demons to try unearthing information on one another—it was that whole "knowledge is power" thing. "None could confirm if any of the sentinels had the ability to alter their scent or cause a heart attack."

Beside him, Larkin blew out a breath. "Sadly, I got nothing."

Keenan dug his flask out of his inner coat pocket. "Same here."

Standing with his hip propped against the wall, Levi shook his head in the negative. "From what I did learn about their personalities, I'd say you could label the four sentinels Cocky, Surly, Dicey, and Robotic. The latter is Sloan's most trusted sentinel, Colm. He's also the one who's typically sent to execute those who wrong the Prime. Very little is known about Colm, his roots, or his abilities."

"Then it might be worth taking a much closer look at Colm just in case there's something more interesting to find," Knox mused. "Perhaps the demons that Sloan planted in our lair will have something noteworthy to tell me."

"Do you still intend to spend some 'quality time' with them?" Levi asked the Prime.

"Yes, I do. Later tonight, in fact. And I plan to question them while I do." Knox's gaze danced from Larkin to Keenan. "After we're done here, I want you to find and bring them both to my Chamber. There are plenty of delightfully torturous devices there that will get them talking."

"Consider it done," said the incubus. Larkin simply nodded.

Knox leaned back in his chair and turned his attention to Tanner. "Tell me what happened at the Damned last night."

"I don't have much to add to what I already told you," said Tanner. He'd telepathed Knox and each of the sentinels the previous evening after his meeting with Maddox.

"I want all the finer details," Knox told him.

"All right." Once Tanner had finished recounting the events, he added, "I can't say for sure whether Maddox was telling the truth that he didn't broker the deal—he's too good a liar—but I still think it's wise to question Sheridan and Lockwood. Jolene and Ciaran are going to meet me at Urban Ink near closing time. The three of us and Devon will then go speak with Sheridan as he finishes work."

"It's possible that Maddox just gave you those names to divert the attention from him," said Levi. "He's usually not so cooperative. It makes me suspicious that he didn't dance around your questions."

"I wouldn't call exchanging info for hellcat venom 'cooperative.'" Larkin fiddled with the end her long braid. "But, yeah, I agree that he's not normally so forthcoming."

Keenan shrugged. "Maybe he just didn't like the thought of having Knox and Jolene on his ass, so he didn't bother with his usual games. Whatever the case, I agree it's wise to speak with Sheridan and Lockwood." His gaze cut to Tanner. "If it turns out that Maddox has you chasing shadows, it'll become clear soon enough."

"There's something else," Tanner said to Knox. "It turns out that Maddox is Raini's anchor."

Levi let out a low whistle. "Did they form the bond?"

"No," replied Tanner. "She marched out of the club, and he didn't try to stop her."

"Do you think he'll want to bond with her?" Levi asked no one in particular. "I mean, he rarely concerns himself with demons outside his own breed. She's not a descendant."

"I might have said no if I hadn't felt the pull of the anchor bond myself," said Knox. "It's very strong, and his demon will no doubt be pushing him to seek her out—that's not easy to ignore."

Tanner rubbed at his nape. "I'm not certain he'd have much success convincing Raini to form the bond. She wasn't whatsoever happy to learn that he was her anchor."

"Well, if Raini and Khloë had just stayed at home like they *should* have, Raini might never have known about it," clipped Keenan. "She could have lived with the bliss of ignorance. You should have sent them home, Tanner. *Especially* Khloë. She's a magnet for trouble. Self-preservation is not a priority of hers *at all*. I don't know how that imp has survived this long." He took a long swig from his flask.

Larkin arched a brow at the incubus. "And just what exactly

did she say when you telepathically yelled at her for turning up at the Damned?"

Keenan looked as if he'd deny having done so, but then he sighed. "She laughed and slammed a mental door on me."

Larkin's lips twitched. "She won't reopen it, will she?"

"Nope." Keenan took another long drink from his flask. "Someone needs to save her from herself."

"Khloë's like any imp: a law unto—"

"Can we stop talking about her?" Keenan complained. "I say we talk about Tanner—it's obvious he got laid last night. It's written all over him."

Tanner shot the incubus a narrow-eyed glare.

Larkin huffed. "I'm offended that you think I'd be so easily distracted, Keenan." But she was eyeing Tanner curiously. "Yeah, you got laid all right. Was it Eleanor?"

Mouth setting into a slash of distaste, Tanner replied, "No."

"Well, you'd better warn whoever it was that Eleanor might confront them over it, since she won't want someone affecting her plans for you," the harpy advised.

Tanner stilled. "If she tries that shit, she's dead."

Larkin sat up straight, smiling. "Whoa, whoa, whoa . . . You're protective of this mystery girl, huh? In that case, she must be part of our lair. The only female outside of our lair that you're protective of is . . . " She trailed off, eyes widening. "Oh my God, you slept with Devon."

*Fuck.* Hey, Tanner had no problem *admitting* it happened. He just had no wish to discuss it with anyone—it was between him and his hellcat.

Keenan snorted. "Their demons would fight to the death before they'd allow that to happen." But when Tanner didn't argue with Larkin's claim, the incubus gaped. "Oh my God, you slept with Devon."

Levi's brow wrinkled. "But . . . your hound and her feline are natural enemies."

"They have something in common, though—they're both protective of Devon," said Tanner. "Her feline sees me as an ally and senses that Devon's safe with me."

"Still, I wouldn't have thought that—" Knox broke off as his phone rang. He fished the cell out of his pocket and frowned at the screen. "Well, this is a surprise." Instead of elaborating, he answered the call.

Like the other sentinels, Tanner fell quiet as Knox—

Larkin's mind touched his. *So, what's next for you and Devon? I'm hoping you're not going to say it was just a one-night stand.*

And *this* was why Tanner hadn't wanted to share what had happened with the sentinels; he'd known that at least one of them would stick their nose in. *You usually don't take an interest in my sex life.*

*Your sex life doesn't usually include Devon, who I consider a friend. I just want to be sure you're not going hurt her, that's all.*

Anger edged his words as he echoed, *Hurt her?*

*Come on, Tanner, you have to admit that you don't have a good track record with the female persuasion. You run at any sign of emotion. Kind of like mascara.*

Tanner felt a muscle in his cheek jump.

*Hey, I'm not judging,* Larkin hurried to add. *It's not like you're the only guy who avoids relationships—*

*Devon and I could never have a relationship,* Tanner cut in. *She's a hellcat, I'm a hellhound; our demons would never take each other as mates.* It wasn't just that their kinds were mortal enemies, it was that the hound would never see a hellcat as its equal. And he strongly doubted that Devon's feline would ever feel safe enough with a hellhound to accept it as a partner.

So, no, they didn't have a future. But that didn't mean they couldn't enjoy the "now." He wasn't sure how easy it would be to convince Devon of that, though. She was skittish around him, and his dominant nature often rubbed her up the wrong way. But he could be patient when it came to hunting prey—it was what he did best.

Larkin's sigh drifted into his head. *I just want you to—*

*This isn't your business, Lark,* he clipped.

*You're like a brother to me, and Devon's my friend.*

*Still not your business. This is between me and her.*

Just then, Knox ended the call, his face hard, his eyes darkening with a growing anger. "That was Muriel Tipton."

Tanner blinked. It had been a very long time since he'd heard that name. Muriel and her brother, Dale, had stayed at Ramsbrook House as children. "What did she want?"

Knox took in a long breath through his nose. "Dale's dead."

The news was like a bomb, and pure silence hit the room.

"She called to give me a heads-up because she didn't want us to hear through the grapevine," Knox added. "He was mutilated, like Harry. *Exactly* like Harry. His eyes, ears, and tongue were removed. He was even posed the same way—sitting against the wall, legs crossed, holding the parts of him that had been removed."

Straightening, Tanner spat a vicious curse, his blood boiling with fury. "When did it happen?"

Knox placed his cell on the desk. "Last night."

"Can we visit the scene?" asked Levi.

Knox shook his head. "It's already been cleared up by her Prime." He drummed his fingers hard on the desk. "That's two people from Ramsbrook who've been killed, and both were killed in the exact same way. I'm not inclined to think that's a coincidence."

Neither was Tanner. He leaned forward, bracing his elbows

on his thighs. "We need to find out if Dale and Harry were in contact with each other—it's possible that they reconnected and worked on something together that got them both killed. They were good friends at Ramsbrook."

Knox pursed his lips. "It's possible. Muriel might know if they were in touch." He smoothly stood. "I think we need to pay her a visit."

Tanner had half-expected Muriel to claim she wasn't in the mood for visitors, but she didn't object to them appearing at her home. Antonio, a member of their Force, teleported Knox, Tanner, and Levi to her hallway before then teleporting himself back to the Underground.

Muriel was waiting for them. He remembered her as a frumpy, shy little girl who'd trusted only her brother. A brother who'd fiercely protected her, particularly since she'd sat low on the power spectrum as a child. A brother she'd now tragically lost in the worst possible way.

She was no longer weak—Tanner could sense that easily enough. But then, psi-shields were rarely weak when fully grown. The problem for them was that their abilities were usually only defensive. Muriel was impervious to psychic attacks or intrusions, which was no small thing, since demons were predominantly psychic creatures. But that wouldn't help her in a physical battle.

Face pale and puffy, eyes red-rimmed and raw, she invited them into a small but cozy living room. Although it was warm, she was wrapped up tight in a long, fleecy robe and thick socks. As if unable to ward off a chill.

Her wan smile flickered. "You all look well." She gestured at the sofa. "Sit down. Please."

Knox and Tanner sat, but Levi took up a position against the wall.

She twisted her fingers together. "Would you like coffee or something?"

"No, thank you, we're good," said Knox, flicking a look at the barely touched sandwich on the table that was set next to a mostly full cup of stale coffee.

Muriel sat gingerly in the armchair and slid her hands loosely onto her lap. "I'm afraid I'm not great company right now."

"We won't take up much of your time," Knox assured her. "We're sorry to hear about what happened to Dale."

Drawing her arms closer to her body, she pressed her trembling lips together. "It still hasn't quite sunk in. I guess I don't really want it to."

Shit, Tanner felt for her. He'd never experienced that sort of grief. Or, at least, he didn't recall doing so. He'd been only two-years-old when his parents were killed; he had no memories of his life before being dumped at the home.

"I appreciate you telling me yourself rather than letting me hear it from someone else," said Knox.

"You were always good to him," she said. "I'll need to call a few others to pass on the news. I'm not even sure where they all are. Dale didn't stay in contact with many people."

"Give me a list of people you'd like notified, and I'll find out their contact information and pass on the news for you."

She offered Knox a shaky smile. "Thank you. I heard you're mated now; that you have a son. Dale almost mated a few years ago, but it didn't work out. Not that I'm insinuating his ex-girlfriend had anything to do with his death," she hastily added. "No, she would never have done such a thing." Her dull eyes filled with tears. "He didn't deserve what happened to him, Knox."

"No, he didn't."

"No one deserves that." Her whole posture seemed to

crumple. She covered her mouth with her palm and bit back a sob. "I'm sorry."

"You have nothing to apologize for."

She tipped her head back and blinked hard, as if to fight off the tears. "I just can't understand it. God, he must have been so afraid. And in so much pain." A breath shuddered out of her, and she met Knox's gaze again. "The things I told you the killer did to him ... they did it before they killed him. Who would do something like that? Who could do such despicable things? And why Dale?"

"Your Prime has no suspects?"

She gave a sad shake of her head. "He had no enemies. No crazy exes. All I can think is that it was some sort of indirect attack on our Prime; a way to get at him. But why use Dale? He's not a sentinel or even a member of our Force. He didn't hold a position within the lair."

Knox tilted his head. "Do you remember Harry Tomlinson? He was at Ramsbrook with us."

Her brows flicked together. "Little Harry. Yes, I remember."

"He was killed a few days ago. Killed in the exact same way as Dale."

She stared at Knox, her face slack. "But that's ...Why? Why would someone do that?"

"That's what we're hoping to find out." Knox leaned forward. "Was Dale in contact with Harry?"

She blinked. "No."

"You're certain?"

"Absolutely. He would have told me."

Knox twisted his mouth. "Somebody felt they both needed to die, and my only theory is that they were being silenced; that they both knew something they weren't meant to know."

Muriel shook her head again. "They weren't in contact

recently, Knox. I'd have known if they were." Her eyes filled again. "I don't know why someone would hurt them like that."

"Neither do I." Knox straightened in his seat. "But I'll find out who did it."

"And you'll kill them?"

Jaw set, he gave a slow nod. "And I'll kill them."

\*

Devon's eyes briefly darted to the clock that hung on the wall of what she called "the piercings room." It was almost closing time, which meant Jolene, Ciaran, and Tanner would be meeting her in the reception area soon.

The guy perched on the edge of the bed in front of her had walked in, all arrogance and boldness, as he declared what he wanted. The more she briefed him on the piercing, the less inclined the gargoyle seemed to be on having it done.

"There are many kinds of penis piercings," she told him. "Some are more painful than others. Some enhance sexual stimulation while others can make certain sex positions uncomfortable."

He swallowed. "How uncomfortable?"

"It differs from person to person. Some piercings heal in a short space of time, others take between four to six months to heal."

His eyes went wide. "Six months?"

"Yes. During that period, you can't have sex, masturbate, or engage in any other form of sexual stimulation."

His mouth dropped open. "You're kidding. I didn't—"

The door opened, and Tanner poked his big fat head inside like he had every right. Oh, he could not be believed.

She gave him a sickly sweet smile. "Can I help you with something?"

His eyes sliced to the male on the bed and then back to her. "I need a word, kitten."

"I'm busy here, as you can see."

The gargoyle practically jumped off the bed. "It's fine, I can come back later." Going by the way he scampered out of the room, Devon figured it was unlikely he'd be back.

Tanner strode inside and picked up the leaflet the gargoyle had left on the bed. His gaze snapped to hers and darkened with something that made her pulse quicken. "You are not piercing that guy's cock." It wasn't an angry statement. It was flat. Calm. Resolute. Left no room for argument.

Devon's brow hiked up. "Excuse me?"

Tanner slowly prowled into her personal space, oozing menace even as he said softly, "You heard me just fine."

"Oh, I heard you, I'm just struggling to understand why you're spouting shit."

He put his face closer to hers. "I don't want you touching some stranger's cock, no matter the reason." The dark, velvety whisper slithered down her spine, leaving a pleasant tingle in its wake. It also pissed her off, because it fairly vibrated with possessiveness.

"You do realize I've done this type of piercing before, right? It's sort of my job."

A muscle in his cheek ticked. "It's not a type you'll be doing again."

"Do I venture down to the strip club on Friday nights and tell you how to swing on your pole? No. So don't tell me how to do *my* job."

Tanner almost laughed. Only she could make him switch from angry to amused so fast. Only her. And fuck if she wasn't cute when she jutted out her chin and gave him that princess to peasant look.

His hound technically should have bristled at her attitude—particularly since said attitude came from what it viewed as a lesser demon—but the hound found her ballsy defiance some-what entertaining. Not a lot amused the demon.

Holding her gaze, Tanner gently shackled her wrists and circled her pulse points with his thumbs. "The only cock these hands should be touching is mine." She didn't lift her chin defiantly. Didn't snap at him. Didn't even appear to bristle. She just looked back at him, as if utterly bored. It was a look that said, "Not sure why we're having this conversation because no amount of dictating to me will ever get you what you want." Yeah, he was beginning to realize that.

Devon sucked in a breath as he placed the palm he'd marked right over his dick. It was hard and throbbing within the con-fines of his jeans. And as he curled her fingers around the shaft as best he could, she felt an answering tingle in her clit.

Devon didn't blush or snatch her hand back. She looked him dead in the eye, because *fuck* if she'd let him ruffle her. "You don't want to push me too hard, pooch," she warned, loading the latter word with condescension. She squeezed his cock just shy of pain.

He grunted, and a small smile curled his lips. "You can make that up to me later. With your mouth."

She pulled her hands free and planted them on her hips. "Keep dreaming, asshole. Now don't we have somewhere we need to be?"

"Yes," he said, taking her hand again. "We do."

# CHAPTER EIGHT

Tanner watched from the thick shadows of the parking lot as a lanky male stepped out of the veterinary clinic and locked the door behind him. The guy flicked up his collar, as if to protect his neck from the cool breeze, and then strode toward the parking lot.

Jolene's voice flowed into Tanner's mind. *That's Sheridan. I recognize him from his social media photos.*

Yeah, Tanner had seen the same pictures—he'd looked the guy up too. Recognizing their target, his hound flexed its claws, raring to strike. *Let's move,* Tanner said to Jolene. He positioned himself in front of Devon as they all headed toward the demon who was currently tossing a bag in the trunk of his car.

Jolene's high heels click-clacked on the pavement. "Dr. Sheridan, isn't it?"

He spared her the briefest look over his shoulder and closed his trunk. "The clinic is now closed, I'm afraid." He turned to face them. "You need to—" His eyes widened as they focused on Jolene, and his entire body went stock-still. He gave a whole new meaning to the term "deer in the headlights."

"Ah, I see that I don't need to introduce myself," said Jolene. "That's good, and it will save us some time. We have a few questions for you, Dr. Sheridan. It's in your best interest to answer them honestly."

"Q-questions about what?" he stammered, skimming his frantic gaze along each of them. A cold fear flashed across his face when that gaze landed on Tanner. But it didn't show even the smallest flash of recognition when it slid to Devon. Apparently, the guy was going to play dumb.

"Let's start with your interest in Devon Clarke," Jolene proposed.

"Devon Clarke?" Sheridan gave a quick shake of the head. "I've never heard of her."

Jolene sighed. "There's little point in feeding us lies. Maddox Quentin told us of his dealings with you."

Sheridan's head jerked back. "I've never spoken to Maddox Quentin. I go to his club a lot, I know who he is—most people do. But I've never officially met him, let alone had a conversation with him."

"That's not what he said."

"Well, then, he lied."

Jolene lifted a brow. "You didn't hire him to compile a dossier on Devon for you?"

"No!" Sheridan denied, his voice bordering on hysterical.

"You hadn't considered her as a potential female to breed with?"

"No! I have a mate, for God's sake!"

"Then why did you want that intel?" asked Devon, speaking for the first time. She'd agreed in advance to let Jolene take the lead on this one, but it was hard to stay quiet. She'd come there prepared to rip the guy a brand-new ass hole unless he could prove he hadn't been behind her kidnapping. As she stared at the male, she felt a niggle of doubt slither through her mind. He was either telling the truth or he was an exceptionally talented liar.

"That's a question I think you should answer," Tanner told him, taking a single step toward him.

Eyes flickering, Sheridan backed into his vehicle and licked his lips nervously. "Look, whatever Maddox Quentin told you . . . he was lying."

Devon gave him a bored look. "Really?"

"Yes," insisted Sheridan. "I'm telling you, I never tried making any deals with him."

"Then just why would he name you?" Devon challenged.

"I don't know! I do know I didn't hire him at any point for any-fucking-thing." Sheridan shook his head, swallowing hard. "I swear, I had nothing to do with whatever this is."

Tanner lunged at him and fisted his shirt. "You thought you could use Devon to have Asa freed," he accused.

Sheridan spluttered. "I don't even *know* an Asa! I don't! Swear to God, I had nothing to do with any of this! N-noth . . . "

Devon frowned as his voice faltered and faded away. His face slackened, and a strange glaze fell over his eyes, making them look almost dead—he was staring right at her, but she knew he wasn't seeing her at all. He wasn't seeing anything. But he wasn't dead. No, she could hear his heart beating steadily in his chest. Yet, there was nobody home right then.

Tanner eased back slightly but didn't release Sheridan. "Did one of you brain-fuck him?"

Ciaran and Devon shook their heads.

"I had thought about it." Jolene waved a hand in front of Sheridan's face. Nothing. He gave no response whatsoever.

Tanner gripped the guy's jaw and studied his eyes. "It's almost like he's—"

Sheridan abruptly sucked in a breath, blinking rapidly as he seemed to . . . burst to life—it was hard to describe. His eyes then homed in on Tanner. Sharpened with intelligence. Those eyes no longer glimmered with fear. No, there was sheer arrogance there. Superiority. "Ah, Thorne's hellhound."

Devon's feline hissed, unnerved by what was playing out before it. That was Sheridan's voice, though steadier and pitched lower. But she knew it wasn't Sheridan who was speaking right then. No, someone was speaking *through* him.

"I'm impressed that you made the connections that led you to Sheridan," it told Tanner. "But you really should back away from this matter. It doesn't concern you."

Tanner's grip on the shirt tightened. "It concerns me, you son of a bitch."

"I should probably warn you that hurting this body will not hurt me."

"Who are you?" demanded Jolene.

Arrogant eyes swung her way. "That's not important, Miss Wallis. What's important . . . is standing right there beside you." His gaze cut to Devon, and those eyes smiled at her in a way that chilled her blood. "You and I will meet soon enough, hellcat." Then Sheridan's eyes rolled back into his head and his body shook violently.

"He's seizing." Tanner lowered the male to the floor, who quickly began foaming at the mouth. "Shit, do we—" And then the shaking stopped, and Sheridan's lifeless eyes stared off into the distance.

Ciaran felt for his pulse, but Devon already knew the guy was dead—she'd heard his heartbeat stutter to a halt.

Breathing hard, Ciaran jumped to his feet with a curse. "Well, what the fuck was that?"

\*

For the second time in the space of a few days, Devon found herself sitting at Jolene's kitchen island with Tanner and some of her lair members. All were in a deep debate about—to put it simply—what the fuck was happening.

Her feline was *pissed*. It hated that there was an ongoing threat to Devon, and it absolutely loathed that it couldn't eradicate said threat until it discovered just who and where it was.

Adam sat one side of her, massaging her back. Tanner sat at her other side, his large hand splayed on her thigh. And neither seemed to like that the other was touching her. She'd shrugged them both off several times but, like herpes, they just kept coming back.

It wasn't Beck who'd called Adam this time, it was Devon. Because she knew that Hunter's sister had the ability to speak through others, so if anyone could help them understand how the ability worked, it was Hunter. Tanner had been firing questions at the guy for the past twenty minutes.

Looking somewhat frazzled, Hunter rubbed at his temple. "I know I'm not doing the best job of explaining the mechanics of the ability, but it really is hard to describe. To speak through someone, you basically need to insert yourself firmly into their mind."

"But you said your sister doesn't leave her physical body," said Tanner.

"She said it's a little like putting shoes on over socks."

"I'm assuming that, in this metaphor, the shoes represent the other person's mind."

"Yes, and the socks represent her body. She slips into another mind while still wearing her body, but her consciousness is divided. Shit, that's not making things much clearer, is it?"

"How difficult is it to use the ability?" asked Devon.

"According to Lydia, it's a lot harder than it sounds, and it's a huge drain on the psyche," said Hunter. "In my opinion, utilizing it is just not worth the trouble when it will leave you feeling weak and tired. It's not even a particularly useful ability anyway. More like a parlor trick."

Devon tilted her head. "So it's not like possessing someone?"

"No, because you can't fully take control. Lydia can get people to move their limbs, but she can't make them do anything complex like drive a car—that would require her to get a deep grip on their brain. But she can use them as a conduit. Like they're a cell phone. And they'll have no memory of her doing it."

Devon blinked. "No memory at all?"

"None," replied Hunter.

"So," began Jolene, picking up her mug of tea. "Sheridan could have been telling the truth. If he was used as a conduit, he'd have had no recollection of any deals he might have made with Maddox."

"But why Sheridan?" asked Adam. "Why do you think he was chosen to be the conduit?"

It was Ciaran who answered. "Maybe Asa's little friend went to the Damned wanting to talk with Maddox and then chose a random patron to speak through. Sheridan said he was a regular at the Damned."

"I guess that makes sense," said Adam. "But why didn't he— whoever he is—go back to Maddox when he wanted to hire someone to kidnap Devon?"

Leaning against the countertop, Beck pursed his lips. "Maybe he worried that Maddox would do just as he said he'd do—contact Knox with the info in exchange for a favor. Especially since he initially lied that his interest in Devon was as a potential breeding partner."

"Whatever the case," began Devon, "we know it was Sheridan

who *physically* requested the dossier on me. Now we need to find out who used him to do it."

Tanner rolled back his shoulders, wanting to shake off the restlessness that had gripped him tight. His hunting instincts were badgering at him, dissatisfied because his prey hadn't yet been tracked. And while the identity of said prey remained a mystery, Devon wasn't safe. That *infuriated* his hound.

The demon didn't much like how Adam was fussing over her either. Tanner had always thought it petty that people could be jealous of how close their partners were to their anchors. But he could admit that it did bug him to know that Adam had innate rights to Devon; bugged Tanner that she *needed* another male, even if it were only on a psychic level.

He looked at Hunter. "Asa's friend killed Sheridan after using him as a conduit. How did he do that? Is it part and parcel of that ability?"

Hunter lifted his shoulders. "If extremely powerful, someone *could* theoretically rupture a mind as he withdrew from it."

"Are you still planning to speak with Lockwood, Jolene?" Ciaran asked her.

"Yes," Jolene replied. "If he *did* broker the deal, it's unlikely he can tell us anything about Asa's friend unless said friend didn't speak to him through a conduit . . . but Lockwood can certainly entertain me by dying an excruciatingly painful death for making the mistake of fucking Devon over like that." She lifted a brow at Devon. "Will tomorrow work for you? I'm thinking we should pay him a visit at his office."

"Sounds good to me," said Devon. "The sooner we question him, the better. What time were you thinking?"

"Early afternoon, right after lunch. There's something satisfying about making someone so nauseated with pain that they vomit their last meal all over themselves."

"I had hoped that Asa's friend would back off from you and try to find another way of manipulating Finn," Adam said to Devon, giving her shoulder a comforting squeeze. "But if the bastard said, 'we'll meet soon,' he's obviously not done trying to get his hands on you."

Tanner's jaw tightened. "No one's getting their hands on her. I'll kill anyone who tries."

Adam gave him a considering look. "Yeah, I think you would." He gave a short nod. "Good." Adam pinched Devon's lips shut when she tried to speak. "Yes, yes, you can kill them yourself—I'm not disputing that. I just like that you have backup. Sue me."

Giving him a mock scowl, Devon knocked his hand away. "I wasn't going to needlessly remind you that I'm capable of protecting myself." Okay, maybe she would have prefaced her statement with that, but whatever. "I was going to say that there are far worse things than dying, and that maybe we should make an example of anyone we discover played any part in what happened rather than killing them outright. We should make them suffer; let others know what fate will await them if they make the same mistake."

Tanner looked at her, his mouth curved. "I like that idea."

"Yeah, I figured you would." His kind were as bloodthirsty as hers. Devon downed the last of her herbal tea and stood. "I need to get home."

"You'll be happy to know that your car is back in action," said Jolene. "I had Richie park it in the lot outside your building earlier."

Tanner pushed to his feet. "I'll give you a ride, kitten."

Her stomach plummeted at the "we need to talk" look he gave her. After the weird evening she'd had, she really wasn't in the mood for *that* conversation. In fact, she wanted to just relax on the sofa with a tub of chocolate chip ice-cream and watch TV. But she didn't fight him on taking her home, not trusting he wouldn't say something like "You didn't mind me giving you a different kind of ride last night" right there in front of God and everybody.

Neither of them said a word during the drive to her place. The silence was far from comfortable, since the air was static with the same sexual energy that pulsed through her body. It was an honest to God relief when he pulled up outside the building.

As they climbed the stairwell, she was keenly aware of every move he made—the bunching and flexing of his muscles, the heated glances he sent her, the way his nostrils flared as he occasionally leaned in to inhale her scent. "Stop sniffing me!"

"Stop smelling like candy."

And what could she say to that except . . . "You're an idiot."

Once they were inside her apartment, she headed straight to the kitchen. Mostly because it was the biggest room she had, which meant she could put a good deal of space between them.

Folding her arms, Devon lifted an expectant brow. Standing a few feet away, he stared at her and . . . God, he was just so intent on her. Snared her with a laser-focus that made her feel as if he saw no one else.

He planted his feet. "Time's up, kitten. I need an answer."

Swallowing hard against the impact of the rising sexual tension that was thickening the air, she tapped her arm with her nails. "A month is too long. One more night."

"No." He shook his head. "Another night won't cut it."

"You don't know that."

"Yeah, I do."

God, he was so damn stubborn. "Forty-eight hours," she tossed out.

"A month." Tanner took a single step forward. "I intend to take you every way a man can take a woman. Need more than forty-eight hours for that."

Well damn if her feminine parts didn't pull out the pompoms. "Forty-eight hours is the most I'll agree to."

"A *month*," he insisted.

Devon's fingers flexed with the temptation to grip him by the throat and shake him. "If you're not even willing to compromise, there's no point to this conversation."

He slanted his head. "Why don't you want to give me a month? What are you afraid of, kitten?"

Honestly? That she'd get used to having him around. Devon relied on herself and met her own needs. A guy like Tanner would barge his way into her life and make a place for himself there. He'd insist on doing things for her, on being there for her, and on having her trust. He'd coax and push and badger and entice, set on having exactly what he wanted exactly when he wanted it. And then he'd leave, and she'd be alone again.

"I'm not keen on letting someone into my life who fully intends to walk straight back out of it once he's had his fill of me," she said.

Tanner felt his jaw harden. She made it sound as if he saw her as nothing more than a faceless fuck, which she had to know was pure bullshit. The truth was he'd *never* get his fill of her. "We can't give each other anything more."

"You wouldn't even if you could," she accused.

Tanner ground his teeth. Like most male hellhounds, he didn't like being in relationships. Didn't like having people interfering in his life or treading on his independence and freedom. He also wasn't a person who leaned on people, trusted them with his feelings, or dropped his guard to "let them in.'" And females often didn't like being with a guy who put his job before them. But ... "I'd have given it my best shot." Because it was her.

She sucked in a breath but said nothing.

Closing the distance between them, he idly played with one of her curls. "I'm calmer when I'm with you, you know. Like all the shit in my head just stops for a while. My role as sentinel takes up so much of my day that I find it hard to switch off from it. But you ... I don't know how you do it, but you make it all fall away. No one else has ever done that for me."

Sighing, she lowered her arms. "Tanner—"

"If you think I wouldn't want more of that in my life, you're wrong. But our demons would never go for it. I can't give you what's not in my power to give."

Looking a little off-balance, she licked her lips. "I know, I get it. I'm not turning you down out of spite. But the fact is all you want is impersonal, uncomplicated sex—that's something you don't need me for. My pussy isn't magic or anything. There are billions of others out there."

He breezed his fingers over her folds, feeling the heat of her pussy even through the denim of her jeans, and she almost jumped. "I want this one," he said. "It's snug and warm and fits my cock just right, almost as if it was made to take me."

"I don't want to be someone's plaything."

"You could never be just a plaything to me, kitten ... although I do like to play with you." Tanner grazed her lower lip with his teeth and gave it a sharp nip, breathing in her soft gasp, needing more. "Give me your mouth, baby." He could have taken it, ravished it, but he needed that surrender from her; his demon needed it. She didn't give it to them.

He hadn't exactly expected her to fall in line with what he wanted—things could never be that simple with Devon. And, honestly, he probably wouldn't find her half so interesting if they were. But he also hadn't expected her to believe the whole thing would be meaningless to him; that he'd think of her as nothing more than a sex toy. It wouldn't be like that at all.

"You're putting a dark spin on this because then you'll find it easier to turn me away," he said. "What we'd have would just be sex, sure, but there'd be nothing impersonal about it."

Devon stared at him. Was he being serious? "Taking someone to bed with no real thought other than to fuck her until you no longer want her is impersonal. A whole month of being used that way? I'm not up for that." Engaging in a fun, harmless fling and letting it play out until it lost its charm ... well, that would be one thing. He was suggesting something else. "Besides, my demon would never give you a month of its time. Not when it's on the hunt for a—" His large hand snapped around her throat so fast that she didn't even see it coming.

"Don't say it," he warned through his teeth. "*Don't.*"

Her demon snarled at him, but it didn't push to surface. Likewise, Devon didn't fight him, sure to her bones that he'd never use his strength against her. "I thought you said I calm you."

Seconds of tense silence ticked by, and then his mouth canted up. "You just did," he said, sliding his hand around to cup the side of her neck.

She sighed. "I don't want to argue with you, Tanner, okay? I say we just leave this at a one-night stand and carry on as we were. There are plenty of women out there who'll give you what you want."

"I told you, *this*"—he glided his fingers over her folds again— "is the only pussy I want. You're not keeping it from me. You're gonna give it back to me, Devon. Maybe not right this second, but you will. Soon. I'm getting my month with you. In the meantime, nobody else gets anywhere near this pussy. They don't touch it. They don't taste it. They don't fuck it. Understood?"

She gaped at him. "I've got to give it to you, Tanner, you've got brass-fucking-balls."

"Not a single soul gets near it. Tell me you hear me."

"Oh, I hear you. I just can't imagine why you think I'll bow down to your wishes."

Tanner pitched his voice low as he said, "You don't want to call my bluff on this, Devon. If someone else touches you, they'll pay for it in blood. That's not a threat, it's a promise. If you're thinking I don't mean that, you're wrong. You don't know the things I've done. You don't know the things I'm capable of."

"Is this where I quiver in terror?"

"No, it's where you heed me for once, because we're far from done." He kissed her. Took her mouth like it belonged to him. Licked and bit until the tension began to leach out of her spine. Yeah, she got his message loud and clear.

Tanner pulled back and released her, satisfied by the flush on her cheeks and the need spicing her scent, despite that she was glaring at him. "Remember what I said."

As he turned to leave, she prompted, "Or . . . ?"

He glanced at her over his shoulder. "Or you'll learn just how far I'll go not to share you. Don't test me on this, kitten. I've killed enough people in the many, many years I've walked this Earth. But then, what's one more to add to the tally?"

# CHAPTER NINE

Standing in the airport terminal the next morning, Devon glanced at her watch. Her parents' airplane had landed twenty minutes ago, so she figured they should have appeared by now. Well, they hadn't.

The people around her were just as impatient, letting out heavy sighs, shifting restlessly, and repeatedly glancing at the large digital monitor displaying departure and arrival times ... as if it would somehow tell them exactly when the passengers would walk through the automated doors.

Enzo and Lex were amongst the crowd—no doubt on Tanner's orders. They'd been following her around all morning. She was also being tailed by two members of Jolene's Force, Tyson and Rhonda. None were making any effort to look inconspicuous, clearly wanting people to know she wouldn't be an easy target if they were dumb enough to make a grab for her.

She took another bite of the candy bar she'd bought from the vending machine. Well, *one* of the bars she'd bought. They wouldn't do much for her figure, sure, but Devon was on the seafood diet. If she saw food, she devoured it. Best diet ever.

God, where were the damn passengers? Her feline didn't like it there. Didn't like being crowded by so many people. Didn't like the cloying scents of perfume, cologne, and hairspray. It wanted to—

The automated glass doors slid open. People began to file out, carting luggage and carrying plastic carrier bags.

Devon craned her neck to look for her parents. Some passengers dashed over to members of the crowd while others breezed by and headed out. She danced from foot to foot, waiting. And waiting. And then Russell shuffled through the doors, grumbling to his mate about something while having some sort of fight with the handle of his suitcase.

Warmth blooming inside her, Devon's lips twitched. He often grumbled. And sighed. And rolled his eyes. And shook his head in consternation. Yet, it was all somehow endearing. Russell was like a grouchy but cuddly teddy bear. And he seemed to have made it his life's mission to leave his beloved armchair as little as possible. But every year without fail, the imp took his mate away for the weekend to celebrate their anniversary.

Unlike him, Gertie was always on the move. Cooking, cleaning, doing laundry, pottering around, working as a cook at the local school. She loved flea markets and garage sales; could sniff out a bargain a mile away—which Russell loved, because he was a major tight-ass.

Gertie often called him lazy and bone-idle, but it really didn't bother her much. Probably because the hellcat had her own way of doing things and didn't like anyone interfering. She also didn't look much like Devon's mother, despite that she was Pamela's older sister.

His gaze found Devon and he brightened. "There she is."

Reaching her, he curled his arm around her and pressed a kiss to her cheek. "Hello, beautiful."

Gertie kissed her other cheek. "Sweetheart, how are you?"

"Happy to see you both," replied Devon. "How was New York?"

"Hectic. Rainy. We loved it. Of course, your father got us lost several times."

"I was taking the scenic routes," Russell defended. "I don't get lost. I have a pigeon's instinct."

"You need a sat nav just to cross the street," Gertie teased. "Not that you leave your precious chair often enough to do it."

Russell huffed at her and then turned to Devon, who forced a smile. Whatever he saw on her face made him frown. "Something's wrong."

The man was far too observant. "I'll tell you about it in the car." Devon took the suitcase. "Come on, I'm parked at the terminal." As she drove to their house, she relayed the entire story. Furious, they launched questions at her and berated her for not calling them. "If I'd told you about it, you'd have ended your trip early, and for what? There was nothing you could have done."

"That's not the point," clipped Russell. "You're our daughter— we have every right to know if you're in danger."

"You should have called, Devon," insisted Gertie, her lips thin. "You'd expect the same from us."

Devon sighed. "I'm sorry."

Gertie made a *pfft* sound. "No, you're not. You didn't want us to come home early in case the trouble touched us, did you?"

"I was kind of hoping it would be resolved by the time you got back," said Devon. "Hopefully Lockwood can shine some light on a few things, though I'm not optimistic about it."

Gertie nibbled on her lip. "Have you told Drew about this?"

Devon eased her foot on the pedal as they approached a red

light. "I'll tell him when it's over. The last thing I want is him in the general vicinity of Knox and Harper." Her brother cared for Harper in his way and, jealous that she was mated to Knox, had tried coming between them—that hadn't ended well for Drew at all. And since he wasn't someone who learned his lessons easily, she couldn't trust that he wouldn't try it again.

Finally, she reached her parents' house. Devon helped them haul the luggage inside, doing her best to ignore the disappointed looks they gave her. She'd expected their anger, and she figured they had a right to it, so she didn't comment.

As Russell headed straight to his beloved armchair in the living room, Gertie rolled her eyes. "How did I know he'd do that? It's just typical that he'd . . . What's that on your hand?" She grasped Devon's palm and studied the mark there. Her brows lifted. "Well, I'm guessing it was Harper's bodyguard who marked you. I've seen the way you two are with each other."

Devon had *not* just blushed. "Let's not talk about the pooch."

Gertie's mouth quirked just a little. "Fine. How about some tea? Or maybe vodka. I always feel better after a shot of vodka."

"I'm good with tea—I'm driving."

Gertie's smile faltered. "God, Devon, I'm so worried about you. I can't stop thinking about what happened."

And *this* was another reason why she hadn't called her parents. Gertie was the type to obsess over things. Devon put a hand on her shoulder. "I'm not going to tell you not to worry— that would be stupid and pointless. But please know that I'm being as careful as I can be. And I'm not in this alone. I have more people protecting me than my ego can take, actually."

Russell spoke, flicking through the TV channels with his remote control, "Well, I'll be calling Jolene and demanding to know what else she's doing to find the bastard who's after you.

And Finn needs to pull his finger out of his ass and get this shit sorted *fast*. He's always been absolutely useless."

"Jolene's doing all she can—she always does," Devon told him.

"But she's not doing enough, or the threat to you would be gone." Gertie rubbed at her temples. "Whoever spoke through Sheridan said they'd see you soon. They're not going to stop, are they?"

"Mom, please don't obsess over this."

Russell snorted. "Like she could do anything else. Making me a coffee and something to eat might help keep her mind off it, though."

Gertie sighed at him. "It wouldn't kill you to fix yourself something to eat and drink, you know." She cast a mournful look at the full suitcase. "I've got some laundry to do, and I'm not looking forward to it."

Russell gave her a look that was pure false sympathy. "It's not going to do itself, so you should probably get started."

Gertie shot him a scowl that had no real anger in it. "So freaking lazy."

"I've never pretended to be anything else." He looked at Devon. "Have I, beautiful?"

She raised her hands. "Don't bring me into this."

"Hmm, yes, you know better than to get involved in—" Gertie gaped in horror when Russell elevated one leg and let out a horrid-sounding fart. "Oh, Russ, must you really do that?"

His eyes widened. "If I can't fart in my own house on my own chair, where can I do it?"

"How about the yard?"

"Not a chance." His nose wrinkled. "Oh, that reeks." He took a folded newspaper from the coffee table and started wafting the air with it.

"Come on, Devon, let's go spare ourselves." Gertie herded her into the kitchen. Lowering her voice, she said, "I didn't want to ask in front of Russell, because hearing her name always puts him a bad mood, but has anyone told Pam—?"

"No," clipped Devon, stomach hardening. "There's no need to."

"Sweetheart, she has a right to—"

"There's no need for her to know. It would do her more harm than good anyway."

Sighing, Gertie gave a wan smile. "I suppose you're right. So ... why don't you tell me how you came to be marked by that hellhound."

"Um, how about no?"

"You want me distracted from everything that's happening around you, don't you? So distract me."

Oh, the woman was diabolical at times. "Some other time. I have to get going." She'd agreed to meet Jolene, Ciaran, and Tanner outside Lockwood's office building in just twenty minutes' time. "I'll see you guys later." After an exchange of kisses, hugs, and "be safes," Devon walked down the cobbled path and over to her car.

Since she had time, she made a pit-stop at the gas station near her destination. As she refilled her tank, she noticed that both pairs of her "guards" were idling near the empty squeegee stations, talking with each other through the open car windows. Even with her hellcat hearing she couldn't make out what they were saying over the sounds of engines idling, gas gurgling through hoses, and music filtering through an RV's open door, but all four guards were laughing about something. Apparently, they'd bonded.

With a snort, she turned back to the pump just as it clicked off. She replaced the nozzle, recapped the gas tank, and wiped her hands with paper towels. Then, sidestepping a fresh oil stain on the hot pavement, Devon tossed the scrunched-up paper towels in the half-full garbage can and headed inside the station to pay for the gas. On her way back to the pump station where her car waited, she gave her guards a little wave, making sure they—

Tires screeched as a van came to a stop next to her car. The back doors flew open. Men leaped out and grabbed her.

Heart slamming against her ribs, Devon struggled like crazy as they yanked her into the van. "You mother—"

There was a sharp prick in her arm, an awful feeling of pressure, and then it felt like her blood was fluttering. And she knew ... *liquid mercury*. The bastards had injected her with liquid mercury, knowing it would weaken her and prevent her feline from surfacing. *Oh, fuck*.

*

Rolling up his electronic window to block out the country music blasting from the BMW idling in front of him, Tanner continued to listen intently as Knox telepathically told him what he'd learned of Sloan's most trusted sentinel, Colm. Which was basically nothing helpful.

It wasn't uncommon for people to go to great lengths to delete any paper trails that led to their past—hell, Tanner, Knox, and the sentinels had done that very thing—but it could be fucking annoying at times.

The only thing that pointed to Colm being the one who killed Harry and Dale was that he was often sent by Sloan to execute traitors. But Colm had never been known to mutilate them beforehand. He allegedly liked to get the deaths over with quickly.

*Did Sloan's plants know much?*

*I'm not sure*, replied Knox, his telepathic tone edged with irritation. *They killed each other before either could speak.*

Tanner blinked. *They what?*

*It must have been a suicide pact, or maybe Sloan ordered them to die rather than pass on any information.*

*They obviously didn't trust that they could hold out against any pain you dealt them.* As the traffic light turned green, Tanner switched gears and drove forward. He wasn't far from Lockwood's office building, where Jolene might already be waiting with Ciaran. He knew that Devon hadn't yet arrived there, or Enzo would have notified Tanner by now—just as he'd notified him of every move that she'd made that morning since leaving her apartment.

*Someone silenced Harry and Dale,* said Knox, *but there's nothing to suggest it was Colm, or even that it was someone who worked for Sloan. This may have nothing to do with the other Prime.*

Tanner twisted his mouth. *Muriel insisted that her brother and Harry weren't in contact, but Dale was real protective of her; if he and Harry were involved in something that could have endangered her, Dale would have kept it from her.*

*True. It's not a coincidence that he and Harry were killed in the exact same manner—I'm sticking with our theory that they both knew something they weren't supposed to know.*

*Or someone is targeting people from Ramsbrook. I can't think why anyone would, but it's possible.*

*If that were the case, there'd be more bodies. So far, only Harry and Dale . . .* Knox trailed off, and there was a long pause. *My meeting is about to start. We'll talk again later. Let me know how things go with Lockwood. If he's uncooperative, bring him to my Chamber.*

*Will do.* If the array of torturous machines and sharp implements couldn't convince Lockwood to part with what he knew, nothing would.

Tanner telepathically reached out to Enzo. *Has Devon left the gas station yet?*

*She just went inside to pay,* Enzo replied. *I'll let you know the second she makes a move.* Enzo didn't add, *Just as I've done since this morning,* but Tanner heard it in his tone.

Did Tanner *need* to check in with the other male so often? No. But having someone watch over her didn't give Tanner the reassurance that it should have done, because it meant trusting someone else's eyes and ears and instincts with something as important as her safety. That wasn't so easy to do. Especially now that he knew the person who wanted her wasn't deterred by their past lack of success or by his mark on her palm.

Rolling back his shoulders, he relaxed his death-grip on the steering wheel. She had four people tailing her, he reminded himself. Four people watching not only *her* but her surroundings, ready to act upon the slightest hint of a threat. And yet, he couldn't help worrying about her.

His frustration mounted with each hour that passed when the cloud of danger continued to color her life. It might not have been so hard to stop obsessing over it if Tanner felt close to unearthing the identity of the bastard who wanted her, but he was utterly fucking clueless. He was a hellhound; hunting was in his blood. But his superior tracking senses didn't help much when dealing with someone who was speaking through others.

No matter how hard he tried to focus on something else, his mind just kept turning back to the mystery again and again. He'd been unable to concentrate during his meeting with the other sentinels earlier. He'd found himself sitting there, drumming his fingers on his thigh, his muscles cramping with the strain of fighting the urge to pace with the restlessness that gnawed at him.

The matter of Harry and Dale's sickening deaths deserved a lot more mental space than he'd been giving them. He'd known them since they were small children; they'd looked out for each other at Ramsbrook; had been through tough times together. He'd only known Devon a handful of years, and yet she was dominating his thoughts.

But then, Devon had always had a way of slipping into his mind and fucking with his focus. Nobody had ever snagged his sole attention the way she did. Nobody. And he had the unshakable sense that no one else ever would. His thoughts always strayed back to her . . . just as they'd done now.

He swore. Honestly, he was fucking hopeless. If he wasn't obsessing over the threat to her safety, he was obsessing over *her*. Over her taste and scent and how good it had felt to be inside her—he'd fantasized about it for so very long that it simply wasn't possible to put it aside. She had a hold over him that he didn't like. A hold she couldn't be aware of, or she'd never have believed him capable of coldly using her.

He did see her point, though. There had been nothing smooth about his proposition. Issuing a time-limit, wording it the way he had . . . yeah, he could see how it might have rubbed her up the wrong way. But there was—

A sense of urgency rocketed through him, so strong it might have sent him to his knees if he'd been standing. His scalp prickled, and the hairs on his nape rose. *Devon.* Instinctively, he knew his mark on her palm was warning him she was in danger. And the telepathic call he received right then from Enzo only confirmed it.

*Fuck, fuck, fuck.*

His demon roared.

His heart hammering in his chest, Tanner sharply yanked on the wheel, switching directions, and slammed his foot on the pedal.

*

The van raced off with a squeal of tires even before the bastards yanked the heavy doors closed. They shoved Devon to the floor, clearly certain she was no threat. How fucking wrong.

With a snarl, Devon sat upright and—knowing she had mere minutes before the liquid mercury would render her useless—freed the dark power within her that bashed against her ribs in a bid for freedom. She didn't send out a tendril of it this time. No, she sent it out in a thick wave that struck as fast as a snake.

Eyes wide, one demon slammed up a hand and popped up a defensive shield in time to save himself. The other three yelled as the hazy vapor spread like fingers, snapped around their bodies, and lifted them off their feet. Backs bowed, necks corded, they roared with pain as bones shattered and veins popped.

The driver glanced around his headrest and spat a curse. "Fuck! Do something, Slade!"

Dropping his defensive shield, Slade dived at her, a syringe in hand.

*Fuck that.*

Her heart pounding hard in her chest, she unsheathed her claws and swiped out at the offending hand, slicing deep into tattooed flesh and scraping bone. Warm blood splattered her face . . . and the syringe dropped to the floor.

"Bitch," spat Slade, his green eyes glittering with anger.

"Fucker." She conjured a ball of hellfire and flung it at him. He slammed up his shield again, and the blazing orb winked out the second it met the shield. *Well, shit.*

He chanted something in a monotonous tone that made her skin prickle. It was an archaic language she'd only ever heard Millicent use that—

Pain smashed into her ribs, the breath gusted out of her lungs, and the hazy vapor dissipated in a flash. The other demons dropped to the floor of the vehicle with weak groans, barely able to move. And she ... oh God, he'd put some sort of temporary block on the power, because she couldn't access it.

Fear tightened her chest and made her stomach drop. A fear that grew as an overwhelming sense of heaviness began to settle over her, slow and insidious, thanks to the fucking mercury. Breathing hard, Devon awkwardly tried to scramble backwards as he advanced on her. She would have stood, but she sensed her legs wouldn't support her weight.

She hissed at him. "Stay the fuck away from—" Her head snapped to the side as a psychic punch slammed into her jaw, all but dazing her.

He straddled her and pinned her wrists above her head. "I usually like fighters, but you're starting to really piss me off."

Devon battled against the weakness assailing her and tried bucking him off. She failed. Her feline hissed its fury, enraged that it was unable to take control; it wanted to shift into its own shape and take down this fucker with teeth and claws. *Craved* the taste of his blood in its mouth, longed to see the life leave his eyes. That sure sounded good to Devon.

Never a quitter, she kept on struggling against his tight grip, feeling her strength slowly fading away; feeling a need to sleep jab at the edges of her consciousness. All the while, the van continuously rocked and swayed, tires screeching as it sped through the streets, making one sharp turn after another.

"Fucking quit fighting," he ordered, tightening his grip on her wrists. He scowled at the driver. "You said the mercury would knock her out instantly!"

There was the sound of a horrendous crash somewhere in the near distance.

"Shit!" barked the driver. "The imps just drove Mike's van off the road!"

Mike? Wait, there were *two* vans involved in this shit? *Wonderful*.

Slade bit out a curse. "Tell me you've lost Thorne's demons, Len!"

Len's silence spoke for him.

The van sharply swerved, and Devon heard something skittering along the floor. Then she watched that same "something" roll to a halt near her head. *The syringe*.

Eyes lighting up as he spotted it, Slade transferred both her wrists to one hand and grabbed for the syringe with the other. *Shit*. A double-dose of liquid mercury could kill her. Maybe it was the anger, maybe it was the adrenaline, but Devon managed to scrounge up just enough energy to whip up her head and sink her teeth into his face, injecting him with her venom.

Roaring in fury and pain, Slade grabbed her head and rammed it hard on the floor of the van once, twice, three times.

The world spun around her, making her stomach roll. Suddenly, she no longer felt heavy. A sense of weightlessness took over, and a ringing sound filled her ears. Urgency beat at her to get up and do . . . something, but everything seemed so very far away.

Sleep. She needed to sleep. It was all she—

A mind touched hers, dark and familiar and fairly buzzing with panic. *Let me in, kitten. Now.*

She obeyed without thinking about it. A gasp flew out of her as Tanner seemed to pour himself into her, shocking her back to alertness, his rage and panic mingling with hers. And that gave her just enough strength to break the block that Slade had put on her power.

The dark force wriggled inside her, demanding freedom. With the last bit of psychic grit that she possessed, she lobbed it at the motherfucker. Slade's eyes went wide as the vapor seized him tight.

*Good girl,* said Tanner.

Too tired to keep her eyes open, she could only listen as Slade's bones snapped, his skin tore, and he roared in agony.

The van skidded to an awkward halt, making him topple sideways. Her mind distantly registered the driver's door being pulled open, Len screaming in pain, and the sounds of flesh smacking flesh. And then the back doors of the van were heaved open.

She tried fighting the tug of sleep as people piled into the vehicle, but it was no use. A dark, smoky scent with notes of cinnamon spice wrapped around her just as the lights winked out.

\*

Fighting to keep his touch gentle when all he wanted was to punch something, Tanner carefully scooped up Devon's unconscious form and cradled her against his chest. The warm weight of her in his arms unraveled one of the many knots in his curdling stomach.

Jesus, she was so still and pale. But she was *breathing,* he reminded himself. She was alive. And not on her way to some fucking stranger who may or may not want her dead.

Tanner closed his eyes as a wave of relief hit him so hard that he was surprised his balance didn't waver. *Fuck, kitten, you gave me a scare,* he said, even knowing she wouldn't hear him.

He quietly let out a slow, centering breath. When he identified and found the fucker who was behind all this, Tanner was going to put him through a world of blinding pain. And with his centuries-worth of experience in torture, he knew a great many ways to make someone suffer deeply without killing them too quickly. It was a skill he took pride in.

Sweeping his gaze over her kidnappers, he noticed that the only one still breathing was now trying to army-crawl his way to the doors, bloody and broken. Tanner snarled. *Motherfucker.*

The other male's nails scrabbled at the floor of the vehicle as Tanner yanked him backwards by his broken ankle.

Still holding tight to Devon, he flipped the bastard over and snapped his hand tight around his throat. That was when his hound pushed for supremacy.

Seething, the entity lifted its captive and hauled him so close they were nose-to-nose. Nostrils flaring, the demon chuffed out a breath. A thick, dark gray, noxious mouthful of air dived up the male's nose and poured down his throat. He jerked, eyes wide and panicked. Coughed, hacked, struggled. Then his eyes rolled back in his head.

The demon watched, detached, as violent convulsions wracked its captive's body harder and harder until, finally, the life leached out of him. Satisfied, the entity dropped the corpse. Aware of the four gazes on it, the hound peeled back its upper lip, warning them to keep their distance. Then it retreated.

Once more in control, Tanner cricked his neck. He raised a brow at the four demons who were watching him warily.

Lex blinked hard. "I've heard of hellhounds breathing out smoke or sleeping gas, but nothing so poisonous that it can kill."

Tanner only shrugged. He didn't use the ability often because he preferred combat, just as his demon did. But he hadn't been willing to put Devon down for a second—not even to kill that little fucker. Had the guy not been so close to death, Tanner would have kept him alive to question him.

"Is she all right?" asked Rhonda, flexing her fingers.

Feeling his jaw harden to stone, Tanner held Devon closer to him and glared at the imp. "She's fine."

Rhonda winced at his curt tone. "We didn't do our job, I know. It just all happened so fast . . . "

Tyson put a supportive hand on the female's shoulder. "This

fuck up is on all four of us," he said, his eyes briefly darting to Enzo and Lex, who both nodded.

Yeah, and Tanner wanted to rip them all a new ass hole, but this wasn't the time or place. What they all needed right then was action. Humans would have noticed the kidnapping and the crash, and steps would need to be taken to cover up as much of the demonic activity as possible—which was why he'd telepathically reached out to Knox and the other sentinels, who were now all on their way, as he drove.

They'd done this dance many times before. Knox mostly took care of tweaking memories, Larkin would edit or delete any incriminating CCTV footage, and the others would stage the scenes in whatever ways were necessary . . . just as Tanner often did. Today, though, he was sticking with Devon.

Rhonda scrubbed a hand down her face. "I haven't panicked like that in God knows how long."

Tanner could say the same about himself. By nature, he wasn't an emotionally overreactive person. He was in control of his emotions, and he was always steady in times of stress or danger. But when Enzo told him that Devon had been taken, his mind had turned into a whirl of chaos.

With adrenaline pumping through his veins, he'd sped around the streets like a fucking crazy person, desperate to get to her—his mouth dry, his heart pounding, his ribs feeling too tight. His only comfort had been the knowledge that her kidnappers would have been ordered not to harm her, just as the others had been.

He'd managed to close in on the van just as the imps took the other vehicle out of the equation, but the car collision had caused a block in the road, so he'd had to abandon the Audi and pursue the first van on foot. And when he'd merged his mind with hers and realized how close she was to unconsciousness, he'd nearly lost his shit.

His hound had gone ballistic, demanding freedom, craving vengeance. The only thing that had stopped it from bashing its way to the surface was the shock of the sight it found when Tanner hopped into the van. Three of the bastards that had taken her were dead on the floor of the vehicle, and the other was barely alive—all looked like they'd been trampled on by a freight train. Several times.

Now, he knew just how sharp his kitten's "claws" really were. The power inside her was as dark and hungry for violence as the hound that lived within him.

Enzo picked up a syringe and sniffed it. "I don't recognize the smell."

"It's liquid mercury," Tanner told him. The damn stuff was leaking from her pores, tainting her luscious scent. The injection would keep her unconscious for a few hours, maybe longer. "They already hit her with one dose of it. Looks like they were thinking of hitting her with another."

"Wouldn't that have killed her?" asked Lex, checking the pockets of the deceased and getting a good look at their bruised, bloody faces.

"Yes," replied Tanner. "They probably only brought the second syringe as a spare in case they lost the first. But when they realized they were dealing with someone far more powerful than they'd been prepared for, they were willing to use the second syringe, even if it meant killing her."

Lex sighed. "None of these guys have any ID or cell phones on them."

Because that would be too easy, wouldn't it? Tanner took a brief look around and then spoke to Enzo and Lex. "Find out who this van belongs to and who the fuck they were."

"It'll be done," Enzo assured him.

The van rocked slightly as Keenan hopped inside. His brows

shot up as he took in the scene. "I'm guessing she's fine, since you haven't gone off the deep end."

It had been a close call. "She's fine ... albeit drugged up to her eyeballs with liquid mercury."

"Liquid mercury?" Keenan echoed. "Fuck me."

Hearing sirens blaring in the distance, Tanner said, "I need to get her out of here."

Keenan nodded. "We'll take care of everything and feed the authorities a false story—you concentrate on Devon."

With a nod of thanks, Tanner exited the van with Devon still in his arms. He needed to get her somewhere impenetrable. Somewhere where she could recover in peace. Right then, there was only one place he trusted her to be safe.

# CHAPTER TEN

It was the hum of the ceiling fan that pierced her sleep. God, she was dog-tired.

Floating in the haze of "almost awake," Devon snuggled deeper into her pillow. No, not *her* pillow. Hers wasn't so soft and plump. Just like *her* mattress didn't feel so astonishingly comfortable—seriously, it was like lying on a cloud. Yeah, this was most definitely not her bed. Which meant it was also not her room. But she knew the scent that seemed ingrained into it. *Tanner.*

She managed to force her heavy eyelids open, but they drifted shut before she could properly examine her surroundings. Ugh. She'd obviously drained herself psychically, and the fucking liquid mercury hadn't helped. It was every hellbeast's major weakness.

She swallowed, and there was an audible click of her tongue. Damn if she didn't feel like crap. Her joints ached, and her muscles quivered slightly . . . like when she had the flu. Her mouth was all dry and sticky, and she was excruciatingly aware of the hollow ache in her stomach.

Food. She needed food. And caffeine. Blessed, blessed caffeine.

Although her body was doing a piss-poor job of waking, her mind was a hub of activity. It didn't feel whatsoever foggy, she remembered everything about the kidnapping; remembered the pooch pouring into her mind and giving her the strength that she'd needed to fuck Slade's shit up and save herself from a second dose of liquid mercury.

In other words, he'd saved her ass.

Oh, how humiliating. And nice. Which meant she'd have to *thank* him. And wouldn't he just love that? Especially after her insistence that she didn't need his protection.

Well, she'd just have to suck it up. He'd not only mingled his mind with hers—something demons didn't do often or casually—he'd also gotten her to safety. Hell, he'd even taken off her shoes and tucked her into his bed.

Yeah, she was gonna have to thank him all right. First, she'd have to find him.

Extending her enhanced senses, she picked up *the slightest* echo of voices. She couldn't make out who those voices belonged to, what they were saying, or where they were in what Harper had once told her was a huge-ass apartment.

The thought of getting up made Devon want to cry, but she couldn't lie here forever. Sadly. And she desperately needed sustenance.

Devon peeled back the cover and, squinting against the dim light coming from the ceiling spotlights, awkwardly sat upright. With only slits for eyes, she gave the room a thorough once-over. *Well.* She supposed "lavish" was a good word to describe the open, airy space. The color of the quality bedding and luxury rug perfectly matched the sleek gray walls. The hardwood floors looked polish-smooth, just like the walnut furniture, which was as masculine and solid as its owner.

There was a wide-screen TV mounted on the wall opposite the bed. French doors led to a pretty terrace, and high windows offered a scenic, breathtaking view. There was also some kind of hi-tech little sensor on the wall that appeared to control the lighting and temperature.

Yeah, it put her bedroom to shame. It put her entire apartment to shame. It was really little wonder that he'd been horrified by the condition of hers.

Although there were no bright colors in the room, it didn't look dull or lack personality as she might have expected. It looked stylish and modern.

Devon shuffled to the edge of the mattress, her movements all sluggish and clunky. Then she just sat there, her shoulders bowed over her chest, staring at nothing. She was just *so tired*.

A yawn cracked her jaw as she glanced down at herself. Devon grimaced. Her clothes were all wrinkled, and her sweater was torn and stained with what was probably Slade's blood. Taking stock of herself, she noticed there was some bruising and grazes from when she'd grappled with Slade. Awesome. At least they'd fade fast—most demons tended to recover from minor injuries quickly.

Licking at her dry lips, she pushed to her feet. There was a lot of weaving and stumbling, but she managed to find her way into the attached private bathroom that was all white gleaming tiles and smooth black marble. Oh, she was having total bathroom-envy right now. There was a monster of a bathtub. Hell, you could fit at least three people in there ... which would be weird, but still.

Turning to the mirror over the sink, she winced at her reflection. Bed-head. Smudged lip gloss. Pasty face. Mascara goop at the corners of her red-rimmed eyes. And he'd seen her this way? Devon groaned, mortified. What bothered her more was that he'd seen her looking so *frail*. She didn't want to show any weakness around him or his demon.

Devon finger-combed her hair as best she could, smoothing away the frizz. She fumbled for the toothpaste and scrubbed some on her teeth and tongue with her finger, wanting that tacky taste out of her mouth. Then she turned on the faucet, wet her hands with warm water, and went to work on her face.

Done, she checked her appearance again. Well, the makeup residue was mostly gone, and her eyes seemed a little more alert, but she was still a wince-worthy sight. At least she no longer looked like she belonged on an appeal poster for hurricane survivors.

A little steadier on her feet, she shuffled back into the bedroom. God, she just wanted to curl up on the bed. Or even the floor. Any flat surface would do, really.

Devon almost flinched as the doorknob turned. Tanner slipped into the room, fluid and silent. God, she needed to put a bell around the guy's neck or something and . . . oh, the goddamn gem had brought her coffee. She fairly salivated at the smell of it.

"You're awake," he said in that deep, gravelly voice that reached so deep inside her she felt it in her bones. "Good. Thought you could use this."

She cleared her dry throat and took the steaming mug he held out. "Thank you," she rasped. Her demon pushed against her skin and eyed him closely. Devon got the impression of . . . respect from it. Well, the guy had come to Devon's aid—psychically and physically—when she'd needed help in a mega way, living up to his promise to keep her safe.

Parched, she would have chugged down the coffee if it wasn't so hot. She settled for taking a few sips. "How long was I out?"

"Just over four and a half hours." He slanted his head. "Do you remember what happened?"

Oh yeah, her memories were crystal clear. She nodded. "Are all the bastards dead?"

"Yes. We haven't yet identified them, but we'll have their names soon. Did you recognize any of them?"

"No." Devon glanced around the room. "So . . . this is your apartment?"

He only nodded.

"Why did you bring me here?"

"I trust that you're safe here."

Well, that was nice . . . although being in a confined space with Tanner Cole did not feel "safe" to her on an emotional level. "I, um . . ." She scratched at her head and blurted out, "Thank you. For helping me."

He inclined his head. No rubbing it in her face. No "ha, I told you that you needed my protection." Just a quiet acceptance of her thanks. She appreciated that.

"I need to call—"

"Nobody," he finished. "Most of the people who are worried about you are gathered in my living room. And they won't go until they've spoken with you and are satisfied that you're okay."

If she hadn't been so surprised by his statement, she'd have laughed at the put-out look on his face. "What people?"

"Jolene, your parents, Harper, Khloë, Raini, Ciaran—the list goes on. Are you up to seeing them?"

She frowned at her torn sweater. "If you'll lend me a shirt."

He crossed to the built-in wardrobe and opened one of the mirrored doors. Hangers clanged together as he pulled out a crisp white shirt. He gently lay it on the mattress, putting it within her reach. "It'll be a bit big on you."

Tanner watched her throat work as she swallowed her coffee, and that sent all sorts of X-rated thoughts racing through his brain. She couldn't know it, but he'd lay in bed with her for a while, watching her sleep; wishing she'd wake, even though he'd known it was better for her to get her rest. Then people had started to arrive, and he'd had to leave her alone.

He'd checked on her several times but always found her sound asleep. It had been a relief to walk in and see her up and awake.

His hound didn't like that she looked so fragile; knew she was far from it. The demon had begun to see just how much it had underestimated her strength in the past. Bloodthirsty, it respected the dark power she wielded; respected how hard and mercilessly she'd fought earlier.

"Hey, did Jolene pay Lockwood a visit without us?" she asked.

"She went to the office after she heard someone tried to take you again. Her mood was so foul I think she would have killed him for sport. But he wasn't there, and it didn't look as if he'd been there in days. Ciaran went to the guy's apartment and found that a lot of Lockwood's shit is gone. Looks like he packed up his essentials and took off."

Devon hummed. "Guilty conscience?"

"If you mean, do I think he did in fact broker the deal made for you? Then, yes, I think he's guilty of that. I'm not so sure he *feels* guilty about it, though. I think he panicked when the first kidnapping failed. I think he was scared we'd trace it back to him and so he fled as a precaution." Tanner shrugged. "Someone will find him."

Devon felt her brow wrinkle. "You're not planning to track him yourself?"

"And leave you? No." He loomed over her, his golden eyes smoldering with something hot and intense that made her itch to take a step back and yet also made her want to move closer. "I wasn't sure I'd get to you in time earlier. You gave me a scare, kitten. Don't do it again." And then he was gone.

Blinking at the door he'd closed behind him, Devon cursed herself for being disappointed that he hadn't kissed her. She was her own worst enemy.

Ready to face the world, she clumsily exchanged her torn sweater for his shirt, drained her mug, slipped on her shoes, and then left the room. Arms hanging limply at her sides, she followed the sound of voices, passing an extra bedroom, the master bathroom, a workout room, and an office/library. Everything in sight was top-of-the-line. Damn, the place was awesome.

It was also kept meticulously clean.

Paintings and mirrors adorned the walls, but there were no photographs, just as there were no knick-knacks in sight. Either he wasn't a particularly sentimental person, or he was too private to put the objects on display.

There were also no antiques that she could see, which surprised her, considering how many years he'd been alive—she would have thought he'd have kept some of his possessions over the years, inadvertently building a collection of antiques. Apparently, Tanner preferred the contemporary look. Or maybe he just kept his apartment so modern and moved with the times because he felt it helped him blend better.

Surrounded by so much opulence, style, and elegance, she should have felt somewhat shabby and self-conscious. Honestly, she was too tired to fret about it.

Walking into the living area, Devon felt her brows lift. God, he hadn't been kidding when he said there was a bunch of people here. In addition to those he'd already mentioned, there was Martina, Beck, Knox, Richie, Levi, Larkin, and Keenan.

All eyes flicked Devon's way, and their conversations halted. Then the room pretty much descended on her. She smiled as they told her how glad they were that she was okay, blah, blah, blah. But there were only so many hugs, cheek-kisses, and back-pats she could deal with before she found herself snarling. "Apparently, we've forgotten that I don't like being crowded."

Harper snorted. "Dork."

Gertie rested a hand on Devon's back. "How about some tea?"

"No, thanks, Mom," she replied. "I just had coffee."

Adam scrubbed a hand down his face. "Shit, Devon, I can't deal with any more of this you-almost-getting-taken crap." His gaze slid to Tanner. "Looks like your mark wasn't enough to deter people from going after her. Nor was the sight of her four guards."

"There'll always be people who'll do stupid things for money," said Tanner.

Martina sidled closer to her. "How's your demon, sweetie?"

"It's sulking because it didn't get a chance to join in on the fun," Devon replied.

Richie rolled his eyes. "Typical."

"Yeah," Devon agreed. Too tired to stand, she sank so deeply into the sofa that her body practically conformed to its shape. The spacious room was just as luxurious as the bedroom with its lush three-piece leather suite, heavy drapes, super-wide TV, and solid oak furnishings.

"Damn, you look ready to drop," said Harper. "You can crash in one of my spare bedrooms when we get back to my place."

Devon could only stare at the sphinx. "Huh?"

"You're staying with me and Knox until all this has blown over," Harper told her in a tone that said obviously.

Panic tightened Devon's throat at the mere idea of leading her shit to her friend's doorstep. "You know I can't stay with you, Harper."

"You can and you will."

Adam cut in, "You're better off staying with me and Hunter."

Oh, hell no, Devon wasn't risking them either. "I'm going home."

Harper's face scrunched up. "Surely that's the last place you'd want to be right now."

Devon frowned. "Why? It's my home."

Harper's eyes flicked to Tanner. "You didn't tell her?"

He poked the inside of his cheek with his tongue. "Forgot to mention it."

"Mention what?" Uneasy, Devon straightened in her seat. "What don't I know?"

Everyone looked at Raini, who bit her lower lip and said, "God, I hate being the bearer of bad news." She tucked a blonde strand of hair behind her ear. "Harper said you'd be staying with her for a few days, so I went to your place to pack you a bag and . . . well, someone had ransacked the apartment."

Devon blinked. "Ransacked it?"

"Well, not all of it," said Raini. "The destruction was confined to the living room. I'm talking an *unreasonable* amount of destruction. Ribbons of the shredded curtains were scattered all over the room. The TV was smashed to shit. I don't know what the intruder used to go to work on your sofa, but it was in three pieces, and the stuffing from the upholstery was everywhere. All your pictures were pulled down from the walls. The coffee table . . . it almost looked like someone had karate-chopped it. I don't know what they took with them when they left, though. I'm so sorry, Dev."

Stomach hardening, Devon swallowed. Devastation, anger, and shock pumped through her blood, fighting for supremacy. Someone had not only broken into her home, they'd wrecked her living room and probably stolen some of her things. It was just stuff; she knew that. Stuff could be replaced. And it wasn't as if the furniture had been worth shit. But, dammit, they'd been *hers*.

"I called Jolene, and she sent Ciaran to me," Raini went on. "He snapped some pictures with his cell and then teleported us both out of there. Show her, Ciaran."

Digging his phone out of his pocket, the male imp crossed to Devon. "They're not pretty."

As she skimmed through the collection of photos he'd taken of her apartment, Devon ground her teeth. "Motherfucker."

"The damage seemed personal to me," said Ciaran. "Vindictive. It's like someone had a brief explosion of anger and then managed to get ahold of themselves."

"I'll have someone clean the place, Devon," said Jolene. "In the meantime, you can't stay there."

"The safest place you can be is with me," Harper insisted.

Devon lifted her chin. "I won't take my shit to your door. Think of Asher. Do you really want this touching your son? Because it could, and I'd never forgive myself if anything happened to my little dude. Come on, Knox, surely you're with me on how bad of an idea this is."

Knox shrugged. "I have extreme preternatural security measures in place. No one can penetrate my estate."

"Stay with me and your mom, beautiful," said Russell. "We want you with us."

Again, Devon shook her head. She wouldn't endanger them that way. Couldn't.

"You could stay in the apartment that's just become empty on the floor above mine," said Tanner. "The tenant had a crazy, Freddie-Mercury-style party last night and got himself kicked out of the building. You could stay here with me tonight while the apartment is put to rights, and then you could move there some time tomorrow. That way, you won't feel like you're putting anyone at risk."

Aside from the part where he wanted her to stay *here* for the night, it was a good solution, but ... "You're asking me to let someone chase me out of my home."

"No, I'm asking you to be smart." Tanner crossed to where she sat and stared down at her, determined to make her see reason. "You know it's a good idea, kitten." And if she tried leaving, well, he'd just bring her back. She'd barely got out of the kidnapping alive—he wasn't going to allow her to risk herself yet again.

Devon narrowed her eyes at him, and then her voice flowed into his head. *You'd take advantage of our time alone to coax me into your bed.*

Tanner didn't deny it—it would have been a lie. That he'd make no bones of seducing her while she was worn out made him an asshole, yeah, but he'd always been selfish and ruthless when it came to Devon. He had no limits where she was concerned.

*You shouldn't be alone when you're not at one-hundred percent,* he pointed out to her telepathically, knowing it would prick at her pride if he spoke out loud of how weak she currently was. *You'd say the same thing to others if the situation applied to them.*

He let his gaze roam over her. There was something oddly satisfying about seeing her in his shirt, just as there'd been something oddly satisfying about seeing her in his bed.

He'd only ever had two other females in his apartment before now—Larkin and Harper, both of whom he thought of as family. Never had a woman slept in his bed. He wouldn't have thought he'd like it, but he had. Though that was probably quite simply because it was Devon.

"I think Tanner's suggestion is a sound idea," Levi said to her. "This building has all kinds of security measures—technological and preternatural. Apart from Knox's estate, which you're insisting you won't stay at, this is probably the safest place for you to be that's local to your friends, family, and work."

"I agree," said Jolene. "The attempt to snatch you right in front of your guards was bold, Devon. I don't foresee the asshole behind all this backing off—which makes him stupid, but never underestimate how dangerous stupid people can be. I'd rather you were staying here. Especially since Tanner would be on the floor below you. Having marked you, he'd be alerted if something was wrong and he could get to you in under a minute."

Devon inclined her head because, yeah, that was a good point.

"He could also give you a ride to work in the morning," Jolene added ever so casually. "And give you a ride home afterwards—it would make sense for him to do so."

Devon folded her arms across her chest. "I see where this is going." Jolene wanted him to chauffeur her around. And as her gaze swept the room, she saw that everyone seemed to think that it was a good idea.

"Twice now you've been taken while on your way somewhere," Jolene reminded her. "I want you to have someone dangerous at your side next time it happens. Not in a car behind you, shadowing your every move."

"Think of having Tanner with you as carrying a loaded gun," said Khloë. "A backup weapon, if you will. Only he's too big to slip into a holster on your ankle. Which is good, because the damn things can rub at your skin something awful at times."

Keenan turned to the imp. "You're armed?"

Khloë frowned at him. "We're not talking about me."

"We are now," the incubus snapped.

Khloë ignored him. "As weapons go, a hellhound is mega cool, Dev. Any girl would happily have one."

"So, *you'd* be okay with someone chauffeuring you around?" Devon asked the incredibly independent female.

Khloë snorted, her brows drawing together. "Hell n—yes, yes I would."

Devon shook her head. "God, you're so full of shit."

Raini sat beside Devon. "What sounds better to you—dead and proud, or alive and chafing at the bit? Because I'd go for door number two, in your shoes."

Harper moved closer. "When I was bristling over Knox assigning me a bodyguard, you said it didn't make me weak to have people looking out for my safety, Devon. You said it made me smart. Well, right back atcha, Clarke."

Devon looked at the three girls carefully. "You guys haven't ganged up on me this way since we were eleven and I refused to lie that Khloë dumped Gary Ford when it was the other way around."

Khloë gasped. "I can't believe you pulled that out of the vault."

"Who's Gary Ford?" Keenan asked, but he was ignored.

With a mock sigh, Tanner stepped forward. "Look, kitten, I know it's a struggle for you to deal with the undying love you feel for me and the close proximity only makes it harder, but what doesn't kill us makes us stronger."

Devon glared at him. "Honestly, sometimes it's like your brain takes a laxative or something."

Tanner chuckled, and his hound let out an amused chuff. She was far too easy to rile, which he couldn't help but enjoy. "You're not dumb, kitten, you know you can't go back to your apartment until it's been cleaned. And since someone managed to get past your protective wards, you can't claim that you'd be safe there."

Levi's mind touched his. *I'm thinking that Eleanor could have been the one who wrecked her apartment.*

*Yeah, I had that same thought,* said Tanner, but it wasn't something he'd mention to Devon until he knew for sure.

"I think it would be best if you stayed here until all this is over," Gertie said to her. "Or at least for a few days. Please, Devon? It'll give me peace of mind. Or if you won't stay here, come home with me and—"

"*No*," said Devon. "I can't go with you."

Gertie squeezed her hand. "Then do one thing for me and *stay here*."

Devon sighed. "What about rent money? I can't afford—"

"Your time here will be free," Knox told her. "Don't argue. This is a safety measure. I won't take your money, so there's no sense in putting up a protest."

"If you're really going to refuse to stay with anyone for fear that the danger dogging your heels will clip theirs, this is your best option," said Harper. "Believe me, I *know* it's hard to accept the protection of others. Having a bodyguard claws at my ego from time to time. And I get how important your independence is to you, but you have to admit that Tanner's come in handy a few times."

"*And* he's pretty to look at, which is always a plus," Khloë pointed out.

Keenan's expression hardened as he stared at the imp. "Is he now?"

Khloë tossed him yet another frown. "What is *with* you today? You're all snippy and snarly. Like a lion with a thorn in its paw."

Keenan scowled. "I'm not snippy or snarly."

Khloë put her hands on her hips. "All I heard was *grr, argh, grr, I'm a raging alcoholic with an oversized cock, grr.*"

Raini groaned and buried her face in her hands.

A muscle in Keenan's cheek jumped slightly. "I'm *not* an alcoholic."

"Dude, you drink vodka like it's water and carry a flask of it around with you wherever you go," said Khloë. "Tell me how that's normal."

Larkin smoothly stepped between them. "Anyway . . . yeah, Devon, I think you'd be better off staying in this building for a little while. You can't deny that you'd sleep better with such top-notch security."

"*I'd* sleep better knowing you were here." Gertie squeezed her hand again. "Please, Devon?"

Closing her eyes, Devon tipped her head back and let out an annoyed groan. "Fine."

Tanner's voice flowed into her mind. *Right decision, kitten.*

She chose to ignore him.

The others stayed long enough for Hunter to whip her up some risotto while they tried theorizing on where Lockwood could be or who might be able to point them in the right direction, but the conversation didn't amount to much.

Advising her to rest, people filed out of the apartment. Russell lingered long enough to warn Tanner that he'd get better not let Devon be hurt in any way, shape, or form.

Hunter was the last to leave. He kissed her cheek and said, "I plated your risotto—it's waiting on the kitchen counter for you. *Eat.* You need to get your strength back."

She smiled. "Thanks, Hunter." Then he was gone. And she and Tanner were alone. In his apartment. While she was wearing his shirt.

"You hungry?" he asked.

"I could eat." She followed him into a large, beautiful kitchen that was all cream gloss and gleaming platinum appliances. "Fancy."

He took the plate of food from the counter, set it on the kitchen island, and gestured at one of the chairs.

Devon happily took the silent invitation and, absolutely famished, delved into her risotto. She groaned in appreciation. "Man, Hunter is good."

Tanner put a glass of water near her plate and then straddled the chair opposite her. "How long have you known him?"

"As long as I've known Adam, so . . . six years."

"You seem to get along well with Hunter." He tilted his head. "You two have never had any problems? He's not jealous of the closeness you have with Adam?"

"No. Which makes me lucky." They made idle conversation while she ate. Pushing her empty plate aside, she sipped some water from her glass while sweeping her gaze around the kitchen. The room was as spotless as the rest of the apartment. "You have a cleaner?"

"No."

Whoa, he couldn't be serious. "You're a neat freak?" She hadn't sensed that about him.

He shrugged. "I like to have a tidy home. I wouldn't say it makes me a freak."

"*I* like a tidy home. This kind of cleanliness screams 'obsessive.'"

Standing, he took her plate and cutlery to the sink and rinsed them off before stacking them in the dishwasher. "The staff at the kids' home where I grew up were strict on us keeping things clean and tidy. I guess it stuck with me."

Devon's chest tightened. Damn, it had to have sucked growing up in a home for demonic kids. He couldn't have had much of a childhood since the staff would have *needed* to be strict or the children would have caused utter mayhem. "Is it still standing?"

"No. Knox bought it, demolished it, and then built a hotel over it. It was Larkin who named it 'Crimson Grove Hotel and Spa.'"

She wanted to ask more about the home; wanted to ask how it was he'd ended up there, but the questions seemed far too intrusive. Plus, she could clearly see he didn't want to speak more of it.

Slipping off the stool, she added her empty glass to the dishwasher. "Tell me about the newly vacated apartment you want me to stay in. Is it like this?"

"The layout's pretty much the same. I don't think it has a spare bedroom, though." He leaned back against the counter. "Just so you know, you won't be using my spare tonight. You'll be in my bed."

Her stomach did a little flip. "We talked about this already; we're leaving it at a one-night stand."

"And if I told you that when I left your place last night I went to a club, picked up a random woman, and then went home with her and fucked her brains out?"

Devon flinched, feeling like he'd slapped her.

"I *didn't* do it. But that thing you're feeling right now, that's what you would have felt if I had. And you're really going to tell me that we're done?"

She sighed. "You can get sex anywhere, Tanner. Hell, go down to the Underground, there are pussies galore."

"But there's only one of you. It's you I want."

That hit her right in her core. Her body should have been too tired to react, but damn if her libido didn't snap awake. "My demon won't give you a month of its life, Tanner."

His eyes hardened. "You won't exactly be taking the time to look for a mate while you're preoccupied with finding Asa's friend. Where's the harm in us having our fun in the meantime?"

"You don't have to say 'mate' like it's a dirty word, you know." Her pulse skittered as he pushed away from the counter and slowly prowled toward her. And then all six-feet-plus of untamed power was towering over her, and her mouth went bone dry.

Devon probably should have backed away, but she felt trapped by that compelling gaze. His eyes shimmered with a need so basic and primitive that her nipples tightened. That need called to hers. Tempted her. Invited her in. Drew her closer.

He skimmed the tips of his fingers down the column of her throat. "Be honest, kitten. It's not your demon that's so opposed to this; it's you. You have it in your head that all I want is to use you and then toss you aside."

"Don't you?" she challenged.

He lowered his mouth until it was only an inch above hers. "You want to know what I want to do to you?" he whispered softly. "I want to explore you. Savor you. Possess you. Over and over and over. Until I know every inch of you."

Her stomach fluttered. Clenched. Twisted.

He kissed the corner of her mouth, traced the curve slightly with his tongue. "It would be using you if all I cared about was what I got out of it, but it's not like that. You know it's not. Outside my lair, you're the only thing I give a shit about."

Those words swathed her like a warm blanket. She wouldn't melt. She wouldn't.

"Love your scent." Tanner brushed his nose along her elegant neck and breathed deep, letting himself drown in her sweet scent. The siren-call of it wrapped around him, heated his blood, thickened his cock. She was an enticement he couldn't ignore. An obsession that just wouldn't fade. A drug he'd always crave, no matter how many times he had her. And didn't that just beat all.

There would be no fucking her out of his system—he knew that. Accepted it. And despite how very smart and perceptive his little hellcat was, she just didn't see it. That baffled him.

He sank his fingers into her hair and gently stretched out the curls, loving the silky feel of them. "I've always been good at abruptly disconnecting from all feeling. I do it whenever I'm in an intense or dangerous situation. But when I realized you'd been taken, there was no distancing myself from the rage. Even my hound went ballistic."

Taking her hand, he circled the mark on her palm with his thumb. "There are few people who matter to me, and even fewer who matter to my demon. It sees most people as replaceable. Disposable, even. They're pretty much generic to it—few stand out from the rest.

"But you made it *see* you. Made it see you as an individual, not a hellcat. And now it wants you. I don't know for how long. I don't know if it could ever really acknowledge you as its equal, just as I'm guessing your feline would struggle to see my demon as its equal. But I say we take advantage of however long our demons allow this to go on. They could put up a resistance any day, kitten. We're at their mercy on this."

Devon nearly jumped when he clamped a possessive hand on her hip. She should shove him away. Should refuse his touch. But, dammit, she didn't want to. Wasn't even sure if she truly could. What pulsed between them was so electrically charged that she'd bet they could power his entire building with it. How did you fight something like that?

"Let me give us what we both want. Let me make you feel good."

She closed her eyes as he scraped his teeth over her pulse. Fuck if he wasn't seduction itself. His words, his mouth, his voice . . . It was like he had molten sexuality flowing through his veins.

He lifted his head, locking his gaze with hers, and she felt captivated by the sheer unadulterated hunger on his face. No one had ever looked at her like that. No one. "I *need* this, kitten."

Despite her intentions, she all but melted. "Tanner . . ." She was going to cave. She knew she was. The tips of her fingers tingled with the need to touch him—a need that wouldn't be denied much longer.

"Let's just be done dancing around this thing and take what we want for as long as we can get it."

Devon licked her lips. "It probably won't be long."

"Probably not. So why waste more time?" He swept his thumb over her lower lip. "Your mouth drives me crazy." His eyes snapped to hers, gleaming with demand. "Give it to me."

The note of authority in his voice punched its way inside her. She swallowed. "What will you do with it?"

His lips curled slightly. "Own it." His clever, carnal mouth swooped down and took total possession of hers.

# CHAPTER ELEVEN

Need *exploded* in Devon's stomach. Little sparks played across her skin, as if she'd been plugged into an electric socket. She gripped his shoulders, so shaken by the sheer intensity and ferocity of his kiss that she might have pulled back if she'd possessed the will-power. Instead, she melted against him as his mouth consumed hers; stealing her breath, sucking her into a maelstrom of sensation, relentlessly hacking through every bit of resistance she had.

She lost awareness of everything but him, his mouth, his hands. Felt feverish with the pressing, crushing need to have him inside her again. Filling her. Stretching her.

Tanner groaned as soft hands slid up his shirt and splayed on his chest, sharp nails pricking his skin. He angled his head, making the kiss deeper, harder, wetter. He was lost. Lost in her taste and scent and the searing heat of her mouth.

His cock was so fucking hard it was painful to walk as he herded her through his apartment and back to his bedroom, stripping them both of their clothes as he went. Standing at the foot of the bed, the breath almost left his lungs as he drank her in. She was all wicked curves and soft skin. Had the most phenomenal breasts—round and high. His mouth watered at the sight of those tight, rosy, pierced nipples. Fuck if she wasn't . . . "Perfect."

He fisted her hair and snatched her head back, arching her spine so he could suck one hard bud into his mouth and tug on her piercing. Spurred on by her little moans, he teased her nipples, alternating from one to the other as he licked, suckled, and scraped them with his teeth.

"I'm going to come all over these one day," he told her. Growling low in his throat, he sank his teeth into the side of her breast, injecting his venom into her bloodstream.

Hissing, she straightened and glared at him. "That hurt."

"You liked it." He grunted as she bit into his chest in retaliation. The burn of her venom went straight to his aching cock. Cursing, he tossed her on the mattress. "Lie back. Good girl." He joined her on the bed. "Now stay still."

"Stay still?"

"I warned you I wanted to explore and savor," said Tanner, sliding his fingers over the flock of butterflies that had been tattooed on her side. He also wanted to make some memories that would keep him warm and sane when she was gone. Wanted to make memories for *her*—ones from which she'd never escape.

The mark on her palm wasn't enough for him. He needed to leave some mark on her soul. Needed to make this so good for her that no other man she had in her bed would ever measure up—not even whatever male she took as her mate. That made Tanner a bastard, he knew that, but fuck if he wouldn't claim and keep some part of her. "Just lie back and enjoy."

Twenty minutes, thirty minutes, an hour later—Devon really couldn't be sure—he was still busy indulging himself, and she was so hot and shaky she looked close to feverish. His mouth and hands, so warm and skilled, explored and teased her body . . . but they always skirted her pussy—a pussy that felt so excruciatingly empty it was painful.

Excitement pooled in her stomach. She was hot and frantic for release. Her body screamed out for his, holding its breath in an agonizing anticipation that she couldn't bear much longer. And every swipe of his tongue, every scrape of his teeth, and every proprietary squeeze of his hands only made it that much worse.

She slapped the mattress. "Dammit, Tanner, I think it's safe to say that the time for exploring is *over*!" She might have sounded a lot more imperious if her voice hadn't cracked.

He looked up from where he'd been licking the delicate swirly tattoo that circled her navel piercing. "What do you need, kitten? Tell me."

Well, *obviously* she needed something inside her. His fingers, his tongue, his cock—any would do fine, she wasn't fussed.

"Not fussed, huh?"

Wait, she'd said all that out loud?

Her lips parted as he plunged two thick fingers into her pussy.

He put his mouth to her ear and nipped the lobe. "This isn't going to be a slow finger-fuck, baby. I'm going to pound your pussy with my fingers until you come hard all over my hand."

Those fingers didn't give her an inch of mercy. They drove into her hard and fast. And when he curved his fingers just right and stroked that sweet spot inside her, she did exactly as he'd said she would—she came hard all over his hand.

"Good girl."

She lay there with her eyes closed, panting and trembling . . . until he curled his hands around her thighs and pulled them further apart.

"I didn't get to taste you last time," he said, settling himself comfortably between her thighs. Using his thumbs, he parted her folds, and she shivered as the cool air whispered over her clit. A full body flush swept over her skin as he stared at her pussy, his eyes darkening with hunger, intent, and sheer male possession.

He inhaled deeply, and a growl rumbled out of him. "Fuck, you smell good." He licked at the crease of her thigh. "I'm gonna enjoy this."

Instead of delving right in, he nuzzled her folds and gently nipped at them. And she sensed he wasn't one of those guys who did the bare minimum to get a girl off. No, he was one of those rare gems who settled in and took his time. Damn, he was racking up points by the minute.

Her eyelids fell shut as he fluttered his tongue through her slit. His low growl sent a little shiver up her spine, and then he feasted. Lazily lapped, sipped, stabbed, and drank from her—in no rush whatsoever. That fabulous tongue lashed at and swirled around her clit, first one way then the other.

The whole time, he watched her closely, taking in what made her squirm or moan or gasp, and then he did those things all the more; always alternating between fast and slow, keeping her off-balance.

Her body was in chaos, both inside and out. Feel-good chemicals flooded her. Desperation pumped through her veins. Her pussy blazed and throbbed.

Moaning, she sank into the mattress when the flat of his tongue started rubbing up and down her clit. He was ruthless. Unrelenting. His teeth nipped, his tongue tasted, his fingers traced and probed. And when he started pumping his tongue inside her while growling in the back of his throat, there wasn't a hope in hell that she could last.

Her breaths quickened, her hips bucked, her thighs shook.

And then she was coming with a choked moan, her back bowed, her pussy quaking around his tongue.

She slumped. Damn, the fucker was good with that mouth. Struggling to catch her breath, she—

Sharp teeth dug into her inner thigh, breaking the skin, and she hissed at the sting. "Enough with the biting."

He looked at her, his lips glistening. "I want my venom inside you. I want to be in your blood." He eased his powerful body over hers, giving her his weight, making her feel trapped yet safe. So full and long and hard, his cock pulsed against her clit. "Just like you're in mine."

Devon wrapped her legs around him and went to grab his solid shoulders, but he caught her wrists and then pinned them above her head with one hand. She wasn't gonna lie, it totally pushed her buttons. Her back arched as he swiped the head of his cock between her folds and aligned it just right. But he didn't sink inside. "Tanner . . ."

His gaze dropped to her lips. "I want to feel that mouth on my cock. Want to come all the way down your throat. You'll give me that—don't say you won't." He flexed his hips forward, pressing the thick head of his dick a mere inch inside her. He nipped at her lower lip. "Open for me."

She did, and he all but ravaged her mouth—licking, kissing, biting. He took and took, owning her mouth just as he'd told her he would. *But he didn't thrust inside her.* Not even when she squirmed or clenched her inner walls around what little she had of him.

She hissed, out of patience. "I'm really not into delayed gratification, pooch, in case you hadn't already noticed."

"What do you need, kitten? Tell me."

"I need you to fuck me." Devon sucked in a breath as his fat cock slammed home, sinking so deep it hurt, stretching the walls of her pussy until it burned.

Tanner ground his teeth as her slick, inferno hot inner muscles clamped around him. His cock throbbed with an almost vicious drive to possess and claim. "I told you you'd give this pussy back to me, didn't I?" He slowly pulled back until only the head of his cock was inside her. "You won't keep it from me again." And then he did what he'd been aching to do since he first saw her—he fucked her hard, deep, rough enough to hurt.

He kept her wrists pressed into the mattress as he pounded into her, his eyes never leaving hers. A fevered haze was threatening to fall over his vision, and he was barely holding onto his control. How could any red-blooded male cling to their control when they had the object of their fantasies beneath them, accepting every hard thrust of their cock?

With the taste of her pussy in his mouth, her intoxicating scent filling his lungs, and her blazing hot pussy clutching him so tight, it felt like his senses were drowning in her. He knew he'd never forget the image of her there—her curls fanned around her face, her eyes glossy with need, her lips swollen from his kisses.

"You won't let anyone else near my pussy, will you, baby?"

"Yours?" She snorted. *Snorted.*

He pulled on her wrists, letting her feel the strain in her shoulders, knowing she liked the bite of pain. "It's mine for as long as you're in my bed."

"Deluding yourself again? How sad."

He slowed, eased up on the depth and intensity of his thrusts. "I'm serious, Devon, I won't share you. Tell me you get that."

She sighed. "Can you quit with the chatting and fuck me?"

Devon knew she'd made a mistake when a very inhuman growl vibrated in his chest and his eyes bled to black. A chill breezed over her skin as the room temperature lowered . . . and she found herself the focus of his demon's dark, reptilian glare. *Shit.*

Her feline pushed close to the surface and watched it carefully, but not with fear—it trusted that the hound wouldn't harm Devon. Yeah? She wasn't so confident of that. There was something exceedingly dangerous glimmering in the depths of those eyes. A callousness that no one in their right mind would want directed at them.

Another growl shook its chest, and then it ... nuzzled her neck. Which would have been a relief if its teeth weren't now so close to her jugular.

She swallowed. "What do you want?"

An image flashed in her mind—one of her giving Tanner a slow nod. Apparently, the demon wanted her to yield to the pooch. Not that simple. It wasn't that she intended to date other guys or anything, she just didn't want to encourage Tanner's possessive behavior. He'd be a nightmare to deal with if she let him get away with that shit.

Yet another image flashed in her mind. An image of the hound standing in front of her in its true form, growling at a group of faceless men. She understood the telepathic message—it wasn't going to allow other males to touch her. Wonderful.

She winced as its teeth dug into her throat; knew the entity was waiting for its answer. "You're not being rational." And those teeth dug a little harder. Having no curiosity about how it would feel to have her throat ripped out, she said, "Okay, okay, there'll be no other guys while Tanner and I are together. Now ease off, Fido. I'd like Tanner back—he has a job to finish." She'd been very close to coming when the damn entity made its appearance.

The demon lifted its head. That dark gaze shimmered with something that might have been amusement. It lowered its mouth to hers, bit her lip. And since she had no intention of letting it dominate her, she snapped her teeth at it. Yeah, that was now definitely amusement in its eyes.

It nuzzled her neck again. Nipped at her pulse. Licked over the small hurt to soothe the sting. And then the flesh of her wrists started to burn—the flesh beneath its fingertips.

She hissed. "What the . . . " Her eyes widened as she realized what was happening. "You've got to be kidding me!" The motherfucking psycho was branding her.

The demon retreated just as the burn faded. Golden eyes stared down at her, looking far too satisfied for her liking.

"Your damn demon just—" She cursed as Tanner slammed into her.

"We can chat, or I can fuck you. Choose."

She tightened her legs around him. "Fuck me, you bastard."

He powered into her with a growl and—*Oh, God, yes*. She lifted her hips to meet each brutal thrust as he drove deep again and again, building the friction inside her once more. His expression was cold, but his eyes were so hot they seared her.

Devon struggled against his grip, wanting to touch him, scratch him, fist his hair. But the prick wouldn't let go, and that—warped as it was—only seemed to make her hotter.

"Fuck, baby, I'm close." He moved his mouth to her ear. "Want me to pull out? Or do you want me to come inside you?"

She swallowed. "In me." She felt his mind brush against hers, and she immediately dropped her shields. He poured in, letting her feel an echo of the sensations that were pushing him closer and closer to his release. All of that fueled her own arousal, winding her so tight she couldn't take it.

His pleasure, her pleasure—she couldn't tell the difference anymore—built and built like a pressure cooker. And then it exploded.

Surge after surge of white-hot bliss whipped through Devon and zipped up her spine as she came with a scream. Grunting against her neck, he pounded harder, faster. The headboard thumped against the wall with each feverish slam of his hips as he drove his cock impossibly deep over and over and over.

Tanner spat a harsh curse as he rammed into her one last time. She felt his cock swell and throb inside her, felt every hot splash of his come. Then they both sagged.

Muscles quivering, heart racing, Devon lay there as they each struggled to catch their breath. Her limp body felt utterly sated and deliciously sore. She'd needed a good, hard ride, and he'd given it to her.

Hauling her close, he pressed a kiss to her neck and then rolled onto his back, taking her with him. Draped over his chest, she lifted her head and found him staring at her through languid, heavy-lidded eyes that gleamed with a wicked satisfaction. And then she remembered.

Sitting upright, she examined her wrists. And gaped. "What the fuck is this?"

Lips twitching, he splayed his hands on her thighs. "They look like fingerprints to me."

Because that was *exactly* what they were. "Your hound is out of its everloving mind." If demons became very possessive of someone, they sometimes branded them—hell, Harper had quite a few brands from Knox. To the human eye, they look like tattoos. But demonic brands weren't permanent; they could fade if an entity lost interest in the person. And that meant that until his hound lost interest in her, she'd be walking around with these goddamn fingerprints on her wrists.

Hell, she'd known that the mark on her palm was going to bring her nothing but trouble. It had obviously sparked a possessive streak in his demon, and now she was dealing with *this* crap.

Devon narrowed her eyes. "You think this is funny, don't you?"

"No." Tanner caught her hands and took a closer look at the brands, feeling satisfaction once more swell low in his belly—the same satisfaction his hound was feeling. "I think it's hot." He could be incredibly possessive when it came to Devon Clarke, so seeing his fingerprints on her wrists . . . maybe it made him fucked up, but he liked it. "My demon has never branded anyone before."

"Well you'd better tell it not to pull this shit again."

He gave her hands a sharp tug, drawing her toward him so she was once more sprawled on his chest. "I can't guarantee it won't happen again." Not just because his hound was territorial of her, but because its instinct when she fought that possessiveness was to make it exceedingly clear that it had rights to her.

She made a sound of sheer exasperation. "You only like it because you know no other male demon will dare touch me while I'm branded."

He gave a careless shrug. "All you had to do was agree not to let other men near you while we were sharing a bed—something you could have done, since we both know you wouldn't juggle two males at a time; it would feel like betrayal to you. But you fought me, so my demon took what measures it felt were necessary to be sure no one else touched you. My advice? Don't fight it or me again on this, or you probably *will* find yourself getting branded again."

He watched her warily as she glared at him through eyes that were dark with indignation, her flushed face getting redder and redder by the second, until he was honestly worried about her blood pressure.

She snarled. "I don't know why women have a thing for alphas—no matter the species, you're all a goddamn pain in the ass!"

"I hear the love in your voice, kitten." He quickly caught her wrist when her claws sliced out and she tried swiping at him. "Christ, baby, why do you always go for my eyes?"

\*

Mouth slack, Khloë stared down at Devon's wrists the next morning. "Oh, Lord."

"Fingerprints?" Raini eyed them closely. "Tanner's demon did that?"

"Uh-huh." Devon tugged down her sleeves, casting a quick glance at the front door of the studio. Clients would start filtering in soon, and though Devon knew it wasn't likely that she'd be able to hide the brands from everyone—her luck just wasn't that great—she intended to give it her best shot.

Leaning back against the checkered partition near her station, Harper blew out a breath. "And I thought Knox's demon putting a 'K' on me was possessive."

Raini's brow wrinkled. "It put a 'K' on you? Where?"

Harper averted her gaze. "Um, never mind." She looked at Devon. "How do you feel about the hound branding you?"

A whole host of things. Shocked. Bewildered. Ticked off. Honestly, she was still struggling to wrap her head around it; she just never would have expected his demon to do such a thing.

Okay, maybe a small, girly part of her liked it—the same part of her that enjoyed romance novels, was a sucker for corner-of-the-mouth kisses, had crushed on him for far too long, and believed in the concept of soulmates. Hey, if there were such things as psi-mates and creatures that could wield a shitload of power, the idea that people might have a soulmate doesn't seem so fanciful. But no one else needed to know that a silly, hormonal part of her was secretly thrilled by the brands.

"Well, obviously, I'd like to ring the entity's neck." She really didn't need or want the kind of attention that these far from inconspicuous brands would bring her. Sighing, Devon raised her hand, palm out. "I blame this damn mark—it made the hound all possessive, and now it's behaving like an idiot." Branding its natural enemy was nothing short of idiotic.

"And your feline?" asked Raini. "How's it feeling about this?"

Devon absently rubbed at her arm. "It's weirdly disinterested."

Harper's head jerked back. "Disinterested? How can it be disinterested about being *branded*? That's not exactly a small thing in our world."

Devon shrugged, absolutely flummoxed. "It's like my demon just doesn't take them seriously. Like it finds the brands beneath its notice."

Eyes narrowing in thought, Raini said, "Which Tanner's demon will no doubt sense, right?"

"Right," Devon agreed.

"Then maybe that's why your feline's being so dismissive of the brands; it wants to piss the hound off," suggested Raini. "Which is sort of their normal type of interaction, isn't it?"

Hell, yeah, it was. "It wouldn't surprise me if the feline's just toying with the demon for fun." Noticing that Harper was staring at her with an odd expression on her face, Devon frowned. "What is it?"

Harper's shoulders lowered. "I'm worried about you. You think we don't know that you care about Tanner?" she asked, her tone gentle. "You think we don't know *exactly* how much it'll hurt you when this fling ends?"

Suddenly feeling incredibly vulnerable, Devon let her gaze flit around the room.

"You might not like these brands," Harper went on, "but when you see them start to fade, it's going to hurt, because you'll know it means his demon's losing interest. You'll know it means your time together is coming to an end."

A sharp pain struck Devon's chest. Yeah, she knew this thing she had with him was a dead end; she'd never once let herself forget it. But she couldn't claim that being prepared for the end would spare her any hurt.

Slumping against the wall, Devon weakly threw up her arms. "I tried to push him away."

Harper gave her a wan smile. "Tanner's not a guy who can be pushed anywhere he doesn't want to be."

"Tell me about it," grumbled Devon.

"I'd be pissed at him if I didn't wholeheartedly believe he cares about you, too," said Harper. "Anyone who knows him well can see that you're important to him. You'll both be hurting when this is over."

Devon felt her nose wrinkle. He'd said she mattered to him, but that didn't mean she was *important* to him. Hell, coffee mattered to Devon, but she could live without it. The people she cared for? They were important to her, and she'd do whatever it took to keep them in her life. She simply didn't have that much value to Tanner.

He probably wouldn't be *happy* when it was over, but she highly doubted he'd be hurt by it. Especially since his main objective was to fuck her out of his system.

"Playing it safe and keeping him at bay didn't exactly make me happy," said Devon. "So, I'm just gonna take what I can get while I can get it—knowing it won't last and that there's no HEA in store for me where he's concerned."

"*Or* you're setting yourself up to be hurt," said Harper. "I don't want that for you. I want you to be happy. A short fling—"

"The best thing about all this is that it's nothing more than a short fling," Devon cut in. "It means he won't have the opportunity to make any kind of mark on my life; it won't devastate me when he's gone from my little world because he was never truly in it—he'll simply have existed around it.

"I'm not going to lie and say I won't still be hurting when he and I go our separate ways, especially since I'll have to see him every day. But I've been through worse than losing Tanner Cole.

I survived those things, and I'll survive this. I'll just need you girls to take me out and get me blind drunk a few times."

"We can do that," said Khloë, giving her arm a light squeeze.

"Whatever you need, sweetie," Raini promised. "We're always here for you—you know that."

Yes, she did know that. Damn if she didn't have the best group of friends ever. Forcing a smile for them, Devon said, "Hey, don't fret so much. I've got bigger things to worry about than Tanner. As it happens, so have you, Raini."

The succubus shot her a narrow-eyed look. "It's so typical of you to turn the attention to someone else when you're in the spotlight."

"Yep," Devon admitted, unrepentant. "But I'm right. Have you heard from Maddox?"

Raini sank into her leather chair. "He talks to me," she blurted out, her gaze on the wall. "Mind-to-mind, I mean."

"Saying what?" asked Harper, but the succubus didn't respond. "Is he pushing for you to form the anchor bond with him?"

Raini shook her head. "He just . . . checks in. And stuff. But I never respond."

Khloë lifted her brows. "What do you mean by 'and stuff'?"

"It's not important."

"It is if it's bothering you," said Devon.

Raini forced a nonchalant smile. "I can deal."

"You sure of that?" asked Harper. "Because I could ask Knox to have a 'chat' with him and tell the guy to leave you be."

Again, Raini shook her head. "There's no need. Maddox will get bored when he realizes I'm not going to answer him. Like I said, I can deal. I'll let you know if that changes." She doodled an X over her heart. "I promise."

Harper let out a heavy sigh. "All right, if you're certain?"

"I'm certain," Raini assured her.

Sighing again, Harper turned to Khloë. "What about you?"

The imp's confused gaze darted left to right. "Hmm?"

"What are you going to do when Keenan finally acts on his little thing for you?" asked Harper.

Khloë waved that away. "Keenan doesn't need a girl in his life, he needs an AA sponsor. Or a dick surgeon to make his package more in proportion. Do they have dick surgeons? Or do the doctors have another title? Like Penis Fixers or something?"

"I'm seeing through all this flippancy," Harper told her. "You like him."

Khloë made a face. "He's good-looking, sure, but that's just skin, muscle, and bone. *And* his incubus mojo."

"A mojo you're immune to," began Raini, "so you can't blame your attraction to him even *partly* on that. Besides, you don't just like his looks, you like *him*."

"I like lots of guys," said Khloë with a casual shrug. "I'd prefer one who wouldn't love to permanently hook himself up to a drip of pure vodka. You all know how I feel about alcoholics."

Yeah, she had no time or respect for them. Mostly because her mother was a raging alcoholic. Demons were prone to developing addictions; it was sadly one of their curses. It was also partly why the Underground was so popular with all its bars, casinos, and other gambling events.

"Knox said that Keenan isn't an *actual* alcoholic," Harper told her. "He's positive that the incubus could cut vodka out of his diet if he needed to—he just simply doesn't want to."

Khloë pursed her lips. "Hmm, I'm not buying that. Speaking of 'buying' stuff . . . what do I get our little Asher for his birthday? I have some ideas, but I want to get him something he'll *really* like."

"If it lights up or makes noise, he'll like it," said Harper.

Raini tilted her head. "What time's his party on Sunday?"

"Two pm," replied Harper. "I'll expect to see you all there. Including you, Dev. I don't want to hear any of that 'I can't go because it would lead danger to your door.' I'm asking you to attend a party, not move in. You're going."

Devon saluted her. "I'll be there."

Khloë absentmindedly played with her earring as she turned to Devon. "When are you moving into Tanner's building?"

"Later on." *If* Devon liked the look of the place. Which she probably would, if it was anything like Tanner's apartment.

Harper gave a satisfied nod. "Good. If you need help moving in, give us a call."

The bell above the door chimed, and in breezed—*groan*—Eleanor. Devon tried not to tense, but it was impossible when looking at the woman who wanted the guy you cared for to impregnate her.

Devon's feline bared a fang, recognizing the female who'd falsely professed to having a claim on Tanner. It was a little disturbing that her feline had developed a possessive streak where he was concerned.

Keeping her keen eyes fixed on Devon, Eleanor walked up to the reception desk. Khloë made a move toward it, but Devon touched her arm and said, "I got this."

The girls looked confused. Well, of course they did. She hadn't told them about her previous conversation with Eleanor. Or about what the bitch wanted from Tanner.

Going for nonchalant, Devon casually made her way to the desk with a professional, impersonal smile. Deciding to channel Jolene, she greeted, "Eleanor, always a pleasure."

Stone-faced, Eleanor glanced at the hand that Devon had braced on the desk. "Is it true? Did he mark you?"

Devon could have played the "I don't know who you mean" game, but that would only drag out the conversation. "Yes."

The female hellhound pressed her lips together and took in a deep breath through her nose. "And you two are sleeping together?"

"Now, that's not really any of your business, is it? And for the record, I don't appreciate you turning up at my place of work, just as I didn't appreciate you turning up at my apartment."

Eleanor sighed. "Look, if you were anything other than a hellcat and he didn't have the typical male hellhound commitment issues, I'd step aside. I'm not interested in messing up a relationship. But there can never be anything between you and Tanner other than however many fucks your demons allow. Quite frankly, I'm surprised they allowed it to happen even once."

"I'm not sure at what point you reached the conclusion that I'd give a rat's ass what you think about anything. You can leave now."

Nostrils flaring, Eleanor leaned forward slightly. "You have to know it would be good for him to start a line of his own. It's hard enough for demons to maintain dominance over the entities within us. The older we get, the harder it gets. Tanner's never going to have an anchor to ground or center him. Having a child of his own could do that. I've seen how becoming a parent can change people."

"Just because he hasn't found his anchor yet doesn't mean he never will."

Eleanor very slowly tipped her head to one side. Something that might have been sympathy flashed on her face. "He hasn't told you, has he? It's probably not something you should take personally. I doubt he's told many people. I only found out about it because it came up in the background check I had done on him. A lot of Tanner's past is ... 'off-record,' shall we say? There are probably a great many things that neither of us know about him."

"And yet, you still want him to be the father of your child?" Something that made Devon want to lunge for the bitch's throat.

"Yes, I do. You're young, you may not be interested in having children just yet, but I suspect you might want them in the future. Just think about how dearly you wish to have, hold, and love a child of your own someday. And think about how Tanner could just warm up to the idea of experiencing that for himself . . . if you'd only let him go."

Devon almost jerked back. "I don't have any hold over Tanner."

"Oh, I think you do." Her eyes dropped to Devon's wrist. "Those are his brands, aren't they?" Whatever she saw on Devon's face made her nod, adding, "That's what I thought. It's a shame for both of you that nothing could ever come of it."

The bell jangled as the door opened again. One of the guards who Tanner had stationed outside stepped into the reception area and shot Eleanor a hard look. "Time to go, Miss Owens."

The female haughtily lifted her chin. "Excuse me?"

"I've been ordered by Tanner to escort you out of here," he said.

Which meant Harper had given the pooch a telepathic heads-up about Eleanor.

"There's no need for that," Eleanor told the guard.

"Because you're ready to leave, right?" It was a pressing suggestion, not a question.

Lips thinning, Eleanor spared Devon one last look as she headed for the door. "Think about what I said."

As if Devon could do anything else.

The moment the other female was gone, the girls crowded around the desk.

"Did I hear correctly that, in a nutshell, she wants Tanner to 'sire' her kid?" asked Raini.

Devon sighed. "Yep."

"And if my ears didn't deceive me, she once turned up at your apartment," said Harper, eyes narrowed. "That true?"

"Yep," Devon admitted, too tired to play dumb.

Khloë put her hands on her hips. "Okay, Clarke, I think it's time you fessed up the rest."

# CHAPTER TWELVE

Later that day, Devon stood in the newly vacated apartment that Knox had offered for her to use as a temporary base. Just as Tanner suspected, it had a similar blueprint to that of his own but didn't include a spare bedroom. The latter didn't bother Devon. She didn't need a spare bedroom. Hell, she didn't need half the space, but she had no complaints about its size. She had no complaints about it at all.

The apartment was stylish and chic. It also had a very welcoming feel with the warm paint colors, soft rugs, cozy fireplace, and maple hardwood flooring. Better still, it came partly furnished, and the kitchen had every appliance she'd need. And the bathroom was to die for.

She'd sure enjoy her temporary stay there. It would be kind of like spending a few days at a luxury condo while on a city break.

Her demon had examined the place carefully. It found the apartment aesthetically pleasing and much safer than their home, so it approved of their new temporary territory.

Having taken a full turn around the place, she rejoined Tanner in the hallway. He was leaning back against the wall, his hands stuffed in his pockets, his mouth downturned ... making her think of a sulking toddler. Though he'd been glued to her side since picking her and Harper up from work, he hadn't insisted on accompanying Devon as she wandered around the apartment—mostly because he was too busy brooding.

He raised a brow. "Well?"

Devon inhaled deeply, drinking in the scents of citrus cleaner and wood polish. "It'll do."

Any other time, the pooch might have snorted at her effort to downplay her excitement. Not this time.

Thanks to the whole Eleanor-turning-up-at-Urban-Ink thing, he'd already been in a foul mood when he arrived to take Devon home. It had only made him more pissed that she'd vetoed his suggestion to stay with him until Asa's friend was found.

Snarly and surly, he'd claimed it made sense for her to stay at his place as they'd be sharing a bed every night anyway. She'd quite rightly pointed out that their demons could protest to their fling at any given moment, so it would be better for her to have a separate living space. He hadn't been able to argue that—hence the brooding.

"Larkin telepathed me while you were looking around," said Tanner. "She was able to identify the men who were involved in the attempt to kidnap you." He rattled off a bunch of names. "Recognize any of them?"

"Other than when the driver mentioned a guy called Mike and referred to Slade by his name—who in turn called the driver Len—I'd never heard of them before." Devon slanted her head. "What lair do they belong to?"

"They're strays." He let his gaze wander around. "It makes more sense for you to stay with me."

And here they were again. "You're not getting bored of this conversation? Not even a little?" Devon sighed. "Look, I agreed to stay at your building, let that be enough."

Tanner pushed away from the wall and crossed to her. When it came to this female, "enough" was something he never seemed to get. He wanted everything from her, even as he knew he wouldn't get to enjoy it for long. He curled an arm around her waist and drew her to him. "Is it really such a bad thing that I want you close?"

She rolled her eyes. "Stop being a spoiled brat, Tanner. You can't always have your way. I'm on the floor above you—that's a damn fine concession and you know it. Learn to love it, because it's the best you're gonna get."

As amused as he was frustrated, he snapped his teeth at her. His demon wasn't quite so annoyed with her for sticking to her guns; it respected how ballsy and independent she was. It would still rather that she was staying at *their* domain, though. "Things would be a lot simpler if you just did what I said at all times."

She snickered. "Like that would ever happen. And if it did, you'd be bored."

He had to concede—if only to himself—that she had that right. Pulling her closer, he nuzzled her neck. "I thought about you a lot today."

"Did you?"

"Hmm." He kissed the hollow beneath her ear. "It's not a good thing. I'm supposed to be focused. You keep creeping into my thoughts and distracting me."

Devon huffed at his accusatory tone. "I don't see how that's my fault."

"I didn't say it was your fault. I'm just blaming you." He nipped her lip. "I wouldn't be so distracted by worry for you if you were staying with me."

"Not dropping this, huh?" She gave him a raised brow and *fuck* if it didn't go straight to his cock. "Listen here, pooch, I won't be guilted into doing something I don't want to do. I agreed to temporarily live here because it was smart. There'd be nothing smart in staying with you, considering we don't know how long it'll be before our demons—"

"I know." Tanner sighed, hating that he couldn't argue her point. He'd had a sick feeling in his gut since the day she was first kidnapped, and that feeling hadn't gone away. Wouldn't.

He'd checked in regularly throughout the day with the demons he had stationed outside her studio. Other than Eleanor turning up, nothing untoward had happened, but he hadn't been able to relax. Even now, when he had her right there in his arms, he couldn't fucking relax.

It didn't help that he was quite sure that it was Eleanor who vandalized her apartment. Tanner had paid it a short visit while Devon was at work. Some of her lair members had been there, clearing away the destroyed furniture. He hadn't picked up Eleanor's scent, but that meant nothing, since enough time had gone by for it to fade. He thought it significant that the one room that was ransacked was the very room in which he'd taken Devon against the wall.

He'd heard that Eleanor could pick up echoes of events by touching objects—a similar gift to Levi's ability to pick up echoes of events at death scenes. If that were true, it was possible she'd touched something in the living room that showed her what had happened there. Eleanor would have had one hell of a damn tantrum . . . which was exactly what the scene of destruction had looked like to him when he'd viewed it on Ciaran's cell phone.

The only thing that brought Tanner any comfort was the mark on Devon's palm. As he looked down at it, he got a glimpse of his fingerprints on her wrists. And he couldn't help but smile.

"You can stop looking so smug about the brands," she muttered.

"I could. But I won't."

"Yeah, I figured you'd say that," Devon grumbled. "They sure raised some eyebrows. All day I had to field off nosy-ass questions from clients. I need to buy some wristbands or something to cover—ow, that hurt!"

He licked over the delectable lip he'd bitten, soothing the sting. "No covering the brands. I like to look at them. I like that other people can see them. And if you try hiding them, there's a high chance my demon will decide to just brand you again."

She stilled, and her gaze turned thoughtful. "That point sadly holds merit."

He hummed, satisfied that she wouldn't conceal them. Cocking his head, he stroked his hand over her hair. "You going to tell me what's bothering you now?" He tapped her temple, adding, "I know something's going on up here. What is it?"

She bit her lip, so he used his thumb to pull it free from her teeth.

"Is it something Eleanor said to you? You were very vague about her little visit." He could ask Harper about it, but he'd rather Devon told him. He wanted her to trust him. To trust that she could be open with him. He caught her face with his hands. "Talk to me. You know you can."

Devon sighed. "She said some things that annoyed me, yeah. She also made me realize something I'm not whatsoever happy about."

He tucked her hair behind her ear. "What?"

"My demon's becoming possessive of you."

Tanner fought a smile, knowing she wouldn't appreciate his smugness. Especially since this was clearly hard for her to admit. "Possessive?"

She nodded. "It was exponentially pissed when Eleanor made it clear just how much she'd like you to impregnate her."

He snorted. "That's not going to happen."

"Would it really be so bad to start your own line?"

"Some time in the future, no. Right now? It's not what I want."

God, it made her such a bitch that that relieved her, didn't it? But the thought of him fathering a kid to another woman was just a little too much for Devon to bear right then. In the future, long after they'd gone their separate ways and she'd licked her wounds, it wouldn't be so hard to handle. Hopefully.

"Parenthood has been known to center people who don't have an anchor. Eleanor said—" Devon clamped her mouth shut and averted her gaze, thinking how unfair it was that she was fishing for information on a subject that could be a sore one.

He gently cupped her chin. "Eleanor said what? Tell me, kitten. What did she say?"

Knowing he wouldn't drop it, she said, "That you'll never have your anchor. I didn't get what she meant. But you don't have to tell me; it's fine. Really." It wasn't as if she didn't have secrets of her own.

Scraping his jaw with his hand, Tanner looked away. "Eleanor must have done a real thorough check on me." He sighed, sliding his gaze back to Devon's. "I found my anchor shortly after I became a sentinel. We didn't form the bond, because her mate was jealous. He didn't want her having such a close tie to another man. He made her choose—me or him. She chose him, which was understandable."

"But you've kept watch over her, haven't you?" Devon guessed, because she knew him too well.

"I did until she and her mate died in a plane crash."

Devon winced, wishing she hadn't brought it up. "Shit, I'm sorry. Maybe it was a blessing, then, that you hadn't formed the bond. I've heard the breaking of it is painful." She gave his shoulder a squeeze. "Thank you for telling me." One large hand spanned the back of her head, fingers sifting through her hair to dig into her scalp—God, that felt good.

"Eleanor only told you about it because she's trying to make you feel that I keep shit from you. She wants you to feel unsure of me." He briefly brushed his mouth over hers. "Forget about her. Ignore the crap she says. She's not important. Okay?"

Devon gave a slow nod. "Okay."

"Good girl." He gave her ass a pat. "Let's go get your things."

\*

As she didn't have an awful lot of stuff and plenty of people pitched in to help, it didn't take long to move her things into his building. In terms of furniture, she only took her bed and a few other pieces, since her stay would most likely be a short one. Her helpers also assisted her in unpacking once she arrived, which was very much appreciated.

As a thank you, she later bought a takeout for everyone, which was quickly demolished. People slowly began to leave over the following hour, until only Devon and Tanner were left. It was while they were cleaning up the kitchen that Finn called her, and it quickly became apparent that he wasn't happy with her for not calling him about the second attempted kidnapping.

"Jolene told me that she'd call you with the entire story," Devon told him.

"And she did. *Five minutes ago.* I should have been told of it immediately. I'm your father. You think I wouldn't want to know that you went through hell yesterday?"

Her father? Biologically, sure, but that was all. "I did send a text message to your phone last night," she reminded him.

"Oh yeah—*Finn, some shit went down between me and a group of demons but don't worry I'm not dead.*"

She shrugged. "I thought it was pretty succinct."

"You know it can take me a while to sift through my text messages—it's why I tell you to leave a voicemail if it's urgent. This counts as urgent. Look, I can understand if you're upset with me for not handing Asa over to Jolene to be interrogated, but I shouldn't have heard about the attempted kidnapping from her. I should have heard it from you. And I should have heard of it *straight away*."

A growl rumbled out of Tanner, who was bagging up the trash, *totally* eavesdropping. "If he yells at you one more time, I'm ending that fucking call."

No, Devon would do that herself. "Finn, you'll be kept in the loop, but Jolene isn't going to be in any rush to call you with news, because she feels that you're not invested in finding out what's going on here. If you were, you'd have given someone else a shot at Asa."

A brief pause. "It's not that simple, Devon. I'd make myself look weak if I surrendered him to another Prime for questioning. No Prime can afford to demonstrate weakness."

"She said you didn't need to hand him over; she said she'd be content enough with going to wherever you're keeping him and having a chat with him."

He made a sound that was close to a snort. "Jolene is an imp. Imps can get in and out of anywhere. If she knew Asa's location, she'd send some of her lair to retrieve him. We both know that."

Okay, that most likely *would* happen.

"Believe me when I say we're doing everything we can to get answers from Asa." He paused as a female voice spoke in the background. "In a minute, Reena, I'm on the phone."

An acidic smile curved Devon's mouth. "I'm sure she's devastated that I got free."

He sighed. "I know you two don't get along well, but she wouldn't like to see you dead."

Devon snorted. "Don't kid yourself."

Another sigh. "Devon—"

"Look, I have to go." Because, really, what more was there to say?

There was a long pause. "All right. If something else happens, I'd like it if you could notify me immediately."

As she couldn't make him any promises, she simply said, "Take care." Devon rang off and took a deep breath.

"I don't like the way that asshole speaks to you," said Tanner. "Like he's *entitled* to know what goes on in your life when he's never made himself a real part of it."

Devon shrugged. "He's a Prime. They're spoiled and used to having their way. Kind of like you."

"I can't even deny that." Sensing that she didn't want to talk more about Finn, Tanner prowled towards her and said, "Cleaning's done. Did you manage to unpack all your things?"

"Yes. I had some help."

"Good." He hauled her close, loving how her heartbeat instantly kicked up. Just that easily, hunger slammed into him, as if her need could in an instant become his. "I've never wanted anything the way I want you." He snaked a hand around her throat and tipped her head back. "Tonight . . . I want to fuck you here, in this apartment."

Devon hummed, not seeming to feel the least bit uncomfortable exposing her throat to him. He fucking loved that. "Why?" she asked.

Because he wanted her to have that memory of him in *her* bed. Wanted her to think of him as she lay on it, even if there was someone else lying beside her.

He dipped his head and pressed a kiss to her pulse. "We could sleep at my place, but I highly doubt you'll want to leave this apartment after all the trouble you've just taken to get it ready."

"You're right on that."

Knox's mind touched his, buzzing with a sense of urgency. *Tanner, we need to talk. Where are you?*

Brow wrinkling at the Prime's curt tone, Tanner replied, *The apartment where Devon's staying for the time being.*

*Meet me at your apartment as fast as you can.* Just that quick, Knox was gone.

Both curious and put-out by the interruption, Tanner lifted his head and pressed a kiss to her mouth. Unable to tell her about Knox's ability to pyroport, he said, "I need to go grab some things from my place." He slowly pulled back, hesitant to leave her for even a minute. "I won't be long."

Strolling into his own apartment no more than a minute later, he found Knox and the other sentinels waiting in his living room. Knox stood near the fireplace, his muscles taut, his expression hard. Except for Levi, who'd propped his hip against the wall, the others were seated. One glance at each of the sentinels' faces was enough to tell Tanner that they had no clue what the emergency meeting was about.

Uneasy, Tanner didn't take a seat. "What is it?"

Knox's nostrils flared. "I'm sure you all remember Mattias Ranger."

Kind of hard to forget someone who Knox once flung into an ants' nest after the kid tried hurting Larkin. Mattias was Ramsbrook House's biggest bully.

"He's dead," clipped Knox.

Shock stiffened every muscle in Tanner's body, and all he could do was join the other sentinels in staring dumbly at their Prime.

"You may remember that I told Muriel to give me a list

of whoever she wanted to be notified of Dale's death," Knox added. "Mattias's name wasn't on that list, but his cousin's name was."

"Noah," Levi remembered. "Both their parents died in a car accident. Noah's father was the driver."

"Yes," said Knox. "And Mattias blamed Noah's father for the deaths, so he made that kid's life a misery. Dale and Muriel befriended Noah, and I think they made things bearable for him to an extent. When I contacted him to inform him of Dale's death, he wasn't just horrified, he was shocked. Because Mattias was mutilated in the exact same way as Dale and Harry."

Larkin sucked in a breath while Levi spat, "Fuck."

Keenan pulled his flask out of his inner pocket. "That makes three people from Ramsbrook who've been—"

"Four," corrected Knox.

Keenan did a double-take. "What?"

"Joseph Morgan was also on Muriel's list," said Knox. "He wasn't taking my calls, but I didn't think much of it until Noah told me about Mattias. On a hunch, I paid Joseph a visit. All I found was his mutilated, decomposing corpse. He's been dead weeks."

"Weeks?" echoed Larkin.

Knox nodded. "Looks to me like he was the first to die. And I'm not sure about any of you, but my view is that we were wrong in what we initially thought. Harry wasn't killed because he knew something that Sloan wanted kept quiet. Someone is targeting people who stayed at Ramsbrook."

"It makes the most sense," granted Keenan. "But . . . why would they?"

Knox snorted. "I have no clue. I can't think why anyone would want to remove someone's eyes, ears, and tongue—nor why they'd prop them up against the wall in a very specific way.

Is it some sort of message to the victim? Is it supposed to be somebody's fucked-up idea of poetic justice?"

Poking his tongue into the inside of his cheek, Levi rubbed at his jaw. "It comes across as a punishment to me. The killer mutilated them while they were alive."

"You know, other ex-Ramsbrook kids could be dead," said Larkin.

"Yes," agreed Knox. "But there's no fast way to trace the whereabouts of all of them to find out—there was simply too many of them. Kids came and went from there all the time."

Some were adopted, some died, some ran off, and some even committed suicide. Ramsbrook was no easy ride. "It's possible that the killer's just randomly picking off ex-Ramsbrook kids and employees, but it seems unlikely," said Tanner.

Nodding, Larkin idly toyed with her braid. "There must be a specific reason why Harry and the others were chosen. It could have been something they did or something they failed to do. Something that made somebody feel the need to track down and kill them."

Tanner perched himself on the arm of the sofa and folded his arms. "Either something occurred there that we don't know about, or we're making the mistake of thinking the killer is operating on logic."

"You think they might be deranged or near-rogue?" Larkin asked him.

Tanner shrugged. "I'm just making the point that the motive only has to seem logical to the killer."

Lips pursed, Knox inclined his head. "True enough. We know from our experiences with other near-rogues like Crow that, even though their minds are splintering, they truly believe they're rational and in the right."

"Personally, I don't see how Mattias, Harry, Joseph, and Dale could have been jointly responsible for some sort of crime or accident that they were recently 'punished' for by some fucked-up vigilante." Keenan took a long swig from his flask. "Neither Dale nor Harry had any time for Mattias or Joseph. *No one* had time for Joseph—he was almost as bad a bully as Mattias."

"If the victims were staff members, I could understand it," said Knox. "The punishments that some of them dealt out were quite severe. Severe enough to leave scars. And they were constantly fucking *preaching* at us . . . "

Knox's voice faded away as something in Tanner's brain clicked. His eyes fell shut as realization hit him like a ton of bricks. He rubbed at his face. "Shit, I should have seen it before."

"What?" asked Levi.

Unfolding his arms, Tanner said, "I thought that gouging out the eyes, slicing off the ears, and cutting off the tongue was a symbolic punishment for being a plant. But it's not that at all. What did the tutors always preach to us? *See no evil, hear no evil, speak no evil.*"

Keenan's mouth fell open. "Fuck, fuck, fuck, we *all* should have seen that."

"But what does that mean?" asked Larkin, leaning forward.

"It means the killer has to be someone from Ramsbrook—either one of the kids or one of the staff. Nothing else makes sense to me." Levi looked at Knox. "I know it's unlikely that Dale and the others were involved in something as kids, but it might be worth asking Muriel. If something *did* happen, she'd probably know about it—Dale confided in her a lot, from what I remember."

"Does anyone know if Ernest Milton is still alive? Or Milton, as he preferred to be called?" asked Tanner, referring to the home's caretaker. "Very little went on in that place that he didn't know about."

Knox's eyes sharpened. "I'll look him up. If he's alive, we'll pay him a visit tomorrow."

"What about the Primes of Matthias and the other victims?" Keenan asked Knox. "Have you spoken with any of them about the murders?"

"Briefly," replied Knox. "They're each looking into the deaths. I thought about bringing them in on our investigation, but none are our allies, and I don't trust them enough to work closely with them—especially when it would mean disclosing a lot of information to them about our pasts. Besides, they'd more than likely be offended that I'd suggested they needed my aid. And unless Primes get along well the way Jolene and I do, coming together on something often isn't very productive."

They spoke for a few more minutes and made plans to meet at Knox's office in the morning. The Prime then pyroported the other sentinels away, and Tanner headed back upstairs to Devon.

*

Squinting up at them from his bunk in the cramped quarters of the fishing boat the next day, Milton echoed, "Secrets?" He grunted, scratching at the stubble on his tanned cheek. "Yes, there were secrets at Ramsbrook. Secrets I didn't even know of for what might have been a long time."

The guy had been washing the deck with a hose when they appeared on the dock near his house and asked to speak with him. It had probably been more curiosity than anything else which made the ornery male invite them inside. He'd gestured for them to take the small sofa, but only Knox and Tanner took a seat. Levi was leaning against the counter in the tiny galley kitchen.

Tanner's demon didn't like the cramped space. Didn't like the scents of brine, motor oil, coffee, and a faint hint of fish guts. It also didn't like being around someone that reminded it of a bad time in its existence.

The demon hadn't minded being around Muriel—she'd just been a child back then, couldn't have helped. But Milton had been an adult, a member of the staff. And though Tanner understood that, as a caretaker, Milton hadn't had enough power or influence to make changes to the shitty place, his hound wasn't so understanding.

"We want to know if something could have happened at Ramsbrook that would explain why someone is killing people who once stayed there," said Knox. He'd called Muriel to notify her of Mattias and Joseph's deaths. She'd claimed there was no way that Dale and the other victims could have been involved in something together.

Milton's brow furrowed. "Who was killed?"

"Harry Tomlinson, Dale Tipton, Mattias Ranger, and Joseph Morgan."

A shocked silence seemed to descend on Milton, making the exterior noises of the creaking of the taut rope outside, the flapping of the mast, and the cries of seagulls that much louder.

Finally, Milton's eyes clouded, and he expelled an audible breath. "Ah, shit."

"The only common denominator we can see is that they stayed at Ramsbrook. We need to know if they were involved in anything that could explain their deaths."

Sighing, Milton rubbed at the back of his nape. "Yes, the boys were . . . I don't know if you'd use the word 'involved.' Something happened to them. I don't even know how long it had been happening. But it came to an end about a year after you left. I might never have known anything about it if it hadn't been for Harry."

"What did Harry tell you?"

"He didn't tell me anything. But one night he asked me to stay in his dorm; to use my ability of camouflage to conceal myself. Said there was something I needed to see. It was the same small dorm that Dale, Mattias, Joseph, and some other kids slept in. I did as he asked. Only Harry knew I was there, from what I could tell. It was about midnight when they came."

"Who?"

"Two of the tutors, Mr. Giles and Mr. Shephard. They ordered the children to get out of bed and form a line, facing the tutors. The kids were pale and trembling, clearly terrified out of their minds, and I knew this wasn't the first time it had happened."

A sliver of unease snaked up Tanner's spine, raising the hairs on his arms and the back of his neck.

Milton fiddled with the collar of his tee. "Mr. Giles asked, 'So, who will it be tonight?' He made the children *vote* on who would go with him and Mr. Shephard. Then the tutors dragged whichever child received the most votes out of the room. I followed them, still camouflaged. They took him down to the basement. Chained him up. Probably would have done despicable things to him, only I slit both their throats and then released the boy."

Disgusted, Tanner ground his teeth to bite back a curse. He remembered the tutors well. Remembered how staid, stringent, and authoritarian they'd been. They'd had no patience for error or idleness; hadn't seemed to take any joy in teaching. But he wouldn't have suspected them capable of such cruelty. That was the thing about evil fuckers like that, though—they were very good at hiding what they were.

The thought that those poor kids had been subjected to such abuse and felt they had nowhere to turn ... Tanner's blood boiled. He hated that it went on right under his fucking nose. If he'd known, if he'd even *suspected*, that such things were happening, he'd have acted—teen or not. And Knox and the other sentinels would have been right at his side when he did.

"I notified the rest of the staff," said Milton. "They were hor-rified. You might find that hard to believe, since they were so cold towards all the children. The punishments were harsh, yes, but the staff never took any sadistic pleasure in them. They did what they thought was necessary to control a whole building of orphaned, angry, gifted children. And maybe sometimes they were harsher than they needed to be, but they didn't get a kick out of it."

Tanner had never got the feeling that any of the staff *enjoyed* what they were doing. They'd never punished anyone for the sake of it or for some imaginary slight. But then, he'd never got the feeling that Giles and Shephard would take delight in abusing kids. "The tutors made the other kids choose which child would go with them because the bastards wanted to make the kids feel partly to blame, didn't they?"

"Yes, I suspect they thought the guilt and shame would keep the kids quiet," said Milton. "And it did. They wouldn't even talk of it much after the truth was out and the tutors were dead. They seemed to just want to forget."

"What happened afterwards?" asked Knox.

"The manager swept the whole thing under the rug because they didn't want to risk that the place would be shut down. I voted against that," Milton quickly added, "just as some of the other staff did, but we were overruled. We didn't hold enough power to overturn their decision." And he appeared to be pissed at himself for that.

"I never noticed any injuries on those kids to suggest abuse," said Levi.

"Shephard could undo wounds, so he'd healed the children afterwards, leaving no evidence of what they'd been through," said Milton. "From what the staff could tell, the abuse was isolated to that one dorm. The reason Harry and the others were placed together was that they were low on the power spectrum—the staff didn't believe it would be fair to place them with children who they'd be unable to defend themselves against. I think that was probably also why the tutors chose that dorm—in terms of power, the kids were too weak to fight back." Milton let out a sad sigh. "And now some of them have been victimized yet again. How were they killed?"

Knox gave him all the details, including Tanner's belief that the mutilations reflected the *See no evil, hear no evil, speak no evil* saying. "How many other kids were in that dorm? Because I'm thinking that one of them is holding the others to blame for whatever they went through, and they're intent on making them pay for it."

Milton pursed his lips. "Other than the boys I mentioned, there were three other children. Patrick Stephens, Royal Foreman, and Donnie Ramirez. I can tell you that Ramirez is dead—he turned rogue while at Ramsbrook; had to be taken down. I'm not sure what happened to the other two. Dale's sister might also be a target."

Tanner's brows pinched together. "Why?"

"Well, she didn't sleep in Dale's dorm—the girls were kept separate—but she told one of the staff members that she snuck in there one night after she'd had a nightmare and the tutors came in and forced her to 'take a vote.'"

Knox stilled. "Muriel told us that there was no way the victims were involved in anything together."

Milton lifted a brow. "Then Muriel lied."

# CHAPTER THIRTEEN

"She's gone," said Tanner, standing in the middle of Muriel's living room a short while later.

Larkin perched her hands on her hips. "It doesn't seem like any of her things are missing. Her wardrobe and drawers are full. Her door keys are in the bowl in the hallway. Her purse is near the sofa. The TV's on." Her nose wrinkled at the bowl of stale soup on the table. "Looks like she sat down to have lunch some time yesterday and then ..."

"And then someone came and took her," finished Knox. His nostrils flared. "*Fuck.*"

"I just skimmed through her phone," said Levi. "She's had a lot of missed calls. The last one she answered came yesterday morning at 10am. Her first missed call was at 2:30pm, so she was taken some time before then."

"There's no point ignoring the reality that she's been taken by whoever killed her brother and the others. God knows where they'll leave her body." Knox sighed. "We need to get back to my office."

Flames erupted around them and licked at Tanner's skin as the Prime pyroported them back to his Underground office.

Planting his hands on his desk, Knox said, "Larkin, Keenan— I'm going to need you both to try to locate Royal Foreman and Patrick Stephens. One of them has to be the killer. It's the only thing that makes sense of everything that's happened."

"Finding them might not be a fast process, especially with respect to the killer," Larkin warned. "He's probably taken precautions to hide his identity just in case anyone worked out what was happening and started to hunt him. He might have changed his name, moved away, switched lairs."

"I'm not under the illusion that you'll find the killer in time to save Muriel," Knox assured her. "He's had her in his grasp too long."

"We'll find Stephens and Foreman," Keenan stated.

Knox sat on his leather chair. "What do we remember of Stephens?"

Levi pursed his lips. "He was a quiet kid. Kept his head down. Made no effort to draw attention to himself. He was also an illusionist. Could force people to believe they could hear, see, smell, taste, or touch something that didn't exist. He didn't have a good handle on his ability back then, though."

"He had cold eyes," Tanner recalled.

Larkin nodded. "Yeah. He could chill your bones with just a look, and he wasn't even frowning or scowling. His face would always be blank."

"Foreman was the opposite," said Keenan. "Loud and brash. Always acting out. But then, ensnares are natural-born tricksters, aren't they? I remember he used to create traps to amuse himself. Sometimes the traps were physical, like nets or tubes.

Other times, he'd trap people's minds *inside* their bodies, stopping the brain from communicating with the body—it meant they couldn't move or speak."

"His snares never stood up well to attacks, though," Tanner remembered. "And they usually only lasted twenty seconds or so. But his ability would have strengthened with age."

Levi folded his arms. "The question is . . . which one is most likely to be the killer?"

"I'd say Stephens purely because I found him creepy," said Larkin. "But I don't think we can really base our suspicion on how they acted as kids. People change."

"Whoever it is, something must have happened recently in their life to spur them into suddenly going after the people they hold responsible for their pain," said Tanner.

Knox nodded. "There must have been some sort of trigger."

Tanner took a deep, pained breath that tightened his chest. "If one of the kids had just told us, just *hinted* at it . . . " He'd have obliterated the abusers in an instant.

"You can understand why they didn't talk," said Larkin, her mouth downturned. "But I sure wish they had."

Yeah, Tanner could understand it, because shame was crawling through his system. He'd noticed the haunted expressions Harry and the others sometimes wore, but he'd never wondered at it. He'd always attributed their hurt to the other shit that went on there. Plus, everyone had a sad story of how they'd come to be at Ramsbrook—it hadn't occurred to him that something else could be going on.

"Harry got them help, in his way," said Levi. "It didn't save him from whoever's been hunting kids from his dorm, though."

And that only made it worse. Tanner was glad the tutors were dead, but slit throats? They'd deserved a fuck of a lot worse than that. "Giles and Shephard died too easily, too quickly. *They* should have been the ones who fucking suffered, not Harry and the others—they were victims."

"So is whoever killed them," said Larkin. "That's the worst thing. We'll be killing someone who's already been through enough."

Exhaling heavily, Knox pushed to his feet. "I need to speak with Harper about something."

Tanner suspected that his Prime didn't have anything in particular to speak with her about. Suspected that Knox simply wanted to see her, wanted to touch the one thing that calmed him. Just the same, Tanner was itching to see the person who had the singular ability to still the chaos in his head. *Devon.*

Anger, guilt, and disgust were clawing at him. The only thing that would give him any relief from it was her. He knew it, because she'd done it for him several times in the past. She just had no idea she'd done it.

They'd slept in her apartment the previous night. He'd taken her in her bed, just as he'd told her he would. Earlier that morning, he'd dropped her and Harper at Urban Ink before leaving with Knox and the other sentinels to visit Milton. She'd be finishing work soon, but he didn't want to wait that long to see her.

"I'll come with—" Tanner cut off as a familiar male mind reached out to his.

*Thought you should know that Devon is on the move,* said Dez, one of the two members of Knox's Force who Tanner had assigned to watch over her. He'd relieved Lex and Enzo of guard duty, since they'd messed the fuck up by taking their eye off the ball long enough that she was snatched right in front of them.

*She's leaving work early?* asked Tanner. Her shift didn't usually finish for another hour.

*Two guys came to the studio to see her. She introduced them to me as Adam and Hunter; said all three of them were going for a fancy dinner to celebrate the anniversary of the day she and her anchor bonded—apparently, it's an annual thing.*

Oh, was it now? What he'd very much like to damn well know was why she hadn't forewarned him about it. Feeling a muscle in his cheek jump, Tanner asked, *Where exactly are they going for dinner?*

\*

As the waitress set their drinks and complimentary hot bread on the table, Adam shot the blonde a winning smile that had her blushing. "Thanks so much," he said.

The ice tinkled against the glass as Devon picked up her soda and took a sip. This restaurant was highly popular within the Underground, so only those who made a reservation a week in advance stood a chance of getting a table. Adam had pre-booked their table, just as he always did this time of year to celebrate the anniversary of their anchor bond. To her shame, she'd forgotten about it. Adam thankfully wasn't upset by that, but she still felt bad.

Although the place was full, it wasn't rowdy. The chatter was mostly soft, and the music played low in the background. None of the servers looked flushed or frazzled. They were calm yet efficient, which added to the relaxed atmosphere.

A door on their left swung open, and a waitress breezed out of the kitchen, effortlessly balancing several trays on her arms. Devon shook her head in wonder. "I have no idea how they do that."

"Practice," said Hunter, expertly slicing into the crusty bread.

Each time the kitchen door opened, a cloud of mouth-watering scents filtered into the room. If she hadn't been hungry before arriving here, the scenes of grilled meat, spices, hot peppers, and garlic would have wakened her appetite.

Setting down her glass, she raked a hand through her hair. "Damn, Adam, I still can't believe I forgot our anniversary."

Adam snorted. "I can. You have all kinds of crazy stuff going on. I'd have been surprised if you were thinking clear enough to remember. It's a relief for me that you're not—it assures me that you're taking the threats to your safety seriously. You have a habit of brushing off danger."

She lifted her chin. "I do not."

"You totally do." Hunter handed her a piece of the bread he'd buttered. "But we love you anyway."

She bit into the bread a little too roughly, tossing her anchor a haughty look that only made him smile. But that smile faltered when his eyes once again landed on the fingerprints on her wrist. Both males had noticed the brands pretty much straight away. Adam looked concerned. Hunter seemed amused.

"I'm guessing those brands are courtesy of the hellhound," said Adam.

"You guessed correctly." She took another bite of her bread rather than elaborate. She adored Adam, she truly did, but this simply wasn't his business. Not that it would do any good to remind him of that. As her anchor, he saw it as his right to interfere in her life in whatever way he saw fit. Sometimes it was cute, other times it was annoying, but she knew his actions came from a good place.

"And you're okay with it?" he asked.

Not at all. But if she said that, he'd see it as the green light to confront Tanner about it. That would not only be utterly pointless, it would run the risk of Adam getting his ass whooped.

She shrugged. "The brands will fade soon enough."

"Don't think I'm buying the casual act. Your emotions have always been all over the place where this guy is concerned."

How she wished she could deny that. Chewing the last of her

bread, she used a napkin to wipe crumbs from her fingers and mouth. "Look, Adam, I already had this conversation with the girls. I'd rather not have it again."

"Hmm, I'm sure you wouldn't. But I'm not just a friend, Dev, I'm your *anchor*. I'm one of the most important people in your life."

The hurt in his voice made her chest tighten. "I know, I'm not trying to blow you off."

"Feels like it."

She grabbed his hand. "You're worried I'll get shit on, I know. I love you for it. But this just—"

"Isn't his business," finished Hunter. Slurping his milkshake through his straw, he shrugged at his mate, who was now glaring at him. "Well, it's not. Come on, Adam, you're her anchor, not her keeper. She's not dumb; she knows exactly what she's gotten herself into. She'll get herself out of it once she's ready. And then, if need be, we'll dig out the shotgun and see how fast the canine can run."

Adam sighed. "I just—"

"No 'justs,'" Hunter told him, wagging his finger. "Let it go. Get rid of the frown. Let's enjoy our meal." He gave her a subtle wink that said, "I got your back."

Adam licked his front teeth and then let out a heavy sigh. "Fine. Tell me what it's like to live in an apartment that costs more than my house."

Smiling, she smoothed a wrinkle out of the soft, white table-cloth. "Well, it's pretty awesome."

Just then, the waitress appeared and set their plates in front of them.

"I just *have* to snap a photo of this," declared Hunter, his eyes bright as he stared at his meal. "I'm going to have a bash at recreating this at home."

Just then, the happy birthday tune began to play out of the loudspeakers. Servers surrounded a circular table, clapping and singing along with the people seated there.

Forking some of her food, Devon smiled at the celebratory spectacle. And that was when the hairs on her nape stood up. Her gaze unerringly shot to her right, and her pulse skittered as she saw Tanner breezing toward her, his muscles rippling and bunching, every inch the predator. And his gaze was firmly locked on her.

Devon swallowed and put down her fork. His feet didn't make a sound as he prowled along the hard, tiled floor. Eyes followed him, of course. Some people shrunk back, as if not wanting to earn themselves the attention of one of Knox's deadly sentinels. Other people, mostly women, tossed inviting smiles his way. *Bitches.* Okay, that wasn't nice, but she hadn't said it aloud.

His golden eyes raked over her face with blatant possessiveness, glittering with something dangerous that made her scalp prickle. Even so, that good ole visceral, ever-present sexual chemistry pulsed between them like a heartbeat.

Unease snaked through her. If she hadn't come to know him so well, she'd have been fooled by his cool expression; wouldn't have picked up on just how pissed he was. Had something else happened? Was someone hurt? Or was it something to do with whatever was going on in his lair that he, Knox, and the sentinels seemed to spend a lot of time debating in private?

He didn't stop at their table and say his hellos. He slid into her booth as if she'd been waiting for him; sat so close that his side was practically fused to hers. Before she could say a word, he leaned in and took her mouth. Just like that, her unease gave way to the need she harbored for him that always seemed to hum beneath her skin, as if lying in wait for him. That need crawled over her, pulled her under, drowned out her awareness of her surroundings and—

Someone cleared their throat.

With a nip to her lower lip, Tanner pulled back and tucked her hair behind her ear. "Hello, kitten. Miss me?"

"Like I'd miss a root canal." She kicked his foot under the table. "Move over." He didn't. Well, of course he didn't. Why would he?

His mind slid against hers just before his voice breezed inside, cool and gravel-rough. *You didn't tell me you were going out for dinner.*

Such a casual comment, such a soft tone. And yet there was something so *dark* there that goosebumps swept down her bare arms. *Something's wrong. What is it?*

He breezed his thumb over her jawline. *You said you'd tell me if you ever had plans to leave the studio while I wasn't with you.*

He didn't trust anyone else to escort her anywhere safely, yeah, she got that, but . . . *I didn't know about the dinner plans—Adam surprised me with them.*

*Hmm.* He took her hand and circled his mark on her palm with the tip of his finger. *You really think it was a good idea for you to go waltzing around the Underground when someone's after you?*

Maybe not, but . . . *I'm not letting the son of a bitch stop me from doing something as important as celebrating the anniversary of—*

*Yeah, yeah, Dez told me why you're here. No celebration is more important than your life, kitten.*

Okay, he had her there. *Tell me what's really wrong.* Because something was going on with him right then. *You're worrying me.*

His expression softened. *It's not related to what's happening with you.*

"Fancy seeing you here, Tanner," said Adam, a forced curve to his mouth.

Hunter's smile, on the other hand, was far from fake as he stirred his milkshake with his straw. "Yeah, what a coincidence."

Tanner draped his arm over the back of the booth. "No coincidence. I came to see Devon."

Adam's expression hardened just a little. "You don't trust that we'll keep her safe?"

"I don't fully trust anyone but me with her safety. It's nothing personal," Tanner added with a lazy shrug.

"Does this mean you're not leaving?" her anchor asked.

"That's exactly what it means."

Well wasn't that just super. Devon nudged him with her elbow. "At least move over so I can have a little more space while I eat my meal." But he didn't. So she gave him a psychic shove, making him skid a few inches along the leather.

His brows hiked up, and he looked nothing short of impressed. "Sheathe those claws, kitten."

"Or?"

"Or I'll do what I always want to do when you use them on me—I'll bite you hard enough to leave a mark."

In public? She narrowed her eyes. "You wouldn't dare."

"Wouldn't I?"

"Not unless you want to find yourself choking on your own testicles."

His mouth quirked. "You have such a short fuse."

"In the exact words I used when we were in bed last night discussing something wholly different ... it's okay, sweetie, we can just imagine that it's bigger."

Adam started choking on his drink, and a laughing Hunter had to slap his mate's back several times.

Shooting the pooch one last scathing glare, Devon turned her attention to her meal.

Tanner wouldn't have thought he had it in him to smile right then, but she always had a way of loosening the grip of whatever bullshit was crippling him. Like it was her fucking super power or something. Or maybe it was just because she was a surprisingly restful person to be around. She just made you feel at ease. Accepted. Relaxed. Honestly, he'd swear he breathed easier when she was with him.

The waitress scrambled over and asked if he wanted to order anything, but he waved her away. He was content to simply watch his kitten while she dug into her food. Content to watch her throat work, her tongue swipe over her lips, and her eyes go heavy-lidded each time she ate something she found particularly flavorsome.

He knew she was keenly aware of his gaze on her, but she said nothing. Well, she said nothing to *him*. She easily kept up a light conversation with the other two males as they ate.

His hound brooded, not liking that it had to share her attention. But Tanner found her struggle to ignore him amusing ... because it *was* a struggle for her while an electric sexual tension purred in the air between them. Neither of them stood a chance of ignoring it.

Waves of disapproval radiated from Adam, but Tanner paid him no attention. If the guy had something on his mind, he'd just need to come right out and say it. Not that it would make Tanner leave, if that was what the male wanted. Tanner was going nowhere.

Finally done with her meal, she slanted him a put-out look as she lifted her glass. "Stop staring."

"Nah." He watched the block of ice bump her lips as she sipped her drink, and he couldn't help but picture the head of his cock bumping her mouth that way.

With a cute little huff, she swiped one of the lemon-scented handwipes that the server had left on their table and tore it open. "God, that meal was amazing."

"It really was." Slumping into his chair with a dreamy smile, Hunter sighed. "I am so stuffed. I don't know about you guys, but I have no room for dessert."

"Neither do I," she said.

Adam snickered. "You're both lightweights. There's *always* room for dessert."

"Then you'd best order yourself one." Having wiped her hands, she drained her glass and then slid out of the booth. "I need to use the restroom."

With no intention of allowing her out of his sight, Tanner flowed to his feet. *Before you try telling me you don't need me to walk you there, know that you'd be wasting your breath. Harper was once taken from a restroom, remember? I'm not taking the risk that the same could happen to you.*

She shot him a dirty look and then flounced off. He followed her to the restroom, passing tables and booths, and carefully skirting a caution cone.

Once she disappeared inside, he stationed himself near the door, satisfied that he was close enough to hear if things went to shit. He also had a good view of the restaurant, so he instantly noticed when Adam exited the booth and began making his way over. Ah, it seemed that the male was ready to spit out whatever was on his mind.

Tanner slowly raised a brow. "Problem?" Even he heard the note of challenge in his tone.

Adam slanted a look at the closed restroom door. "That girl is very important to me. I don't want her hurt."

Bristling, Tanner flicked up his eyebrow. "You think I'd hurt her?"

"Not on purpose. But you're a hard man, Tanner. It's obvious you don't like emotional attachments. Devon is warm and kind and caring. She'll give her partner everything she has, and she deserves to get that in return. In some ways, you seem good for her. But I don't know if you could ever give her what she needs."

Tanner's eye twitched. The words far too closely echoed those that Larkin had spoken to him not so long ago. Just like he'd told the harpy ... "This is between me and Devon."

Face hardening, Adam leaned toward him. "She's my anchor—"

"That's great," said Tanner with mock enthusiasm. "But it makes no difference."

"It does, because she's very much my business."

Thinking it would be fun to stab a claw right into the fucker's eyeball, Tanner ate up the space between them in one smooth stride. "You don't want to get in my way where Devon's concerned," he warned, his voice whisper-soft. "You really, really don't."

Looking remarkably calm, Adam gave an innocent shrug. "I'm not in your way. *You* are. Whatever issues you have about relationships are in your way. Typical male hellhound, really."

He flexed his fingers. "And, what, you're going to tell me to end it?"

"I don't need to. I'm certain you'll end it yourself at some point. Another guy will come along who's willing to give her everything she deserves, of course. The question on my mind is ... will you let him live long enough to make a place for himself in her life? If the answer to that question is no, well, I have to wonder what it is that you'll do about it."

The hinges squeaked as the restroom door swung open. Devon sauntered out, her gaze dancing from him to her anchor. "Something wrong?" she asked.

Adam smiled. "No. We were just talking."

She twisted her mouth. "Hmm."

Tanner seized her hand. "Time to go."

Devon barely got a chance to say her goodbyes to Adam and Hunter before the pooch was dragging her toward the exit of the restaurant, where there was a long line of people waiting to be seated. And that was when she noticed *them* gathered near the front of the line. *Shit.*

She would have looked straight ahead and pretended she hadn't seen them if Finn hadn't then turned ... and instantly spotted her.

He blinked. "Devon."

Stopping in front of him, she forced a smile and let her gaze sweep over Leticia, Spencer, Reena, and Kaye. "Hello."

Smiling, Spencer stepped out of the group. "Hi there, you look good." He gave her a brief pat on the back and then turned to the male at her side. "You must be Tanner. I heard you were guarding Devon." He held out his hand. "I'm Spencer, her brother."

Brother? It wasn't often that he used that word when referring to their relationship.

Tanner shook his hand and gave him a curt nod, but his eyes turned flinty when he slid them back to Finn.

Sensing the two people who'd come up behind her, Devon gestured to them and said, "This is Adam, my anchor, and his partner, Hunter."

His smile weak, Finn nodded their way. "Devon's mentioned you a time or two."

"It's good to meet you both," Spencer told them.

"Same to you," said Hunter, but Adam didn't speak. Considering his utter distaste for her paternal relatives and how fiercely protective her anchor was of her, it didn't surprise Devon that he didn't conjure up even the slightest bit of civility for them.

"We were just, um ..." Finn cleared his throat. "We came here to celebrate. It's Reena's birthday."

"I know," said Devon, her tone even. "I sent her a birthday card with a gift card in it."

Surprise seemed to ripple around the group, and Reena averted her gaze.

Leticia shot her eldest daughter a hard glare that she didn't see. "That was very nice of you, Devon. Thank you. Reena's very grateful."

Kaye snickered. "Reena's very embarrassed."

"*Kaye*," her sister hissed.

"You're welcome to join us," Finn said to Devon.

She didn't miss the way Reena tensed, or the way Kaye's nose wrinkled.

"We've eaten," said Tanner, tightening his grip on her hand.

Purely because Devon knew it would annoy her, she said, "Happy birthday, Reena. I hope you all enjoy your meal."

Outside, Adam gave her shoulder a supportive squeeze. "I wish we'd picked another restaurant."

"It's our ritual to come here. They don't get to ruin that." Devon gave both him and Hunter a kiss on the cheek. "Thank you so much for dinner. Love you both."

Adam smiled. "Love you, too."

"Back at you, Clarke," said Hunter, pinching her cheek.

And then Tanner was literally dragging her down the Underground "strip." When he didn't head in the direction of the studio, she frowned. "Harper—"

"Is riding with Knox tonight," he finished.

People cast them curious stares as they walked through the Underground toward the elevator, hand in hand, his body language as boldly possessive as it was protective. And it was a true struggle not to plant her palm in his face and shove him out of her personal space.

He didn't say a word during the short elevator ride. Nor did he speak as he led her to his Audi. He maintained said silence as they drove to his apartment building.

She sighed. "You gonna tell me why you've got a bug up your ass?"

"I'm fine," he clipped.

"Oh. Okay." She turned to the window, deciding to let him brood.

Finally inside his building, they slipped into the elevator. And he was still a silently seething mass of anger. When the elevator paused at his floor, she didn't step out. "I'll be upstairs—hey, let the fuck go." But he didn't. He all but dragged her to his apartment and into the kitchen, where he switched on the coffee machine. "Christ, pooch, what is your damage?"

He didn't answer. Just stared out of the window.

She slipped onto a stool and rested her folded arms on the island. "What did Adam say to you? You've been pissy ever since you spoke to him outside the restroom."

He glanced at her over his shoulder, his brows drawn together. "I don't get pissy."

"Dude, you're pissy." She tapped her nails on the counter. "If you're not going to tell me what he said, you can at least tell me how serious this thing is that you and the other sentinels are all in a tizzy over."

His face blanked. "It's lair business."

Yeah, she got that. And she wouldn't expect him to share such information with someone outside of his lair. "I never asked you to tell me what it is. I asked how serious it is."

He turned to fully face her. "Very."

"Then you should be concentrating on that, not on what's going on with me."

"I'm focusing on both."

"But you feel disloyal dividing your attention this way."

Sensing he didn't like that she'd read him correctly, she shrugged. "It's not hard to sense. And it's understandable."

Tanner almost laughed. Understandable. Levi's ex-girlfriend had used that word, too. She might have even meant it. But it hadn't been long before she'd grown resentful of the time, attention, commitment, and loyalty that Levi showed to Knox. Neither Levi nor his inner demon had been able to accept someone into their life who didn't truly understand and accept their dedication to the role of sentinel.

Devon was a very different creature from Levi's ex, though, wasn't she? His hellcat didn't rely heavily on others. Didn't hold them responsible for her happiness. Didn't need a man to feel "complete." Devon had her own life, and she lived it fully.

It hadn't been easy for Tanner to wangle his way into said life—even now, she held him on the periphery of it. He didn't like that, but he couldn't exactly blame her for it. What reason would she have to open her life fully to him when he wasn't offering her what she needed?

Tanner crossed to her and twisted her stool so that she was facing him. "Next time you feel like going somewhere during work hours, you tell me," he said, his voice low.

"So that you can tag along?"

"Yes." Insinuating himself between her thighs, he placed a kiss on the gentle curve of her mouth. Her lips parted on a soft sigh, but he didn't accept the silent invitation. He pressed a kiss to the other corner, breathing in her delectable scent.

Catching sight of the small black infinity symbol on the hollow of her ear, he flexed his grip on her hip. Whenever demons formed the anchor bond, they left such symbols on each other as a message to the outside world that these people were under the protection of someone who'd fight to the death to avenge them—any anchor would.

He brushed his thumb over the symbol. "I don't like that you wear someone else's mark on your skin." Nor did his hound, as it happened.

"It's an anchor mark," she said patiently.

"I still don't like it." He gently collared her throat, deliberately concealing the symbol with his thumb, and her pupils swallowed the color of her eyes. "Didn't like it before I knew how it felt to come deep inside you. And I really don't like it now."

He swooped down and took her mouth, sinking his tongue inside. He ravished and feasted until his head spun with her taste and his cock was hard as a steel spike. Keeping his hand curled around her throat, he slid his other down her arm, took her hand, and dug his thumb into the center of her palm right over the mark. "It'll always be there, you know."

"You can't be sure of that."

"I can."

She shook her head. "Your demon will pull away from me soon enough."

"But it won't cease being protective of you. Not now that you matter to it." Not even if her feline pulled away first. He brought her hand to his mouth and nipped the heel of her palm. "And I really don't think it'll cope well when you take someone as your mate. I know I won't."

She swallowed. "One day, you'll find someone who matters enough to you that the idea of having a mate won't seem so bad."

He knew his smile was somewhat bitter as he said, "Some people are better off alone, kitten. They're just built that way."

"And some people, especially when they've been alone for as long as you have, just get so used to it that they don't know how to be part of something. But that doesn't mean they can't be."

He rested his forehead against hers. "I'm a lost cause, kitten."

He wasn't lost, Devon thought. He was just surrounded by so

many protective walls that he'd emotionally isolated himself, and now he didn't know how to be any different. "I still maintain that someday someone will come along and change things for you." Devon would probably hate her on principle, but she'd like to think she'd still be happy for him. "And she'd better be good to you, or I'll kick her ass."

His lips curled slightly. "You'd kick someone's ass for me?"

There wasn't much she wouldn't do for him, which was just plain sad. "If the situation warranted it, sure. You'd do the same for me."

"I'd kill for you. I *will* kill for you." His eyes went so cold and flinty she almost shivered. "As soon as I find out where Asa's friend is, I'll fucking destroy him."

And then he closed his mouth over hers. She instantly caught fire, and in mere minutes they were both naked and more than ready to fuck. He took her right there on the kitchen floor, yanking her body to him each time he thrust forward, burying himself as deep as he could go.

The tension built and built until neither could take any more. His cock thickened, her pussy quaked, and then they were both coming. Coming hard and long, until every bit of pleasure was wrung out of them, and all they could do was collapse.

# CHAPTER FOURTEEN

For a while, they simply lay on the kitchen floor, their fingertips idly stroking one another. Once they caught their breath and recovered, Tanner carried her into the bedroom, flicked back the covers, and settled her on the mattress. He then slid in beside her and pulled her close. "You all right?"

She danced her fingers over his sleek, solid chest. "Why wouldn't I be?"

"That scene at the restaurant wasn't fun. It can't have been nice to see that your paternal relatives were having a cozy, celebratory meal they didn't bother to invite you to."

"Why would they? We're not close."

"Because they do shit like that—deliberately exclude you. And it pisses me off that they blame you for the lack of closeness just to make themselves feel better. They could instead oh, I don't know, treat you like family."

"I've *never* been part of their family, Tanner," she said without bitterness. "I don't expect to be. I was not part of Finn's plans, and I was certainly not part of Leticia's. Why should they make room for me in their lives when I'm nothing more than a result of a one-night stand he should never have had?"

"That hurts you," he said softly.

She shrugged one shoulder. "A little. No one likes being made to feel unwanted, especially by their own blood. But it's not a big thing. Take away Finn's penchant for cheating on women, he's an okay guy. But he's not my dad. He's not the man who loved and supported and raised me. He's just a guy who forgot to use a condom. For him, I'm a mistake that almost cost him his family."

"No, baby, what he *did* was a mistake." Tanner caught her face with his hands. "You are far from a mistake. And I'll beat the shit out of anyone who says differently."

She smiled. "It always feels weird when you're nice to me." He just chuckled. "Will you tell me a little about your parents? You don't have to," she quickly added.

Tanner could tell by her expression that she truly wouldn't be upset with him for evading the question. Wouldn't judge or sulk or accuse him of being too closed off. Honestly, he'd rather avoid the subject, but he heard himself say, "My father was Prime of his lair—a lair which is long gone now. When someone killed and usurped him, they also killed my mother and the other two women he'd bred with."

Eyes clouding with horror, Devon gasped.

"It gets worse. In total, my father had three other offspring as well as me. They were teenagers. The new Prime snapped their necks, but he didn't kill me. Maybe he just found the act of killing infants distasteful, or maybe he knew no one in the lair would pledge loyalty to someone who'd kill a toddler—who knows?" But Tanner suspected it was the latter. "He dumped me at Ramsbrook House instead."

She stroked his chest. "Do you remember any of it?"

"No. I don't even remember my parents. The staff told me the story when I was old enough to understand." His only childhood memories centered around Ramsbrook. In some ways, he figured that made his stay there easier than for those kids who'd come from a happy home or were grieving people they loved.

"Is the bastard alive now?" she asked, eyes hardening.

"What do you think?"

"I think you wiped him from the face of the Earth pretty soon after you left the home." Her tone said she hoped he did.

Yeah, that was exactly what Tanner had done. "He got what he had coming to him."

"I don't disagree." She sifted his hair through her fingers. "Is that part of why you're reluctant to have kids? You don't want them being hurt by people who seek to hurt you?"

Tanner blinked. "Maybe. I never really thought about it." He wasn't much into self-reflection. "You want kids?" Something flashed in her eyes—something dark and ... sad? Whatever it was, it raised his hackles.

She swallowed hard. "Yeah."

Fuck if the thought of her pregnant with another man's kid didn't make his stomach roll. "But you want a mate for that, huh?"

"Yep."

"What triggered your demon's want of a mate?"

"Seeing Harper and Knox so settled. It envies them. Wants to be important to someone. Wants that same loyalty, trust, and commitment."

He gave a slow nod of understanding. It happened to all demons at some point. It had just happened to Devon's feline a lot sooner than he'd banked on. "And that's what *you're* looking for as well?"

"Is that so bad?"

"No. But you're already important to a lot of people, kitten." Including him. "You have their trust and loyalty."

"It's not the same," she said with a weak smile. "I'll bet the loyalty and trust that exists between you, Knox, and the other sentinels has kept you all reasonably grounded. But I'll bet it also doesn't fulfill Knox in the same way that his relationship with Harper does."

"It's not the same," he agreed, thinking of how much more balanced and whole Knox was with Harper in his life. The guy's inner demon was no less cold and brutal, but its mental state had stabilized since it had taken her as its mate.

The mental state of Tanner's own demon was going to take a downfall when they were forced to watch their hellcat mate with another. Honestly, it would even sting that her feline had formed an attachment to another male. He was finding that he was possessive of both woman and entity.

He stroked his hand down her spine. "I want you to do something for me."

"What?"

"I want you to let out your feline."

She did a slow blink. "What's that now?"

"I've never met it in its true form. I want to see it." He'd seen hellcats before; they were beautiful creatures. Each time he'd encountered one, every instinct he'd possessed had urged him to growl, chase, take it down. He was certain that wouldn't happen with her demon.

Devon snickered. "Uh, no."

"Why not?"

"Is that a trick question?"

"It won't hurt me." Well, probably not. "It considers me an ally, remember. Come on, I want to see it."

She bit her lip. "I don't know, Tanner."

"Does it want out?"

"Well, now that you've put the idea in its head, yes."

"Then let it out," he coaxed.

She sighed. "This could be a real bad idea."

"I'll be fine, it won't hurt me." He sat up as she reluctantly edged out of bed and closed the bedroom door.

"You sure about this?" she asked when he'd pulled on his jeans.

"I'm sure," he said, sitting on the floor in the center of the room.

She gave him a look that called him crazy. "All right." And then it was like she got hit with a smoke bomb. The air misted with something thick and gray.

He'd never seen a hellcat shift before, but he'd known it happened differently with them than it did with hellhounds. There was no popping and reshaping of bones. The change was instant. Fast. Mostly painless.

The mist cleared, and now a hellcat stood a few feet away. He sucked in a breath. It was, in a word, magnificent. Red, amber, and yellow shimmered like flames in its eyes. And those eyes locked on him like nothing else existed. Having that laser-focus on him lifted the hairs on his nape.

In terms of animals, hellcats were close to black panthers. They had a broad head, sleek muscular body, and short soot-black fur patterned with charcoal rosettes so faint you'd only see them if you were looking for them. Its paws were shrouded in faint, dim flames . . . as if someone had set them alight.

Whereas hellhounds were born to guard the gates of hell, hellcats were born to defend those that dwelled within it—which was easy to see in the regal, predatory, dauntless air they possessed. This feline had that in spades.

They were also moody, territorial creatures that would attack in the blink of an eye so, yeah, he could see why Devon thought him insane for wanting to meet her demon.

Lithe and sure-footed, it padded toward him, its flaming paws leaving a trail of scorch marks behind them. It didn't move, it *flowed*. All power and grace and spirit.

He thought it would come to him. It didn't. It began to circle him. Didn't snarl or hiss. Just eyed him. Not wary or distrustful. It was just being a typical feline—doling out attention on its own terms in its own time. That made his lips twitch.

His hound moved close to the surface, watched the feline. Tanner braced himself to fight the demon's instinct to chase and subdue. But it didn't demand that of him. It was just content to watch the she-demon, admiring how fluidly it moved. Admiring its grace. Its power. Its air of danger.

"Hey," Tanner said simply.

It chuffed, whatever that meant. Then it gave him its back. Ho, ho, ho, this cat had guts. His hound made a rumbly sound of approval.

The hellcat took a turn about the room sniffing and chuffing and rubbing its body against things, scent-marking the space. But he knew it was aware of him. He also knew it was making him wait.

Yeah, he liked this feline.

He dug his phone out of his jeans' pocket and skimmed through his messages and emails, feigning disinterest in the demon, knowing it wouldn't like it. So, it wasn't long before he sensed it padding his way. He didn't look up, though. Just kept on staring at his phone.

A tail lightly flicked his head as the hellcat skirted around him and then settled on the floor nearby.

He pocketed his phone. "Hello, beautiful."

It just stared at him, tail twitching.

"She thinks you're going to try to hurt me. But you won't, will you? Because you know I'll kill for her."

His hound wanted the freedom to officially meet the feline, but Tanner held tight to his control. He didn't trust that the two demons wouldn't end up fighting. The feline trusted *him* to have

Devon's back, but that didn't mean it trusted his hound as well, despite the mark on her palm.

"You gonna let me pet you?"

An image flashed in his mind of Tanner's hand giving its flank a single stroke. "Once," he understood. "All right." It was better than he'd hoped for. He slowly leaned forward and gently stroked its flank; the fur was softer than he'd expected. Silky soft, and roasting hot ... like the feline had a fever. But he knew it was normal for hellcats.

He straightened. "Thank you. Can I have Devon back now?"

It chuffed at him, but then fog burst into the air yet again. Moments later, Devon was lying on the floor in front of him. All the scorch marks from the demon's paws had disappeared. That was the thing about hellcats—they left no trace of themselves behind.

He settled down beside her and splayed a hand on her stomach. "Your feline was very well behaved."

"It didn't even scratch you," she said, sounding somewhat perplexed.

"I told you, it trusts me."

She shook her head. "It doesn't trust anyone."

"It trusts me with your safety." He brushed his mouth over hers. "And so do you, don't you?"

She swallowed. "Yes."

He felt his mouth curve. "Good."

Standing in the living room of Harper and Knox's stately home, Devon chuckled as Asher dove into yet another gift bag and ripped out the tissue paper. The guests—most of whom were Wallis imps—were scattered around the large, luxurious room, smiling and snapping photos as the little guy opened his birthday gifts.

Each time he tore through wrapping paper, he gave himself a huge clap, grinning when everyone clapped along with him.

Only then did he pay a hint of attention to whatever the gift was. And Harper was right in what she'd predicted; if it lit up or made noise, Asher liked it.

"That kid is too cute," said Khloë.

She wasn't wrong. Just looking at him made Devon's heart melt. Those deep-set ebony eyes danced with mischief and were framed by long, thick lashes. His short, wispy, inky-black hair was as silky-smooth as it looked. And his dimples … oh God, those dimples were just adorable. One little smile from him and people were just a goner.

"I can't believe he's already a year old," said Devon. As demonic babies developed faster than human babies, Asher looked more like an eighteen-month-old. He was also steadier, stronger, and more verbal than human kids of his age.

"I know." Raini sighed. "It doesn't feel like long ago that I held him for the first time." She tilted her head. "You know, although he looks uncannily like Knox, he often reminds me of Harper."

Devon nodded. "He has a lot of her mannerisms." And when he tiredly rubbed at his little eyes or made that little sob that broke her heart, he also sometimes made her think of another little boy. A boy who'd cried and cried and cried while she'd banged on the car window and—

*Not now.* No, she wouldn't let the memories creep up on her on Asher's birthday.

Sipping her soda, Devon let her gaze sweep around the spacious room. In terms of decorations, Harper had gone all out. There were banners, balloons, streamers, garlands, fairy lights, and fun props everywhere, making the room look like a kid's wonderland.

The colorful, three-tiered birthday cake situated under the balloon-arch was like something out of a Willy Wonka factory with its swirly frosting, sprinkles, chocolate ribbons, icing decorations, jelly beans, and edible toppers. Yeah, Devon needed a slice of that in her life.

Across the room, Knox's expression darkened with frustration as something caught his attention. She tracked his gaze and . . . *oh*. She clamped her lips closed, fighting a smile, as she took in the new arrival. Clothed in a worn Harley tee, faded jeans, frayed baseball cap, and shabby sneakers, the Devil clapped along with little Asher as the kid applauded himself yet again. The mercurial, antisocial, entitled male totally dug the little boy.

Knox crossed to Lucifer, who beamed and said, "I came to wish my nephew happy birthday."

"Don't call him that. We've been over—" Knox broke off and stared hard into the guy's eyes. Then he sighed. "Lou, you can't come to a kid's party *stoned*. You can't come to my house to see my son *stoned*. We talked about this, remember."

"I remember. Sort of." Lou's brow pinched. "The memory of the conversation's a little hazy."

"Probably because you were stoned when we had it."

"It's a likely scenario." Lou raised his hands. "Fine. No more booting the gong before I come to see Asher. I'll wait until afterward. Happy?"

"Yes." Knox inclined his head. "Thank you."

Smiling to herself, Devon turned back to the girls. Her brow furrowed as she noticed them staring at the four sentinels, who looked deep in discussion about something.

"What do you think they keep having secret talks about?" Khloë asked. "It's like every time I turn around, they're huddled together and whispering."

Devon shrugged. "It'll be lair business of some kind."

"Well, I know that much," said Khloë. "But would it kill them to turn the volume up so we can eavesdrop a little?"

"I asked Harper about it," Raini told them. "She said

something big happened that's related to the children's home that Knox and the sentinels grew up in."

"Really?" Khloë might have said more, but then Keenan looked her way. She gave a haughty sniff and then cut her gaze back to Devon and Raini. "Anyway, let's talk about something interesting."

"Personally," began Raini, "I find it interesting that the incubus is now heading your way, frowning at the glass in your hand."

Moments later, Keenan sidled up to Khloë. "Should you really be having shots?"

The imp lifted a brow. "This pearl of judgementalism is coming from an alcoholic? Really?"

His mouth thinned. "I'm not an alcoholic. And I'm being serious about this. The last time you had shots at a party, you were contemplating the wisdom of positioning a party horn at the tip of your ass hole to see if you had enough, and I quote, 'fart fire-power' to make it go off. I managed to talk you down, but it took some serious effort on my part."

Khloë patted his arm. "I was just fucking with you, Keenan. As if I'd honestly put a party horn in my ass!" She angled her body away from him just enough to subtly look at Devon and mouth, "Did I really talk of doing that?"

Lips twitching, Devon nodded.

"Whoa," Khloë mouthed.

"Just lay off the shots this one time," Keenan told her. "In fact, give me the glass. I'll go get you a soda or something."

Khloë turned back to him. "I don't want soda."

"And I don't want to have to talk you down from doing dumb shit again."

"You *don't* have to, Keenan. I don't need a babysitter. I'm a full-grown adult."

"With the impulse-control of a child."

"All I'm hearing is *blah, blah, blah, it totally sucks to be me, blah.*"

Devon went to exchange an eye roll with Raini, but the blonde's gaze was focused inward in a tell-tale sign that someone was speaking to her telepathically. Devon gently nudged her and asked quietly, "Everything okay?"

Raini blinked, and the cloud left her eyes. "Yep. Fine."

"Was that Maddox telepathing you again?"

The blonde just shrugged and grabbed a brownie from her paper plate.

"You can't block him?"

"Nope. Either he's a guy who can't be blocked or it's because he's my anchor." Raini bit into her brownie. "I'm okay. It's just frustrating."

"Do you talk to him?"

She shook her head hard. "I know better than to respond to him. He'll get bored soon enough."

Well that was the hope. "And if he doesn't?"

Raini's shoulders slumped. "I don't know."

Hoping to get rid of the lost look on her friend's face, Devon said, "I will say one thing. He's hot."

Raini's eyes lit with amusement. "Don't let Tanner hear you talking like that. He'll growl and snarl and throw you over his shoulder. Which sounds like it could be fun."

Devon laughed. "Yeah, it kind of does."

Soon Asher was done opening his gifts and the party games began. Honestly, it was amazing how competitive imp children could be. Jolene had to step in several times to stop the kids arguing and trying to choke one-another. Khloë's little sister, Heidi, even set a little plastic chair on fire when she lost at musical chairs.

When it came time to light Asher's candles, they all crowded around him and sang happy birthday. Knox helped him blow them out, and then the kid shoved his hand right into the cake.

Laughing, Devon snapped a photo with her phone as Harper wiped his sticky hand. "You're a menace," Devon told him.

He took a blob of frosting from his sleeve and offered it to her. "Kick."

"He means cake," said Harper, her mouth quirking.

Devon took the blob from him. "Aw, thanks little man." And then flames burst to life around her phone, which then disappeared in a blink.

Fire erupted out of Asher's clean hand. The flames died away, revealing her damn cell. "Ooh, mine."

Devon twisted her mouth. "Ah, so he was trading the frosting for my phone."

"No," sighed Harper. "I think he was just trying to keep you distracted so he could take the cell. Asher," she drawled in her "you're in trouble" voice. "Give it back to Auntie Devon."

He mimicked his mother's frown. "Mine."

"No, *not* yours. You can't take people's things." Harper took the phone from him and handed it back to Devon. "Stuff it in your pocket fast."

Devon did so, chuckling at Asher's pout. She scooped him up and balanced him on her hip. "I can make faces too." She crossed her eyes, sucked in her cheeks, and stuck out her tongue. His pout melted into a smile, and he tried copying her.

"Now wait a minute," said a voice to her left.

Devon looked to see Lou trailing after Jolene, who was heading toward them.

"Are you insinuating that I'm friendless?" he demanded.

Jolene turned to him. "I didn't imply it. I said it."

He jutted out his chin. "I have tons of friends, thankyouverymuch."

"Asher and your pets don't count."

Lou ignored that. "I even have a BFF. He and I go *way* back."

"Oh yeah?" Jolene folded her arms. "What's his name?"

Lou's mouth bopped open and closed. "Bart. He's tall. Always wears a suit. Has great teeth."

"You're talking about your shrink. And his name's Garth."

"Well, I call him Bart. It's a nickname. BFFs have nicknames for each other."

Rolling her eyes, Jolene pivoted on her heel and held her hands out to Asher. "Come to Grams." She snatched him before Devon had the chance to object.

Lou scoffed. "Why would he want to go to you when he can come to Uncle Lou?" He tried taking Asher, but Jolene tightened her hold. And then flames roared to life around his little body and he disappeared from his grandmother's arms.

Hearing a burst of flames behind them, they whirled to see him sitting on the table next to his birthday cake. Once again, he shoved his hand into it.

Harper growled. "Dammit!"

Devon's chuckle faded as she *felt* Tanner's attention settle over her. Her gaze instantly found him prowling toward her with little Heidi at his side. The little girl was babbling about something or other while waving a form at him.

Tanner sighed down at her. "I tell you what, kid. I'll sponsor your school run—even though I think you're just making this up to get money out of people—if you'll stop stealing my wallet. Now give it back."

Heidi blinked, all innocence. "Wallet? Why would I have your wallet?"

"Hand it over."

"Fine." Mouth setting into a disappointed pout, Heidi gave him back the wallet and stomped away.

"Typical imp," Tanner said to Devon, curling an arm around her waist. "If you're dumb enough to not pay attention, they'll rob you blind."

Devon shrugged. "If it makes you feel any better, she probably would have given the wallet back to you at the end of the party. I'm not saying all your cash would still have been in it, though, or that she wouldn't have scribbled down your bank card details."

Tanner shook his head. "Unreal."

Hearing Asher's infectious laugh, she turned to see him running from Lou, who was demanding to have his cap back. "He looks more and more like Knox every time I see him."

"He does," Tanner agreed. "You love the little guy, don't you?"

"Hell, yeah," she said. "Who wouldn't?"

"Then why do you sometimes seem so sad when you look at him?"

The unexpected question hit her right in the solar plexus, making her feel like she'd had the breath punched out of her. Had she really been that obvious? Or had he just come to read her well? "It has nothing to do with Asher. It's also not something I can talk about here."

His gaze drifted over her face. "All right." He put his mouth to her ear. "Do you think it would be rude of me to put you flat on your back on that table and eat you out?"

Once again, he'd shocked her. But this time a laugh bubbled up. "Given the amount of people here, it could get awkward. Maybe you could do it in your apartment later."

He pulled back and arched a brow. "Yeah?"

"Oh, yeah. Your services will be appreciated. And rewarded."

His smile faded as Jolene appeared at their side wearing a sober expression. "Something wrong?" he asked.

"Wrong?" echoed the Prime. "No. In fact, I have news I think you'll both be pleased to hear."

# CHAPTER FIFTEEN

Jolene tugged on the small string hanging from the bare bulb, casting just enough light across Richie's dark basement that Devon could clearly see Roth Lockwood strapped to a chair. The podgy, balding male blinked rapidly against the brightness of the light. Sheer unadulterated fear flickered across his mottled face as he spotted her, Jolene, and Tanner.

"Well, hello, Roth." Jolene's heels clicked along the cement floor as she ever so casually walked toward him. Apparently, her sentinels had found him holed up in a motel in Reno. They'd hauled his dumb ass to Richie's basement and, if the bruises and swellings on his face were anything to go by, had roughed him up in the process. Well, good.

Devon followed Jolene and Tanner further into the basement, her nose wrinkling at the scents of must, mildew, and something even more foul. *Pain.* Yeah, these walls had seen a lot of people hurt.

Unlike other kids, Devon had never thought there was

anything spooky about basements. It was just the place where her parents kept the washing machine, dryer, and some boxes. Khloë, however, *hated* them. And maybe this was why, given she'd once lived with her father.

The large space was dank and cold and eerie with shadowy corners so black they looked like voids of nothing. This basement was the kind you saw on horror movies where a sweet little family moved into a haunted house and then had to call out an exorcist when their darling child got possessed. Oh yeah, an evil poltergeist would fit well down here. Or a serial killer.

Her skin suddenly felt so clammy and chilled she almost shivered. Devon had the feeling that Richie deliberately kept the space so moldy, musty, and dreary. Because if the blood stains on the cement floor were anything to go by, he sure didn't do his laundry down here.

"It's ever so good to finally meet you," said Jolene, standing in front of Roth while Devon and Tanner flanked her.

"Yeah, I've been looking forward to it." Heat roiled low in her stomach as Devon glared down at the son of a bitch. Face ashen, lips trembling, he stared at them wide-eyed, reeking of sweat and fear. Her demon liked the smell of the latter. Liked seeing that glint of terror in his eyes. So did Devon, because she was certain just from the way he looked up at them like a boy caught with his hand in the cookie jar that he was guilty as sin.

His heart was beating *frantically*. She could hear it pounding and pounding like hooves galloping on a racetrack. Yeah, the guy knew he was fucked.

He jumped as water gurgled in one of the rusty, exposed pipes.

"You're not looking good, Roth." Shoulders back, fists clenched, Tanner stared down at the pathetic piece of shit, sure to his bones that Roth was the broker they were looking for. Why else would he have run? Why else would guilt be plastered all over his face?

Wrestling with the urge to lunge and slice open Roth's throat, Tanner inhaled deeply through his nose. No, he wouldn't lose it. The bastard *would* die tonight, but not yet.

He'd expected his demon to fight him on holding back—it wasn't a creature that liked to bide its time, didn't care to wait until Tanner had answers. But right then, it didn't push for supremacy or demand instant vengeance.

Oh, it wanted to lash out. Maim. Destroy. Not simply because Devon was under its protection. It had developed a sort of ... well, something as close to a "fondness" for her as the entity was capable of feeling. The hound didn't view her or her inner entity as prey anymore. Didn't think of itself as superior to them. It liked her fire and spirit and that she kept Tanner on his toes. And now it wanted to rip apart this person who'd dared to play a part in the danger surrounding her.

But it remained still for the time being, its muscles straining against its skin as it locked its unblinking stare on Roth. It intended to deliver the killing blow, though—Tanner could feel it.

Tanner briefly flicked his eyes to the particularly ugly gash on the other male's temple. "Bet that hurts." He telepathically reached out to Jolene and asked, *How is it that the rope has held him for so long?* Roth didn't sit high on the power spectrum, but he could escape a damn rope.

*Devon's godmother, Millicent, spelled the rope so that it would restrain any preternatural creature, no matter their strength or breed,* the Prime replied. *It's come in handy many times over the years.*

Exuding a calm she didn't feel, Devon took a single step forward. "You brokered the deal that had me kidnapped. *Twice*." She cocked her head. "Did you really think no one would trace it back to you?"

Sweat beaded on Roth's lip. "I get why you'd think it was

me," he said, his voice trembling as hard as he was. "But you're making a mistake."

Devon's brow hitched up. "Am I?"

Roth nodded hard. "Yes. Maybe there's someone out there who's stupid enough to broker a deal that would largely piss off two Primes, but that person ain't me."

"You were stupid enough to betray Knox," Tanner pointed out.

Roth licked his lips. "I didn't broker the deal."

"Then did why you run?" Devon challenged.

"Because I knew you'd blame me! Maddox Quentin is the guy you should be talking to."

Jolene idly toyed with her necklace. "We already had a chat with him."

"I'll bet he pointed the finger at me, didn't he?" Roth sneered, shaking his head.

"He certainly considers you a person of interest, given that you'd happily do something that would infuriate both Knox and Richie," Jolene replied. Her face hardened as she added, "You became more than a person of interest when we realized you'd fled."

Wincing, Roth squeezed his eyes shut. "I know it looks bad, but I had nothing to do with the deal." His eyes snapped open and landed straight on Devon. "I didn't. You have to believe me."

Devon sighed. "I really hate it when people try to blow smoke up my ass."

Roth's lips thinned. "I'm not—"

"Each time you lie to us, I'm going to slice into you," Tanner told him, cool and calm, as if they were merely discussing the weather. "Every cut will be that little bit deeper than the one before. I don't need to worry about you bleeding out, because the wounds will heal in seconds."

Devon pursed her lips. She hadn't known he had that

delightful ability. It wouldn't be so useful in battle, but it would be *real* helpful when it came to torture.

"In other words, Roth, this process can be as painless or agonizing as you want it to be," Tanner went on. "Your death won't be painless—I won't lie about that. But even a sadist would be sickened by the sort of pain I'll put you through if you don't quit lying to us."

She almost shivered. Damn but the guy could be scary. As for Roth ... Shit, she hadn't thought he could get any paler. It was like every drop of blood just left his face. His leg muscles seemed to tighten, and she had the feeling he'd have tried to flee if he could have moved.

"I only agreed to broker the deal because I knew the attempts to take her would fail!" he burst out. Roth jerked with a loud cry as three ugly rake marks appeared on the side of his face. Devon heard his skin tear, saw his blood seep to the surface. And then the wounds healed, leaving no sign that they were ever there.

Her brows shot up in surprise. Her feline twitched its tail, impressed. "You didn't give a rat's ass if they failed or not," Devon accused.

Breaths bursting in and out of him, Roth shook his head hard. "No, I planned to contact Jolene and tell her everything if someone managed to get their hands on you, I swear!"

There was the horrid sound of skin tearing as Roth once again jerked against the rope. Claw marks spanned his upper chest, deeper and more jagged than the last. Yet, they healed just as quickly.

"Who came to you to broker the deal?" Devon asked.

A drop of sweat dripped down the side of Roth's face. "I never met him before. He's a cambion. A stray. He said he wouldn't harm you."

"His name?" demanded Jolene.

He hesitated, averting his gaze. Then he cried out again as his head whipped back and rake marks appeared on his throat—they'd sliced so deep she thought he'd choke on his own blood. But then they healed.

Jolene leaned toward him slightly. "*His name?*" The words seemed to bounce off the walls they echoed so loud.

Roth took a shuddering breath and rasped, "Ryder Flanagan."

Devon didn't recognize the name. There were three possibilities, as she saw it. Sheridan had used a different name, Flanagan was the person behind all this, or Flanagan had merely been used as a conduit just like Sheridan. "Describe him."

Panting, Roth swallowed. "He had a buzz cut. Tall. Well-built."

*Not* Sheridan then, Devon thought.

"Where do we find Flanagan?" Tanner asked Roth, the urge to hunt once more pounding through him.

"I don't have his full address. He said he lived in Nevada." Roth licked his lips. "I tried warning him not to go through with it; tried telling him about all the people who'd try to avenge the hellcat, but he cut me off. He said he knew more about her than I did. Said he knew *all* her secrets, including where she's hiding her real mother, and that 'that bitch Pamela needed to pay for the pain she'd caused.'"

Everything in Tanner stilled. Hiding? As far as he knew, Devon's biological mother was dead. He looked at his hellcat, and his hackles rose. She was staring at Roth, her expression carefully blank, her posture rigid.

The fuck?

And then it occurred to him that Devon had never once told him that her mother was dead. He'd taken "gone" to mean deceased, and she hadn't corrected him. Maybe he had no right to be pissed that she'd kept such a secret from him, but Tanner found that he was. His chest expanded as he took in a deep, centering breath. Later, he'd question Devon and Jolene later.

He turned back to Roth. "Did you notice anything strange about Flanagan?"

"He moved all slow and clunky," Roth replied, sweating copiously now. "Like he didn't have good muscle control."

Which meant that Flanagan was most likely used as a conduit, just like Sheridan.

Sensing that Tanner was done, his hound pushed for supremacy with a feral growl. It didn't want to take over Tanner's body, though. No. It wanted the freedom to rip Roth apart with its own teeth and claws. And Tanner decided to let it.

Muscles tightening in readiness for the shift, Tanner said, "You've been very helpful, Roth. Now it's time for you to die."

Devon flinched as a wave of Tanner's power swept outwards, carrying with it the faintest scent of—*oh fuck*—brimstone. And she knew what he meant to do before he even started shedding his clothes. *Shit.*

"Jolene, edge over to the wall," urged Devon even as she grabbed the woman's arm and subtly herded her aside. Her heart pounded as bones popped and cracked. And then Tanner was gone, and his hellhound stood in his place.

It shook its head and snorted. Raked the floor with one paw, leaving claw marks on the cement.

Keeping very still, Devon watched it warily. Jesus, it was one big, beautiful bastard. Broad and fierce and badass, it had muscles upon muscles. Its thick, coal-black fur stood on end as it growled at Roth, glaring at him through blood-red eyes. Nothing so savage and vicious-looking should possess a majestic air, but it just did.

It could also very well decide to attack her, hence why she slowly unsheathed her claws. Her feline? It wasn't the least bit perturbed. In fact, it was eager to watch the hound rip their enemy to shreds. It even wanted to join in. *Fuck that*. The two entities would end up fighting to the death over their new toy.

A pitiful whimper escaped Roth. "Oh, God," he said, his voice a mere whisper. "Please don't—"

The hound let out a guttural roar that seemed to rattle Devon's bones. Its veins suddenly glowed as if filled with liquid fire, and tiny red embers danced around its body like pixie dust—signs of its growing rage. And then it lunged, sending Roth's chair crashing to the floor.

Roth let out a primal, bloodcurdling scream as the snarling hound brutally ripped into him. It clawed. Mauled. Slashed. Mangled. All the while, it ignored his cries, shrieks, and pleas for mercy.

She had a strong stomach, but she wasn't gonna lie, the sounds of claws shredding flesh and teeth crunching bone made her stomach churn—especially when coupled with the sight of the hound digging Roth's organs out of his body as if it were digging bones out of the ground.

The hound didn't just kill Roth. It *butchered* him. And it didn't back off until he was nothing more than a bloody mass of broken bones, severed limbs, and mushed organs.

And then it turned to face her, pinning her gaze with those blood-red eyes. Her skin tingled, and the hairs on her nape and arms rose. *Shit*.

"I'll pop up my shield if need be," Jolene whispered, "but I don't think it will harm you."

Yeah? Devon wasn't so sure. Not while it was stalking toward her with its lips peeled back, exposing blood-stained teeth. It had the look of a predator that had chased down its favorite prey. Figuring that "Nice doggy" wouldn't wash down so well, she instead said, "I'd like to have Tanner back now."

Oh, that earned her a growl so rumbly it resembled an idling motorcycle.

Her feline gave it a half-hearted snarl, but it didn't rise to protect Devon—didn't believe it needed to. She took a deep breath. "Look, I appreciate you making mincemeat out of Lockwood—"

Little red embers floated around its body once more, and she figured it hadn't been the best idea to remind it of Roth. The hound snapped its teeth, making blood and foam spatter on the floor . . . *and on her shoes.*

That was it, Devon had had enough. "Fuck you, Fido, I haven't done *shit*! Now quit snarling and spitting at me, I'm not in the fucking mood."

The growling faded. The embers winked out. There was pure silence. And then it was butting her hand with its big fat head, wanting . . . attention?

"Oh, you cannot be believed." But she sheathed her claws and cautiously stroked it, ready to snatch her hand back if it tried to bite her. Instead, it leaned against her, rumbling a contented growl. In seconds it had gone from a killing machine to a big, shaggy dog.

She skimmed her fingers over the scar on its muzzle. "You're not so bad."

A rough tongue licked her hand, and then bones began to pop and crack once again.

Standing before them, Tanner cricked his neck. "So, kitten, why don't you tell me about Pamela?"

\*

A short while later, Tanner stood in front of Richie's living room fireplace staring down at Devon. "You told me we'd talk up here, away from the mess in the basement. Well, we're here."

Not liking how pale she was, he softened his voice as he said, "Kitten, talk to me."

But she didn't speak. Didn't even look at him.

Tanner felt his nostrils flare. "The only way we're going to untangle this fucking mess is if we're all straight with each other. So . . . ?" Again, no one spoke. He crouched in front of his hellcat and rested his hands on her knees. "Where's Pamela, and why would someone believe she needed to 'pay' for something?"

Standing beside the sofa, Jolene put a hand on Devon's shoulder. "Pamela's in the containment ward beneath my lair's penal complex. She's been balancing on the knife-edge of a psi breakdown for a long time now."

Okay, well he hadn't seen that coming. A psi breakdown occurred when a person's psyche fractured under the strain of maintaining dominance over the entity within them. He'd met people hovering on that edge before; they tended to live very sad lives, considering they were only a few mental steps away from being rogue.

"Part of the reason Pamela doesn't have enough control over her inner demon to lead a normal life is that she finds it difficult to block her main ability," Jolene went on. "It has affected her emotional *and* psi state."

"What is her main ability?" asked Tanner.

Jolene sank onto the sofa. "Pamela can see right into a person. One touch, and she sees their worst sins, their worst memories, their darkest fantasies. She says it's hard to know that there aren't truly any 'good' people in the world. Hard to so often see the very worst in people. She did learn to shield herself, but the more intimately she knew a person, the more difficult it was for her to block them. And so, she's had no real peace. If it wasn't for Devon, Pamela would have either killed herself or given in to her demon's demands for dominance long ago. She loves Devon, she's just unable to take care of her.

"There were times when we were able to bring Pamela so far back from the edge of a psi breakdown that she could function well enough to be released. But after a while, she'd start to digress again, because she doesn't have the strength or psychic stability to maintain dominance over her demon for long periods of time without help. We're not *hiding* her existence. We just don't speak of her much."

"Okay," said Tanner. "How long have you kept her in the containment ward?"

"She was in and out of it throughout Devon's childhood, which is why Devon thinks of Gertie and Russell as her parents. They loved and raised her right alongside their son, Drew."

Tanner looked back at Devon, who still had her eyes on the floor. Was it fair of him to be pissed that he hadn't known any of this before now? Probably not. But he wanted her to trust him. Didn't like that she felt that she couldn't.

He stood upright and asked Jolene, "When did you last commit Pamela to the ward?"

"When Devon was six. There was an ... incident."

"Incident?"

"Yes. About eight months prior to that, Pamela dumped her outside a grocery store and called me; said the voices in her head were telling her to kill Devon and she was terrified she'd hurt her. One thing I can say for Pamela was that she never fought us on committing her if we thought it was necessary. But later that same year, Pamela escaped the ward, convinced Devon was in some sort of danger—such delusions were commonplace for her. Things ... went badly."

Tanner narrowed his eyes. "What does that mean?"

Devon slid her fingers into her hair. "I was at a party," she

said, her tone flat. "A kid's party. One of the moms was giving
me a ride home. She went back into the party venue so that
her son—my friend—could use the restroom. That was when
Pamela hijacked the car. She said she was all better now, that we
could be a family again. She just . . . kept driving.

"I asked her over and over where we were going. She just kept
saying that we were almost there, but I don't think she had a
destination in mind. I don't think she'd thought that far ahead."

This was going to be bad, he could feel it. "What happened, kitten?"

She swallowed hard, and the movement looked painful. "I
fell asleep. When I woke up, I realized the car wasn't moving
anymore. Pamela had parked it outside a crummy-looking casino.
She did love casinos. It was baking hot, and I was so thirsty. Felt
so sick. And the baby just wouldn't stop crying."

Tanner's brows snapped together. "Baby?"

"Pamela had just ignored the fact that I wasn't the only child
in the car when she hijacked it." Devon sniffed. "See, my friend's
baby brother had been sleeping in his child seat. I told her a few
times that we had to take him home, but she never responded.
Anyway, I kept watching the door of the casino, waiting for her
to come out. But she didn't.

"The car seemed to get hotter and hotter. Every breath I took
in seemed hot and thick in my lungs. I tried to get out, tried to
get the baby out. But the woman who owned the car was an
incantor, and she'd put protective wards all over it. I couldn't
open the doors or windows. Couldn't even smash my way out."
She swallowed. "The baby had been dead for hours before Jolene
found us. Heatstroke. Pamela was inside the fucking casino,
playing blackjack. She'd lost track of time, she said."

Tanner's eyes fell closed. Fuck, so many things about her made
sense now. The nervousness she showed when someone else was

driving. The way she sometimes gazed at Asher with sadness in her eyes. Her reluctance to speak of her biological mother. And maybe even the reason she didn't feel that she *should* have been loved by Finn—part of her felt undeserving, just like many who experienced survivor's guilt.

"Beck hauled Pamela outside," Jolene added, picking up where Devon left off. "She looked at the baby like she'd never seen him before. She asked us to commit her to the ward permanently, and she's never asked to be free; never tried to escape. I suppose she's punishing herself, really. She's deteriorated since then. I think knowing that she was responsible for the baby's death and that she'd caused Devon such trauma . . . it just broke something in her."

"I go to see her sometimes," said Devon. "She's not insane, but she's not totally rational either. She has days when she's lucid. Other days . . . they're not so good. Sometimes she remembers why she's in the ward, other times she's confused and just can't piece everything together. But she always knows who I am, no matter how muddled her mind is at the time."

Probably because Devon was the woman's one constant; the very thing she clung to in order to center herself as best she could. "Has anyone told her of the recent kidnappings?" asked Tanner.

Jolene shook her head. "It would be very harmful to her state of mind. What she doesn't know can't hurt her."

"Is there anything else I need to know?"

"That's the whole story," Jolene told him. "We wouldn't have kept it from you if we thought it was relevant to what was happening right now."

"Well, I think that it is relevant." He cut his gaze to Devon. "I don't think the reason you were kidnapped had anything to do with Asa. I think whoever wanted you used him as a smokescreen."

Devon's brow creased. "A smokescreen to hide what?"

"You heard Roth," he said. "Flanagan—or whoever spoke through him—claimed they knew where Pamela was, and they stated that she needed to pay. Even called her a bitch. Someone targeted you to get at *Pamela*. Why?"

"It won't be someone looking to avenge the baby, if that's what you're thinking," Jolene cut in. "The mother killed herself and her older son not long after the baby's funeral. The father wasn't in the picture. And there's nobody in the lair who would feel a need to avenge them or they'd have done it long before now."

"I wasn't thinking of the baby's family," said Tanner. "Someone heartsore over his death would have used stronger wording than 'that bitch Pamela.' That phrase sounds pettily bitter. Resentful. So, who else has Pamela wronged?"

Jolene pursed her lips. "People tended to pity her. She isn't a bad person. Never was. She's just weak."

"*Someone* didn't pity her," Tanner pointed out.

Jolene stood and began to slowly pace. "If this was just about hurting Pamela, why not demand something from me? Why bring Finn into it? He's not part of our lair."

"Exactly. It makes me wonder if someone was using Devon to punish them both. The people who'd want to do that? Well, you have four, as I see it. Leticia, Spencer, Reena, and Kaye."

# CHAPTER SIXTEEN

Rocked by his words, Devon stiffened. "I'm not saying they don't hate Pamela or that they're not pissed at Finn. But they love him, Tanner. They wouldn't concoct a scheme like—"

"People betray each other all the time, kitten," he softly reminded her. "And they'd see it as fitting, considering *he* betrayed *them*."

"Okay, but they could have hurt him in a billion other ways."

"Yes, they could have, but this isn't just about him. You, Pamela, and Finn shook their world. I think at least one of them wants you all to pay for that."

"But whoever's doing all this made it very clear that the kidnappers weren't to harm me," Devon pointed out.

"This is about revenge, kitten. They probably want to be the one who makes you pay. Especially since they can't physically reach Pamela. They can only hurt her through you. You're the only thing that matters to her. Take you out of the equation, and she'd have no other reason to live. No other reason to hold on to what semblance of sanity she has. It would wreck her."

Devon's stomach bottomed out. He made sense, and she hated that.

"The person behind all this didn't bank on me marking you; they'd expected to have their hands on you by now. Think of what would have happened if their plan *had* worked."

Devon licked her lips, running through the scenario in her head. "If I hadn't escaped the incantor, then I'd be in the grasp of whatever fucker hired him. They would have asked Finn to make the trade, but he wouldn't have handed over Asa."

"That's right, he wouldn't have. Primes need to be ruthless. They can't afford to show weakness. Can't be seen to give into terrorist actions. Despite understanding that, Knox and Jolene would have pushed him to make the trade. And if he refused . . ." Tanner trailed off, allowing her to finish.

"They'd have killed Finn," said Devon.

Tanner nodded. "I think it's safe to say that our prime suspects are Leticia, Spencer, Reena, and Kaye."

"Leticia already punished Finn, though," said Devon. "She left him shortly after Jolene contacted him to tell him about me. Took the kids with her. She then made him grovel for two years. Made him watch her have relationships with other men to give him a taste of how she felt."

"That doesn't mean she's forgiven him," said Tanner. "And I doubt she's forgiven Pamela. Did your mother know he had a partner when they had their one-night stand?"

It was Jolene who replied. "She said she didn't, but her gift would have allowed her to see the darkest parts of him. Maybe that's why she didn't tell him about Devon. Maybe she felt guilty and didn't want to hurt his family."

Tanner rubbed at his chin. "Reena doesn't make any secret of how much she dislikes you, kitten."

"She senses that he's proud of Devon—that's her problem," said Jolene.

Devon made a face. Was the woman high? "Proud of me?"

"He might not approve of your job, but he does respect your determination to rely on yourself," said Jolene. "Out of all his children, you're the most like him. Reena only wants Daddy's approval. Kaye is a free, directionless spirit. Though Spencer works hard, he only does it because he wants to take over the family business one day—he doesn't want to build anything for himself. But you work hard and go after what you want in life. He can relate better to you than he can to the others."

Devon blinked, having never looked at things from that angle before. "Well, if he feels pride in me, he has a real funny way of showing it. I really don't see Reena wanting Finn dead. We shouldn't point the finger her way just because she doesn't like me."

"I agree," said Jolene. "She isn't the only one who dislikes you. Don't forget you had that falling out with Kaye a few years back."

"Falling out?" echoed Tanner.

Devon sighed. "Like I told you, Kaye's always been pretty much indifferent to me. But shortly after Harper mated with Knox, Kaye turned up at Urban Ink and asked to take me out to lunch. She said it was time we 'bonded.' About an hour into our lunch, she asked me to use my close connection to Harper to get her boyfriend a job interview with Knox; said it was time I did something to help 'the family.' I was so pissed. She was pissed that I was pissed. Things got heated. A lot of ugly shit was said—apparently I'm a loser and a slut."

A growl rumbled out of Tanner before he could stop it.

"I pointed out that everything she owns was either bought by Finn or paid for using the credit card that he gave her, whereas

*I've* never accepted a handout from him and have worked for everything I have. She yelled at me, accusing me of thinking I was better than her. I said I *knew* I was better than her, because I'd never use people the way she did."

Devon shrugged. "Honestly, I don't think she has the smarts to come up with such a complicated plot. She'd come up with something much simpler. As for Spencer? I wouldn't count him as a suspect—he and I don't clash or anything."

"But let's not forget that he'll get a bigger piece of the inheritance pie if you're not in the picture, kitten—many people have killed over greed. Demons mostly kill over power. He'll take over the lair when Finn dies. Anyone can see just how much Spencer's looking forward to ruling."

Jolene folded her arms across her chest. "In other words, they're all viable suspects. I'll have my sentinels track down Flanagan. We should find out if there's a connection between him and Sheridan. It's possible that both were randomly chosen as conduits, but I'd like to be sure there's no link at all between them."

"We should also see if we can link either of them to Leticia or one of your half-siblings, kitten. Do you know if any of them have the ability to speak through another?"

Devon shook her head. "Finn would know, wouldn't he? Jolene told him that Sheridan was used as a conduit. He didn't mention that Leticia or any of his children had that ability."

"Maybe because he knew, given the strained relationship they have with you, that we'd consider them suspects," mused Jolene. "Or perhaps they have the aid of someone who does have that ability." She shrugged. "I don't think there's any sense in telling Finn of our suspicions. He wouldn't believe us. And I'd rather not give the others a heads-up that we've put some pieces of the puzzle together."

Devon gave a slow nod. "Let them think we're still chasing shadows. We'll find out which one of them is behind this, and they won't even see us coming."

*

It didn't surprise Tanner that his hellcat didn't speak much throughout the journey back to his complex. She seemed in a daze as she allowed him to lead her into the elevator and up to his floor. She also didn't comment on him taking her to his apartment rather than her own.

Inside the living room, he pulled her close. His chest tightened as he stared down at her. She looked all hollowed out, like she hadn't eaten or slept in a while. No surprise. She'd had a shit evening. Had been forced to go for a hike down memory lane—a lane that was rocky, treacherous territory. And then she'd had to face the very real likelihood that one of her half-siblings could be the person who'd tried to have her kidnapped.

His demon let out a disgruntled growl, not liking that she wasn't her usual fiery self. Rather than trying to shake her out of her funk, since Tanner figured she was entitled to indulge in one for a while, he took her to his bathroom and slowly shed her clothes. They didn't speak much as he bathed her, but he sensed the tension leaving her muscles. Her eyes closed in contentment when he began massaging shampoo into her hair. By the time he was plucking her out of the bath and patting her dry with a lush towel, she no longer looked so lost.

In his room, he brushed her hair and then slipped one of his shirts on her. Fastening the last button, he asked, "You hungry?"

She gave a weak shake of the head.

He curled his hands around hers. "Talk to me, kitten. What's going through that head of yours?"

She licked her lips. "I want to argue that you're wrong; that

Leticia and the others aren't involved in this. I want to believe your theory is way off-base."

"But you know it's not."

"I tried to stay out of Finn's life. I never asked him or any of them for anything. I never bemoaned not having a place in their family or—"

"Listen to me, baby. This isn't about you; it isn't about what you did or didn't do. Whatever emotions are driving this fucker—anger, hate, resentment, all three—are *nothing* to do with you. People feel those emotions every day and don't plot to kill. Their actions are on *them*. Not on you. Not on Pamela or Finn."

She bit her lip. "You were mad that I didn't tell you the truth about Pamela."

"At first, yeah, but I get why you didn't. It just bothers me that you don't feel you can trust me with whatever's in here"—he tapped her chest and then moved his finger to her temple—"or up here."

"It's not about trust."

"You didn't trust that I wouldn't judge Pamela for what happened."

"It's not that. It's just . . . strong people can't always see things from the perspective of someone who's so emotionally vulnerable."

"My opinion? Your mother isn't weak. A lot of people in her position would have turned rogue a long time ago. She held on. And she held on for *you*. That's not weak, baby." The woman was resilient, just like her daughter. Fuck, his hellcat had been trapped in a car with a dead body—a dead *baby*—for hours when she was only a child. That would fuck anyone's head up, but she'd worked through it as best she could. Even had enough softness in her to feel sympathy for the person who put her through that shit.

"I really did try to get out of the car. I just . . . couldn't."

He caught her face in his hands. "You hold no blame in what happened."

"I know, but I can't help feeling that I should have tried harder to make Pamela listen to me about the baby. She kept ignoring me, no matter what I said or how many times I said it."

"Give your six-year-old self a fucking break, kitten. You couldn't have known what would happen. You hold no blame. If our positions were reversed, you'd say the same thing to me." He curled her hair behind her ear. "You've got to let that shit go. It taints the way you look at Asher, and it could taint the way you look at your own children."

She opened her mouth to say something, but then she swiftly clamped her lips shut and averted her gaze. And something about the way she did it made his alarm bells ring.

"What is it?" He cocked his head, trying to read her expression. "You can tell me anything, kitten. You know that."

But she slowly shook her head, her eyes glinting with a pain he didn't understand the source of.

"I swear to Christ, you're safe with me." But she didn't say anything and, yeah, that hurt. Tanner was a hard man to get close to—he owned that. But Devon had just as many protective shields in place. Or maybe she only raised those shields with him.

"Don't give me that look," she said when he took a step back.

"What look?"

"That wounded look. Like I'm holding back from you."

He lifted a brow. "Aren't you?"

"Well, yeah, but not in the sense that you're stuck in a one-sided relationship where I'm not living up to my part of the deal. This isn't a relationship. That means you can't be mad when I won't bare my soul to you."

He felt his nostrils flare. "I just want you to trust me. Is that so fucking bad?"

"No, it's not. And I do trust you. That doesn't mean I have to expose all that I am to you. And it's not like you don't have your own secrets, is it? Do I push you to tell me more than what you're comfortable sharing?"

"There's no reason for you to feel uncomfortable sharing things with me, no matter what they are."

"That isn't the point, and you know it. You want too much from me." She narrowed her eyes. "Sometimes . . . sometimes, I even get the feeling you're trying to leave some sort of mark on me—not one I can see, but one I'll *feel*—so that I'll never be free of you."

Because he was. "A part of you will always belong to me. I'm not giving it back. It's mine now. You don't need it as much as I need it."

And he'd take more pieces of her if she let him, Devon thought. God, what was she doing? How could she have thought she could really have a simple, shallow fling with this male she'd grown to care for? There was nothing simple or shallow about what she felt for him. Never had been. And every protective instinct she had was telling her to cut her losses and leave.

Just the thought of it made her chest pang, but what choice did she really have? He'd demand more and more of her, make himself more and more important to not just her but to her demon.

She hadn't thought there was a chance of the entity ever forming an attachment to him, but she'd been wrong. The threads of an attachment were there already. It liked him, respected his strength, trusted him to protect Devon. She needed to walk away while she still could. "I think we should end this now."

He went rigid, eyes darkening to flint. "What?"

"I told you, you want too much from me. You're not a guy who'll settle for anything less than what you want, and I'm not willing to give you any more of me than what you've already had." And by dragging out this whole thing, she was only hurting herself. "My demon isn't just possessive of you, it's starting to become attached to you—I can't let that happen, Tanner, I can't. It's best if we end this now."

His jaw tightened. "You're serious?"

Sadly ... "I'm serious. We need to go back to the way things were."

*

Stomach rolling, Tanner fisted his hands. He'd known this would only ever be temporary and that he'd have to give her up at some point. He'd thought he'd readied himself for it. Thought he'd accepted it. Thought he'd be able to calmly walk away when the time came. But as she stood before him declaring that it was over, everything in him rebelled.

His hound roared and prepared itself to lunge. Not to hurt her—no, never that—but to subdue her; to demand her submission; to prevent her from leaving.

They needed to *go back to the way things were*, she'd said. He couldn't imagine going back to no longer having the right to touch her, taste her, and take her whenever he wanted. Couldn't imagine taking a backseat in her life and becoming nothing more than a fucking observer—a mere figure in the background while she chose a mate, set up house, and then later had kids.

And him? He'd have nothing. He knew Devon; knew how deep her loyalty ran. If she took a mate, she'd no longer engage in her little games with Tanner, no matter how harmless he claimed they were. Their banter and flirting would have to end, so he'd no longer even have *that* much with her. All they'd have would be a strained, awkward mockery of what a friendship should be.

He'd never have suspected that the thought of walking away

would hurt so much. His aversion to relationships wasn't a simple case of commitment issues. Tanner had been alone since he was two-years-old—he didn't know how to be anything else. The Ramsbrook staff had ensured he was fed and sheltered, but they hadn't raised him. He'd raised himself, and he hadn't done the best job of it.

"Alone" was familiar for him and his demon. Felt safer. Meant they didn't have to rely on anyone or lay themselves bare. But right then, being alone didn't seem safe to either of them. Didn't feel comforting. It felt *wrong*. And his hound was having fucking none of this "going back to the way things were" shit.

The demon couldn't give less of a fuck that she was a hellcat. Few things piqued the interest of his easily bored hound, but Devon did. She amused it. Impressed it. Surprised it. Had earned its respect and loyalty. It liked her company. Liked that she played with it. Liked that she made Tanner laugh. It wouldn't permit another male to come along and claim her. No fucking way. She was his demon's choice just as much as she was his.

As a sense of resolve settled over him, Tanner crossed to her, his jaw set. "You're not leaving me."

She sighed. "Tanner, be fair—"

"You're not leaving me."

"Oh, I am. Look, I don't want to argue with you or . . . why are you looking at me like that?" Devon felt her pulse quicken as he began to circle her like a predator. The glint in his eyes made her skin prickle. He didn't seem angry. He looked strangely satisfied. Relaxed, even. As if he'd made peace with something, maybe? She wasn't sure. Didn't get it. Just knew it was weird. And she was done with "weird" for the night. Devon raised her hands. "I'm gone."

She turned toward the bedroom door, and a wave of power swept out and slammed it closed. "Oh, very mature."

Behind her, he leaned in just enough to sniff at her hair. She snarled. "Don't make me hurt you, pooch."

"Do your worst, kitten," he said, eyes lit with something close to mischief. Oh, the hellhound wanted to play. Well, she didn't.

"I won't do this with you. I'm out of here." She skirted around him, marched to the door, and—

She spluttered as an invisible force gently pushed her backwards. Devon whirled on him, gaping. The bastard was smiling. "Are you fucking kidding me right now? You can't keep me here."

"Sure I can. And I will. It's where you belong."

Where she belonged? Devon stared at him. "I'd ask if you were on dope or something, but I don't smell drugs on you."

With just a few slow, fluid strides, he ate up the space between them. "There's no point in fighting me. It's done."

"Huh?"

"You know the males of my kind can take a long time to mate. But once we make our choice, it's permanent. There's no going back, kitten. Not for me, not for you, not for our demons. Like I said, it's done."

Feeling a little dazed, Devon put a hand to her head. "I feel like I'm only hearing one side of a phone call."

He skimmed his fingertips down her arm. "The first time I saw you was through the window of your old Urban Ink studio. I thought . . . *Christ, what an ass.* Then you turned around, and the view got even better. And I just had to have you. But then I realized you were a hellcat, which meant I couldn't make a move on you. I figured I'd get a handle on this thing between us. Figured it would fade. But it never did."

"Because I was forbidden fruit."

"Because you're *you*. Sweet. Restful. Bitchy. Fierce. Independent. So strong and unbelievably stubborn. I fell hard, kitten. But there was nothing I could do about it."

Throat thickening, Devon bit her lip as he slid his hand up her spine and curved it around her nape. "Tanner—"

"Back then, I didn't expect that my demon would eventually get so used to having you around that its instinct to harm you would fade. Didn't expect it to ever be protective of you. But it was the kind of protectiveness a person would feel toward a small, vulnerable animal. A kind of 'aw, this creature is cute and needs to be guarded for its own sake'—which sounds insulting, but that's more than what my demon feels toward most people.

"You showed it that it was wrong to view you as weak. Showed it that you were its equal. And then the type of protectiveness it felt toward you changed into a whole other kind. More of a 'I will bite the fucking face off anyone who tries to hurt what's mine' kind."

The hand cupping her nape slid up to palm the back of her head as he added, "I don't know how you earned its trust—my demon watches everyone closely, waiting for them to fuck up—but it trusts you. Wants to collect and claim and own you. Wants you to be as attached to it as it is to you."

Overwhelmed, Devon closed her eyes. She should have been elated at what she was hearing. Instead, she was afraid. Afraid to believe it was true, even as she knew Tanner would never lie about something like that. But it was scary to have someone hand you something you'd wanted for so long—something you'd thought you'd never have—because you knew how much it would hurt to have it snatched away.

"Look at me, kitten."

Oh, God, that soft tone undid her every time. She opened her eyes, and the hand cupping her head gently tugged her so close her body was pressed to his.

"Why do you look so scared?"

She licked her lips. "In a very short space of time, you've gone from wanting a fling to wanting everything. How do I know you won't change your mind again?"

"Baby, I've always wanted everything. Just didn't think I'd ever be able to have it. I couldn't change my mind even if I wanted to. As for my demon? I told you, it's already formed an attachment to you. It will never let you go. Not ever." His eyes drifted over her face. "You can feel I'm telling you the truth. Can't you?"

Devon swallowed. "I feel it," she admitted. But the fear didn't leave her system, which made her feline roll its eyes, the heifer. It wasn't in the least bit spooked by what it was hearing. It thought him a suitable, worthy partner for Devon; liked his demon's strength and viciousness.

It sent her an impression of the feline standing in front of her, on guard. Not a reassurance that it would protect her; a reminder that it would never support any situation that it thought could later cause her harm.

"I'd be lying if I told you we've got an easy road ahead of us," said Tanner. "I've never been in a relationship before. I'm gonna fuck up regularly, and there may be times when you'll ask yourself why the hell you took a chance on me. But I'll give this everything I've got, kitten, I swear that to you. Can you promise you'll do the same for me?"

God, she wanted to. She really, really did. But how could she reach for this when she hadn't yet told him that she might never be able to give him the kids he might later want? "There are things you don't know, Tanner."

"I don't care. There's nothing you could tell me that would change my—"

"I've never gone into heat," she blurted out. "Not once."

His face went all soft, and he stroked his free hand up her arm. "That doesn't have to mean anything, kitten. A hellhound from my lair didn't have her first heat until she was in her late thirties. She has four kids now. Even if that didn't happen for us, it would change *nothing*. There's no one else I could ever want."

He flicked up a brow. "You hear me? No other woman could ever be what you are to me. That's no word of a lie. You will *never* have to worry about me walking away. When I decide something belongs to me, I keep it close. I don't share my possessions well. Never did."

"Your possessions?"

"Yeah. You're by far the finest one I own."

Devon went to speak, but then his mouth dropped on hers. His tongue dove inside and licked at hers, coaxing it to play. He didn't kiss her, he greedily ravished her mouth. Just like that, the air ignited with a need so raw and powerful it was almost palpable. That need punched its way inside her, coursed through her veins, and settled deep in her core.

She tore her mouth from his as he ripped open her shirt. "Wait—"

"Fuck, kitten," he groaned, staring down at her breasts. "My kitten." His eyes snapped to hers. "You've always been mine." His warm, calloused hands roughly palmed her breasts as he again closed his mouth over hers.

She arched into him, moaning as clever fingers pinched and rolled her tight nipples, tugging on the piercings just right. Every erotic flick of his tongue pulled her deeper and deeper under his spell, until every rational thought in her head simply scattered.

Devon gave as good as she got, shoving her hands under his tee and digging her nails into sculpted abs she'd traced with her tongue more than once. He growled as she dragged her nails down, scoring his flesh. His strong hands were sure and confident as they roamed over her body, his fingers splayed wide, flooding her system with all kinds of delicious feel-good chemicals. She wanted . . . *more*.

She tackled his fly just as he whipped off his shirt. His cock sprang toward her, thick and hard. She fisted his shaft and squeezed, eliciting a deep groan out of him. God, he was so hot and heavy in her hand.

His mouth took hers with renewed vigor as she pumped his cock with a firm grip, having already learned exactly what he liked. His sleek, solid chest drew her eyes, and she just had to take a bite. She sank her teeth into one pec.

He hissed, tangling his hand in her hair. "Fuck, yeah, harder."

She obliged him, deepening the bite so the mark would linger for a—

The hand gripping her hair snatched her head back, and then he walked her backwards, herding her toward the bed. "Sit down, kitten."

Sitting on the edge of the mattress, she found herself almost eye level with his cock. Yeah, she saw where this was going.

Tanner brushed his thumb over her plush lower lip, making a mental note to leave an imprint of his teeth on it later. "You have no idea how many times I've imagined having your mouth wrapped around my dick." No idea how often he'd envisioned fucking said mouth and coming down her throat. "Are you going to give me that?"

"The reality surely can't live up to the fantasy," she said, and he realized she was teasing him. "Are you sure you want to risk spoiling it?"

His mouth curved. "I'll take my chances." She fisted his cock again and looked up at him, sure and cool and hungry. This wasn't a female who'd ask for direction or want any instruction, he thought.

She flicked out her tongue and lapped at the head, sweeping up the drops of pre-come. And then she closed her mouth over the head and sucked. Eyes drifting shut, he drove his fingers into her hair and bunched it tight. Fuck, it already felt ten times better than he'd imagined.

"Take all of it, kitten."

She bopped her head, swallowing more of him, leaving behind a tiny trace of lip gloss as she pulled back. That only seemed to make the whole thing hotter.

He traced the outline of her lips with his finger as she swallowed him down over and over, keeping the suction perfectly tight, making little purring sounds that ate at his control. Her wicked little tongue sporadically danced around his shaft and flicked the sensitive spot beneath the crown.

Just when he thought she couldn't take any more of his length, she swallowed a little bit more, driving him closer to orgasm. And then she deepthroated him. The breath slammed out of his lungs. "Jesus *Christ*."

Composure gone, he roughly thrust into her mouth, keeping his grip tight on her hair. She didn't struggle. She sucked harder, purring. Glazed, hungry eyes locked with his, and his balls drew up tight.

Her mind fluttered against his. *Come*, she whispered.

That sensual invitation slid up his spine and acted like a trigger. He fucking exploded, swelling and pulsing inside her mouth. "Yeah, baby, drink my come." She swallowed it all, holding his eyes the entire time.

Feeling rather pleased with herself, Devon pulled back and licked at her lower lip. Tanner was staring down at her, his eyes heavy-lidded, his cheeks flushed. She was just about to ask when it was her turn to come, but then she found herself flat on her back on the mattress.

He dropped to his knees at the foot of the bed and clamped his hot mouth around her pussy. Inhaling sharply, she fisted the sheets as his tongue fluttered through her slick folds. God, that felt good. Too good.

Tongue, teeth, lips, fingers—he used them all as he wound her tighter and tighter until, finally, she shattered. And then he did it again, licking and probing and biting as he drove her into a mind-blowing orgasm that rendered her a shaking, whimpering mess.

His cock hard and heavy once more, Tanner flowed to his feet and flipped her onto her stomach. Flames of need licked at his skin. Only she could inflame and entice him this way. Only she could make him so fucking greedy and hungry.

He palmed her nape and dragged his hand down her spine, over the intricate lotus flower tattoo, smiling as she arched into his stroke just like a cat. He swatted her ass. "Up. I want you on your hands and knees. That's my good girl." He knelt behind her. "My demon wants me to take you like this. Wants me to fuck you so hard and deep it hurts. But it wants to do one little thing first . . ."

Devon jerked forward when a thick finger slammed into her. A cold draft swept over her back, making her shiver, as an inhuman growl rattled out of the body that blanketed her. A calloused fingertip probed her g-spot, and she almost jumped. Then the flesh beneath the tip of that finger began to burn . . . and she understood.

It hurt in the best way, but she was so stunned she tried moving away. Sharp teeth sank into the crook of her neck and held her in place. All she could do was cry out in pleasure/pain as the bastard branded her.

Finally, the burn faded, and a hot tongue bathed the bite on her neck. The air lost its chill, and Devon snarled. "Pooch, you need to do something about your demon. It's fucking warped. It just *branded my pussy*."

More aroused than he could ever remember being, Tanner wrapped her hair around his fist. "I know." He snatched her head back and rammed his cock deep, bumping her cervix hard. He groaned through gritted teeth as her pussy clamped down on him and squeezed tight. "*Fuck*."

Nothing cool or calm about him, he powered into her, filling the air with the sounds of grunting, snarling, and the slap of flesh. Every thrust was brutal. Forceful. Unrelenting. She went wild beneath him as his cock slid over the brand again and again, her moans a mix of both pleasure and pain. "Want me to stop?"

"Don't you fucking dare stop!" Spine arched, Devon pushed back to meet each hard thrust as he slammed in and out of her. The friction that came from his cock dragging over the hypersensitive nerve endings of her newly branded flesh was like nothing she'd ever felt. Already her body was wound excruciatingly tight as the friction built and built. And then her pussy began to quake.

Tanner groaned. "Yeah, kitten, fucking come. Milk my cock."

A shockingly powerful orgasm barreled into Devon, sending an avalanche of sensation washing over her. She came with a scream, bucking and pulling at the bedsheets, as rope after rope of hot come splashed her quaking inner walls. And then she was floating.

She slumped to the mattress, mouth dry, chest heaving, body shuddering. And one-hundred percent sated.

Dropping beside her on the bed, he pressed a kiss to her shoulder. "You okay?"

She opened one eye. "Not happy with your demon," she slurred. The corner of his mouth canted up. "You like it when the demon brands you."

Yeah, but . . . "Not when it weirdly and inappropriately brands *seriously* sensitive places. And God only knows what the brand looks like." At least she wouldn't have to worry about anyone seeing it.

"My hound sent me a telepathic snapshot of it." He took her palm and pointed at the mark there. "It looks like this, but it also has my fingerprint layered over the little tribal-like lines in the center of the circle."

That was just weird, whatever way you looked at it. "Speaking of fingerprints, are these ever going to fade?" she asked, gesturing at the ones on her wrists.

His mouth twitched into a wider smile. "No."

"I can't walk around with fingerprints on my damn wrists, Tanner. I'm going to have to ask Raini to tattoo over them. You know that, right?"

The smile slipped from his face. "There'll be no tattooing over them. Imagine if your feline branded me and I wanted to cover it. How would you feel?"

As if he were rejecting its claim on him, which she'd hate—psycho or not, her feline was part of her. *Dammit.* She sighed. "Fine, I'll leave them be."

"Good girl." He laid a soft, languid devastating kiss on her that melted her bones.

She bit her lip. "You're sure about this? About us?"

"You wouldn't even think to ask that question if you knew what I feel for you. There's nothing soft or soppy about it. It's dark and intense and scares the shit out of me." He cupped her neck. "I told you that I own you, but you own me just the same. You never leave my mind for even a second, no matter how much is going on around me. I don't like leaving you. Don't like other men being near you. Don't like that you have an anchor because I selfishly want to be all you need.

"It should be annoying that you're on my mind so much, but it's not, and I don't even know why. What I do know is that there's no going back."

Warmth bloomed inside her and the backs of her eyes

prickled. She took a deep breath. "You have to be *one-hundred percent* certain about this, Tanner. You say I'm on your mind all the time. Well, right back at you. You made yourself important to me a long time ago. Now you're offering me something I never thought I'd have. I don't mind admitting I'm scared to believe you won't change your mind. If you ever stopped caring for me or wanted to end this, it would absolutely destroy me."

"You don't ever have to worry that I'll stop caring about you, just as you don't ever have to worry that I'll leave you. I'm going nowhere. You're mine. All rights reserved."

"Even if I can't give you kids?"

"Even if," he replied without hesitation. "The female hellhound from my lair went to see a specialist, you know. He told her that the causes of these things can sometimes be psychological. Maybe that knot of guilt sitting heavy on your stomach for not saving that baby has had an influence of some kind over this. We're demons, our minds are seriously powerful things." He palmed one side of her face and swept his thumb over her cheekbone. "You've got to let that senseless guilt go, kitten."

She swallowed. "It's not that easy."

"I know, but my guess is that you cling to it because you'd feel cruel for laying to rest what happened ... as if that's the same as saying it didn't matter. It's not the same. Just as it's not bad to live and enjoy your life. You don't need to cart these memories and that needless shame around with you. You've got to find a way to let it go. Especially because I won't tolerate anything or anyone—that includes you—causing my girl pain."

Devon took in a long breath through her nose. "I'll work on it. I promise."

"Good." Wanting to lighten the mood, Tanner added, "Now that you've got regular access to superior sperm, I can't see pregnancy being a problem."

A laugh bubbled out of her. "Did you honestly just say that?"

"Well, you have." He brushed his nose over hers. "So, what time are you moving your stuff in here tomorrow?"

She sighed. "Tanner, seriously, would it kill you to *ask* me to move in instead of making presumptions? I mean, if I tried telling you what—"

"Okay, okay, so that didn't come out right. Look, I'm not always going to phrase things in a way you like. I've been a sentinel for centuries, I'm used to issuing orders and being direct about what I want. It doesn't mean I see myself as in command of you. You're my equal, my match, and I respect the hell out of your strength. I don't want to control you. But it's in my nature to take control of situations."

That made Devon's hackles lower, because she knew he was right. There was no sense in viewing his take-charge demeanor as a sign of disrespect.

"I want you to move in. I like starting my day with you right here. I like that the first words you'll hear will be mine. So, will you please give me that?"

Quite frankly impressed he'd asked her so politely, she said, "Yes, I'd like that. Happy now?"

He hummed. "Ecstatic. And I'm positive you're just as happy right now. I mean, we both know your heart has longed for this since the day you met me. Longed and pined and yearned. All that emotion you've been trying to hide—" He laughed when she hit him with a pillow. "I'm feeling the love, kitten. I'm seeing it right there in those pretty green— *Shit! Do you always have to go for my eyes?*"

# CHAPTER SEVENTEEN

Standing in the VIP glass box of the hellhound racing stadium a few evenings later, Devon put a hand to her fluttering stomach. Floodlights illuminated the large oval dirt track that had just been prepped for the next race—one in which Tanner's hound would partake.

She turned to face the girls and Keenan, who were relaxing on the row of leather seats. "God, I'm so nervous."

An announcement was made over the intercom only moments ago, informing the spectators that the race would soon begin. Lots of people milled about the tiered grandstands, private boxes, and spectator area overlooking the track. Gambling addicts often frequented the place, but they weren't the only attendees. There were also couples on dates, clusters of women having a girls' night out, and even groups of men casually discussing business ventures.

"Tanner's hound will be fine," Harper assured her, perched on the edge of the seat directly beneath the ceiling fan. "It always is."

"Yeah, and if hellhound racing wasn't so brutal and rife with cheating, vicious motherfuckers, I'd be a lot less tense."

"You've been edgy all day," said Khloë, slurping on her soda and pointedly ignoring that Keenan—who was on bodyguard duty—was frowning at her.

"People keep looking at me." Devon scratched at her arm. "I don't like it." Which was why she was glad to be in the private box. It was sweet with its comfy seating, multiple TV screens, floor to ceiling view, and personal server who came and went.

Raini smiled, dipping a nacho in the cheese dip. "Well of course you keep getting funny looks. It's not every day that a hellhound claims a hellcat, is it?"

No, it wasn't. Tanner had instructed members of his lair's Force to pass on the news, so it hadn't been long before it became widespread. And it was clear to see that most were stunned.

Harper and Raini had been just as shocked when she told them. Khloë, however, had nodded and said, "I knew the canine would pull his head out of his ass sooner or later, now where're the donuts?"

If the girls had possessed Devon's sense of smell, they'd also know that she now wore his scent on her skin. Literally. The smell of Tanner was faint, but it was there, and no amount of soap would wash it away. That kind of thing happened sometimes with demons, but only when they were intimate on more than one level. That was why her scent was now embedded into his.

"Your feline is definitely okay with this?" asked Raini.

"Very okay with it, which surprises me. It wasn't so long ago that it was directing lazy snarls his way. There was no aggression or malice in them. Just plain exasperation." Devon's brows lowered. "Now it's sort of smug. But not smug that it has a mate. It's something else, I'm just not understanding it."

"Huh." Harper twisted her mouth. "You don't think your feline was testing him, do you?"

Devon tilted her head slightly. "What do you mean?"

"Well, hellbeasts look for strength in their partners," the sphinx pointed out. "They tend to test them to be sure they're worthy. Your demon would have known how interested you were in Tanner, and it would have sensed his interest in you. But it would also have considered any inaction on his part to be a show of weakness, right?"

"Right," Devon agreed.

"So, maybe it started driving you to find a mate merely to see what Tanner would do about it. Your demon would have needed to know you were important enough to him that he'd push aside all his bullshit to have you. It would have needed to be sure you'd be his priority and that he'd be someone it could trust to give you what you needed."

"That would explain your feline's current mood," said Raini. "It's smug that its plan paid off."

A smile tugged at Devon's mouth. "That ruthless little shit."

"It'll always be ruthless when it comes to your well-being." Harper shrugged. "That's just the way our entities are."

"What I really like is that you won't have to worry about any other people trying to kidnap you." Khloë slyly took one of Raini's nachos. "The broker's dead, so the deal is void. Whoever's behind it—and I agree with Tanner's theory that it's probably Leticia or one of her vexing spawn—might make another move of some kind, but I doubt they'll be able to recruit someone into helping them. Not now that Tanner's made it clear to God and everyone that you're his."

"Whoever it was must have been responsible for the damage to your apartment," said Keenan, stretching his legs out in front of him. "That seemed more like a feminine tantrum than a masculine one. Was there something in your living room that could have set them off? Like a photo of you and Finn together?"

Devon bit the inside of her cheek. "There were a few pictures of my mother in the framed collage I'd hung on the wall. There was also a pretty vase that Finn once bought me. It came with the bunch of flowers he sent for my birthday."

"Maybe Finn also sent one to Leticia, Reena, or Kaye and they recognized it as a gift from him," Keenan suggested. "Whoever it is, they're probably of the view that you have no right to anything from him. Seeing your mother's face on your wall would have exacerbated whatever anger or spite they were feeling."

Khloë licked salt from her finger. "I think Kaye's our guy. Well, girl. She wants Daddy to spend all his money on her. And she's petty enough to have a tantrum like that."

Harper nodded. "Whoever it is, I don't think they'll like that Tanner's claimed you, Dev. Not just because it'll make it harder for them to get to you. But because they resent you; they won't want good things happening for you. How do Gertie and Russell feel about it?"

"They didn't sound all that surprised," replied Devon. "My dad asked me to hand the phone to Tanner. I don't know what he said—I'm guessing it was a threat—but Tanner's mouth twitched, and then he assured my dad that he had no need to worry."

"Have you told Adam yet?" asked Raini.

"Yep. I called him after I spoke with my parents. He said, 'interesting development.'" Devon had heard the smile in his voice; sensed he was happy for her. "Then he made me promise to bring Tanner for dinner next weekend."

"Is Adam planning to switch to my lair like you?" Harper asked. "You *are* planning to join my lair, right?"

"I love being part of Jolene's lair. Always have done. But it's not like I won't still see everyone or that I'll be far away. Plus, being in the same lair as you again will be no hardship at all. And I'd be an asshole to not consider how hard it would be for Tanner to switch. It would be a much bigger deal for him than it would be for me, so I don't mind compromising on this. I just feel shitty leaving the people I love behind."

Harper grimaced. "Yeah, the feeling isn't a great one. But you know you'll still be as welcome at their homes as you were before. That's what's important."

Sighing at Khloë, Keenan asked, "You gonna take that off yet?"

The imp frowned. "What?"

He gestured at the empty cup she'd earlier balanced on her head to prove how good she was at it. A cup she'd clearly forgotten about.

"Oh! Right!" Khloë grabbed the cup and threw it in the trash can.

They all swerved their heads as the door swung open. A devastatingly good-looking male strolled in, all swagger and smolder.

Khloë beamed. "Teague!" She handed her soda to Raini and then rushed over to the male hellhorse who was also her anchor. The guy was no less unstable than Khloë. But then, his kind were *wild*. Hellhorse racing was even more brutal than hellhound racing.

"Hey, gorgeous." He pulled the imp into a tight hug. "I was just talking to Knox and Levi, they told me you were in here."

"Did you bet on Tanner's hound?" asked Khloë, looking at the ticket in his hand.

"I only ever bet on the best." Teague greeted each of the girls and then gave the other male in the room a cool look. "Keenan."

"Teague," the incubus greeted, his voice even.

Teague's gaze swung to Devon. "Heard Tanner claimed you. I wasn't sure if I should believe it or not."

"It's true," said Devon. "He—"

The door opened again, and Knox and Levi stalked inside.

"Thought you were never gonna get your epic ass in here," Harper said to her mate.

Knox's mouth quirked. "And miss Tanner's demon run? I think not."

A bell rang, and Devon's stomach dropped. "Shit." She blew out a shaky breath as she turned to the window, and the others all fanned out around her. The outdoor crowd cheered as eight hellhounds fluidly stalked onto the dirt track, all kingly and impressively well-built.

It was easy to recognize Tanner's hound due to the scar on his muzzle. It was broader than the others, but those extra pounds of sheer muscle never slowed it down. His hound was a regular winner. Which was no doubt why, according to the electronic boards scattered around the stadium, it was favorite to win.

The hellhounds positioned themselves on the track, growling and snapping their teeth at each other. Corded with muscle and exuding confidence, Tanner's hound braced its legs wide apart and held its head high and proud.

Small fires suddenly sparked to life in random places on the track. Hot, oily pits appeared in others. But it was the sporadically placed puddles of boiling water that concerned her most—they apparently burned like holy hell.

Yeah, nothing about a hellhound race was easy or straightforward. Which was why she wasn't reassured by how badass, superfast, and agile Tanner's hound was. Especially when there were some dirty, cheating bastards out there.

Another bell rang, and the hellhounds burst to life. They galloped across the track, kicking up dirt and leaving clouds of dust in their wake. Tanner's hound fell into fourth place, its pace fast and steady.

"It's got this, it's got this." Bouncing lightly on her toes, Devon cheered the hound on. The whole thing was so intense, her heart was in her throat.

The hellhounds leapt over fires, swerved around oily pits, and neatly avoided the bubbling puddles. They also body-slammed and bit into each other's flanks as they warred to take first place.

Inside the box, Devon and the others urged Tanner's hound on. Outside, spectators chanted names, shouted words of encouragement, and cursed any hellhounds that tried to cheat.

Oh, and they *did* cheat. One mercilessly shoved a competitor straight into a sticky pit. Another leapt onto the back of the hellhound in front of it; sending it smack bam into a bubbling puddle and using the body as a bridge to avoid it.

Tanner's hound kept its focus firmly on the race, but that didn't stop it from almost ripping off the ear of its competitor when said competitor tried tripping it up.

As Tanner's hound skated into third place, Devon grabbed Harper's tee. "It's closing in on the others."

Harper put her fist to her mouth. "It can do this. It can *so* do this. Come on, come on!"

Raini slapped her hands to her cheeks as the hellhound behind it chomped down on its tail. "Oh my God, what a little fucker!"

Tanner's hound roared but didn't slow down. Didn't retaliate. It just kept on running, its legs a blur as it rocketed along the track.

The voices of the spectators became louder and more frantic as the hounds approached the final part of the track. Which was right around the time that Tanner's hound veered around a pit and picked up speed, hurtling into second place.

Khloë danced from foot to foot. "Second! It's second!"

An orb of hellfire whizzed through the air and smashed into one of the other hounds, almost sending it skidding off the track. Then another ball was hurled. And another. And another.

Devon snarled. "Whatever sicko came up with the idea that the spectators could shoot at the hellhounds in the last section needs— *Motherfucker!*" she cursed as an orb smacked into the head of Tanner's hound. Its pace faltered ever so slightly, but it kept on going.

Harper patted Devon's arm. "See, the hound's okay. It's fine. The track-people allow the orb-throwing because they like that the race is—"

"Pretty much anyone's race, yeah, it makes it more exciting," finished Devon. "But I don't have to like it."

She almost jerked back when a ball of hellfire hit Tanner's rear leg so hard that it was a sheer miracle the leg didn't crumple beneath it. Even more amazing was that the hound put on a burst of speed, its paws thundering along the dirt track . . . and bolted into first place.

The whole room exploded into applause as it crossed the finish line.

Devon literally jumped up and down. "It won! The crazy fucking canine won!"

Most of the spectators outside cheered and bounced on their feet. Others roared in annoyance, crumpling their tickets.

Smiling so hard her face hurt, Devon put her hand to her chest and let out a relieved sigh. "Okay, this is just far too intense for me. I don't think I'll be coming again."

Harper snorted. "You always say that, but you always come back."

Totally true.

It wasn't long before Tanner joined them in the private box.

He made a beeline for Devon, even as he accepted congratulatory nods and back-pats from the others. "Hey, kitten. Did you miss me?"

"You mean when I was hurling balls of hellfire at you? Yeah, missed every time." She went easily into his arms. "How's your head?"

"All right."

"And your leg? It looked like those orbs hit you pretty hard."

"I'm fine." He pressed a long, lingering kiss to her mouth. "You hungry? I need something to eat, I'm starving."

"Tanner, you have a visitor," Levi called out, his voice carefully neutral.

Devon turned toward the open door . . . and stiffened at the sight of Eleanor standing there.

Tanner growled. "The fuck?"

Eleanor raised her hands in a gesture of peace. "I'm here to apologize."

"Apologize for what exactly?" he clipped, crossing to the doorway with Devon at his side.

"For pushing you both so hard," Eleanor replied. "I genuinely hadn't thought anything serious would happen between the two of you. If I had, I wouldn't have—"

"Wrecked Devon's apartment?"

Eleanor gave him a somewhat haughty look. "I'm not so petty as to anonymously vandalize a woman's home merely because she stands in the way of something I want. I did, however, see the extent of the damage." Her gaze slid to Devon. "I went to your building that day, intending to talk with you. I'd considered making you a generous financial offer if you'd back away from Tanner at least temporarily." She slanted him a quick look when a guttural growl rumbled out of him.

"Then what?" prompted Devon.

Eleanor's eyes sliced back to her. "The front door was open when I arrived, and I noticed that the lock was busted. I walked in and saw the mess. I also have an idea of who caused it. That's the main reason why I'm here. I don't want you for an enemy, Tanner. I'm hoping that giving you this information will ease any hard feelings between us."

He lifted his chin slightly. "What information?"

"As I was walking up the stairwell toward Devon's floor, I saw somebody coming down. They were coming fast, looking somewhat frazzled."

"Who?"

\*

Clenching his phone tightly, Tanner paced the VIP box as he relayed Eleanor's information to Jolene. Devon leaned against the wall, staring off into the distance, looking deep in thought.

"What was Eleanor's excuse for not coming to you sooner about this?" Jolene asked.

"She said she hadn't considered that Reena could be responsible for the ransacked apartment because she hadn't known there was any connection between Reena and Devon," said Tanner. "But when she heard from someone earlier today that Finn Moseley was Devon's father and that her relationship with Reena was rumored to be a very rocky one, it made Eleanor wonder if the sentinel could be responsible."

Jolene hummed. "She may be right. You will be interested to know that I found Ryder Flanagan. Sadly, he's dead, so there's nothing he can tell us. Someone slit his throat from ear to ear. I found no connection between him and Sheridan, but I did find one between *Reena* and Sheridan. Turns out he's a cousin of Reena's ex-partner."

Tanner ground his teeth. "Finn failed to mention that." The

guy had failed to pass on a lot of info. But then, they weren't always totally upfront with him either.

"It's possible that he didn't know," said Jolene. "If he did, I imagine he kept it to himself for fear that we'd point the finger at Reena. He won't want to believe that one of his children could have anything to do with this. And who could blame him for that?"

Tanner twisted his mouth. "I think we need to have a long conversation with Reena."

"I agree, but she's a sentinel. She's strong and well-protected. We can't just pluck her off the streets the way we did Lockwood. Unfortunately."

"I heard from a member of my Force that she frequents the Underground sports bar near the mall," said Tanner. "I'll give the owner a call. If Reena's there, we can go have a friendly chat with her."

\*

Nose wrinkling at the feel of the sticky hardwood floor clinging to the soles of her shoes, Devon followed Tanner further into the dim sports bar while Jolene took up the rear, passing crowded tables and a long bar lined with wooden stools. The scents of yeasty beer, cigarette smoke, and greasy food tainted the air. Waitresses zigzagged around tables, carrying trays, while one was poking at a patron who seemed to have passed out.

The bar was dingier than most, boasting scarred wooden tables, waning neon signs, old-looking pinball machines, and lots of empty glasses that had yet to be collected. The mirrored wall behind the bar reflected the sports paraphernalia that hung crookedly on the wall opposite.

Most patrons were facing the TV, avidly watching the football game and yelling at the screen. Others sat talking and laughing and glugging down beer.

The sounds of a table being upended and glass breaking were soon followed by the bartender yelling for a server to intervene. Honestly, it wasn't a place she'd expected to find Reena, who'd always seemed too hoity-toity to even consider entering a dingy sports bar.

As the neared the rear of the space, there was the sound of a ball smacking into another, so it was no surprise to see a row of pool tables. It was, however, a surprise to see Reena hanging near one of them with her fellow sentinels, twirling a pool cue. She was also holding the neck of a beer bottle between two fingers. Hmm, no colorful foo-foo cocktail for Reena.

There appeared to be some playful shit-talking going on, but Reena wasn't part of it. She was merely listening, a half-smile fixed on her face, seeming more relaxed than Devon had ever seen her. Huh.

As if she felt the weight of someone's gaze, Reena looked their way. And tensed, smile fading. With a put-out sigh, she set her bottle on the high table beside her and leaned her cue against the wall. She murmured something to one of the guys who was munching on a hot wing. He only nodded, and then she headed toward Devon, Tanner, and Jolene.

Jaw hard, Reena folded her arms as she came to stand in front of them.

Jolene's smile was all teeth. "Reena, always a pleasure." Although she was no longer Devon's Prime, they'd decided to let her take the lead, since Devon's new Prime couldn't be with them.

"What do you want?" the other female asked, annoyance written all over her features.

"I was hoping you could answer a question for us," said Jolene. "See, we've wracked our brains trying to understand . . . but the answer just eludes us."

"If you have questions, you should talk to my father. He's Prime of the lair; it's up to him what he does and doesn't share with outsiders."

"True," said Devon "But I doubt he'll have the answer as to why you wrecked my apartment."

Reena froze, then quickly forced a disbelieving snort. "Why would I even go *near* your apartment?"

"Don't bother playing games, Reena," Tanner warned. "We have a witness who says you came running down the stairwell of Devon's building. A witness who then went up to Devon's apartment, only to find that it had been ransacked."

"That doesn't prove anything," Reena maintained, eyes flickering.

"It proves you were there," said Devon, sounding dangerous even to her. "Maybe you'd like to explain why that is."

Reena lifted her chin. "I don't have to explain anything to—"

"*Do not* be under the mistaken impression that your being female will keep you safe from me," rumbled Tanner. "I could kill you where you stand and think nothing of it. Nor would I give a hint of a fuck how pissed that made Finn. He wouldn't be the first Prime to come at me—they all died, too."

"Be smart, Reena, and tell us what we wish to know," said Jolene.

Reena's nostrils flared. "I went to see her that day, yes," she told the Prime. "I wanted to ask her some questions about the conduit, Sheridan. You were vague to my father, and I suspected you were holding back. But when I got to her apartment, I found the front door wide open. I rushed inside, saw the mess in her living room, and thought someone had taken her. I called my father and asked if he'd heard from her. He said he'd just gotten off the phone with her, that she was at the airport."

"He didn't tell us you went to her apartment," said Jolene.

Reena cheeks flushed. "He doesn't know. I didn't tell him, because I knew what it would seem like. I knew people would suspect *I* ransacked the apartment. It wasn't me."

"What was it you wanted to know about Sheridan?" Devon asked. "Were you curious about if he'd mentioned you? Because he did know you, didn't he? He was your ex-boyfriend's cousin. You failed to mention that as well."

"Because I knew you'd think I had something to do with this. *I didn't.*" Reena clenched her fists. "I wouldn't come up with some messed-up plot to have you kidnapped so I could force my father to release Asa. I mean, what possible reason could I have for wanting him released?"

"We all know that Finn never would have made the trade. You could have then killed me and made it seem like it was *his* fault for not releasing Asa."

Reena's jaw hardened. "I don't want you dead."

"Because you care so much about her," Tanner deadpanned.

Reena ignored him. "I don't like you much, Devon, that's true. But there are lots of people I don't like. That doesn't mean I want them all dead. All I ever wanted was for you to stay out of our lives—that's it."

"And this *would* have ensured I was no longer in your life, if only the kidnap attempts had worked," Devon pointed out.

"I didn't vandalize your apartment, and I didn't play a part in any scheme. You'll all see that for yourselves when my father finally gets a name out of Asa. He won't give up until he does."

Just then, Eric sidled up to Reena, bringing with him the scent of cloying cologne. "I just wanted to check if everything is okay over here," he said.

Reena took a centering breath. "Everything's fine, Eric. We were just discussing the investigation."

Eric didn't look convinced, but he nodded at them in greeting.

"It's good to see you all again. I heard you two claimed each other," he said to Tanner and Devon. "Congrats."

Reena didn't pass on that same congratulations. She just looked at the floor. Maybe Devon should have been hurt by that but, honestly, she was beyond caring.

"Can I get you a drink? You're welcome to join us." Eric gestured at the pool table with his thumb.

"No, thank you," said Jolene. "We're leaving now. You know, Reena, I wouldn't have thought this was your scene. It makes me wonder what else we don't know about you."

Something flashed in Reena's eyes. Unease, perhaps?

"Come on, kitten." Tanner took her hand and led her outside. "You all right?" He didn't like the strained smile or barely-there nod she gave him. It had to be downright dispiriting to hear your own sibling tell you they didn't want you in their life when you hadn't done a damn thing wrong.

Devon glanced over her shoulder at the bar. "If anyone asked me if Reena drank beer, played pool, and hung out at places like this, I'd have laughed in their face."

"Same here," said Jolene. "She always came across as very high-and-mighty. Yet, she looked right at home in there."

"So, do you believe her?" asked Devon.

"That she wasn't the one who went crazy on your apartment?" Tanner pursed his lips. "My gut says she was telling the truth, but it's clear that she's very good at deception. I doubt her own parents would guess that this is how she sometimes spends her free time. They'd probably be appalled." Tanner went to speak again, but then Knox's mind touched his, buzzing with frustration.

*We have Patrick Stephens' location*, said the Prime.

Tanner's mouth snapped shut. *Where is he?*

*A cemetery in Ohio. He was killed—and mutilated—a week before Mattias.*

*Which makes Stephens the first victim,* Tanner realized, silently cursing to himself.

*The killer has to be Royal Foreman—there's no one else left. He hasn't returned Muriel's body to her home. I can't think of where else he'd put her.*

Tanner rubbed at his jaw. *Is Larkin still struggling to locate him? Yes, but she'll find him. She always comes through.*

A thought occurred to him. *What if it isn't Foreman? What if the reason Muriel's body is nowhere to be found is that she's the one who's been doing the killing? Foreman could be her last intended victim.*

Knox paused. *She seemed to be genuinely grieving her brother's death. Then again, she also seemed to be genuinely sure that Dale, Harry, and the others couldn't have been involved in anything. I'll have Levi look at what was happening in Muriel's life over the past year to see if there's anything that could have acted as a trigger.*

Tanner gave a satisfied nod, even though his Prime couldn't see it. *As a child, she was too low on the power spectrum to be able to subdue people or cause heart attacks, and I've never known her capable of altering her scent, but she may have grown in power as she aged and developed other abilities. I'd like to think she's not the killer, but my instincts won't let me dismiss the idea.* And his instincts had never let him down before.

# CHAPTER EIGHTEEN

The following evening, Tanner strode into Knox's home office with Levi at his side. Tanner had received the telepathic summons from his Prime just as he and Devon were finishing dinner. He'd brought her with him to the mansion and left her in the living room with Harper and Asher, where the two females were now discussing the arrangements for the "Welcome to the Lair" party that Harper was insisting on throwing. It would also double as a "Congrats on Your Mating" celebration.

With the help of the other sentinels, he and Devon had moved her things into Tanner's apartment after they got back from the sports bar. It was as they were unpacking her stuff that Finn had called, grumbling to her that he'd heard about the mating through the rumor mill rather than from Devon. He'd also passed on his congrats, though. Her brother, Spencer, had left her a congratulatory voicemail, but she'd heard nothing from Kaye—nor had Devon expected to.

She and Tanner had talked a lot the night before. They'd lay in bed exchanging stories from their childhood and divulging things that seemed easier to share in the dark. They'd also made each other come several times before falling into something close to a sexually-induced coma.

Knox tapped a few keyboard keys and then pushed out of his leather chair. "Close the door."

Tanner did so and then crossed to the black U-shaped executive desk that looked smart with the high-tech computer and multiple monitors. Maybe the room should have seemed dreary with the flint-gray walls, but the contemporary geometric rug, backlit glass shelves, and three abstract art canvases of mechanical clockwork gave the space a lift.

"Larkin found some info on Muriel that I think will interest you both." His footsteps muffled by the rug, Knox skirted the desk and came to stand in front of them. "We're still finding it difficult to locate Foreman, but it's only a matter of time before we do."

Whether they found him alive or dead was a whole other matter.

"Three months ago," Knox began, "Muriel was attacked in her home by a human. According to the police report, he drugged her drink at a club, followed her home, and then broke into her place. He sexually assaulted her, the bastard."

Levi squeezed his eyes shut. "Fuck."

"The drugs kept her close to paralyzed, but she was aware enough throughout the assault to give the police a thorough description of him," Knox went on. "Two nights later, a male of that description was found dead in an alley. Someone sliced his dick off before stabbing him multiple times. The police questioned Muriel but later cleared her. Dale gave her an airtight alibi. But I believe one, the other, or both of them found and killed the human."

"I don't blame them." Tanner wouldn't have done anything less.

Knox pulled open a desk drawer, leafed through some papers, and then plucked out a single sheet. "Keenan found this in her dresser when he did a search of her apartment. It's a letter from Harry. A letter begging for her forgiveness."

"Forgiveness?" Tanner carefully took the sheet of paper. It was so badly crinkled it was hard to read the words, like someone had scrunched up and then reopened it again and again. He read the date. "He sent this a month before she was assaulted?"

"Yes." Knox slipped his hands into his pockets. "According to Milton, Muriel told the staff that she snuck into Dale's dorm one night after a nightmare, unaware of what would happen, and was then forced to vote. Going by what's in that letter, it seems that she also received the most votes that night."

Levi stiffened. "The boys offered up a little girl like a fucking sacrifice?"

"It would seem so. Worse, it wasn't an isolated event. Mattias convinced her that the tutors used to go to all the dorms; he would tell her he'd heard rumors that they'd be going to *her* dorm that night and so she should stay with them. Sometimes she would, sometimes she wouldn't."

Tanner swore. "How could Dale *not* have made sure she didn't believe that bullshit?"

Knox shrugged. "Maybe he tried, maybe he didn't—there's nothing in Harry's letter that would suggest one way or the other. In any case, she was forced to vote on more than one occasion. And she was abused on more than one occasion."

Tanner rubbed the back of his head. "Shit."

"In the letter, Harry repeatedly mentioned 'that night;' said it haunted him. I'm not sure what he was referring to, only that something particularly bad seemed to have happened to her one night and it was what gave Harry the guts to—in a roundabout way—go to Milton for help. Apparently, Harry couldn't shake off the guilt that he hadn't gotten help sooner."

Levi tilted his head. "But why would he contact Muriel after all this time?"

"The woman who Harry was seeing has a four-year-old daughter from another relationship. He told Muriel in the letter that each time the little girl smiled, hugged, or looked at him with trust, he felt like a fake. Said it killed him that she trusted him to protect her, because he didn't feel that he deserved that trust. He was frightened that he'd fail to protect her just as he'd failed Muriel at Ramsbrook."

"He was only a kid himself back then," said Levi.

"Harry obviously didn't think that meant anything, because 'that night' was something he couldn't forgive himself for. He said he didn't expect Muriel to forgive him either, but he hoped there might come a time when she could; he hoped that his apology might mean something."

Tanner placed the letter back on the table. "So, this would have brought back all the memories for her; made them fresh in her heart and mind. And then she was sexually assaulted in her own home. During the attack, the past and present probably mingled in her mind; it would have left her feeling weak, small, and helpless all over again. Killing her attacker might have made her feel strong, restored her sense of control."

"That could have been what sparked her to go after the others she feels are responsible for her pain," said Levi. "She couldn't kill Giles or Shephard—they're already dead—so she went after the boys from the dorm."

"She killed them all, even Dale." Tanner frowned. "Does that mean they all voted for her at one point or another, including her own brother?"

Knox's mouth set into a flat line. "I suspect it does."

"But he was very protective of her," Levi reminded them.

"He was also a terrified, traumatized child," said Knox. "He might not have voted for her. She might simply have blamed him because he didn't make the abuse stop."

Tanner scrubbed a hand down his face, hating to think what had happened to them all those years ago. Now that Devon was his mate and officially part of his lair, he'd been able to share the recent Ramsbrook business with her. And he'd watched her heart break for those poor kids who'd been abused. She'd also agreed with him that Muriel could be the person picking off those children one by one.

Tanner folded his arms. "Devon thinks it's possible that the killer may also intend to end their own life after completing their 'mission.' They'll know that the alternative is being tracked and punished by you or the Primes of their other victims."

Knox gave a slow nod. "It's certainly possible. The hope is that we locate both her and Foreman before such a thing can occur. I'll have Larkin use facial recognition software—our system is tapped into most CCTV footage available. I don't have a recent photo of Foreman, but I have one of Muriel. Surely it won't be that hard to find her and . . . "

The Prime's voice faded into the background as Devon's mind practically slammed against his, vibrating with anxiety. *Tanner, something's happened.*

He rushed out of the office, down the stairs, and into the living area. She was standing in the middle of the room, rubbing at her pale face.

Devon winced when she saw him. "I'm sorry, I shouldn't have interrupted your meeting. Calling out to you was instinct—"

"Fucking good, it should be." Tanner gripped her forearms. "Now tell me what's wrong."

"I just had a call from Jolene. Pamela's . . ." Her lower lip trembled, and she bit down hard on it. "Someone poisoned her, Tanner. They tried to *kill* her. The doctors pumped Pamela's stomach, and she seems to be stable, but . . ." She paused, breath hitching. "I have to go see her."

"I know you do. And I'm coming with you."

\*

The containment ward looked much like any hospital with its plain white walls, fluorescent lighting, and shiny tile flooring. Devon would wager it was more secure than San Quentin State Prison. She and Tanner had had to pause at several doors while someone punched a long-ass code into a security pad, allowing them entrance. It was no easy thing to get in or out of the ward, and security personnel constantly patrolled the long hallways.

In the daytime, patients often walked the hallways. But they were usually secured in their rooms no later than 7pm, so it was almost eerily quiet as she and Tanner made their way to the crisis unit where Jolene was waiting for them.

The astringent scents of bleach and disinfectant filled the air, irritating her feline. It didn't like the ward; didn't like being in a place that it knew it would have a hard time escaping if need be. But it never protested to Devon visiting Pamela.

The ward wasn't exactly a cheery place, but it was the best place for Pamela. Jolene had once given Devon a tour, respecting that she wanted to know her mother was in a safe, clean environment. It was *massive*. There were counseling rooms, cafeterias, observation rooms, recreational areas, and common rooms. Devon usually spent time with Pamela in the visitation area, but she'd seen her mother's room once. It was sparse and sad, especially with its fake window.

The ward was clean and well-kept, given the circumstances.

There was the occasional dent here and there in the walls or floor, courtesy of the patients who liked to upend furniture, fling their power around, or throw shit. But there was no dirt or mildew or shabby furnishings.

"Devon?"

Hearing Jolene's voice, Devon turned to see the Prime standing at the nurse's station looking weary and downright *pissed*.

"You got here fast," Jolene added, crossing to her.

"How is Pamela?"

"Stable." Jolene sighed. "Her heart stopped once, but the doctors were able to get it going again."

A harsh breath whooshed out of Devon. "Is she in there?" Her gaze flicked to the closed door behind Jolene.

"Yes. She's sleeping, but you can see her in a moment."

Flexing her fingers, Devon stepped closer to Jolene. "You have the person who did this to her, right?"

Jolene's face hardened. "I wish I did. Nobody saw anything, none of the cameras picked up anything suspicious. But one of the nurses who works on the ward left early and is now missing. My guess? She was paid or blackmailed to poison Pamela and she left before anyone could notice that something was wrong. The other staff said she'd been acting strange all day. Said she was edgy and impatient." Jolene rubbed Devon's arm. "She'll be found, sweetheart."

Tanner raised a brow. "But will she be alive, or will she have her throat slit like Flanagan?"

"Hopefully, she's alive, because I have some delightful things in mind for her," said Jolene, her voice pure silken menace. "This whole thing has shaken up everyone. We're not used to our own betraying us this way." Jolene gestured at the trauma room. "Go see her."

Pushing open the door, Devon stepped into what closely

resembled a hospital emergency room. Pamela lay very still on the bed, eyes closed, lips parted, her skin so pale it made her orange hospital bracelet look almost neon—orange being "code" for patients who could be a danger to themselves.

A slender woman looked up from her magazine and smiled at Devon and Tanner, but she didn't leave her chair until Jolene reassured her that they'd be fine alone with Pamela.

Swallowing, Devon crossed to the bed and took her mother's limp hand. It was cold and thin. "Mom." Her voice cracked, so she coughed to clear her throat. "Mom."

Pamela's eyelids fluttered open, revealing bloodshot eyes that quickly lit with recognition. "Devon," she breathed. Her lips slowly curled into a blinding but shaky smile, as if she lacked the energy to keep it on her face. "I don't feel too good," she added, her voice weak and subdued.

"I know." Devon gave her hand a gentle squeeze. "You're going to be okay." God, it was horrible seeing her this way. Her mother never looked fully alert. Her eyes always seemed cloudy and could sometimes be disturbingly vacant. But she was never groggy or physically weak. Right then, Pamela looked like she'd had the life sucked out of her.

Pamela squinted, eyes dancing from object to object. Confusion marred her features, and it was clear she didn't know where she was or why she was there. "Who's the man by the door? Don't recognize him," she slurred.

"That's Tanner Cole. He's my mate."

"Mate," Pamela quietly echoed, but it was like the word didn't really penetrate in her mind because she didn't otherwise react. "Do you remember when we went sailing with Beck and Richie? You were four, I think. It was a beautiful day. You were convinced you saw a whale."

A faint nostalgic smile crept onto Devon's face. "I remember."

"Beck stopped the boat at a cove. It was all dark and shiny and magical. He told you to throw a coin into the little spring there and make a wish. You made a wish that I'd get better." Her eyes drifted shut, and she forced them open. "I tried, you know. Tried over and over. Never could make your wish come true, though."

Devon's throat thickened. "It's okay."

"It's not." Her eyes slid to Tanner. "My girl's special."

"I know," he said.

"You treat her like she's special." Her eyes involuntarily drifted shut again. "I would've done it, but I couldn't."

"Sleep now," Devon whispered. "You need it."

"You'll come back?" she asked, eyes still closed, sounding half-asleep.

"I'll come back."

Once Pamela had drifted off to sleep, Devon slipped out of the room and took a deep breath. "I'm gonna kill the fucker for this, Tanner. Blood relative or not, I'll fucking kill them."

"I'll help you," he said.

# CHAPTER NINETEEN

"A naked day?"

Lying beside his mate on the bed the next morning, Tanner smoothed his hand down her bare arm, marveling at how silky-soft her skin was. His ego got a real kick out of seeing her all loose and lazy and sated. "Yeah. We've both got the day off work, you don't want to go anywhere, we've got no visitors coming, so why not just spend the day naked?"

"And what could we possibly do to keep ourselves occupied while naked?" she asked, eyes sparkling.

Mouth curling into a lopsided smile, he lowered his face to hers and whispered, "Wicked, wicked things."

"Wicked? I like wicked."

Chuckling, he kissed her, licking into her mouth and savoring her. She tasted like sin and the coffee he'd made earlier in the hope that the smell would lure her out of sleep. He'd wanted to wake her by lashing her clit with his tongue, but he'd learned early that his hellcat needed caffeine before she'd be amiable to . . . well, anything.

After making her come with his mouth, he'd fucked her slow and hard until she came with a choked cry that he felt in his balls. They'd then lay there for a while—kissing, stroking, whispering, and teasing.

It didn't seem possible that one person could wrap around his soul, but she had. And, if he was honest, she'd done it a long time ago—he'd just taken some time to accept it. Now that he had, now that he'd dropped the walls that she'd been hammering at for years just by being her, she'd filled him up in a way he couldn't explain. Brought peace to his demon, which was plain miraculous.

Currently, the hound was still and quiet, content to just be with her. And, of course, it relished being the center of her attention—something it didn't like to share.

Tanner stroked her arm again. "So smooth." Tracing her navel tattoo with his finger, he asked, "Are you going to put some ink on me?"

She blinked. "You want a tattoo?"

"I want a tattoo from *you*." Wanted her to mark him.

Surprise lit her eyes, and she smiled. "Hmm, that's doable. What do you have in mind?"

He hummed. "I want your hellcat on the back of my shoulder. I want it prowling out of high grass or flames or something like that."

Face softening, she asked, "Why on the back of your shoulder?"

"Because my hellcat watches my back," he said softly. "And I trust it to do so." He dropped his mouth to hers and gave her a quick kiss. "I did think of having a tattoo of it clawing its way out of my skin, because you and your demon are firmly under there. You always have been. Like a splinter."

She snorted, eyes gleaming. "Oh, thanks." Doodling circles on the back of his shoulder, she said, "I'll draw up a few designs for you to look at." Hearing her phone beep, she grabbed it from the nightstand and swiped her thumb over the screen. "It's a message from Jolene. She says Pamela's condition is improving."

"We can go see her again today, if you want."

Devon returned the phone to the nightstand. "Can't. Jolene's put the ward on lockdown until she's caught whoever poisoned Pamela—no one's getting in or out. I'm glad. I want to see Pamela, but this puts my mind at ease."

Just then, Levi's mind touched his, humming with anticipation. *The facial recognition software got a lock on Muriel. Get this: she's at fucking Crimson Grove. She checked in an hour ago.*

Tanner stilled. *Fuck, we should have guessed she might go back to the beginning.*

*I don't see the point in her doing it. Knox tore Ramsbrook House down; there's nothing left of the original building. The hotel is something wholly new.*

*I'm not sure that matters to Muriel. The hotel was built on Ramsbrook grounds—that will probably be enough for her, even if it all now belongs to Knox and looks totally different.*

*Knox had security personnel detain her. I don't know what she meant to do there—possibly commit suicide or something. Antonio is going to teleport me, Knox, and you to the hotel. Larkin is going to hold the fort here, and Keenan will stay with Harper and Asher. We could ask Antonio to teleport Devon to Harper if you like, but I think she'll be safe in your building.*

The thought of leaving Devon made his stomach knot. It played on his mind constantly that the threat to her hadn't yet been eliminated. But Levi was right, she'd be safe at his building. *I'll ask her what she wants to do and get back to you.*

Looking down at her, he saw a grim realization on her face.

"We're not gonna have our naked day, are we?" she asked, but it wasn't really a question.

"No. Knox found Muriel."

Her lips parted on a soft gasp. "Really? That's good."

He quickly brought her up to speed. "I'd rather stay here with you, but this needs to be dealt with."

"Well, of course you have to go." There was no aggravation or resentment in her words, just pure understanding. "You're looking at me like you expect me to curse you for leaving. I knew coming into this that your position of sentinel is super important to you; I knew you'd be on call, even on your days off. I'm not mad that you need to go, I get it."

He let out a long breath he hadn't even realized he'd been holding. "Hopefully, I won't be too long."

"I'll be fine here."

"Are you sure?" He palmed her cheek. "You could spend some time with Harper and Asher while I'm gone."

Her nose wrinkled. "That would require getting dressed and slapping on some makeup. I don't have the energy for that. I'd rather just stay home, and maybe binge watch a TV series."

That made the corner of his mouth hitch up. "I like that you call this 'home' already."

"It *is* home."

"Yeah." He sipped from her mouth, silently cursing the fact that he had to leave. "I had plans for this body this morning. So many, many plans."

"You can carry them out later," she whispered.

"Later." He kissed her again and then edged out of bed. In the bathroom, he went through his morning ritual, telepathed Levi to say that Devon would be staying here, and then returned to the bedroom. She was sitting cross-legged on the bed, the sheets pulled up to cover her breasts, reading something on her phone.

Pulling on his clothes, he asked, "You're sure you'll be okay here?"

She looked up at him—didn't give him a brief glance or answer without moving her gaze from her cell. No, she gave him her full attention. He fucking loved that.

"I'm sure," she said.

He liked that she'd be in the building, where she'd be safe, but . . . "I don't like that you'll be alone."

"If you're worried that I'll get lonely or bored and decide to go out, don't. I'm not stupid. Venturing out alone while I have danger lurking isn't on my list of things to do. I'm not going to make it easy for the fucker to get to me."

Finally dressed, he crossed to the bed and planted a fist on the mattress either side of her. "If for some reason you *do* need to go somewhere, call Ciaran and ask him to teleport you wherever you need to go. Also tell him to give me a telepathic shout-out so I know exactly where you are. Okay?"

She turned her face upward and rolled her eyes. "If it'll make you feel better, okay."

He dropped a kiss on her mouth. "Thank you."

Knuckles rapped on the front door and then a familiar mind slid against his. *It's me,* said Antonio. *You ready?*

*Yeah,* replied Tanner. "That's Antonio," he told her, straightening. "I have to leave now." His hound rumbled a dark growl, not wanting to go, even as it knew its Prime needed it. "I might be a few hours," Tanner warned her.

She crossed her eyes. "Yeah, pooch, I get that. *I'll be fine.*" She flapped her hand toward the door. "Now go. Shoo. Good dog."

Lips twitching, he narrowed his eyes. "You'll pay for that later, kitten."

She smirked. "Sure I will."

Shooting her a mock glare, Tanner spun on his heel and left the apartment.

\*

A short time later, he and Levi flanked Knox as they stalked
through the lavish hotel lobby that was all gleaming marble tile,
domed stained glass ceilings, and designer rugs. Some people
were in a line near the front desk, hauling luggage. Others were
relaxing on the designer couches in the sprawling seating area
beyond the bank of elevators.

The uniformed staff had a habit of rushing to Knox with
queries the moment he stepped into the building, but not today.
Probably because he was exuding a "You really don't want to fuck
with me right now" vibe.

Knox made a beeline for the head of the security team, who
was unobtrusively leaning against a marble column near the
water fountain, taking in everything.

The male straightened as they approached. "Mr. Thorne."

"Derek," Knox greeted. "Is Muriel still contained?"

"Yes, sir." Derek fell into step beside the Prime as Knox immediately headed in the direction of the security office, since it was
the only room that provided access to the detention room—a
space specially designed to hold demons. Like both Knox's home
and their lair's prison, it was safeguarded by a myriad of spells
that kept the prisoner contained and stopped anyone from teleporting inside. In addition, each of those spells were covered
with protective wards to prevent them from unraveling.

"Did she give you much trouble?" Knox asked Derek as they
all turned down a long, carpeted hallway.

"A little, but nothing we couldn't handle," replied Derek.

"Is anyone with her now?"

"No, but we've been monitoring her from the office through
the camera." Derek grimaced. "We noticed something."

"What?"

"Well, she was sobbing for a while, rocking forward and backward while sitting in the corner with her legs tucked up to her body. Then, at one point, she stopped. Went completely still. She took a deep breath, closed her eyes, said she was 'done.' And then her demon surfaced. It has been driving the wheel ever since, so to speak."

Entering the security office, they crossed straight to the monitor that was linked to the camera in the detention room. Muriel was standing near the rear wall, her back straight, her chin high . . . and her eyes pure black.

"Thank you for your assistance, Derek. We'll take it from here." There was no bloodthirst in Knox's voice, and Tanner knew the Prime hated that he'd have to kill this person who'd been through more than anyone should ever have to endure.

Levi opened the door, and all three of them filed inside. Knox stood directly opposite Muriel while Tanner and Levi flanked him. And it was right then, as Tanner stared the demon in the eye and saw the malicious gleam there, that his instincts went on high alert and his hound let out a snarl.

Tanner froze. So did the others, which meant they'd obviously sensed what he and his hound had: Muriel hadn't just retreated to allow her demon to surface temporarily. No, Muriel had given her demon *full*-control. She'd turned rogue.

*Fuck.*

This wasn't good. Not at all. The entities were all essentially cold, unfeeling psychopaths. But sharing their soul with an actual person gave them a sense of balance. Without that balance, without an element of goodness touching their souls, they were as close to pure evil as anything could get.

Rogue demons weren't insane in the literal sense, but they didn't behave rationally . . . purely because they didn't want to. They would kill without thought or discrimination. Would just as easily slaughter or torture an infant as they would an adult, and they wouldn't even need a motive to do so.

It wasn't that they became rampant serial killers who craved the sight of blood ... But they were always looking for the next high—something they got from drugs, alcohol, destruction, inflicting pain, causing misery, and stealing the lives of others.

Many people died whenever a rogue was on the loose. They cared for nothing, couldn't be reasoned with or controlled. Didn't care if their actions attracted the attention of humans.

There was only one way to deal with a rogue: you had to kill it.

"Thorne," the demon greeted, its tone flat and cold.

"I'd like to talk to Muriel," said Knox.

The demon lifted its chin slightly. "Muriel is gone—you can sense that much for yourself."

Recalling what Derek told them about how Muriel claimed she was "done," Tanner said, "She willingly handed over control to you, didn't she?"

"She was done with this world," it replied. "Too weak to handle it. She knew I was stronger."

"She gave over control to you because she didn't want to deal with us herself," Knox corrected. "She was escaping the consequences of her actions. It was cowardly, really."

The demon shrugged one shoulder, clearly not giving a hot shit what they thought.

"What happened to Royal Foreman?" asked Knox.

A glimmer of humor briefly glittered in its obsidian eyes. "You will find him eventually. I doubt you will like the state you find him in."

"Did you help her kill him and the others?"

"No. She wanted to punish the boys herself."

"For voting for her?"

"Yes. They all did it at least once, aside from Foreman."

But Muriel had still killed him. Tanner wondered if that meant she'd developed a taste for killing. After all, demons craved power. There was no greater power than that over whether someone lived or died.

"Dale didn't try to protect her from the tutors?" asked Levi.

"No," said the demon, its voice seeming even flatter than before. "He never offered to go in her place. Never told her not go to the dorm. Never tried to help her. He even voted for her more than once. He would tell her afterward that the other boys made him do it, but that was a lie."

Knox slanted his head. "How many times was she taken down to the basement?"

Black eyes sliced back to him. "Six, in total. Six times too many."

Yeah, Tanner could agree with that.

"What happened the last time?" asked Knox. "Why did Harry want her forgiveness?"

"Ah, you found the letter," the demon realized. "Muriel could not decide whether to be furious by his request for forgiveness or comforted by the sheer knowledge that he was haunted by his decision. She wanted him to suffer."

*Is it just me wondering why it's being so talkative?* Tanner asked Knox. *Rogues usually have a more "fuck you, I don't explain myself to people" attitude.*

*I'm guessing it's either under the illusion that it will get free and is simply biding its time before it strikes or it's been wanting to get this shit off its chest for a very long time,* said Knox. "What exactly was Harry haunted by?"

"The night before Milton intervened," began the demon, "Muriel and Dale received the same number of votes. The tutors decided to take them both to the basement." Its eyes hardened to stone as it added, "They hurt the children. Forced the children to do vile things to each other. Then they brought Harry down and gave him the choice to take Muriel's place. I could smell his fear; knew he would not agree, but she had hoped he would. He didn't."

Tanner liked to think he'd have offered to trade places with Muriel to spare the little girl further pain, but he couldn't blame Harry for not wanting to do so. He'd only been a child himself. You couldn't really know what you'd do in such a situation unless you were in it.

"The tutors were not surprised by his refusal," the demon went on. "They laughed. I think they had noticed how the guilt of voting for others again and again was eating at Harry; they had worried he might tell someone, and so they had added to his shame by making him the offer to save Muriel, knowing he would refuse. But it did not have quite the effect they had hoped for. It made him more determined to make the abuse stop for good."

Knox's nostrils flared. "Why didn't you push her to tell me? You must have sensed I'd have done what I could to stop it."

"I urged her to speak with you. She would not listen, and she was far too ashamed to speak of it."

Scrubbing his hand down his face, Levi softly cursed.

"You would not pity Muriel so much if you knew she was not so innocent," said the demon. "She once convinced another female child to go the boys' dorm, hoping she would be taken instead. The child received the most votes, and she was taken to the basement. She did not come out of it alive. The tutors made it seem to the other staff like she was yet another runaway. But Muriel liked to block that memory—she could not deal with the guilt. Not feeling so sorry for her now, are you?"

"She was still a victim," said Knox.

"Yes. But she had no problem making someone else into a

victim. No problem voting for those boys. She even voted for Dale a time or two. Not that I blamed her."

Staring at the demon, seeing how little sympathy it now had for Muriel, Tanner couldn't help but think that *this* was what would have become of Devon's mother if she'd given control to her own demon. Pamela could have surrendered to the inner entity to escape her pain and guilt, but she hadn't, even though the pull of it had to be strong. Pamela might have done some messed up shit, but it said a lot about her that she hadn't tried to escape it.

The demon gave Knox a bored look. "I suppose you are going to kill me."

"You can't be allowed to live," said Knox, conjuring a lethal ball of hellfire.

The entity spared the blazing orb a brief, disinterested glance. "Are you not going to ask why Muriel came here?"

"We know why."

"Do you?"

"She intended to kill herself here; to die where she'd no doubt wished she'd died as a child rather than suffer what she'd suffered."

"You are partly right. She wanted to die here. But she also wanted to purge the ground as she did so. There is no clock in here, so I am not sure how much time you have left before the bomb detonates, but I doubt it will be long."

*Motherfucker.*

\*

Devon frowned as the intercom buzzed. Honestly, she was in too lazy a mood to get up and see who her visitor was. But she was also far too curious to not check. Draining her mug, she set it on the coffee table and pushed to her feet.

The intercom buzzed again just as she reached the small screen that showed who was on the doorstep of the building, hoping to be admitted. Finn. And he did not look happy.

She pushed the speak button. "Hello?"

"Let me up, we need to talk," said Finn, curt. He had one of his sentinels with him, but no Leticia, Spencer, Reena, or Kaye. Hoping he had some damn good news that might clue her in as to who was fucking up her shit, she pressed the button that would unlock the front door for him.

Devon glanced down at herself, frowning at her sweatpants and old tee. She looked far from presentable. Oh, well.

Minutes later, she was opening the door to find Finn standing there, his shoulders tense, his brows drawn together.

"Wait here," he told Eric, who inclined his head at Devon and then adopted an on-guard position.

Finn surged past her, waiting for her to close the door before he spoke. "I heard about what happened at the sports bar."

Ah, so this was about Reena. "And what is it exactly that you heard?"

"You accused her of being the one who broke into your old apartment," he hissed.

"It wasn't just broken into; it was vandalized."

His mouth set into a white slash. "You can't truly believe she did it."

"Why not?"

"She's your blood."

"Not in her mind. She wants me out of her life, out of your life—she told me that herself. Not that I hadn't already received that message long ago." Devon headed into the living area, aware he was following her.

"Reena's not a person who would find any satisfaction in vandalism."

"She's also not a person who'd hang out at a sports bar drinking beer and playing pool," said Devon, sinking into the sofa. "Or, at least, I wouldn't have thought so, but she looked really relaxed there."

He dismissed that with a flick of his hand. "She probably goes there with the other sentinels as a sort of team bonding exercise."

"Hmm."

"Your old apartment was in a bad area where crime is pretty much rife. You can't live in a place like that and expect not to be robbed."

Devon felt her expression go hard. "It wasn't a robbery. It also wasn't a simple case of vandalism. It was a fucking tantrum. Jolene sent you copies of the photos that Ciaran took. Did you notice that the vase you bought me was shattered?"

"Reena wouldn't care about a vase."

"No, but she'd care that you buy me things. She always has, and you know it." She tilted her head. "You don't find it the tiniest bit freaking suspicious that she was at my building on the same day that the break-in happened? Something she kept from you, I might add."

"She just wanted to *talk* to you."

"She wanted to check if Sheridan had mentioned her name or if he said anything that could implicate her," Devon corrected. "Did she tell you that she knew him?" His eyes flickered, and she tensed. "You already knew, didn't you? You knew, and you said nothing."

He rubbed at his brow. "I didn't see it as relevant. There's no way Reena would have any reason to want Asa released."

"I don't think anyone wants Asa released. I don't think they ever did." Devon draped her arms over the back of the sofa, deciding it was time to test her theory out on him. "I think the reason he hasn't given you any more names is that he's been telling you the truth all along—he has none left to give you."

"What are you saying?"

"Probably something you've already considered. You're not stupid. Surely you've wondered if this is even about Asa at all. Surely you've asked yourself if maybe someone used him to muddy the waters and hide the real motivation behind what they're doing."

Finn's gaze slid briefly to the side. "It occurred to me, yes. My sentinels and I all discussed it. We agreed it's possible that someone was trying to hurt me through one of my children."

"I think it's more than that. So do Tanner and Jolene." She twisted her mouth. "Lockwood said something that got us thinking."

"I knew you were all holding back something," he said, a muscle in his cheek jumping. "Go on, what did he say?"

"He said the person who hired him told him they knew where I was hiding my mother, and that—and I quote— 'that bitch Pamela needs to pay.' If this was only about hurting *Pamela*, there would have been no reason for anyone to bring you into it; they could have asked Jolene to make some sort of trade for me. If this was only about hurting *you*, someone would have been more likely to kidnap Reena, Spencer, or Kaye. But it was *me* who was taken. It was you who would have been asked to 'save' me. And it was Pamela who was poisoned just yesterday."

His confrontational manner slipped away in an instant. He blinked slowly. "Poisoned?"

"Her heart even stopped at one point, but the doctors managed to stabilize her." Feeling her nails pricking her palms, she forced her hands to unclench. "This whole tangle of shit has been woven around the three of us. As I see it, there are only four people in our lives who would truly wish us all such harm."

Her jerked back, mouth slack with shock. And then he vigorously shook his head. "No."

"Push through that denial, Finn. It isn't going to help us. Don't you want this to be over?"

He slanted his body away from her. "No. My children wouldn't do this. Leticia wouldn't do this."

"You hurt them, Finn. You betrayed them. Broke their trust. Fathered a child to another woman. Probably even lost a little of their respect. They had a cushy life, and the discovery of my existence swept the rug right out from under them. Everything changed—"

"Leticia forgave me! They all did!"

"Did they really? How certain are you of that?" Personally, Devon wouldn't have found any of it so easy to forgive. In fact, she wasn't sure she could truly forgive Tanner if he betrayed her that way. Wasn't sure she'd ever be able to take him back.

"None of them have the ability to speak through people," he pointed out.

Knuckles rapped hard on the door. "Mr. Moseley?" Eric called out.

Finn sighed. "Give me a moment, Devon."

It was pure nosiness that made her walk to the far end of the living area so she could hear what Eric said. Finn opened the door, and a familiar figure barged past him right into the apartment. It wasn't Eric.

\*

"Where is the bomb?" Knox hissed at the demon.

"You know I will not tell you that," it said.

He hurled an orb of hellfire at the demon, knocking it to the ground. "*Where is it?*"

The demon sat upright, chest sizzling where the hellfire ate at its flesh. "You are wasting time asking me what I will not tell you."

The Prime conjured another blazing orb. "You *will* tell me."

Tanner didn't believe so. "It's not afraid of pain or of dying; it's not going to tell you anything. We need to kill it and then search Muriel's room."

"He's right, Knox," said Levi. "It wants this place to blow, it's happy to die knowing it took a whole building full of people with it. Let's just get this part over with fast and find that fucking bomb."

The orb in Knox's hand brightened, grew, and buzzed louder. And then, jaw set, he tossed it at the demon. The orb smashed into its head, caving in three-quarters of its skull, killing it instantly. The demon flopped to the floor like a ragdoll, and the hellfire ate at its flesh. Tanner knew the corpse would be ashes in moments.

"We need to get everybody out," said Knox.

After sealing the detention room, Knox ordered his staff to evacuate the building. He, Tanner, and Levi then searched every inch of Muriel's room. They rummaged through her suitcase, upturned furniture, rifled through the wardrobes and dresser, checked every nook and cranny.

"Nothing," said Levi, breathing hard. "Where else would she have placed the bomb? Or is there some chance the demon was just fucking with us? Because, honestly, I don't even know why Muriel would bother planting one here. It's not the original building."

"I didn't get the feeling that the demon was playing a game with us," said Knox. "But yes, it's possible that it was lying. Still, we need to be certain. We have to keep looking."

Tanner squared his shoulders. "I can find the bomb. I just need to follow her scent trail to see where else in the building she's been. If there's a bomb here, I'll locate it."

Knox gave a sharp nod. "Do it."

Planting his feet, Tanner rolled his shoulders and closed his eyes. Latching onto Muriel's scent, he stripped it of the hairspray, perfume, and other smells that tainted it; needing it in its purest form. *Frosted cherries and cream.*

His eyes flipped open. "Got it." The call of the hunt trickled through his veins, pounded in his blood, wrapped around his bones, and filled every part of him all the way to his fingertips and toes.

With his demon close to the surface, Tanner followed Muriel's scent out of the room and down the hallway, aware that Knox and Levi were following him. Adrenaline pumped through him, sharpening his senses, readying him for action.

Tanner cursed as they reached the bank of elevators. "We're going to have to pause at every floor so I can step out and test the air for her scent." And since there were eighteen floors, that was going to be a motherfucking bitch.

"Then that's what we'll do," said Knox, jabbing the down button. "There are two floors above this, but that's where the luxury rooms are located. Guests who are staying up there need to insert their keycard in the elevator panel before pushing the buttons for those floors or the elevator simply won't take them up. That means Muriel could only have gone down, so we only need to check the fifteen floors below us."

Well that was something.

The silver, metal doors opened with a chime, and the three of them stepped inside the empty elevator. With the call of the hunt still nagging him to move, move, move, Tanner jabbed the button for floor fifteen. He blocked out the soft music and hum of machinery, keeping a tight hold on Muriel's scent. When the doors slid open, Tanner stepped out and breathed in deeply. "Nothing. She didn't stop here."

They stopped at floor fourteen. Still nothing. Then thirteen.

Still nothing. And on and on it went. As the building had been evacuated, there were no guests trying to join them in the elevator, so Tanner was free to concentrate solely on his task.

Finally, they reached the ground floor. Tanner stepped out and inhaled deeply. *Frosted cherries and cream.* "Here. She stopped here."

"Either that or this leads outside—you could be simply following the trail she left on *entering* the building," Levi pointed out.

"Only one way to know for sure." Tanner latched onto the scent again and followed it, prowling through the lobby. He halted, because there were *two* threads of Muriel's scent. One led to the reception area, but it was faint. The other thread was fresher, and it seemed to head in a whole other direction.

Honing his senses on the fresher thread, Tanner stalked out of the lobby, passing the sitting area, bar, gift shop . . . and walked right into a small café.

Dozens of distracting scents assaulted him. *Fresh-brewed coffee. Ground beans. Baked goods. Orange juice. Chocolate. Vanilla. Cinnamon. Herbal tea. Tomato soup. Sweet desserts*—it went on and on.

A sharp pain struck him right between his eyebrows that felt much like brain-freeze. A pain he wouldn't have felt if he hadn't been extending his sense of smell so much. It was like when you strained to hear something, and then a loud noise came at you from nowhere and hurt your ears.

Tanner shook his head. "I think she came in here hoping I'd lose her scent."

"Have you?" asked Knox.

"Yes. But I'll find it again." He was a fucking alpha hellhound, for Christ's sake.

Closing his eyes, Tanner dragged the surrounding scents into his lungs, filtering through the café-scents in addition to the perfume, cologne, hairspray, lemon cleaner, air conditioning, fresh flowers—

*Frosted cherries and cream.* Tanner opened his eyes. "I've got her."

He clung to the scent with metaphorical hands and followed it out of the café, passing the restaurant and conference room, before turning down a carpeted hallway where the scent became stronger.

Blood buzzing with the thrill that always came with being close to his prey—whether it be a person or object—Tanner quickened his pace, following the trail to the end of the hallway. He shoved open the fire exit door and found himself in a stairwell.

The scent took him down two flights of steps toward ... "Fuck, the basement. We should have fucking guessed she'd plant it in the one place that destroyed her fucking life." Even if it *wasn't* the exact same basement where she'd suffered the abuse.

Knox cursed. "Step aside. I'd sure like to know how she got in here without knowing the code. Then again, it wouldn't be impossible. I can do it easily enough." He didn't punch a code into the keypad near the basement door. Just sent out a brief wave of power that pushed it right open. Inside, he flicked on a switch.

Tanner glanced around. It was nothing whatsoever like Richie's basement. It had been converted into a clean, bright storage space for hotel supplies—including food, bedsheets, towels, complimentary toiletries, and gift shop stock.

Locking onto Muriel's scent once more, Tanner advanced further into the basement. The scent took him deeper and deeper into the large space. "I hear a faint beeping." And the scent was leading him right to it. He hastened his pace, his heart beating fast, his blood still buzzing with—

There was an audible *click* in the air. A glass wall slammed up in front of them. And on their left. And on their right. And behind them. And above them. It happened in under a millisecond.

And now they were fucking contained by a glass fucking cube.

No, it wasn't glass. The transparent wall seemed fluid, like water. He touched it. Hissed. The fucker was ice-cold. And it buzzed with power.

Levi hurled balls of hellfire at it, but the water instantly doused them, making them sizzle as they faded to nothing. "The fuck?"

Then a bulky figure stepped out of the shadows. It took a moment for Tanner to place that familiar face. "Foreman." And if his expression was anything to go by, he wasn't there to help them. He was there to stop them. No, *trap* them … like any good ensnarer. Well, fuck.

*Muriel spared him,* he said to Knox.

*Her demon said he never voted for her,* the Prime reminded him. *She must have convinced him to work with her. As an ensnarer, he could have kept the victims still for her while she hurt them. Shit, I can't pyroport out of this. Royal has definitely gained in power over the years if he can form traps that block forms of teleportation. That's not to say we can't get out of here, just that it's going to take time.*

Which meant they were dead if they didn't find some way to get out *before* the bomb detonated. *Fuck, fuck, fuck.*

# CHAPTER TWENTY

Jaw hard, Finn followed the newcomer as they headed toward the living room. "We agreed that you should wait in the car." Hearing footsteps behind him, he glanced over his shoulder and frowned. "Jo, what are you—"

"Jo is with me," said Leticia just as this Jo person closed the door behind her.

Leticia smiled. "Hello, Devon. You're a hard woman to get alone. Eric let me in the building, gentleman that he is. I'm afraid he won't be joining us."

Finn planted his fists on his hips. "I told you I would deal with this, Let—"

"I'm not here to confront her over the accusations she slung at Reena," Leticia told him. Then she nodded at her friend. "Jo."

Just like that, a heavy weight clamped around Devon's body, pinning her still. She tried moving. Failed. Seriously, it was like someone had encased her in steel from her shoulders all the way down to her toes. *Fuck.*

Panic struck her hard, making bile rise in her throat and causing her breathing to turn quick and shallow. The feeling of being trapped would never be something she handled well. It always took her back to that sweltering hot car.

Her feline went berserk. Wanted freedom so that it could rip Leticia apart limb from fucking limb. The dark power inside Devon's belly was just as wild, eager to be released; eager to protect and defend. But it, too, was trapped.

Her ribs suddenly seemed too tight, and she felt like she just couldn't get enough air. She squeezed her eyes shut, trying to shut down the panic before she hyperventilated. She forced herself to take a deep breath. And another. And another. And another.

"I know you got away from that last incantor, Devon, but I can assure you that Jo is far too powerful for anyone other than another incantor to take on," said Leticia.

Maybe, thought Devon, opening her eyes. But that didn't mean she wouldn't get free sooner or later. Leticia didn't need to know that, though. She also didn't need to know that Devon's demon intended to rip out her throat. "Tanner will come."

Smugness glittered in Leticia's eyes. "No, he won't. You see, the magick surrounding you won't just keep you still, it will put a block on whatever psychic link the mark on your palm gives you to him. He has no idea just how badly you need him right now."

Panic threatened to consume her once more, but Devon forced it back down. When the magick finally lost its hold on her—which it eventually would—he'd feel that she was in danger. She could only hope that it happened before Leticia had a chance to kill her, which she clearly intended to do.

Realization hit Finn, who also appeared unable to move, and his eyes widened in horror as he stared at his woman. "No."

Leticia gave him a smile filled with mock pity. "Oh, yes."

"Why?" he demanded, voice cracking.

"You really need to ask that question?" She sniffed. "That doesn't surprise me. You never really saw any wrong in the things you did over the years. So many women you cheated on me with," she mused, circling him. "Cheating was one thing, and I made you pay for it every time. But impregnating another woman? Giving her something that you refused to give me? *I don't want any more children*, you said. *Three is enough*, you said."

His nostrils flared. "It wasn't planned."

"Oh, I know."

"I agreed to try for more. We tried."

"And then I found out you'd had a *vasectomy*," she spat, venom in every syllable. "You knew there was no chance of us having more children unless you had the operation reversed, *which you didn't*. You let me think that the problem was me. And let's not forget the other lies you told. 'I love you more than life itself' is probably my favorite. But you told me there would be no more cheating if I came back to you. You *promised* me. You lied."

"Leticia—"

"All those years I stuck by you. Forgave you again and again. But did you ever declare me your mate? No. No, you wouldn't share your precious power, would you? The only reason I stayed with you is that I thought you one day would. *You owed me that*."

"And then you would've gotten rid of me," he accused. "You'd have ruled the lair alone."

"Only until Spencer became old enough to take over. I'd say that time has come." She looked down her nose at him. "My son will be better at ruling than you ever were."

The steel-like weight around Devon fluttered against her skin, and then it loosened *ever* so slightly. Not enough for her to move or send out any tendrils of power, but enough that a cautious hope flickered to life in her belly. She didn't let that show on her face; just continued to watch the spectacle before her play out.

Finn inhaled deeply. "Leticia, please listen to me."

"You have nothing to say I want to hear," Leticia clipped. "I promised myself I'd never go through what my mother went through; never fall for a man who didn't love and value and respect me. But you're no better than my father, are you? A cheating, lying bastard. Pamela was right in what she said about you. She had herself a lucky escape, in my opinion. Didn't save her from a shitty life, though, did it?"

"What does that mean?" The question burst out of Devon.

Leticia turned to face her. "Ah, so Pamela never told you. You weren't the unlikely product of a one-night stand between strangers, Devon. He and your bitch of a mother had known each other for a long time. They used to date when they were teenagers. But she wouldn't commit to him; said there was too much potential for sin in him. She was certain he'd hurt her over and over."

Devon could only stare at the other woman, utterly stunned.

"You hear that?" Leticia snarled. "She gave. Him. Up. She could have had him, but she let him go. *I* found him. *I* gave him the children he wanted. *I* was his advisor and more as he worked his way to the position of Prime. She had no right to have a for-old-time's-sake fuck with him—a man who had a *family*. He belonged to me. But she fucked him, and then she had *you*."

"Leticia, please listen to me," Finn beseeched. "I hurt you. Took you for granted. Cheated on you. But that cheating ended after you came back to me, I *swear* I—"

"You were planning to leave me, weren't you?" It was a quiet accusation, and it made Finn stiffen. Leticia fingered the button of his shirt. "I found out about the little slut you keep in that condo in New York. It was bad enough you were up to your old tricks again. But then I realized you weren't just having an affair with her. It was more. Hmm, I wonder if she knows about all the other sluts you keep housed all over the US."

Leticia went nose to nose with him. "If you think I've put up with *years* of your bullshit, years of humiliation and betrayal and pain, only for you to leave me ... Well you're *very* much mistaken. I paid my dues with you. I *had* hoped that Knox or Jolene would kill you for me but, alas, that did not happen, so I'll take care of the matter myself." She lifted her chin. "I say it's time to clean house. All those sluts you have secretly tucked away for when you're on business trips will all be meeting untimely deaths. Some already have. And, of course, your illegitimate child will do the same."

Ignoring Finn's appeals for her to listen to him, Leticia crossed to Devon and tilted her head. "To your credit, you never asked him for anything. Never tried to impose yourself on us. I might have left you alone if the attempt to poison Pamela had worked—after all, I know what it's like to be the child of an adulterer. But she survived the poisoning, and I can't reach her now. The only way I can make Pamela suffer is by taking away the one thing she loves; the one thing she holds onto her sanity for."

"Jolene won't tell her I'm dead," said Devon. "Pamela will never know."

"But she'll start to notice that you haven't visited. She'll either believe you're dead or that you've abandoned her—either one of those things will send her over the edge. As such, I have no choice but to get rid of you."

"Don't bullshit me, Leticia. You wouldn't have let me live," Devon accused. "Like you said, you're cleaning house."

Leticia only smiled.

A knock came at the door.

"*Help!*" Finn bellowed toward the door. "*We need help in here!*"

Leticia rolled her eyes. "The walls are demon-hearing proof, idiot."

The magickal weight confining Devon fluttered once more

against her skin, and she felt it loosen a little more. Devon subtly tried to move her toes, and her heart slammed in her chest when she managed to wriggle them just a bit. Yeah, the magick's hold was wearing off. Not enough to release any of the power demanding freedom, sadly, which meant it was probably still blocking Tanner from sensing that she was in danger.

No sooner had Jo opened the door a crack than Eric barged inside.

Finn's gaze went soft with relief when he spotted his sentinel. "Eric!"

"You haven't done it yet?" he barked at Leticia.

She gave the sentinel a haughty sniff. "I'm not going to rush something I've waited so long for."

"Thorne's hound will be back at some point," said Eric, nostrils flaring. "If you want to make them suffer, you'd best get it done."

"Eric," began Finn. "What are doing?"

"He's been on my side for quite some time, darling," Leticia told Finn, stroking her hand down Eric's chest. "He kept an eye on you for me. He was even good enough to broker deals for me using conduits. Yes, I know you had no idea he possessed that nifty ability to speak through others. There are lots of things you don't know about me and Eric."

"Tanner will know you were here," said Devon. "He'll pick up your scent." And then hunt the bitch down and gut her open. The thought was so cheerful it almost made her smile.

"I don't plan to run out and pretend I was never here. Eric and Jo will both back up my story that all four of us came to the building but that only Finn went inside to see you; he wanted privacy. Whenever Finn goes anywhere alone, he regularly checks in with Eric telepathically, assuring him that he's fine. But this time, Finn didn't contact him or respond to Eric's telepathic calls. So, concerned, Eric went inside. He heard you two arguing—Finn was furious with you for the accusation you made against my Reena, you blamed him for your mother almost dying, you hated that he was refusing to hand over Asa, maybe you even blamed him for your mother's mental state ... Oh, yes, I like that. And then maybe he told you that you were a mistake; that you should never have been born; that Pamela was better off dead.

"Eric, so focused on trying to calm you both down, didn't realize he'd left the door ajar ... until someone came in and attacked. There was a struggle. Eric telepathed me, and I came rushing up here with Jo only to find you and Finn dead. I'll have to injure Eric a little to make it look real, of course, but that can be done." She patted the sentinel's cheek gently. "I'll make it up to you later."

"You won't pull it off," clipped Devon.

"We'll pull it off, I assure you." Leticia sighed. "Sadly, I don't have time to torture you, and it would certainly mess up my story if you had all sorts of injuries. However, that's not to say I can't still make you both suffer before I kill you. I've suffered plenty. So why shouldn't you?" She glanced at Jo and clicked her fingers. "Give it to me."

Devon would have backed up if she could have fucking moved.

"Here," said Jo, putting a tiny bottle into Leticia's hand.

The bitch opened the bottle and sprinkled the contents onto her hand. Dust. It was just dust. Leticia blew it at Devon and—

*Six-year-old Devon plastered her small sweaty hands on the window, gasping for air. She's not coming, she thought. No one was gonna come. No one was gonna get them out of the car. No one was gonna help them.*

*She dropped her forehead to the glass, breathing hard and fast. Her hands hurt so bad from punching the window, and her knuckles*

*were all swollen and bloody . . . like Drew's were when he had a fight
with a boy on their street. Drew hadn't minded how sore they were.
He'd thought his knuckles looked "badass."*

Devon didn't want badass knuckles. She wanted to go home.
Wanted to get out of the baking hot car and change into clothes that
weren't all patchy with sweat.

Her chest burned each time she breathed in the thick hot air. It
was like breathing air right out of a hairdryer or something.

She stared at the building on the far side of the parking lot, wishing
the front door would open and Pamela would walk out. Why wasn't
she coming? Devon hadn't actually seen her go inside, but there was
nowhere else out here for her to go.

Had Pamela forgotten about them? She forgot about things sometimes. A lot of times. But then she'd remember, and things would be
okay. For a little while.

Her mother would remember to come back outside soon, right?
She would. She had to.

Devon licked her chapped lips, wincing at the sting. She needed
water. Her throat was so dry, and it hurt from screaming. She'd
stopped, because it hadn't helped. No one had heard her. No one
had heard the baby crying.

He wasn't crying anymore. Wasn't fussing or kicking. Wasn't
doing anything.

*He's asleep,* she told herself, refusing to look at him. *Babies slept
all the time; that was all he was doing. She didn't need to check on
him. He was fine. Just sleeping.*

But she knew it wasn't true. She couldn't hear his little heart
beating anymore. Couldn't hear him breathing.

A sob wracked her body and she punched at the window
again. "Help!"

Devon gasped like she'd just come out of the ocean for air,
tears pooling in her eyes while her heart bled. It occurred to her

that she probably shouldn't have been able to fight her way out of the memory. She'd have worried that more dust would have been blown her way, but no one was paying any attention to her. No, they were focused on Finn while Leticia berated and cursed him.

Devon felt the pull of magick on her psyche once more, knew the dust still had some hold on her. Fuck, no. No, no, no, no, *no*, she couldn't go back there again. Couldn't go—

*Devon stopped slapping the window and collapsed against the car door with a weak cry. She'd gotten excited when she saw the guy on the bike. Thought he'd see her, thought he'd help. But no matter how hard she'd hit the glass or how loud she'd screamed, he hadn't noticed her. And now he'd gone inside the building where Pamela had to be.*

Maybe he had heard Devon, *she thought, hope kindling in her* chest. Maybe he'd ask the people inside the place who the car belonged to and then Pamela would remember.

*Devon swallowed, and there was a weird clicking sound. She rubbed at her throat. It felt all scratchy on the inside, and her tongue felt swollen.*

*She tried reaching out with her mind to touch her mother's, but again it didn't work. Devon could only talk to people telepathically if they weren't too far away.*

*Tears stung her eyes, and she wiped them away with her clammy fingers. She was tired. Felt all dizzy and heavy. Wanted to just sit down and close her eyes. But that would mean turning away from the window. It would mean turning . . . and seeing . . . seeing him.*

*He hadn't started crying again. Hadn't sniffled or moved.*

*He's. Just. Sleeping.*

*Devon weakly banged her head on the window, wishing somebody would come, wishing the baby boy would move or whimper or something. But none of those things happened, just as she'd known they wouldn't.*

The breath gusted out of Devon's lungs as she once more

snapped back to the present, her heart pounding, her cheeks wet with tears. The others were still focused on Finn, who was screaming while Jo chanted something at him. Devon tried moving, was able to flex her fingers, wriggle her toes, and squirm slightly, but that was as good as it got. Still, she could sense that the magick was wearing off fast.

Darkness yanked on her psyche again, and panic seized her tight. No, she could not go back there again. Just couldn't. She fought the magick, fought to stay with the present, but the memories sucked her under and—

*Devon's eyelids fluttered open, and she squeezed them shut as the sunlight stabbed at her eyes. She hadn't meant to fall asleep.*

*She realized she was still leaning against the car door but, too tired to move, she decided to just lean on it a little longer. She didn't really want to move her head anyway. It felt light but it ached at the same time. Like someone was stabbing her in the head with something real sharp. Her cheeks were burning so bad it was like they were on fire.*

*She felt her eyes drift shut but didn't fight it. Didn't bother trying to punch the window or shout for help, because . . . No one is coming.*

Maybe something had happened to Pamela. Or maybe she'd come outside to check on them, found Devon asleep, and figured she'd be okay a little longer. *The thought made Devon's heart slam against her ribs, and her eyes snapped open.* She hadn't missed her chance to get help, had she?

Oh God, maybe she had. She should have stayed awake.

*A sob built in her throat, but it didn't come out. Her breaths were just soft, shallow pants now. Like her body didn't have the energy to take a full breath.*

*She didn't know it was possible to be this hot. Or this thirsty. Or this tired.*

*Her eyes almost slid to the side to get a look at—no. No, she couldn't look at him. If she looked at him, it would make it real.*

*She needed to pretend that he was okay. Needed to pretend they'd both be okay.*

*Her eyelids fluttered shut again. She wouldn't fall back asleep, but she could just rest her eyes for a few minutes.*

*Tires screeched outside. Doors opened and closed. Footsteps thundered along the cement. And then a hand slammed on the window.*

*Devon forced herself to look up, saw . . . "Jolene," she rasped.*

*The Prime tried yanking the door open, but it didn't work. And then one of the lair's incantors was there, telling Jolene to stand back. The woman then waved her hands and did some sort of chant.*

*The door was roughly pulled open seconds later, and then Devon was being scooped up by Jolene. "Devon. Oh, sweetheart." Jolene kissed her cheek. "Please tell me somebody has a bottle of water! Beck, get the baby out." She kissed Devon's cheek again. "It's all right, sweetheart, you're going to be—"*

*"Jolene," said Beck. The word was flat. Somber. Devastated.*

*"What is it?" Jolene peered into the car. And tensed.*

*"I don't think he's just sleeping," Devon rasped. "Can we fix him?"*

*Face crumpling, Jolene just palmed the back of Devon's head and held her close.*

The heavy weight of magick disappeared from Devon's body, making her suck in a sharp breath. She didn't hesitate to release the dark power that had been bashing against her ribs. It lunged at the incantor and snapped around her body, squeezing the breath right out of her lungs.

Jo's eyes widened with first shock then pain. Her mouth opened in a silent scream as the hazy vapor slithered around her like a serpent, tightening and tightening, crushing bones, causing veins to pop, tearing skin, and rupturing blood vessels. Then her head flopped forward, and the power released her corpse in an instant. It was over in mere *seconds*.

Devon was vaguely aware of Finn leaping to his feet and

diving at Eric, taking him down, as she threw a ball of hellfire at Leticia, who'd been staring at Jo in shock.

Leticia stumbled backward, colliding with the wall. "Bitch!"

"Aren't I, though?" Devon's inner demon charged to the surface with a snarl, appearing in an explosion of smoke with only a flash of pleasure/pain. It blinked its eyes at its prey, blood boiling with rage, leg muscles quivering with the urge to lunge and maul and kill.

*

"You're wondering why you didn't scent me," Foreman said to Tanner. "I can hide my scent. Make it literally vanish. Hiding the scents of others isn't as easy—I usually only manage to cover them in a fake scent."

Which was why Tanner hadn't recognized Muriel's scent at Harry's crime scene. "You didn't change Muriel's scent today, though."

Foreman shrugged. "There didn't seem any point. You still would have followed the scent down here. I just had to be ready to stop you from disabling the bomb."

None of them would know the first fucking thing about disabling a goddamn bomb, but Knox would easily dispose of it . . . if only they could get out of this fucking snare.

"You really want to die, Royal?" asked Knox.

Pain shadowed Foreman's eyes. "I died here a long time ago. Muriel's right; this ground needs to be purged of the evil here." He frowned. "I didn't help her kill the others. Just kept them still for her. Can't aim that ability on more than one person at a time, though, so I figured it'd be best to cage you all."

"It wasn't," said Knox.

Foreman jumped back as flames shot out of the ground and lapped at the fluid walls of the snare. Flames that were a mix of red, gold, and black that gave off no smoke. "The flames of hell." Foreman stared at Knox, his face slack. "It's true, you really can conjure them."

"They'll eat this snare, Foreman," Knox told him, speaking loud enough to be heard over the crackling, hissing, spitting flames. *Nothing* was impervious to them. "They'll devour it, and then they'll consume you just before they consume the bomb if you don't let us out *right fucking now.*"

"You'd never spare me." It was a quiet, shaky whisper.

"I would if you released us. I don't want to kill you, Royal. I think you've suffered enough. But I will end you if you don't back the fuck down."

Foreman swallowed hard. "I'm sorry. I just can't. This has to be done." He shook his head. "You all should have just stayed away."

A familiar, raging sense of urgency struck Tanner hard, making his knees buckle, his scalp prickle, and his hackles rise. *Devon.* His heart began to pound like a drum, every muscle in his body went tight, and his hound just about lost its shit.

"Something's happening," he told Knox. "I *have* to get to Devon." He snarled at Foreman, his eyes briefly bleeding to black. "Open this fucking thing. *Open it!*"

The male stepped backwards. "I-I can't."

"You listen to me," Tanner ground out, fighting his hound for supremacy when all it wanted was to surface and lunge at the prison it had no chance of smashing through. "My mate needs me. If I don't get to her now, she could *die.*"

Foreman licked his lower lip. "I'm sorry." He genuinely looked like he was, and then Tanner couldn't see him at all, because the flames spread to the front of the prison and blocked his view.

Breathing hard, Tanner spat out a curse and hurled one ball of hellfire after another at the fluid walls. All the orbs disintegrated. *"Fuck!"* Nostrils flaring, he started pacing up and down. His hound roared and raged, *demanding* freedom even as it knew there was nothing it could do—they were fucking trapped.

"I'll get you to her soon, Tanner, I swear that to you," said Knox. "As soon as the flames destroy this snare, we'll be out. It won't take long. There are already fractures in the walls."

It didn't take long for someone to die either.

"I tried notifying Larkin and Jolene," said Levi, "but I can't touch the minds of anyone outside this prison. It's fucking blocking me, just like it blocks teleportation."

It was also blocking Tanner from touching Devon's mind to be sure she was alive. Snarling deep in his throat, he punched the fluid wall in front of him. It was like punching an iceberg, and it hurt like a motherfucker. He pulled back his fist with a hiss.

A wave of Knox's hand made the flames part just enough for him to look at Foreman. "Last chance to let us out, Royal. It'll mean death by the flames if you don't."

His expression both grave and determined, Foreman shook his head. "I truly am sorry." And then he started edging away, clearly intending to make his escape. He might be content to die in the explosion, but he clearly didn't want to go through the agony of being devoured by the flames of hell.

Knox sighed. "Bad decision."

A black flame flicked out and hooked around Foreman's throat. He screamed and kicked his legs as it lifted him high, and then it dragged him down. His howls of pain cut off as the flames swallowed him whole.

"The gaps in the walls are getting bigger," said Levi.

Big enough to fit an arm through, but not a body. And if the flames didn't destroy the snare before the bomb detonated, they were totally fucked.

Urgency riding him hard, Tanner again tried reaching out

with his mind to touch Devon's, needing to know if she was alive. But, again, the fluid prison blocked his attempt.

Even as they all knew it was likely pointless, the three of them battered at the walls with everything they had—orbs of hellfire, raw strength, waves of sheer power. Nothing worked, but they didn't stop. Still, it was likely thanks to the flames alone that a break finally formed in one of the walls that was almost wide enough for them to squeeze through.

"I know you're eager to get to Devon," Knox said to Tanner. "I'll pyroport you right to her the moment we take care of the bomb—that can't wait. Foreman seemed to be guarding that portion of the wall over there," he added, pointing to their right. "Which was exactly where Muriel's scent seemed to be leading you. The second we get out, you get your ass to the bomb. I'll direct the flames at it, and then I'll get us the fuck out of here. Agreed?"

Tanner nodded, even though the only thing that mattered to him was getting to Devon. He'd heard the ticking; knew the bomb was close.

"We can fit through the gap now, but it won't be easy," said Levi.

His prediction proved right. Knox ordered the flames to move away from that part of the wall—they'd cause him no harm, but they'd eat Tanner and Levi alive. The prison walls were so cold they burned Tanner's flesh as he awkwardly struggled through the large crack. Although they were fluid, they scraped and scoured him, just as a huge block of ice would.

When he was finally free, he hurried his ass to find the bomb, but didn't bother to check how much time they had once he found it. Didn't need to, because Knox called on the flames, and they rippled along the ground toward the bomb, consuming it.

"*Now* we leave," Tanner growled.

# CHAPTER TWENTY-ONE

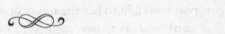

Prowling towards Leticia, the feline peeled back its upper lip, baring its venom-tipped fangs. It snapped its teeth, and she flinched.

"Oh no, there's no way you're getting near me with those teeth." Leticia pushed off the wall. "You're one scary-looking bitch, I'll give you that. You'll also be a dead scary-looking bitch when I'm done with you." She flicked her hand, and power slashed out like a knife. The feline moved fast, avoiding the blow. Porcelain shattered as the scalpel-sharp energy sliced right through the empty mug.

The feline sneered at her poor effort but didn't retaliate. It wanted to play with its prey a little before it killed this bitch who had sent Devon back to a time in her life that had almost destroyed her. Oh, the female would pay for that.

Control and power were important things to her——the demon could sense it. So it would show her just how much weaker she was than the feline; would take away the control she needed;

would make her feel a terror so thick she could choke on it, just as Devon once had.

Backing away, Leticia made an exasperated sound in the back of her throat. She flicked out her hand again. The feline ducked, and the curtain rod behind it clanged to the wooden floor as the power severed it.

Leticia's fingers retracted like claws. "For fuck's sake!"

She struck out again and again. Wicked fast, the feline ducked and dodged, evading each one. Glass splintered as pictures fell to the floor. The coffee table toppled after one leg was shaved off. The sofa dipped after it was almost sliced in two. Each time the harbinger missed, the feline would sneer or let out a chuff of disgust.

Still, Leticia redoubled her efforts. Items fell, crashed, shattered, and snapped. But the feline remained untouched.

It sniffed at her and twitched its tail, communicating how very unimpressed it was. The harbinger's heart was pounding hard and fast now with a fear that the feline delighted in. The scent of said fear was wafting from her like the sweetest perfume, making satisfaction unfurl in the demon's belly.

Licking her lips, she looked to Eric for the briefest moment, as if to ask him for help, but he was still engaged in a struggle with Finn. "Will you just fucking die!" Leticia flicked her hand hard, and a wave of sharp power slightly scoured the feline's flank, shaving off fur but not cutting into flesh.

The demon bared its fangs and scratched at the floor with its paw. It sent Leticia a telepathic image of herself lying dead in a puddle of her own blood. Then it pounced.

Leticia backpedaled fast and skirted the sofa, placing it between them as if it would protect her. The feline chuffed in disdain at her cowardice.

A loud cry of sheer agony burst out of Finn. The hellcat

looked to see the male clutching at a heavily bleeding chest wound. Devon pushed to the surface, worried for him; urging the demon to help—

A blazing pain sliced the feline's ear, almost ripping it off. Red-hot fury surged through its veins. It leaped on top of the sofa and roared, letting out a thin stream of fire that rippled along the rug and licked up Leticia's pants, chewing the material.

She squealed in shock. A wave of Leticia's hand put out the flames, but the feline could smell charred flesh, knew it had scored a hit.

Cheeks flushed with anger, eyes bright with fear, Leticia tossed a series of hellfire orbs in quick succession—one, two, three. The first two missed. The third slammed into the feline's shoulder; it was like being bit by a boiling hot rock, and it made the demon awkwardly slide off the sofa. It landed on its feet, hissing at the burn on its shoulder.

Ignoring the pain, the demon leaped over the sofa and roared again, directing more flames at its prey. But Leticia had already scrambled backwards and put distance between them. Still, the fire licked at her bare arm.

She screamed as the searing heat scorched her, making blisters pebble her flesh. "You fucking—"

The feline dived at Leticia, knocking her flat on her back. She held the feline's head in place with both hands, screaming as it clawed at her belly; ripping, burning, and charring her skin with its flaming paws. The smell of her blood and terror only spurred it on.

It shook its head hard, trying to break free of her grip so it could sink its teeth into her throat, but she held it firm. The feline kept on shredding her stomach with its claws, slicing it open and tearing at her insides until its paws were slick with her blood.

Her screams faded, her eyes clouded, her grip weakened . . .

and the demon sank its hard-as-steel, razor-sharp teeth into her throat and yanked, ripping it out.

*"Fuck, no!"*

Something heavy careened into the demon's flank, sending it skidding along the floor. Seeing Eric bent over Leticia, the demon righted itself and bared its blood-stained fangs at him.

Eric's fists clenched as he turned to the feline, his eyes blazing. "You fucking killed her."

The feline's head whipped to the side as a psychic blow slammed into its head, almost dazing it. With a chuff, the demon gave its head a little shake, clearing its cloudy vision ... and saw that every bit of glass from the floor was hovering in the air. A muscle in Eric's cheek jumped, and then the pieces of glass rocketed toward the feline and sank into its skin.

The feline bucked with a roar of agony as pricks of pain stabbed its head, flanks, neck, legs, and paws. The shards sank deep, one even went down its ear. The larger pieces were wedged into the feline's skin, but there was nothing the demon could do to pull them out. Blood soaked its—

A psychic blow to its spine made its legs crumple, and the feline landed on its stomach. Then Eric was straddling its back, pummeling it with fists that felt like slabs of granite, driving the pieces of glass deeper—so deep some scraped bone and pierced organs.

"Fucking, fucking, *fucking* bitch!" He yanked out a large chunk of glass from the feline's paw, making it roar. "She was *mine*." He stabbed the glass deep into the feline's neck. Roughly pulled it out. Stabbed it again. And again. And again. And again.

Curling his arm around the feline's head, he wrenched it back and pressed the sharp piece of glass to its throat. "She wanted to slit this right open, you know. That's how she wanted you to die, so that's what's gonna happen."

The feline roared fire into his face. Screaming, he dropped the glass and fell back. The demon righted itself, turned—

Eric was snatched from the floor by some unseen force and flung at the wall. A familiar guttural growl split the air just as a large hellhound launched its body at Eric, its veins glowing as if filled with liquid fire.

Breaths sawing in and out of its body, scratching at its dry throat, the feline watched with grim satisfaction as its mate mauled and mangled the other male, chomping through bone, digging out organs, and tearing off limbs. It butchered Eric just as it had butchered Lockwood, even stripping the skin from his face.

Then, chest heaving, muscles quivering, the hellhound turned to the feline, who only stared right back at it. Tiny red embers danced around the hound's body as it stalked toward the feline, sniffing and rumbling.

"We need to get the glass out," Knox said.

"I can do it with my telekinesis," said Levi. "But it's gonna hurt the hellcat, so Tanner's hound had best make sure its mate doesn't go for my throat."

Then it was like a vacuum was aimed at the feline, ripping every bit of glass right out of its body. It roared, legs trembling. And then the hound was there, licking the feline's wounds.

"Sorry, but it's just plain weird seeing a hellhound tend to a hellcat like that," stated Levi. "Plain. Weird."

"Hopefully Devon can explain what happened here later," said Knox. "First, we'd better call in some people to clean this place up. And someone needs to check on Finn—he seems to be out cold, and he's in a bad state."

*

It was the feel of fingers playing with her hair that woke her. Lying flat on her stomach, Devon forced her heavy eyelids open.

Tanner was sitting beside her on the mattress, toying with the ends of the clump of curls in his hand.

As if he felt her eyes on him, he looked down at her. A warm, lazy smile softened his mouth. "Hey, kitten. Nice to see you awake." He bent over and pressed a lingering kiss to her temple.

"Hey," she breathed. It was all she managed to get out. God, she was *dog-tired*. She could only guess that he'd brought her to bed, since she didn't remember much after shifting back to her own form. The mix of psychic exhaustion, blood loss, and the adrenaline crash had knocked her clean out.

"Brought you coffee. Think you've got enough energy to sit up and drink it?"

"No," she pretty much grunted. Okay, fine, she just didn't *want* to get up yet. "But I can prop myself up on my elbows." Devon went to push herself upwards, but then she winced as she felt the pull of several injuries.

Tanner softly cursed. "You need to move slow or you might reopen some of those wounds. It pisses me off that I can only heal injuries *I* inflict."

Devon carefully propped herself up on her elbows and then gratefully took the mug he handed her. She took a sip and almost groaned with happiness. He made damn good coffee. After a few more sips, she asked, "Was I out a while?"

"Six hours straight," he replied, lying on his side and planting his elbow on the pillow. "You started fussing a few minutes ago—you always do that about ten minutes before you wake up."

"You watch me sleep?"

"Sometimes." He slid his hand up her bare spine and hooked it around her nape. "You purr in your sleep. It's cute. I like it."

She grunted again and took another sip of her drink. He didn't natter away while she finished her coffee; he gave her a few minutes to shake off her usual morning mood. But he also didn't give her any space. He burrowed closer, tracing her skin with his fingers, snaking his hands over her, and pressing kisses here and here—careful never to touch her injuries.

Normally, she'd grumpily bat his hand away until she'd had a chance to properly wake. Today, she allowed it, because she sensed he needed this. Needed to touch her and reassure himself that she was fine.

"I'm sorry I didn't get to you sooner."

She frowned at the dumb, gruffly spoken apology. "You have nothing to apologize for."

"I should have gotten here sooner," Tanner insisted, feeling his chest tighten as he remembered the state her feline had been in when he arrived—patches of her fur were soaked in blood, her unique eyes were dull with pain, and pieces of glass were sticking out of her like porcupine quills. "I would if I could have done." He told her what happened at the hotel, and her face paled.

"You were almost *blown up by a bomb*?"

He massaged her nape and soothed, "I'm here, I'm fine, same as you."

"That's not the point. You could have fucking *died*. Shit."

He rested his forehead against hers. "You have no idea how horrible it was to be unable to reach you when I knew you were in danger." The guilt, panic, and fear hadn't yet left him. It was only the sight of her there—alive and well—that kept him calm.

"You'd have felt that I was in danger sooner if it wasn't for Leticia's incantor-friend. She used magick on me and Finn . . ." Devon's eyes widened. "Shit, how is he?"

Hesitating to answer, Tanner stroked her hair. "I'm sorry, kitten, it's not looking good. Eric savaged him. But Finn has doctors from his lair working on him. Spencer promised to keep me updated."

She swallowed. "I should have helped him instead of toying

with Leticia. I didn't realize Eric was that strong—I thought Finn could take him."

"Of course you'd assume that—Finn's a goddamn Prime, for God's sake. Don't be stupidly feeling guilty." He took the empty mug from her hands and set it on the nightstand. "Want to tell me what happened earlier?" he asked, skimming his hand down her arm. "You don't have to yet if you don't feel like talking about it."

She took a deep breath. "Well, Finn came to visit . . ."

Tanner listened intently as she gave him the full story. His stomach twisted tighter and tighter with each word she spoke. "Fuck." He pressed his lips to her head, exhaling hard out of his nose. "Should've stayed with you."

She grabbed his wrist. "No, you shouldn't have. You're a sentinel, it's your—"

"You're more important to me than a fucking position, kitten."

Her breath seemed to catch in her throat, and she bit her lip. "You couldn't have known what would happen when you left. You thought I was safe. I *should* have been safe. Everything that happened was because of Leticia, not because you weren't here. Besides, you got here in time to deal with Eric."

His eyes flared. "The fucking asshole died too easily."

"Your hound *butchered* him."

"He deserved worse. I swear, my vision went red when I got to the apartment and saw him stabbing your feline. My hound lost its fucking mind and took over before I had a chance to fight the shift. That pissed me off, because I wanted to kill the son of a bitch myself."

"Don't start mentally kicking your ass. I'm okay. You're okay. That's what matters."

He massaged her head, digging his fingers into her scalp just hard enough to feel good. "Fuck, I love you."

Devon's heart slammed against her ribs, and she felt her nose prickle. "Yeah?" It was a shaky question.

He smiled. "Yeah."

"Good. I love you right back." He kissed her, licking into her mouth, demanding a response. She gave it to him, moaning as he took her mouth in a soft, deep, drugging kiss that made her toes curl.

Then her phone rang.

Pulling back, he sighed. "I've been fielding calls from people, telling them you'd call them back when you were awake. Gertie has called eight times. I assured her that you're okay, but she's worried about you. I think she'll need to hear your voice before she believes you're truly fine."

"I'll return the calls after you've made me come."

He smiled. "Later. Some of your wounds are still a little raw. Don't pout," he added, chuckling. "Come on, let me feed you and then you can make your calls. My guess is some of those people, especially your parents, will want to see you. After they've all gone, I'll put you to bed and make you come with my fingers and mouth before I fuck you. Deal?"

She pursed her lips. "Works for me."

# CHAPTER TWENTY-TWO

Her eyes glazed and heavy-lidded, Khloë raised her hand. "Wait," she slurred. "You're saying my tongue print is different than yours?"

"I'm saying *everyone's* tongue print is different," said Devon, setting her glass on the table but almost tipping it over. "Like fingerprints."

"Wow. If I was blitzed right now, my mind would be *blown*. Good thing I'm sober." Swaying just a little, Khloë chugged down the rest of her drink and burped loud. "How cool would it be if I could fart confetti?"

"Fart confetti?" echoed Raini, slumped in her seat, twirling the little umbrella from her cocktail.

Khloë frowned at the blonde. "You can't honestly say you've never wondered about it."

"I honestly can," Raini told her.

Khloë just snorted.

Staring into her empty glass, Harper pouted. "I miss Asher. I always feel so *guilty* when I leave him behind."

Devon patted her shoulder. "The party's almost over. You'll see your bambino soon."

Harper and Knox had thrown the "Welcome to the Lair" slash "Congrats on Your Mating" party in the Underground. Most bars and nightclubs on the strip took part, and a lot of food vendors set up stalls outside those venues to help celebrate, so it was kind of like a street party on crack.

There'd been lots of eating, drinking, and dancing as Devon and Tanner hopped from venue to venue, accepting well-wishes and all that jazz—the girls, Knox, and the other sentinels were with them every step of the way, of course.

Now that the mingling was done, the girls were settled at a table in their favorite bar. Tanner, Knox, and Keenan were near the restrooms, talking with a group of people Devon didn't recognize. But it was good that they were all the way over there, because then they wouldn't notice that the girls had exchanged their bottles of water for yet more alcoholic drinks—apparently, the guys thought they needed to sober up. Pfft. They were *not* drunk. Really.

Everyone in the lair had all been very welcoming, which was nice, but Devon was still sad to leave her old lair. She also didn't like living so far from her parents. Nonetheless, she had no intention of living anywhere but with Tanner. And it wasn't exactly a hardship to live in his—no, *their*—condo.

Harper nudged Devon with her elbow. "On the subject of bambinos, what did the specialist say about the whole you-not-going-into-heat thing—something you should have mentioned *years* ago, heifer. And I say 'heifer' with all the love in my shriveled heart."

"You know why I didn't tell you." Devon awkwardly elbowed her right back. "The doc said nothing's wrong; thinks it's all psychological."

Khloë clasped her hands together. "So there could be hellkitties or hellpuppies in your future?"

"The doc thinks so," said Devon.

Khloë's eyes went super wide. "Cool. If I had a flag, I'd totally wave it. Ooh, can I have pick of the litter?"

"Khloë, I love you for realsies, but I'm not gonna give you one of my kids."

"It doesn't have to be your firstborn or anything—I'm not Rumpelfuckingstiltskin."

Devon's brows dipped. "Rumpel who?"

"You've never heard the story of Rumpelstiltskin? Girl, you haven't *lived*." Khloë gave her a quick recap of the fairy tale. "The moral of it is ... don't make deals with strange little dudes—they'll fuck you over every time."

"Gotcha." Devon picked up her glass and knocked back the last of her Cosmo. She had a real good buzz going on. Felt all warm, cozy, and tingly. "I could totally crash right here I'm so relaxed."

"Me, too." Raini tipped her head back and closed her eyes. "You've gotta love that transcendent state of pure happiness that's devoid of tension and strife. Know what I mean?"

"I was just gonna say exactly that," said Harper. "Not gonna lie, I was drunk off my ass earlier, though."

Yeah, so was Devon. But after a few bottles of water and several thousand pees, she was simply a little buzzed; basking in the atmosphere and delighted that the world was such a beautiful, wondrous place filled with love and laughter. Even better, it was no longer spinning. Just kind of blurry, that's all.

"Shit, the guys are heading our way!" hissed Khloë.

Devon and the girls quickly put their empty glasses under the table and planted innocent smiles on their faces.

Reaching them, Levi frowned. "Those smiles are making me nervous."

Snorting, Tanner plucked Devon out of her seat, sank into the chair, and then perched her on his lap. "Hi, kitten. Did you miss me?"

"Like an idiot misses the point," she replied.

Chuckling, Tanner pressed a kiss to her mouth. "You always make me feel so adored." He peeked down her dress, getting a good look at her cleavage. "How are Holly and Molly doing?"

She sighed. "It's not normal that you've named my boobs. You know that, right?"

"It seems so impersonal to refer to them as Leftie and Righty."

Unable to stifle a smile, Devon shook her head. "You're an odd one, pooch."

He gave her another kiss. "Party's almost over, so we'll be leaving soon. I've gotta say, you impressed me tonight. People fussed and crowded you, but you only hissed a few times. Didn't draw blood once."

"I *did* lunge at the slimy lawyer, though."

"Him I don't like, so it doesn't count."

"Oh. Good." She rested her head on his shoulder, smiling as his arms tightened around her. He'd been a little clingy since the whole her-almost-getting-killed thing. She figured his protective streak might be on fire for a few more months at least.

He'd been in a good mood today, though. Mostly because he was smug that her demon had branded him that morning. Twice. He now sported a tribal band on each of his upper arms. If anyone looked close enough at the design, they'd notice that each of the black curved lines were in fact claw marks.

His mind brushed hers. *Love this dress you're wearing,* he said, sliding his hand up her side over the lattice design. The white, smooth, slinky number clung perfectly to her body. *Can't decide whether I'd rather flip it up when I fuck you or just claw the whole thing off.*

*There will be no tearing this dress*, she asserted. *It's one of my favorites.*

*There'll be plenty of fucking, though, as soon as we get home.*

*I'm counting on it. Hey, on another note . . . I meant to ask you earlier, what's up Keenan's butt?* The incubus had been glaring at a completely oblivious Khloë all night—something he was doing again now.

*Not sure*, replied Tanner. *But I'm getting the feeling that the imp has done something to piss him off.*

It seemed likely. But if Keenan thought that Khloë would even notice those glares, he was wrong. Her shields were solid, and passive-aggressiveness often went right over her head.

"Teague's racing tomorrow," Khloë announced. "He said he'll sort us a private box if we want to go. You girls up for it?"

"Sure," said Devon.

Raini raised a hand. "I'm in."

"You can count me in, too," Harper told her.

"Awesome." Khloë sank into her chair with a happy sigh. "I feel like I could float right now. How cool would that be? I mean, think of the possibilities. I could pee on people. Say hi to birds. Sleep on clouds like a Care Bear."

Raini wrinkled her nose. "What's a Care Bear?"

Khloë did a slow blink. "Dude, don't you ever watch cartoons?"

"No."

Khloë shook her head. "I feel like I don't know you right now."

"You're not going to apologize, are you?" Keenan asked, his voice clipped.

The table fell silent. Khloë looked up at him and seemed surprised that the question had been directed at her. "For . . . ?" she prompted.

Keenan's lips thinned. "For what happened last night when I gave you a ride home from the Xpress bar."

Khloë bit down on the inside of her cheek. "I'm not sure what answer will bother you more. That I can't remember what happened, or that it's unlikely I'll apologize, since annoying you is always fun."

Curious, Devon lifted her head from Tanner's shoulder and asked, "What did she do?"

Keenan didn't even look Devon's way. He was still glaring at Khloë, his neck corded. "It was irritating enough that you wouldn't get in the car without bringing a road cone with you. Listening to you sing the wrong lyrics to 'Wake Me Up Before You Go-Go' was equally irritating—especially since you were using a tampon as a microphone. I can only thank God it was an unused tampon, because you tried shoving it down my ear. Oh, and then there's the part where you were texting yourself. And yes, I had to listen to you read aloud a text-conversation you were having *with yourself* about how annoying it is that donuts have holes in them."

Biting back a laugh, Devon snuggled into Tanner, whose shoulders were shaking.

"I wish I could say it ended there," Keenan went on. "But no. You refused to get out of the car when I parked in your driveway. You swore it wasn't your house and accused me of trying to hand you over to sex traffickers. When I *finally* convinced you that it *was* your home, you kept insisting I kiss the road cone goodbye. I refused, of course, so you threatened to post on social media that I'm a road cone bigot. Only *you* could turn a simple car ride into a crazy-ass episode—something you topped off by trying to unlock your front door with a tampon. I mean, seriously, *what is up with that?*"

Khloë blinked. "Wow. That explains why I woke up snuggled into a road cone."

Keenan gaped. "That's all you have to say?"

She narrowed her eyes at him. "I feel you and your monster cock judging me. I don't like it."

Honestly, he looked like he wanted to grab the imp by the throat. *"Would you stop commenting on my—?"*

"What's with all the yelling over here?" asked a new voice.

Knox sighed at the newcomer. "Lou," he greeted simply.

The devil smiled down at Devon and Tanner. "So, a hellcat has mated with a hellhound. Off the top of my head, can't think of anything weirder. But hey, I'm all for it. I like weird. Most do."

*"You* are weird," said Harper.

"And likeable, which proves my point." Lou glanced around. "Where's my favorite nephew?"

"Asher is at home," said Knox. "And he's not your nephew."

"He is where it counts," Lou insisted, pounding a fist over his heart. "He loves me."

Jolene sidled up to him. "Who loves you?"

Lou jerked away from the female Prime like she'd burned him. "Asher, *obviously.*"

Patting her hair, Jolene made a *pfft* sound. "My grandson merely tolerates you like the rest of us do."

Lou shot her a petulant look. "You're just being bitchy because he loves me more than he does you."

"You lie to yourself far too often," said Jolene.

"You really think he loves you more? Oh, wake up and smell the joint in my pocket—"

"You have a *joint* in your pocket?" Knox cut in, his eyes hard.

Lou's eyes went wide. "Of course not," he scoffed. "Jeez, would it kill you to trust me?"

"Kill me?" asked Knox. "No. Make me extremely naïve? Yes. Considering you're a chronic liar, a drug addict, and the most untrustworthy person I've ever met."

Lou cupped his ear. "Sorry, could you repeat that? It's hard to hear you from all the way up here on this pedestal you've put me on."

Looking at Tanner, Devon rolled her eyes. "Interesting company we keep."

Lips twitching, Tanner inclined his head. "'Interesting' is one word for it."

Tanner almost let out a sigh of relief when the party finally reached its end. He had to hold in a laugh as, with a lot of staggering and weaving, his mate dished out hugs to her friends. He kept his arm curled around her waist as he led her drunken ass out of the Underground, smiling at the mad shit she was chatting—some of which he was convinced she hadn't meant to say out loud.

Since he hadn't consumed any alcohol, he drove them home in his Audi. Their friends had helped put the apartment to rights after the Leticia debacle. The blackened, broken furniture had been replaced. The fallen pictures had been reframed and rehung. And the scorch marks and patches of bubbling paint on the walls courtesy of the hellfire had been taken care of.

Other things, however, hadn't been so easy to fix. Pamela had recovered well from the attempted poisoning, but she seemed to have retreated a little more. The nurse who poisoned Pamela was eventually caught, thanks to Jolene's sentinels. She'd admitted that Leticia paid her to do the deed, hoping that being honest would earn her a quick and painless death. It didn't.

He and Devon had paid her mother a few visits. Pamela never remembered him, and it was unlikely that she ever would, but he still intended to go with Devon on future visits. He wanted to get to know her mother, even if her mother would never really know him.

Finn's situation hadn't been so easy to fix either. He'd physically recovered from his wounds, but he was emotionally shattered. It was clear he blamed himself for all the shit that had happened—even for Leticia's actions. He'd chosen to step down from his position of Prime.

Spencer had taken over, but he hadn't seemed excited about it. Like his siblings, he was gutted by Leticia's death but also angry with her for almost killing their father. Reena was feeling guilty, since she'd begun to suspect her mother might have been involved but hadn't said anything. Tanner figured she therefore *should* be feeling guilty, but Devon wasn't holding her accountable for anything.

When they *finally* entered their apartment, Tanner steered a humming Devon into their bedroom and held her tight. She looked up at him, her face all soft, her eyes glassy and hooded. She was *blitzed*. He had to smile.

"You're gonna crash hard tonight for sure," he said, skimming his knuckles down her cheek, drinking in every feature. "So gorgeous. I remember I once came on this pretty face, didn't I?"

"You got it in my hair—I wasn't impressed."

He chuckled. "You sure you're up to taking my cock tonight?"

Her eyes darkened with a naked, sensual hunger that matched his own. She fisted his shirt and pressed herself tight against him. "Oh, I'm sure."

"Then I guess I'll take your word for it." Tanner sank his tongue into her mouth, and the flare of need was instant. It blasted through him with the force of a fucking freight train. His body tightened. Nerves sparked to life. Chemicals raced through his bloodstream.

He kissed her over and over, unable to get enough of her taste. The atmosphere was thick and static with the same sexual tension that had taunted them both from day one. He roughly palmed her breast, swallowing her soft moan, growling at the feel of her nipple piercing. "Can't look at you without wanting to fuck you. Do you know that?"

Devon groaned into his mouth as his tongue again licked and tangled with hers. The kiss was hot, wet, and so damn carnal. Hell, he pretty much fucked her mouth with his tongue. Molten lust dazed her thoughts and swept her under, making her so frantic to feel his skin against hers that she impatiently tore off his shirt.

His hands were sure and confident as they roamed over her body, stirring it to life. So much sexual energy bounced between them it almost made her dizzy. Electric sparks seemed to leap from him to her, making her skin tingle and her nerve endings hypersensitive. Her nipples beaded into hard painful points that throbbed, desperate to be touched and tasted.

Tanner hiked up her dress, just as he'd been aching to do all damn night. "Lie down flat on your back. That's it." Kneeling on the mattress between her spread legs, he skimmed his hands up her silky-soft inner thighs. "I want to see those tits, kitten. Show me." She scooped them out of her dress. "Good girl."

Tanner bent over and drew as much of her creamy breast into his mouth as he could. She raked her fingers through his hair, pricking his scalp with her nails, as he sucked and licked and toyed with her piercings. He bit her nipple, injecting his venom into her bloodstream.

She hissed. "One day, I'm going to bite you right on the cock." She glared at him when he chuckled. "Don't think I'm kidding, pooch."

"I consider myself warned," he said, sliding her panties off her legs, baring her glistening pussy to him. "So pretty." She jerked when he slipped the tip of his finger between her slick folds. "And so very sensitive. I like that." Her lips parted on a soft gasp of surprise as he plunged two fingers *hard* into her pussy. Tanner groaned. "Jesus, kitten, you're so fucking hot."

He drove his fingers inside her again, humming as she

rocked against his hand and ground her clit against the heel of his palm. "Yeah, that's it, baby. Take what I give you." Tanner pumped his fingers into her pussy, clenching his teeth as her tight walls spasmed. He wanted to feel her pussy rippling around his cock, wanted all that slickness wrapped around him.

Soon, her walls began to flutter and tighten. "You ready to come?" he asked, scissoring his fingers. He didn't wait for an answer. He hooked his fingers just right and thrust deep and hard over and over, watching her buck and moan and bite on her lip. And then she was coming, her hands fisting the sheets, her thighs tremoring.

Tanner slipped his fingers out of her and sucked them clean. He growled. "Fuck, I want you."

Panting, she licked her lower lip. "You have me."

"And I'm keeping you." Tanner angled her hips, snapped open his fly, freed his cock, and slammed home. *Sheer fucking heaven.* Her blazing hot pussy clamped down on him so tight it should have hurt. She writhed, trying to fuck herself on him, but he held her still. "Shh, I got you."

Tanner began to slowly thrust in and out of her. Watching her inner walls cling to his cock was fucking hot. Feeling those tight muscles try and suck him back in again and again was even better. "Never had a pussy this sweet." He swiveled his hips. "If I could, I'd be in you twenty-four/seven."

She tried to take over and quicken the thrusts, but Tanner wouldn't let her. He kept the pace slow and easy, ignoring her demands of "harder" and "faster."

Her nostrils flared. "If you're going to ask me to beg—"

"I don't want you to beg. I'm not interested in taking hits at your pride." He swiveled his hips again. "I just want to make you come while I take you like this, all soft and slow. Then I'll give it to you hard." Maybe it was messed up, but her snarl went straight to his cock.

"Slow just makes me cranky. It doesn't do anything for me."

Which was why he was determined to make her come that way. And it wasn't long before she did. Her hot, slick pussy contracted around his cock. It took everything he had not to explode right along with her.

Draping himself over her, Tanner hummed into the hollow beneath her ear. "I like watching you come." He grazed her earlobe with his teeth. "I think I'll do it again." He slowly pulled his hips back, loving how her tight muscles clenched his dick. Then he slammed deep. "This time, I'll fuck you hard. And then I'll fill this pussy up with my come."

Digging her nails into the smooth flesh of his broad shoulders, Devon held tight as he fucked in and out of her body with blatantly possessive thrusts. So many sensations assailed her—the burn of his thickness stretching her, the dig of his fingertips in his hips, the slap of his balls on her ass, the heat of his mouth as it ravished hers with so much greed it stole her breath.

He groaned. "Fuck, kitten, your pussy is strangling my dick."

Devon bit her lip as he spread her folds with his fingers, exposing her clit to every brutal, branding slam of his cock. She dug her claws harder into his flesh, scratching the hellcat she'd tattooed onto the back of his left shoulder. "Harder, Tanner."

He gave her what she wanted, grunting and breathing heavily down her ear. Every heavy pound of his cock wound her tighter and tighter, driving her closer and closer to coming . . . until she was teetering on the knife-edge of what she knew would be a mind-blowing orgasm. She felt his cock throb and swell; knew he was close as well.

"You love me?" he ground out.

"Yes."

"You belong to me?"

"Yes."

"Will I ever give you up?"

"No."

"That's right. I couldn't even if I wanted to. Need you more than you'll ever know. And right now, I need you to come for me." He slipped his thumb between her slit and thumbed her clit hard. "Do it, kitten, milk my cock and . . . yeah, that's it."

Devon's head flew back as white-hot pleasure blasted through her body, making her muscles spasm, her pussy ripple, and her spine arch like a bow. Tanner cursed into her neck as he slammed harder, faster. His teeth sank into her skin just as his cock roughly sank deep one last time. He exploded with a growl, and she felt jet after jet of hot come splash her quivering walls.

Devon slumped into the mattress, breathing hard, shaking with aftershocks. Damn if the pooch wasn't good at—

Her brow furrowed as he slid something cold onto her third finger. A little dazed from her orgasm, she blinked at her finger. It wasn't a ring. It was two. One was a black gold band that had a row of small garnet stones. The other black gold ring was thinner and had an emerald-cut black diamond in the center.

Her heart slammed against her ribs, and she met his eyes. "This is a *black diamond*."

His lips twitched. "Well I know that."

Pulse racing, she could only gawk at him. It was no casual thing for a demon to give their mate a black diamond. It was the ultimate brand of ownership; a symbol of commitment. And since demons didn't commit easily or lightly, a lot of couples waited a long time before exchanging rings.

It took male hellhounds *far* longer than other breeds to settle down, if they ever did—it still amazed Devon that he'd taken her as his mate; the last thing she would have expected was for him to give her a black diamond so soon. Especially when "alone" was what he knew best.

She licked her lips. "Tanner—"

"You're thinking this is too big a step for me; that I haven't thought this through," he said, looking more peaceful than she'd ever seen him. "You're wrong. We haven't been together long, that's true. But you've been mine since the day we met, kitten, and we both know it. It just took us a while to get where we are now."

He rested his forehead against hers. "I've never felt what I feel for you for anyone else, and I know I never could. I love every part of you, inside and out. Every inch of this body, every hair on your head, everything that makes you who you are. You're irreplaceable for me, and there isn't a single thing I won't do to keep you. I've told you before; once a male hellhound chooses a mate, it's permanent. I mean it when I say I will fucking obliterate anyone or anything that tries to come between us."

Nose prickling, throat thick, Devon bit her lip. "Then I'll wear these rings with pride." She hugged him tight, breathing him in, so far gone for him it wasn't even funny. "Love ya, pooch."

Looking down into eyes glistening with unshed tears, Tanner felt warmth radiate through him and swell in his chest. Fuck if those simple words didn't have the power to bring him to his knees, even if he'd heard them before. "Love you right back, kitten."

"Where's the male version of the ring? I know they come in a set. And no, I'm not asking you to put it on just because you slipped these on me. I *want* you to wear it. And I'll shove it up your nostril if you don't—it'll be a tight fit, but I'll make it work."

He chuckled. "No need to convince me to wear it."

"Well, then, what are you waiting for?"

"So impatient." He plucked a box out of the nightstand draw

and pulled out a thick, masculine black gold band that had a single, small garnet stone in the center. He slid it onto his third finger. His chest expanded as he took a deep, satisfied breath. "Happy now?"

"Yep."

He rolled them onto their sides, keeping her close. "What about your demon?"

"Content. It likes shiny things, and it's smug that you've laid such a massive claim."

"My demon is rather pleased—it likes seeing those rings on your finger; likes that everyone, including humans, will know you're taken. And it's just as pleased that you want me to wear the masculine band."

"Then all is good in our world."

"Yep, it is." Unable to refrain from teasing her, he said, "So, all your dreams have come true. You're officially my mate, you're living with me, you're wearing my rings, I'm wearing yours. Your heart must be close to bursting with the sheer joy of it all." He almost laughed when her eyes narrowed. "I mean, let's be honest, it was a case of love at first sight for you, wasn't it? You've adored me for so long, it must be sometimes hard to believe that this is all truly real and that—"

He laughed when she swiped at him, her claws out. "Now, now, kitten, we've talked about this—you need to leave those claws sheathed. If you want, we can forget that you've been obsessed with me all these years; we can pretend that you didn't compare other guys to me and find them all lacking so— *Fuck, stop going for my eyes!*"

# Acknowledgements

I should take a moment to thank actor, Chris Hemsworth, for his input on this book—Ha! Kidding. Never met the guy, but my daughter dared me to add this to the acknowledgement section and I'm not good at ignoring dares.

I absolutely have to thank the most important people in life—my husband and kids, who support me every step of the way and keep me sane when the voices in my head get too loud.

I also need to thank my unfailingly patient assistant, Melissa, to whom I will be forever indebted for saving me from myself at numerous author signing events.

A huge thanks to everyone at Piatkus, especially my fabulous editor, Anna Boatman, who is everything a writer would want in an editor.

Last but not whatsoever least, thank you to everyone who has taken a chance on this book. You're all. Seriously. Awesome. Don't let anyone tell you different.

S :)